What If?

Martina Reilly

W F HOWES LTD

This large print edition published in 2013 by
W F Howes Ltd
Unit 4, Rearsby Business Park, Gaddesby Lane,
Rearsby, Leicester LE7 4YH

1 3 5 7 9 10 8 6 4 2

First published in the United Kingdom in 2013
by Hachette Books Ireland

A CIP catalogue record for this book is available
from the British Library

ISBN 978 1 47123 983 0

Typeset by Palimpsest Book Production Limited,
Falkirk, Stirlingshire
Printed and bound by
www.printondemand-worldwide.com of Peterborough, England

From the extended O'Shea/Hand family

To our beautiful mam, Doris.
Alzheimer's has stolen your memory
but it can never take away our loving
memories of you. I hope you still know
how much we love you, Mam. x

From the Shanagher family

In memory of Aiden Shanagher
one of life's rare masterpieces and a true
success story. Loved and missed every
day from all the Shanagher family.

Also dedicated to all who donated
anonymously to CanTeen Ireland as a
result of my online auction.

PROLOGUE

In her dream, she was five. It was late spring and the field of rapeseed stretched far, far away, farther than she could even see. A yellow-brick road leading up to the horizon and beyond. She stood at the stone wall waiting on her daddy, her feet getting hot in her black wellies and her arms getting cold in the breeze. It was a funny old day, as her daddy would say.

She saw him walk towards her. He seemed impossibly tall, the tallest man in the whole world and his wellies were way bigger than hers. They made a funny sound too as he marched along. Whoosh, whoosh, whoosh.

Deirdre scrunched her eyes to look up at him, because the sun was behind him. There was a halo around his head, like Jesus.

A robin caught her eye as he hopped on the wall in front of her. Deirdre sucked in her breath but knew enough to be statue still. The robin cocked his head, staring her up and down. Deirdre remained frozen, fascinated by this tiny creature. He hopped nearer her and she held her breath. Her daddy stopped too and put his finger to his lips. Eventually, the robin plucked an insect from the wall and flew off.

'Did you see that?' Deirdre shrieked. 'He came *this* close.' She made a little space with her thumb and forefinger to show her daddy how close the robin had been.

Her daddy told her that he had. Then he took her hand in his. His hand was big and warm and rough. She skipped alongside him, almost on tiptoes because he was so tall and she was only five. He told her about the robin. He'd told her that the robin was a cheeky fellow, a real 'Jack the Lad'. He said it in amusement, his mouth turned up in a smile. In contrast, the humble and boring jackdaw, who he pointed out to her, was a faithful chap, not as cute as the robin but a better bet as a friend. She'd asked him why the birds were so different. He'd shrugged and said that that's just the way they were. Then added, his face scrunched up, 'I suppose now, that the robin is a sort of solitary bird, which means he lives alone, so I suppose he never gets to find out about families and how nice they are. Maybe he's scared. The jackdaw lives with lots of others and they're close. Maybe that's why.'

Deirdre nodded. She felt sorry for the robin. 'I'd like to be a jackdaw so,' she said.

Her daddy laughed and lifted her up and swung her around and told her that she could be anything she wanted and that he'd always love her because she was his lovely girl.

His lovely girl.

Deirdre woke with a jerk. It was her new producer, Suzi, letting her know that she had half an hour before she was expected in the studio to talk about the rare sighting of a semipalmated sandpiper. It was her first time fronting a radio show and she was dreading it. But it was a great opportunity, everyone said so. Psyching herself up, Deirdre brushed the tears from her face. Having that dream always made her cry in her sleep, which was weird.

FIVE YEARS AGO . . .

'How did it happen?' Abe sank into a chair and looked up at Zoe. He even looked sexy when he was in shock, she thought, all dark hopeless eyes and tense shoulders. His mouth hung open, reminding her of the door in her apartment that he'd promised to fix and hadn't. She bit back a grin. This really wasn't a funny situation.

'Well, we had sex. Obviously.'

'Zoe, this isn't a funny situation,' he said.

'I didn't deliberately get pregnant,' she defended. 'It wasn't exactly on my five-year plan.' Ten-year plan maybe but, hey, she and Abe had only known one another eight months.

'I bet I know what it was,' Abe said sounding suddenly energised. 'It was those cheap condoms you bought. What was it? Five thousand condoms for four euro?'

'Four euro for fifty condoms actually,' she corrected, trying and failing to sound superior. The thought had crossed her mind too. 'And if you think about it, it was good value. The other ones are way too expensive.'

'Yeah, probably because they *work*.'

'I never saw you buying any.'

'You never asked.'

'Well, I shouldn't have to.'

Stalemate.

They glared at each other.

Abe was the first to drop his gaze. He heaved a great sigh. 'I'm sorry.'

'It's OK.' She smiled at him.

He gave a watery smile back. He looked impossibly young. 'So what now?'

Zoe felt guilty seeing him look so dejected. Abe, despite his reluctance to embrace impending fatherhood, was a good guy. He spent a lot of time in foreign countries bringing water to people and helping them grow crops. He even built their houses. He gave generously to collections and there was nothing he didn't recycle. In fact, Audrey, her flatmate and best friend, was going mad because Zoe, having listened to Abe bang on about leftovers, had large amounts of compost in a bag in the kitchen. Abe had called to collect it and so Zoe had taken the opportunity to tell him that she was pregnant. She'd started with the statement, 'I have some positive news.' It had been a joke that fell spectacularly flat.

'Well, what happens now is that the baby grows, I get fat and then in a few months we become parents.'

Abe swallowed and choked out, 'Please don't make jokes.'

'It's not a joke,' Zoe stopped smiling. 'I was being flippant, but it's not a joke.'

Abe winced.

'I'm scared too, you know.' She slid into the seat beside him and tentatively took his hand.

'Good,' he muttered, but he didn't pull away. 'We're only twenty-two.' He sounded like a kid who'd had his best football card nicked.

'I know, but I think we'll cope, don't you?'

He didn't answer.

'We can take it one step at a time,' Zoe said carefully. 'See how it goes.' She paused and when he still said nothing, she added, 'I am going to have this baby, Abe, and if you want to be involved, great but if not, walk away now.'

She didn't know how she'd managed to sound so confident. If Abe walked, her mother would have a big 'I told you so' face on. She didn't like Abe ever since he'd refused an invite to her fiftieth. 'Men who don't "do" family, don't do family,' she'd said at the time. At least if Abe was around, it gave Zoe some credibility. And, besides, children needed a family around them.

'I'm not someone who walks away,' Abe said, in a surprisingly loud voice, sounding offended. 'I'm not walking away from anything.'

'I never said—'

'No, no, I'll stick around,' Abe nodded, half to himself. He sounded as if he were about to do ten rounds with Ali. He smiled in that unexpected way she loved, his mouth curving up at the

9

corner, 'It makes it easier because you're so damn gorgeous.'

She smiled back. She hoped that she'd still be gorgeous when she got fat.

Lily was losing her mind. Day by day, bits and pieces of it were floating away. Things she should know, names of familiar people, places she'd been, all disappearing like sugar in tea. There was one time, long ago, when she'd wanted to lose her mind, to forget things that had happened, but now, quite suddenly, that seemed the most precious thing to hold on to. She wanted to remember, she needed others to know now – to understand, to forgive – and so she lifted herself up from the sofa, her frailness reminding her that she was in her seventies and not the bright young thing she sometimes thought she was, and shuffled her way into the kitchen.

She found the diary in a drawer, bright blue, her favourite colour. Most of it was filled in, written in her neat flowing script. She'd written it after getting it as a present for her fifteenth birthday. There were gaps in its narrative, sometimes years, because it had been hard at times to confront events, let alone write them down, and so, just a few months ago, she'd attempted to fill in the missing bits and to conclude her story, but then the memories had washed over her and she hadn't been able to go on. But she would now. She was losing her mind and she did not want to lose those memories – not before passing them on. And her girl needed to know the whole story. She needed to know why Lily had done what she'd done. Maybe then they could understand one another better. It was important to write it down before she forgot . . .

Then she would make the phone call.

PRESENT DAY . . .

CHAPTER 1

'You'll freeze,' Zoe said, eyeing up her co-worker Carrie, who was wearing a tiny denim mini and white blouse. Outside, thunder boomed and rain drummed relentlessly, bouncing off the windows of the large reception area of Lakelands Nursing Home.

Carrie ignored her. Instead, almost defiantly, she pulled on a white cardigan and belted it with a skinny blue belt.

'Is that all you're wearing?' Zoe asked. 'You'll be drowned by the time you get to the pub.'

'You look like Zoe,' Carrie eyed her suspiciously, 'but are you sure you're not my mother?'

'Ha, ha.' Zoe grinned before asking teasingly, 'Does Harry let you go out like that?'

'Harry *told* me to go out like this, he's joining us later.'

'So you always wear what the husband-to-be tells you, do you?' Dominic said, catching the end of her remark as he came up behind them. 'I thought women these days were liberated and do ridiculous things like dressing for their own self-worth and shit like that.'

Dominic, like Zoe, was dressed for the thunderstorm raging outside. But Dominic rode a motorbike and so was always in black docs, jeans and a leather jacket. A number of earrings studded his right ear lobe. He was the resident chef in Lakelands Nursing Home, a sort of handsome not-so-hairy biker, Zoe always thought. The nurses were mad about him but mostly he tended to hang out with Zoe and Carrie.

Carrie rolled her eyes as she led them towards the door. 'Dominic, I wish you dressed for your own self-worth, the state of you.' She eyed his jacket, 'How long have you had that thing?'

'About as long as you've worn very few clothes,' Dominic answered, and then laughed as Carrie belted him. 'Where's June?' he asked them. 'Is she not coming?'

'She's got a new resident arriving later,' Zoe said. 'So she's bailed.'

'Phew,' Carrie said. 'I like June but I prefer it when she's not around. I can't relax when she's with us, her being the boss and all.'

The others echoed her sentiment as Zoe pulled open the door.

Carrie squealed as she stepped into the rain and the other two laughed.

Six miles away across the city, Lily allowed the man to help her on with her coat. He had black hair, parted in the middle, and a very nice smile. He hunkered down to her level. 'Now, Lil,' he said, and his voice was kind, 'you're all set.' He patted her arm. 'All set,' he said, before turning away.

Lily wondered if he was sad. There was a droop to his shoulders, a sort of reluctance on his part to meet her eyes. She wished she could remember who he was. She knew she knew him, like the way a child knows how to read without actually remembering how they learned. She adjusted her coat, fumbling with the buttons. She looked around and found her blue book on the seat beside her. That was important, she had to have that. She picked it up and held it close. Something fell out.

The man heard and he turned. That was good because Lily didn't have the words to ask him to get it for her. These days words, like her memories, got caught somewhere inside and refused to come out whole. Like a runner, exhausted at the end of a race, collapsing just as the finish line was in sight.

'You dropped this, Lil,' the man said, handing it to her. She liked that he didn't look too closely at it. He had manners. He could be trusted. 'Would you like me to put it back in your book?'

It was a brown envelope. She remembered quite suddenly that it was for Deirdre. At the end. She couldn't give it to Deirdre just now because Deirdre would open it and that wouldn't work. Lily looked at the man. Memory stirred like a fish deep in the ocean. He was polite. He hadn't seemed curious. She pushed the envelope towards him.

17

'For me?' he said.

She just kept holding it out. She tried to nod but even that went wrong.

The man turned the envelope around, 'For Deirdre at the end,' he read aloud. 'Do you want me to give this to Deirdre,' his voice went funny, 'at the end?'

Lily nodded.

'OK,' he said gently as he crouched down and smiled right into her face. He fastened up her coat again, she must have unbuttoned it. 'You, darling,' he said, 'are not going anywhere for a long, long time.' His voice caught. 'You wanted to go to Lakelands when you couldn't manage food anymore, remember you told me that?' He paused. 'That's the only reason you're going. Me and Deirdre, we'll be in as much as we can, you know that, yeah?' He tipped his head to hers.

Lily pulled back. Who did he think he was? Family?

The man smiled. A sad smile. He pocketed the envelope. 'But I will hold on to this until you,' he faltered on the word, 'die, and give it to her. But that's not going to be for a long time.'

Lily flinched. Die? That's not what she meant. Not what she meant at all. She tried to say the words and they wouldn't come out. The man told her it was OK. To relax.

Lily knew she had to remember. Remember the envelope.

★   ★   ★

Zoe watched as Harry slipped an arm about Carrie and unselfconsciously caressed her shoulder with his thumb. Carrie twisted herself towards him and he kissed the tip of her nose. She pushed him off laughing and he started to nuzzle her neck.

Had she and Abe ever been like that? Zoe wondered. All touchy and snuggly. Though Abe, it had to be said, was not a snuggly person. He liked sex, he was very good at that, but he wasn't so hot on the rubbing of shoulders or the ear nibbling. She took a gulp of whiskey, felt it warm her inside. She'd been happy enough with Abe until she'd come face to face with Harry and Carrie's passion for each other.

'Great, isn't it?' Dominic whispered, startling her. He was lounging back in the seat, slightly drunk, eyeing the pair of them in amusement.

'Huh?' For one second Zoe thought he had read her thoughts. 'What?'

'The Harry and Carrie show.'

Zoe smiled and whispered back, 'You make them sound like a sitcom.'

Dominic raised his eyebrows as if to ask 'well, aren't they?' which made Zoe giggle. It was true, Carrie and Harry's relationship had played out like a soap opera. The older residents of Lakelands Nursing Home had eagerly awaited every Monday's thrilling instalment of Carrie's weekend. Zoe had often thought that wondering what was going to happen next was the only thing that kept some of them alive. Harry was moving abroad with his job,

19

then he wasn't moving, his father had died so he was forced to stay in Cork to look after the business, oh, hang on, he could run it from Dublin. Weren't computers great? Harry's ex was after him, Carrie's ex was after her. And on and on.

'Still,' Zoe smiled, 'they are mad about each other, it's nice.'

'It's nauseating,' Dominic smirked, elbowing her. 'I feel ill, right now.'

'That's only because you've got no one,' Zoe teased. The nurses in work had a saying that if Dominic were a house, he'd fetch top dollar even in a recession. All high-class fixtures and fittings with a gorgeous exterior. It was hard to believe that he hadn't been snapped up.

'No one has got *me*, you mean,' Dominic clarified with a wink.

Dominic's winks were very sexy, everyone, even the residents of Lakelands, agreed. It was something to do with his long lashes.

Zoe made a face at him and said with false sarcasm, 'I doubt anyone gets *you*, Dom.'

'Oooh, good one!' He lightly punched her. Just then his phone rang and he took a few slightly inebriated seconds to extract it from his pocket. 'Shit,' he said when he saw the caller's ID. 'Rosie, what's up?'

It was his urgent tone that made the others look at him anxiously. Dominic had paled and was darting furtive glances at them.

'OK, be right there.' Dominic ended the call and

stood up quickly, pulling his jacket from the seat. 'Gotta go. Sorry. Something's come up.'

'You OK?' Harry asked. 'You need a lift?' He indicated his pint, 'I've only had the one.'

'No, thanks anyway. I'll get a taxi.'

'Nothing serious I hope?' Zoe said.

'Nah.' He managed a grin that didn't quite cut it. 'See you both in work.'

'A lift's no problem,' Harry insisted.

But Dominic didn't answer as he sprinted from the pub.

They spent the rest of the night wondering what could have happened.

'OK, here we are,' Deirdre said, adopting a heartily cheerful tone as she pulled her car into Lakelands' small car park. It was after nine, a late hour to be booking her mother into the nursing home, but work had been quite stressful. And, if she were honest, she'd tried to stall this trip for months now, inventing reasons why it didn't suit her to bring her mother in. When she'd rung Rick with her latest excuse, he had sternly told her that Lily's place in the home would be gone if Deirdre didn't pull her finger out. And, he added, as Lily had picked the place herself, it'd be a crying shame if she lost it. Deirdre realised that Rick was right – and so here they were. A sad little threesome. She switched off her engine and her blue Yaris was plunged into silence. Nobody moved, as if afraid to take the next step. After a second, Deirdre turned around. In the back, Rick, her mother's cousin, had his hand on her mother's arm. He shot Deirdre a sad smile and she knew that she'd never forget that moment or the picture the two made in the back. Despite her illness, her mother still had a regal air. Her hair, white and soft as lamb's wool, was scooped into a bun and showed off a long slender neck. The royal blue coat she wore emphasised her still-bright blue eyes. But it was the expression in them that gave her away, a childlike wondering mixed with confusion.

'Mammy,' Deirdre said softly, trying to keep her voice level and calm, trying desperately to keep a lid on the churning doubt inside her, 'are you sure you want to be here?'

'Here?' her mother repeated. 'I want to be at home.'

Deirdre shot a look of desperation at Rick.

'This will be your home,' Rick said in his husky smoker's voice, pressing Lily's hand gently. 'It's called Lakelands and it's a nursing home.'

'Who are you?' her mother demanded querulously.

Rick hesitated so Deirdre answered, 'He's Rick, your cousin. And I'm Deirdre. I'm your daughter.'

'Rick is dead,' her mother said dismissively. 'And Deirdre is—' she paused and frowned and said with a mixture of pride and sadness, 'On the radio. That's when I get to hear her.'

'No, I'm here,' Deirdre bit back a sob. She couldn't cry, not now. This wasn't about her. This was about getting her mother settled in Lakelands. She put on her hearty voice, 'Now, come on and we'll get out of this car.'

Rick helped Lily from the back seat and Deirdre took her mother's arm as Rick popped the boot and took Lily's case from it.

As Deirdre led her mother through the car park and into the stunning reception area of Lakelands, she thought the guilt would bend her over.

'Out late, aren't you?'

Zoe jumped at the sudden voice from behind. Turning around she saw Marty, the neighbour from hell; in fact, if Zoe had to bet on it, he was Satan himself. He was old, she couldn't even begin to guess how old he was, and he walked with the aid of a walking stick. He was kind of famous in that he was on every radio and TV talk show complaining about things. Radio shows rang him up for his bigoted and extreme views and, because he was old, he got away with saying the most outrageous things.

'Ten o'clock isn't late,' Zoe said breezily as she stuck the key in her door. 'Anyway, you're out late yourself, aren't you?'

'I've just come from RTÉ. I was debating the behaviour of children in schools on Pat's show.' He said RTÉ like it was the Holy Grail.

'Are you teaching in schools on a regular basis?' Zoe enquired, knowing full well that he wasn't.

'No,' he sounded belligerent, 'but I read the

23

papers and I see on the internet what's happening in America. Children bringing AK47s into the classroom.'

Zoe gave a polite smile, not wanting to get caught in a debate in the middle of the smelly rundown corridor of Dodder Gardens. Her brother often joked that it should be rechristened Dodgy Gardens and she had to agree. The apartment name gave the impression that they stood on the Dodder, a picturesque river in south Dublin. And, indeed, if one stared very hard out the window with a pair of powerful binoculars, one could see a flash of shining blue. But mostly, all the average person saw was apartment block after apartment block, with a few junkies thrown in for good measure. All of life's emotional cripples seemed to live in her block. Marty was just one of them. She unlocked her door and shut it on Marty's assertion that he could smell a strong smell of drink from her. She leaned her back against the front door and heaved a sigh. It would be nice to think that coming home would make her feel enveloped in safety and security but, in truth, as she looked around the messy cramped living room, it was like visiting Iraq.

She and Abe had moved here before Lee was born. The plan had been to rent it temporarily until they had more time to look around, but somehow, they'd never found the time. 'Isn't Dodder Gardens handy for your job?' Abe would ask each time she broached the subject. 'Isn't it cheap?' And he was right. Dodder Gardens let them have a life without much commuting or expense – or comfort, Zoe thought a little glumly. Still, the two people she loved most in the world were here so that counted for something. She tiptoed across the room and opening the door of Lee's room peeked in on her son. He was curled up in his duvet, a thumb in his mouth, fast asleep. Zoe's heart spilled over with love and she smiled. She had a sudden urge to cuddle him but resisted, there was no point in waking him. Pulling off her coat and scarf, she shut the door quietly and made her way into her and Abe's bedroom.

Abe was lying sprawled across the bed, limbs everywhere, also asleep. He liked to go to bed early because he believed it kept him healthy. She undressed and slid in beside him, dodging his arms as, sensing her presence, he flailed about a bit. Then he settled on his side, his back to her. Zoe curled herself about him and he woke briefly, turning to kiss her. 'Good night?' he asked sleepily.

'Weird night. Dominic left early, I played gooseberry to—'

'Well, don't forget you've work tomorrow,' he mumbled. 'You told me to set the alarm before you came back. Night. Love you.'

Aw shit. She had forgotten. Once a month she worked Saturdays, because as entertainment manager she had to be there whenever she booked an outside act for the residents – tomorrow, there was a magician coming. She'd meant to spend the day planning Lee's birthday on Sunday.

'Abe?'

'Mmm.'

'Can you sort out Lee's party for Sunday? Just get some balloons and stuff.'

'Uh-huh.'

'Thanks. I'll leave a list.'

He didn't answer. Five seconds later he was asleep.

June, the manager of Lakelands, seemed very capable, Deirdre thought. She was smartly dressed and she carried a clipboard. Clipboards said a lot about a person. June's clipboard was blue and shiny and the paper affixed to it was neat, straight and aligned. June was telling them to leave Lily for now. Deirdre wasn't sure that she could.

'We'll have Olive watch her for the night,' June said. 'If you'd both like to come to my office, we can go through some paperwork.'

Deirdre took a final look at her mother as she lay in her new bed. She looked so tiny, the covers pulled right up to her neck. She watched as Rick gently smoothed the covers down. 'She likes things to be smooth,' Rick said.

Deirdre swallowed a lump in her throat. How was she just going to leave her mother there? Leave her to the care of these strangers? She knew she hadn't been the greatest daughter in the world sometimes but just to abandon her . . .

'She really will be fine,' June said gently. 'And we'll contact you immediately if she gets upset.'

'Yes, yes, of course you will,' Rick said, as if he was trying to convince himself. Deirdre noted that even his tall frame seemed diminished by the act of leaving Lily. 'Come on, Deirdre, let the experts mind her now.' He offered her his arm and she let him lead her out, every instinct in her wanting to stay in the small room. But what good would I do by staying? Deirdre wondered. What would it achieve? It seemed wrong to leave her mother and step back into the throng of life again. It seemed wrong to have a life while her mother's was suspended between these walls.

Deirdre wondered if Rick felt any of this and could only conclude, by his defeated posture, that he must do. He smiled down on her and, despite her ongoing suspicion of Rick's motives in looking after her mother these past few years, she felt a bond with him. They were both locked together by this deed. It comforted her, reminded her that she was not alone.

Together they followed June back through reception and, taking a corridor to the left, June ushered them into her office. It was as neat as her clipboard, which was a great sign.

'Coffee?' June asked.

They both said they'd have one.

'I know how both of you are feeling,' June said as she handed them their drinks. 'I've been here over ten years and believe me it's the same for everyone. But you are doing the right thing, looking after an elderly relative with Alzheimer's is a twenty-four-hour job and, even then, it's not possible to be there all the time.'

'Lily was the one who decided when to come in,' Rick said.

'She made it easy for you both,' June nodded gently. She looked down at the pages on her clipboard. 'Right,' she began, 'I know you've already told me most of these details, but it's no harm at all to double check. Is that OK?'

Deirdre liked that. Double-checking was professional. She always did it before going on air at the radio station. Triple-checked sometimes. She settled herself into the chair, tucking her feet well in under the seat. She adjusted her cardigan and smoothed out the creases in her blouse.

'Lily has Alzheimer's, is that right?'

'Yes,' Deirdre answered.

'Any idea when it started?'

Deirdre looked to Rick. 'About six years ago now.' A pause as Deirdre admitted quietly, 'Rick would know better than me, he was with her a lot more.'

If June found that odd, she didn't say, instead she turned to Rick.

'About six years,' he confirmed. 'Lily asked me to mind her about two years ago, when she felt she couldn't cope anymore. I moved in with her about eight months ago.' He hesitated slightly, 'I trained as a nurse, so I was the obvious choice. It was Lily who decided that when things got too bad that she'd like to come here.'

'Anything else you can tell me about Lily? I see here that she's had depression.'

'I'm not sure if it was depression,' Deirdre said, glad to contribute, 'I just put it down because I remember, when I was younger, she'd lie in bed and wouldn't get up. It happened on and off through the years. No one ever talked about it at the time.'

'Sounds like depression,' June nodded. 'Were there any reasons for it? Any triggers?'

'Oh, I wouldn't know. It was a long time ago now. It happened quite a bit when I was younger, when we lived in Cavan. She moved to Dublin some years ago and it hasn't happened since.' Thank God, Deirdre thought.

June jotted down notes. 'Anything else we should know?'

Deirdre frowned. Other than those curious episodes, her mother had been as healthy as brown bread.

'Her diary?' Rick prompted.

'That's right!' Deirdre wondered how she could she have forgotten about that. 'She has a blue diary with her. She holds it during the day, like a security blanket. She won't let anyone near it. Sometimes she likes to open it and read it, though I don't know if she can read anymore. And also, though it's not so much now, she can be really lucid at times.'

June took a note of that. 'Well, I think that's fine for now,' she said softly, standing up. 'If you think of anything else, ring anytime. Don't be afraid.'

'Thank you,' Deirdre put her mug down and stood up too. Leaving Lily here was unbearable. For the first time she dreaded going back alone to her little cottage in Bohernabreena. If only she could share it with her mother, bring her walking in the fields out the back, show her the wild roses and honeysuckle and the amazing plethora of birds that populated the area to the back of her cottage. But it was too late for that now. And, anyway, on the one occasion she had done it, Lily had tried to sound interested but both of them had known it was just an act. It had been an incredibly strained afternoon, the two of them dancing around the explosive subject that had blown their already fragile relationship apart. Showing Lily her house had been Deirdre's attempt to rebuild something from the ruins. Pretending delight had been Lily's. Really, though, it was Jimmy, her dad, who had been the cement between them and he was gone. Deirdre's voice shook as she said, 'Please take care of her.'

'Of course we will.'

'I feel so guilty you see and—'

'Everyone feels the same, trust me, I know.' June smiled sympathetically at her. 'And you did say Lily chose this place herself?'

'She did, yes,' Rick sounded as if he might cry now.

'So, she has great taste,' June said, making them smile. 'We will care for your mother as if she were family. Safe home now.'

They shook June's hand and side by side they walked to the door.

'D'you fancy a guest in Mam's house tonight?' Deirdre asked quietly.

Rick's answer was a tearful nod.

Without thinking, Deirdre hugged him.

CHAPTER 2

It was not going well, Zoe thought, from her vantage point at the door. OK, it was going well for Ronnie Matthews, the eighty-year-old man in the wheelchair who was sitting right up the front of the hall. Ronnie was the reason a lot of acts refused to come to Lakelands. Today, though, Ronnie had stepped up his heckling campaign and the residents of Lakelands were on fire.

Everyone was realising, solely through Ronnie's taunts, that Marvello the Magician was not so marvellous.

'Oh, please,' Ronnie eventually said as Marvello pulled a rabbit from a hat, 'the rabbit is stored in a box under your table.'

'A rabbit in a box under the table?' Julie Lyons, seventy-nine years old but only claiming seventy-five of them, said, appalled. 'How cruel.'

Everyone started to agree.

'Does it spend all day in a box under your table?' a voice asked from somewhere.

Marvello pretended not to hear. He put down his hat and bowed. A few of the more polite audience members clapped. Then they applauded more loudly as Marvello's assistant, Gloria, walked on stage. The more sprightly residents, Ronnie among then, wolf-whistled and Gloria flinched, then scowled.

'Nice legs,' Ronnie called.

Another glower from Gloria. Then Marvello took her hand and led her towards an upright box. Grimacing, she waved at the audience as she climbed in.

'Bye bye, dear,' Lily said from beside Zoe.

Zoe smiled at Lakelands' newest resident, who'd come in late last night. She must have been a bit of a stunner in her youth. There was a man sitting with her.

'It's just a show, Lily,' she explained. 'She's not waving at you.'

'That's what I was trying to tell her,' Lily's visitor said with a charming smile. He was probably quite the looker in his day too. 'He's a magician, Lil.'

'I will now plunge knives into my assistant!' Marvello intoned, with a flourish of his cape.

Lily gasped.

'It's just a show,' the man repeated, taking Lily's hand in his.

'I'm Zoe, by the way,' Zoe held out her hand to Lily's visitor, who shook it. 'Entertainment manager.'

'Rick,' the man said.

'If poor Lily is upset by this, I'm responsible and I apologise,' Zoe gave a sheepish grin.

'Oh, it'd take more than that to upset Lily, she was a tough cookie in her day,' Rick grinned, before turning to Lily and saying, 'You gave everyone the run around.'

Lily ignored him. She was studying Zoe as if trying to work out a puzzle. Finally she said, 'You read the papers.'

'Yes, I do,' Zoe nodded. 'Well done.' Turning to Rick, she explained, 'I read the papers to them in the mornings.'

'That's amazing, she hasn't remembered anything like that for ages,' Rick sounded delighted. 'Deirdre will be thrilled when I tell her.' His voice dropped. 'Deirdre is her daughter. She would have been here only she's working. She works in radio you see and her days can be a bit erratic. She made me come in first thing to see how this one is doing.' He smiled at Lily. 'You always did like your news in the morning, didn't you? She—'

'I will now plunge *six* knives into my assistant,' Marvello shouted, drowning out whatever else Rick had to say as he displayed six shiny sharp knives to the audience.

'What a horrible man,' Lily said loudly and people around her laughed.

'You tell him,' Rick chortled. Then added to Zoe, 'I think Marvello could use a disappearing trick if this crowd get any rowdier.'

Zoe winced. 'What an introduction to Lakelands for you both.'

'Well I actually thought he was good until that

man in the front kept shouting out how he's doing the tricks.'

'That's Ronnie,' Zoe said, 'and I reckon he was a hell-raiser in his day.'

'He was probably also a magician,' Rick laughed as, yet again, Ronnie disputed the veracity of Marvello's claims.

'I shall put this straight through her heart,' Marvello went on gamely, plunging the knife into the centre of the box.

'Big swinging mickey,' Ronnie snorted, causing more gasps than Marvello had managed to achieve.

'I'll kill him,' Zoe clapped a hand over her mouth.

Rick laughed. 'This,' he indicated to the room, the magician, the noise, 'this is great. I needed to see this. Deirdre will be so happy to hear about this.'

'Well,' Zoe smiled, 'I'm glad the ritual humiliation of our magician has made you see us in a good light.' Then she added, 'She will be happy here, honestly.'

Zoe pretended not to see Rick's eyes grow shiny by turning to look daggers at Ronnie as he urged the crowd to boo.

She was going to give him a piece of her mind after this, wheelchair or not.

Deirdre sighed with relief as she clicked off her mobile. It seemed that her mother was settling in quite well in Lakelands and had even recognised one of the members of staff. As she barely recognised

Deirdre anymore, that was a huge thing. Deirdre rested her elbows on her desk and wiped her eyes with the heel of her palm. She hadn't realised how stressed she was over her mother until Rick had phoned to say all was well. Still, she knew she wouldn't relax properly until she'd seen it for herself, and that wouldn't be until Wednesday afternoon, which was her half day from work, barring emergencies. She was only in work today because the director general had asked to see her and basically you did whatever he asked. He usually met with her and her team when he wanted her to 'bumf' – his word – up her programme. He never asked her to come in on a Saturday though, so it was very puzzling.

Deirdre opened the window of her office before lighting a cigarette. Puffing contentedly, she thought about the first time she'd been shown this office. It had been five years ago, she'd been a gardener in Dublin's Botanic Gardens and had been asked by RTÉ to comment on some disease that had been rampaging through the trees in Dublin's parks. After that interview, to her surprise, she'd been inundated with offers to do her own radio show. She'd plumped for Dublin Live. She missed gardening though. Missed it like Christmas.

Deirdre yawned – God, she was tired. She had spent a sleepless night in her mother's house. Even though Lily had lived in Dublin for over a decade, Deirdre still couldn't get used to the fact that the two-bedroom house in the middle of a terrace on a busy street was her mother's home. In Deirdre's mind, it would always be her childhood house in Cavan that was her refuge, but that was gone, sold to an uncle. Just another thing that Lily had done to cause friction in their relationship. In the middle of the night, when Deirdre was sure Rick was sleeping, she had pulled on her fleecy dressing gown and crept into her mother's room. In the half-light, the bedroom had appeared a little alien, shadows being thrown by the light on the landing lending everything a slightly menacing air. Nothing was familiar. Her mother had sold or discarded most of the furniture from the old house when she'd moved. The only thing she'd kept was the big brass bed frame, which Deirdre climbed onto. Turning her head to the pillow, she had been assailed by the scent of lavender, a perfume that Lily had worn all her life. That smell, more than anything, had made Deirdre's body ache with longing to be back with her mother and father in Cavan. Just for one day, to tell them how much she loved them both. She'd never wanted to leave Cavan to live in Dublin, but her parents had been so proud to see her get a place in college that she hadn't wanted to disappoint them. She'd never gone back to live at home. The lavender reminded her of the times her mother had cuddled her to her, the times Lily had nursed her when she was sick, the times she'd kissed away her night-time fears. *If she could just go back and tell her that she did love her. That even though they barely knew what*

37

to say to each other any more, she still loved her.
But time was cruel, it just marched on, trampling
all before it. If only time were a book or a diary
that you could reread until you understood the
significance of something, Deirdre thought; instead,
time was a teacher that ploughed on regardless of
your understanding. At fifty-five, Deirdre still felt
a little lost in an adult world. She had been playing
catch-up her whole life.

Rick had startled her by tapping on the door.
'OK in there?' he asked.

'Yes,' Deirdre answered, a little abruptly. She
wasn't too sure how she felt about this man.
She was grateful for what he'd done for her
mother but the man was hitting eighty and he
still dyed his hair, for God's sake.

'I'm downstairs having a glass of wine if you
want to join me,' Rick said and she heard him
move away from the door and shuffle off.

After a few minutes, still unable to sleep and
craving company, she threw on her dressing gown,
pulling the belt tightly, and joined Rick in the
kitchen. He said nothing to her, just found a glass
and poured. Deirdre wasn't a drinker, but the wine
was smooth and it relaxed her. She hadn't asked
Rick why he was still up, she knew that after almost
two years of caring for Lily, Rick must miss her
too.

They'd stayed up until four, not talking much,
just sitting together. Two people unable to find
any words for what they'd just done.

The ring of her office phone sent her thoughts scattering. 'Hello, Deirdre here,' she said in her best professional manner, hoping she didn't sound as flustered as she felt.

'Hi, Deirdre, this is Lorna, Michael Allen's PR. Can you come to his office?'

'Of course,' Deirdre said, trying to sound upbeat when in fact the opposite was true. Michael was intimidating. His presence was like a cushion pressed hard against your face. 'No problem. Be there in five.'

'OK, I'll tell him.' Lorna hung up.

Deirdre did a quick check in her office mirror. She couldn't exactly say that she was pleased with what was reflected back to her, but as she told herself many times, it was like the weather, just there and impossible to change. She was stick thin, with birdlike arms and childlike wrists. Straight up and down and tall as a pole. Her hair was cut. She never quite knew what to do with it, so she just got it 'cut'. And it was a salt-and-pepper grey where it once had been a tumbling black. Her eyes were her best feature, she supposed. A dark chocolate-brown, they were almost too large for her small pixie face. At least she was well turned out in a calf-length brown wool skirt, beige tights and flat beige shoes. She liked beige, it was warm and safe and didn't scream look at me. She had a horror of being noticed, of people thinking she was an attention seeker. To complement the skirt, she wore an expensive cream silk blouse with puff

39

sleeves and pearl buttons and a beige cardigan. Taking a deep breath, she promised herself that whatever Michael Allen had to say, she would not say anything stupid in reply.

It was dinnertime and those who were able had it in the small dining room. It had the air of a hotel, with tablecloths and polished cutlery. Zoe wandered into the room and looked around. Dominic was serving and she gave him a wave. Whatever that phone call was about last night, he seemed to have recovered from it. 'You seen Ronnie?' she called.

He cracked a grin and crossed towards her. 'I heard about this morning. He's probably hiding away, afraid he'll meet you.'

'That'd be very sensible of him,' Zoe agreed grimly. Then she asked, 'Are you OK? That call last night – we were worried.'

His eyes slid away from her gaze and rather than answer, he gave a subtle nod, 'Here he is, go easy on him.'

Zoe looked and saw Ronnie, head down, wheeling himself past as quietly as he could. 'Oi! You!' She stood in front of him and the canteen quietened, 'Troublemaker!'

'If I was able bodied, I could march on past you,' he snapped. 'Being in this bloody thing, I have no choice.'

Zoe ignored his bad temper. He was always giving out about his chair, always moaning about

40

his lack of mobility. There comes a time, she thought, when he'd just have to accept the way things were. It was obviously not going to be any time soon though. And since he'd come to Lakelands eight months ago, after his daughter and son-in-law had put him in before scampering madly in the other direction, he'd played on everyone feeling sorry for him.

'What you did this morning was unacceptable,' she told him.

'I know,' he grinned. 'But that act you booked was crap.'

'Really? And you'd know that, how?' Zoe had read his file. He used to be an 'entertainer', whatever that was.

Ronnie scowled at her. 'I'd like my lunch now,' he said.

Zoe threw Marvello's magic hat onto his lap. She hoped this worked, as Ronnie was going to find himself out of a place to stay if he didn't stop. And she would have hated to see that happen. Behind all the bluster, Zoe was sure there was a decent, though unhappy, man. 'Marvello gave you this. He was a bigger man than you. He said he respected you for showing him up.'

'Wow,' Dominic patted Ronnie on the back. 'Go you.'

The residents of Lakelands murmured appreciatively.

'He gave this to me?' Ronnie looked sceptically at the hat before glancing up at Zoe.

'Yep. Though personally I think he should have kicked your arse.'

Ronnie laughed a little before reaching out a finger to touch the soft velvet hat. After a second, he reverently picked it up. He kept his face averted as he stroked it, examining it from every angle.

'You're on your final warning though, Ronnie.'

It was a moment before he raised his eyes and Zoe was shocked to see how moved he was. 'Long time since someone showed me a bit of respect.' His tone was a mixture of emotion and complaint.

Zoe grinned and poked his arm with her finger, 'Yeah, well, maybe if you showed others respect, Ronnie, that would be good too.'

He made a face at her.

'An apology would be a great idea right now,' Zoe hinted.

'OK.' He heaved a sigh. 'I guess I better apologise to you then. Sorry about this morning.'

'Forgotten, don't let it happen again.'

Someone down the back cheered. Others shouted out, 'Well done, Ron!' Some sporadic clapping broke out. Ronnie turned and bowed to the room. Then wheeled himself off.

'How much did you pay for that hat?' Dominic spoke out of the corner of his mouth.

'Thirty-five shagging euro, bloody man tried to sew it into me for trauma.'

'Ouch.'

'It'll be worth it if it works,' Zoe smiled. 'And I think it might.'

'You old softie.'

They grinned at each other.

'Oi! Baker Boy! Stop chatting Zoe up and dole us out some dinner, would you? None of your fancy shit though,' Ronnie called.

Grinning, Dominic gave him the two fingers.

Ronnie laughed.

Dublin Live had started out as a small radio station, but because of its mix of popular culture, arts and nature, its listenership was growing year on year. There was now a staff of sixty and Deirdre's show *Wild* aired each weekday for an hour. It was an ironic name, seeing as Deirdre was not wild at all. She had three people on her production team. Suzi, the producer, was forty, single and, like Deirdre, showed no signs of ever getting married. She'd been with Deirdre from her very first show and they really clicked. Emma and Matt were the two researchers in their twenties and Deirdre really wasn't sure what they were there for. Emma was shy, blushing every time Deirdre asked her a question, while Matt spent most of the time with his feet up making coffee for them all. Deirdre ended up doing most of the research herself, but at least it was done properly.

She arrived outside Michael's office and his PR, flashing her a look that she couldn't make out, told her to go on in. As Deirdre entered, Michael rose up from the chair behind his desk and gave her a wide smile. His teeth had been whitened to an unnatural dazzle and his face looked quite weird, with its folds and wrinkles. 'Hello, Deirdre,' he said heartily, 'thanks for coming, sit down there.' He indicated a chair.

Deirdre sat warily, tucking her skirt neatly under her. Michael was smiling too much. He was the director general and did not have to smile at anyone. He very rarely smiled at her so this was alarming. She wondered idly if she was about to be fired. Well, it was either that or she'd won a prize. Radio hosts were only ever called to his office for these reasons.

'I have some news for you,' Michael sat back behind his desk and steepled his fingers. 'I've told Suzi already.'

Deirdre wondered why Suzi hadn't told her. She felt Michael was studying her, like a specimen in a Petri dish, for a reaction. 'Yes?'

'You've been here five years, isn't that right?' Michael began.

Deirdre nodded. It felt longer.

'Well, as you know from all the figures from the past few years, your listenership has stagnated,' Michael said. Deirdre sighed inwardly, he always began every conversation with her in this way.

'Yes, I know,' Deirdre said. 'We keep our listeners.' That was always her response.

'So,' Michael said as if she hadn't spoken, another thing he always did, 'in order to give you the boost you need, we've decided to take on another producer to head up the team. We think some fresh eyes could turn your show around.'

This was quite disturbing news. 'My show doesn't need turning around. Suzi is great.'

Michael didn't respond. He just let her protest float away. Then after a beat, his teeth shining like tusks, he said, 'We've poached Paul Maguire from RTÉ.'

'Paul Maguire?' For a moment the name meant nothing to her and then it hit her. 'Paul?' she blurted out incredulously, her voice rising. 'You can't have.'

Paul Maguire was producer of some of the trashiest, though most popular, radio documentaries. Things like *The Woman who Had Four Breasts* and *Is Sex Dead in Ireland?* Deirdre had never met him and never wanted to. His reputation for procreating and partying preceded him and she knew that he'd be a bad influence on her team and her show.

Again, Michael let her protest die away before saying, 'I know you probably think he wouldn't have a clue about your type of show—'

'Well how could he?' Deirdre felt a light sweat break across her forehead. 'He produced *Porn Unleashed* for God's sake.'

'Yes, exactly.' Michael nodded excitedly. 'Fresh eyes, a new approach. Paul says he can't wait.'

'And what about what I have to say?' Normally she'd never talk like this to her boss, but really how could he humiliate her and her team by employing the master of sleaze to produce her show?

45

'What do you have to say?' Michael asked, his voice not sounding very encouraging. 'We want listeners, Deirdre. Our shows have to produce them and, frankly, yours doesn't. Paul is also going to head up a couple of other shows too but yours will be his baby.'

'His baby?' Deirdre spluttered out. She pulled her cardigan around herself and folded her arms. 'From what I gather he doesn't need any more of them.'

Michael actually laughed. 'I wouldn't have thought you read the tabloids, Deirdre.'

Now honestly, what was that supposed to mean? Of course she did. 'Do you think we can't up our listenership ourselves?' she asked, diverting things away from her reading habits.

'Paul will be here in two weeks.' He stood up to show that the meeting was over.

'That's a "no" then?' She was surprised at her doggedness. So was Michael.

'Yes,' he sounded annoyed. 'I happen to think your show needs a good kick up the arse, Deirdre. Is that frank enough for you?'

She flushed and swallowed and pulled her cardigan in even tighter. 'There's no need for that,' she said before turning on her heel and walking out.

She badly needed a smoke.

Or ten.

CHAPTER 3

Since finding out that her mother was ill, eight months ago, Deirdre had developed a habit of calling in to see her on the way home from work. Now that her mother was in the nursing home, Deirdre wondered if she should call on Rick. It was all a bit odd, she barely knew the man and yet, having seen him with her mother on the times she had called, Deirdre knew that he'd played a very important role in her mother's life these past few years. He'd been indispensable and Deirdre would never have managed without him, much as she thought she might have. To heck with it, she thought, turning the car and heading towards her mother's, she'd call in today and see how things were. It wouldn't be right to discard the man after what he'd done, though her feelings towards him were ambiguous. He was family, but not close family. Her mother's cousin, so *her* first cousin once removed or something like that. She was not very good at figuring out family connections or relations. Deirdre had the uneasy feeling that Rick wanted something out of all this. Why would he just drop everything to look after her mother?

OK, he was a nurse and he got food and lodging in return for his care, but what he had contributed far outweighed that. *Was* he after something? Deirdre suspected that he'd been down on his luck and her mother had taken him in out of pity. But the things he had done for Lily were not what one would do just for a clean bed. Had he persuaded Lily to change her will? Deirdre felt bad for thinking it but, as her mother would have said, Deirdre's always on high alert in every situation. A good thing too if her mother was going to be fleeced.

Two months previously, Deirdre had thought she'd had the measure of him when, after the decision to move Lily to a nursing home was taken, he'd asked shyly if he could stay on in Lily's house for a little while. Then he'd scuppered her perception of him as a money grabber by offering to pay the going rent. He'd made some friends in the area, he'd explained, and he would miss them if he had to leave. Deirdre found it hard to believe that he'd made such close friends in such a short time, but as she had been going to rent the house anyway, she was agreeable but feigned a reluctance to take full rent from him. He had insisted, which was a relief and a disappointment.

As Deirdre drove up the M50, her thoughts drifted back to the first time she'd met the man. It had followed a phone call from her mother asking to see her urgently. Lily's request had been alarmingly out of character as her mother only

48

ever phoned her in emergencies. The last bombshell her mother had dropped, about fifteen years ago, had been precluded by another such call – and from then on relations had been shaky at best. And so Deirdre had left work, full of trepidation. She loved her mother dearly, but sometimes Lily did things that made it hard to keep loving her.

More quickly than she wanted that day, she was pulling up outside her mother's tiny terraced house. Her mother was already at the door, waiting for her. Behind her mother, there was a tall, elderly man with dark hair. Dyed. Deirdre was immediately suspicious.

'This is Rick,' Lily said smoothly, introducing him. 'Rick, this is my daughter, Deirdre.'

'Hello,' Rick held out his hand. His nails were neatly filed. 'Nice to meet you.'

He'd sounded half-English. Deirdre shook his hand briefly. His handshake was firm so that was good, but any man who dyed his hair, never mind one obviously hitting old age, was someone to be wary of. He was a pleasant-looking man, trim and fit, with dark eyes and sallow skin.

'I have a bit of news for you,' Lily said.

'News?' Deirdre's heart began to hammer ferociously. She needed a handkerchief badly.

'I think you'd better come into the kitchen and sit down,' her mother said, sounding more mature than Deirdre had ever remembered. If she had to draw a picture of her mother, it'd be of light and air, kind of impossible to draw really. This new mature person was alarming and Deirdre felt spidery fingers of fear crawl up her spine as she followed her mother down the hall. Rick shut the door.

Deirdre sat, perched on the edge of a chair in her mother's ultramodern high-gloss kitchen. Her mother had put new curtains in the window since the last time she'd been there, which had to be over a year ago now, she thought guiltily. Light bounced from glossy surface to glossy surface and Deirdre felt the shadow of bad news fall as her mother sat opposite her.

'What?' she asked, trying to sound matter-of-fact.

Rick sat beside her mother. His expression was hard to gauge – he looked at once grave, upset and stunned.

'I'll get straight to the point,' Lily said, 'before I forget.'

This caused Rick and her mother to laugh a little. Confused, Deirdre looked from one to the other.

'Sorry,' Lily said. 'Sorry, pet. Sometimes it's nice to laugh.'

Deirdre sighed. Her mother always told her she was too serious, was always on at her to laugh more. Deirdre was quite happy not laughing actually. 'What's this news?' she'd asked instead.

Her mother's smile faded and Deirdre felt momentarily guilty for robbing her of that smile. 'It's hard to tell you this,' Lily began, her bright blue eyes catching and pinning Deirdre with their gaze, 'but I've been having some problems with my memory.'

'And?'

Rick and her mother shared a look.

'What?' Deirdre asked, her gaze flitting from one to the other. 'What did you forget? Something important?' When Deirdre was young, her mother regularly messed up while grocery shopping. She always remembered just as they left the super-market that she'd forgotten an essential item. Then Deirdre would be left, watching over bags and bags of messages while her mother ran back inside. She'd hated that because what if someone had swiped a bag? What could she have done? Why didn't her mother make lists like normal people? Why—

Deirdre, so caught up in remembrance of that angst, missed what her mother said. She knew because there followed a silence that she was expected to fill. So she winged it. 'What's that? Is it bad?'

Her mother looked a little incredulous. 'Yes,' she'd said, 'eventually. It leads to complete memory loss. You know, of everything, not just of people or places, but of skills like, I don't know, eating.'

It took a few seconds, like sugar in cold water, for the information to sift down until it settled. 'Hang on,' Deirdre said suddenly. 'Are you talking about Alzheimer's?'

'Yes.' Her mother looked at Rick as if to say 'she's not normally so slow'.

Deirdre opened her mouth to speak, but realised that there were no words for news like that. She was just shocked.

'I know it's awful.' Her mother filled the silence. 'And I didn't want to tell you but Rick said you had a right to know.'

Her mother had Alzheimer's and this unknown man had had a say in whether or not she should be told? She wished she had the energy to glare at Rick, but she didn't. 'You weren't going to tell me?' It hurt like a knife, she sounded about six as she added, 'Why don't you ever tell me things that are important?'

Her mother's eyes widened in hurt, then she bowed her head. Her mother's head was so tiny, with such gorgeous white hair, always neatly bushed and set. That day, she wore a tiny little flower in the bobbin. It was that detail that made Deirdre's heart crack just a little. 'I'm sorry. I'm sorry, Mammy.'

'You've nothing to be sorry for,' Lily said softly.

But she did. She'd been a failure of a daughter. Oh, she'd tried her best to make her mother happy and proud, but had never quite managed it. Look at her now, upsetting her mother instead of comforting her. She hopped up and, hunkering down beside Lily, she wrapped her arms about her waist. Her mother laid a hand on her head.

Deirdre closed her eyes and inhaled lavender.

'She just didn't want you to worry,' Rick said quietly after a bit.

Deirdre glanced up at him, 'Who are you anyway?'

'No one really,' he muttered, going red and looking at his hands, 'just a—'

'Rick is going to be my carer,' Lily cut him off. 'He's my cousin, first cousin, and he's an expert on this sort of thing.'

'Yes,' Rick agreed.

'I can care for you,' Deirdre said indignantly. She flapped an arm, 'You look fine to me now. You don't need a full-time carer. I'll move in and—'

'Rick has been caring for me for a while now,' her mother said, and though she wasn't trying to make Deirdre feel ashamed, Deirdre did. Imagine not knowing something as important as that. She might have known if she'd called in more often, she supposed, but there was always some excuse why she hadn't. And in a way, her not calling was a relief for them both, it made it easier to avoid painful subjects. 'He's going to move in now because I'm getting worse.' Lily sounded as if there was no changing her mind. She tipped Deirdre's chin up, 'You have your job,' she said firmly, 'and you do it so well. Rick is retired and willing. He's happy to stay here and spare you the worst of it.'

'You are my mother,' Deirdre said, twisting away. 'I want to do it.' That was directed at both of them.

'You are my daughter,' Lily spoke softly, she even smiled a tiny bit. 'I will not let you become my parent.' A pause. 'Not again.'

Her mother's words hung in the air before they settled about Deirdre's shoulders, making her eyes brim with tears.

'It's what I want,' her mother said softly. 'Please.'

'I can't believe this is happening,' Deirdre whispered to no one in particular.

Her mother stood slowly and embraced her. Deirdre hugged her back fiercely, already wondering how many more hugs they had left before her mother forgot her.

They'd told her everything that horrible evening eight months ago. After that night, Lily's disease had progressed quite quickly, almost as if by telling Deirdre, her mind had finally stopped battling to remember everything. She'd gone missing, escaping from the house in her dressing gown early one morning. She'd upset Rick by insisting that he was dead and refused to acknowledge that Deirdre had grown up, asking her over and over where her little girl was. She became unable to dress herself and spent the day asking Rick if he knew when Jimmy was coming. Or if Patrick was outside. Whoever that was. It was heartbreaking, but inside, sometimes, there were glimpses of the old Lily. That's what kept Rick going, he told Deirdre. Bold, feisty Lily, that was who he saw whenever she smiled at him.

Deirdre wondered if her mother had confided her secrets to Rick during their two years together but Rick never alluded to anything amiss in Lily's life. Maybe he was too much of a gentleman, maybe he didn't know, so Deirdre kept her silence on the matter too.

As she pulled up in front of her mother's house, she was taken aback though amused to see Rick, in her mother's flowery pinny, polishing the windows. He gave her a wave, a delighted smile on his face, and she waved back, surprising herself by smiling too.

But she was still on her guard. Something about him was just not . . . right.

CHAPTER 4

The boys were destroying the apartment. There were only eight of them but it was as if they'd been caged all their lives and had now only been set free. They'd all arrived within seconds of each other; their parents had declined an invitation to join in the festivities, and instead they'd actually fled down the hallway, chatting to each other about the fun they were going to have now that their sons had been bundled off on an unsuspecting Zoe. Not that they'd actually said *that* of course, but it was what they'd meant.

The boys had greeted each other like long-lost allies, flung their presents in Lee's direction, cheering loudly as Lee unwrapped them with all the grace of someone having a seizure. Wrapping paper was flung into the air, boxes ripped open and the gifts were descended upon like crusts of bread in a famine.

Zoe's parents had arrived with a card and were thrown a careless 'hello' by a Lee who was high on excitement.

'Who are those old people?' Tom, the wildest boy, asked.

'No one,' Lee said carelessly, 'just my nana and granddad.'

Mrs Killeen looked miffed. 'Aren't you going to open your card?' she asked.

So Lee opened his card and there had been an awkward moment when his nana had held out her arms for a kiss. Tom had snorted in derision and Lee, looking anxiously at him, had backed off with a muttered 'thanks' to rejoin his friends on the floor.

'Those boys are not a good influence on him,' Mrs Killeen muttered, peeved that no kiss had been bestowed upon her by her grandchild. 'Peer pressure at five years old.'

'Come into the kitchen and have a cuppa.' Zoe ushered them in.

Abe was at the table, a massive pot of tea beside him, totally calm in the face of what was going on outside. He had the paper open beside him. 'Hey!' he greeted Zoe's parents. 'Cuppa.'

'Thank you, Abe,' Mrs Killeen said, sitting down. 'Weak. Only a little milk.'

Abe did as he was told, then poured Zoe's dad one before turning back to the paper.

Zoe bristled. Honestly, she thought, the least he could do is chat to my parents. He was acting like he was still in bloody work, reading reports or something. Her parents, though, didn't seem surprised by Abe. They were used to it, Zoe thought with a slight shock.

'He normally kisses me,' her mother went on

then, shaking her head. 'Your brother, now there was a boy that loved his hugs and kisses.'

'I'll kiss you instead,' Mr Killeen joked, arms open wide but his wife pushed him off.

'There is no point in trying to get into my good books,' she said crossly.

Mr Killeen heaved a sigh and at Zoe's questioning look said, 'Washing machine broke down.'

'That is not the problem,' his wife snapped. 'The problem is that you tried to fix it. D'you know what, it's about time you realised that you can't even fix a simple breakfast never mind a complicated piece of machinery like a washing machine!'

'If you hadn't walked on that spring thing then—'

'Hey,' Lee whizzed into the kitchen, 'Tom wants to know where's my other nana and granddad – he has four, he said. Are they dead or what?'

Behind the paper, Abe jumped.

Zoe flushed, wondering what he'd say. It was a bone of contention between them that had grown over the years. It was only natural Lee should wonder.

'Well?' Lee asked. 'Are they dead?'

'My dad is.' Abe peered over the top of his page, his face was bright red. 'My mother is still alive, I guess.'

It was enough for Lee. He ran back into the room yelling, 'I have three! Three of them are still alive!'

Zoe's dad laughed loudly as Abe went back in behind his paper. Zoe's mother shot Zoe a look which she ignored. She was about to change the subject when the doorbell rang. 'That's probably Greg,' she said, relieved to be escaping from them all, however briefly. 'Hang on.'

She pushed open the kitchen door and waded her way through cardboard boxes, stepping over five-year-old boys to answer the bell.

But it wasn't Greg, it was Audrey, who air kissed her on both cheeks and flung a present in Lee's direction, managing to hit one of the boys on the head as it coasted towards her godchild. 'Happy Birthday, Lee,' she called out, before turning to Zoe saying, 'I'm gasping. And I need a fag.'

'Abe has some in the kitchen, go on, in you go.' Zoe grinned at her best friend. Audrey was in tailored white trousers and a red silk blouse. She was allergic to kids she said, but Lee wasn't too bad. She always remembered his birthday and Christmas, so as far as Lee was concerned she was a top-notch godparent. In high stiletto heels, Audrey minced her way through the mess.

'Hey, where's the sweets?' Tom called from his position upside down on the sofa.

'Coming soon,' Zoe answered, trying to sound upbeat.

'They're taking ages,' Tom said, 'the last party I was at, we had the party first and played later. I think I prefer that.'

I'd prefer if you hadn't come, Zoe thought crossly.

'Yeah, where are the sweets?' Lee called as if he too was used to loads of parties.

The chant was taken up and Zoe thought how bloody exhausting all this was. She had to seriously question Lee's choice of friends. He'd obviously decided to hang around with the most obnoxious section of his class.

'Who is looking for sweets?' Abe appeared in the kitchen doorway, a massive bag in his hands.

Nine boys descended on him and he teased them by holding it high above his head, making them laugh and squeal. He winked at Zoe and she managed a weary smile back.

The bell rang again.

It was Greg, her brother. Great, another man. Maybe he and Abe could keep the lads under control.

'Hey, sis.' Greg kissed Zoe on the cheek. He looked a little pale and stressed, she thought. He'd been looking like that a lot recently. She was about to ask him if he was OK when Tom, jumping back up onto the sofa, piped up, 'Oooh, Lee, is that your mammy's boyfriend? Is she having an affair?'

All the boys turned from Abe and gawked at Greg.

'What's an affair?' some other little boy asked.

'You'll fall off the sofa, Tom,' Zoe said, secretly thinking that it would serve him right if he did.

'I'm Lee's uncle,' Greg announced, grinning. 'And where is he?'

No one reacted at all.

'OK,' Greg said loudly, 'if Lee isn't here, I'm gonna have to leave with my present. There's

60

another boy whose birthday it is today and I'll give it to him.'

'Hey, Lee, you'll miss out on your present from your uncle,' Tom shouted, making everyone wince with the foghorn quality of his voice.

'He's here,' Abe held Lee up and shook him hard, making Lee laugh.

The rest of the boys, taking the cue from Lee, laughed too and Zoe was reminded once again how good Abe was with kids.

'That's not Lee,' Greg frowned, giving Zoe a puzzled look, 'No way! That boy is way too big to be Lee. Lee's about,' Greg made a hand gesture somewhere around knee height, 'that tall.'

Zoe laughed as all the boys, except Tom, insisted indignantly that Lee certainly was himself. Tom just shouted out that Greg was a 'blind bastard', which had Mrs Killeen gasping loudly in the kitchen, while Greg and Abe spluttered with suppressed laughter.

Boys were a funny lot, Zoe thought.

'Not true!' Greg shook his head, 'You're not Lee and,' he swivelled on his heels and eyeballed Tom, saying mock-sternly, 'if you say that to me again, Lee can't have his present.'

'Yeah, shut your cakehole, Tom,' one of the other boys said with a swagger.

Zoe gawped at him. Lee was doomed, there was no other word for it. If these were his friends now, what would he be like as a teenager? '"Cakehole" is not nice,' she said primly.

'Sorry,' the boy flushed, mortified, and looked as if he might cry.

Lee glared at her. 'Mam!'

Zoe felt terrible. Jesus. 'It's not a nice word,' she stammered out.

A big tear slid out of the little boy's eye.

Abe rescued the atmosphere. 'Prove to Greg that you're Lee,' he said to his son.

Lee laughed. 'It *is* me, Greg,' he yelled. As if to demonstrate, he flung his arms wide and stuck out his tummy. 'See.'

Greg peered at him more closely.

'Your uncle is stupid,' Tom snorted.

'Wow!' Greg feigned a stagger. 'It *is* you! You've grown loads since you were four. Well,' he went into the hallway and returned with a massive box, 'I guess this is for you so!'

Four of the boys gasped. Tom looked bored. Zoe felt like strangling him. 'Open, open, open,' the boy who had been about to cry began to chant, clapping his hands, and in response, Lee tore the wrapping off and shrieked when he saw the mini boxing gym Greg had bought him.

'Oh, mega,' he breathed.

'Gee, thanks, bruv.' Zoe fisted Greg's arm. 'That's great. That's all I need.'

Greg cupped his hand to his ear. 'Is that a hint of sarcasm I hear,' he grinned.

'A hint? A hint? A massive big clout across the ear, more like!'

He laughed and she led him into the kitchen and Zoe grinned at the way Audrey perked up.

Abe, meanwhile, began to assemble the boxing gym.

Four hours later, after thanking Greg, Audrey and her parents for their help and dropping some of the boys home, Zoe drove herself and Lee back to the apartment.

Unlocking the door, she saw with a slight annoyance that Abe hadn't even started to clean the place. Paper and smashed-up cakes still littered the carpet. 'Aw, Abe!' she groaned.

'Uh-huh?' he poked his head out of the kitchen.

Zoe bent down and began picking stuff up. 'Would you not think of cleaning up while we were gone?'

He looked at her blankly.

'The apartment? After the party?'

'Yeah, I was going to,' he said easily, 'but I just got caught up watching a news report. D'you know that it takes a thousand—'

'I know that unless you get your ass in gear, it'll take a thousand people to pick you up off the floor,' Zoe snapped.

Lee sloped off to his bedroom, taking his boxing set with him.

'And who rattled your cage?' Abe joined her in the living room with a roll of black bin liners. He pulled one open and started dumping all the plastic wrapping into it.

'Do you really need to ask?' Zoe said. 'You hardly said a word to my parents all day.'

'I was playing with the lads.'

'Not all the time. You could have talked to my folks.'

'They hate me,' he said.

'Plus, you let the kids wreck the house—'

'That's what boys do at parties.' Abe shrugged and dumped a load of wrapping paper on the sofa. 'They had fun.'

'Well I didn't!'

'Eh, newsflash.' Abe crossed towards her and grinned a little. 'Parents don't have fun at kids' parties. They suffer through them.' He stood in front of her and his grin widened, 'And when the party is over, they thank God that the next one is a year away.'

'What if you have more than one kid?'

Abe stared steadily at her. 'We don't,' he said evenly and resumed his cleaning.

'Will we ever?' It just popped out. It wasn't something she'd ever really thought about, but yet she always knew that she wanted more than one child. She didn't want Lee to be on his own.

Abe stiffened. He straightened up and turned to face her. A few seconds passed and then he said, 'I doubt it. This place is too small for starters.'

'Yeah. We *move*, Abe. We get a bigger place, we grow up. We can't stay here forever. This is student-ville.'

'I'm happy here,' he said. His grinned lazily, 'I'm

happy with Lee. With you.' He made to move towards her, but she fended him off and he gave a pissed off sigh and turned away.

Zoe watched him for a bit. Sometimes she didn't know how he put up with her, all she seemed to do lately was grouch at him – but sometimes she didn't know how she put up with him. He was determined not to move on and what was all that about not wanting another child? It wasn't just his decision to make. She watched his broad shoulders moving under the 'Save the Earth, Save Yourself', T-shirt he wore. The back of his neck was deeply tanned from so many months under blazing suns and Zoe felt her heart sort of squeeze up at the sight of it. Abe had a nice neck. Oh, God, he was a good man. Hopeless in domesticity, but good. And a great dad, when he was there. 'Sorry,' she mumbled, surprising herself. 'Sorry for getting cross.' Why she said it, she didn't know. She wasn't sorry.

He turned around again. 'I was going to clean it, honest,' he said.

She knew he was, only he'd have probably left it for about a week. Abe didn't see mess, he created it.

'And my parents don't hate you,' she corrected.

Abe laughed in disbelief as he dumped another armful of paper onto the sofa. 'Yeah, they do.'

'They have you over, they talk to you—'

'That's cause of you, it means nothing.' He was still grinning.

'Well, it's more than your mother does.'

His face darkened. 'Let's not go there, OK?'

'Well, we might have to. Lee is starting to ask questions. You heard him today.'

'So? I will never take him to meet her.'

Abe had never got on with his mother. He'd left Toomevara in Tipperary when he was eighteen and since Lee had been born had only gone back once, with Zoe and Lee in tow. Zoe hadn't even made it past the door. She'd sat outside in the car and when Abe came back, he'd started the car up and told her that they were never going back. Despite her probing, he'd refused to say why and he'd told her quite firmly that he didn't want to talk about it.

'Would you not try to contact her one more time?' Zoe asked, following him as he scooped up all the paper for recycling. She hadn't meant to broach the subject at all, but maybe if Abe made his peace with his mother, he might actually take charge of his life, take charge of his own family. It wasn't right, never to see your family. 'She could have mellowed, she might want to see her grand-child. Family is important.'

'Nope,' Abe said, moving towards the kitchen, a black sack of paper held tightly, his knuckles white.

'I just think Lee deserves a chance to get to know your side of the family,' Zoe said gently, standing just inside the kitchen door.

'He deserves a lot more than that,' Abe shoved

the paper more firmly into the black bag, stuffing it so it wouldn't pop back out. 'Drop it, OK?'

'I can't,' Zoe folded her arms, 'just give it one more try.'

Abe stood very still. It was a second before he spoke. 'Zoe, I told you before I am never going back there.'

'But Abe, just—'

Abe pushed past her out of the room.

'Abe!'

When he came back in, his combat jacket half on, half off, he said, 'I'm going out. Don't wait up.'

'Aw, Abe, come on. I'm sorry.'

His reply was a slam of the front door.

Of course she did wait up. And when Abe came back, slightly drunk, he sat beside her on the sofa and buried his face in her hair. 'I'm sorry,' he muttered, 'I should never have gone out like that.'

'I won't ask you about your mother ever again,' she whispered back.

If she expected him to protest, she was disappointed. 'Thanks,' he muttered, before beginning to kiss her softly on the neck.

She gave herself up to it. OK, he was drunk but it was still nice.

But she wasn't going to give up.

CHAPTER 5

Suzi plonked down in a chair opposite Deirdre in the staff canteen. She was a big woman dressed in leggings and a huge wraparound orange wool cloak. It took her a few moments to settle her large bulk in the small plastic chair but, eventually satisfied, she produced a piece of paper from her pocket and laid it on the table between them. 'I just got this.'

As Deirdre studied the email, Suzi divested herself of her cloak to reveal a T-shirt with two strategically placed sunflowers.

Hi, I'm arriving Wednesday at 4. See you all then. Looking forward to it. Paul Maguire.

Deirdre feigned indifference and pushed the paper back to Suzi. 'Grand,' she said. 'I won't be here, though, it's my half day. I'm visiting my mother in the,' she swallowed, found it hard to say the words, but eventually, like a faulty tap, splurted out, 'home.'

Suzi nodded sympathetically, then said delicately, 'It might not look good for you if you're not here.'

'I don't care how it looks,' Deirdre shrugged.

Suzi sighed and unwrapped her sandwiches. Her usual everyday lunch, six ham and coleslaw on white bread. She took a bite and said through a mouthful, 'I wonder will they put me on another show.' She didn't sound overly concerned, which struck Deirdre as odd. But maybe she was just trying to be brave.

'I doubt it. I told Michael you were great. I have no idea what on earth this Paul person can contribute to the show. It's ridiculous.'

Suzi bit another hunk of sandwich and chewed some more while Deirdre sipped her coffee, thinking about Paul Maguire. Even though she knew him from the tabloids, she'd googled him the other night and it was as bad as she'd feared. He was Irish, from a farm in Cork and he had started his career in pirate radio, gaining a name for himself as a bit of a shock-jock. From there he'd been lured to England and after some success on radio and in the bedroom with some page three girl, he'd produced a son along with numerous popular shows which chronicled the sleazier, tackier side of life in a big city. He had a radar for what the public liked and most of what he did turned to radio gold. He'd moved back to Ireland after a disastrous split with his girlfriend and now worked at RTÉ. Deirdre was puzzled about why he'd bother with her show and she had no idea how the studio could afford him, they must be paying him a lot. Bastard.

'Will you be able to work with him?' Suzi asked. 'He doesn't sound like he will fit in with us.'

Deirdre felt as if someone had just put their warm hands over her cold ones. 'I just have to.'

'I think Matt and Emma are excited. They think he's a legend.'

'Well, hopefully that means he'll be history.'

Suzi laughed and Deirdre grinned back, then drained the last of her coffee. 'Right, I'll leave you to it. I'm going outside for a cigarette. See you later.'

She left Suzi and walked through the double patio doors, passing Michael Allen's lunch table. He was there with his usual man's club, all guffawing and laughing together. Deirdre had never been invited to sit at that table, but had always wondered how you got an invitation. She probably wouldn't have liked it much anyhow. In fact, from all the testosterone floating about she'd probably have sprouted unsightly body hair.

Outside in the smoking area, the day was calm. She lit a cigarette and used a handkerchief to wipe the wooden bench down. It had been donated by a deceased member of staff's family but if they could see it now, they'd have been appalled. It badly needed a varnish and a de-chewing-gumming. Finally satisfied that the bench was fit to sit on, Deirdre laid another handkerchief down and sat on that. Feeble rays of sunshine bathed her face, and she welcomed the first signs of spring. It was a pity that this place was such a mess though. Not much happening in the way of spring here. The ground the unfortunate bench sat on was concrete and, beyond that, the space was littered with cans and other rubbish and tufts of yellow grass. An overflowing bin sat desolately in the centre of the space. Deirdre often thought what a lovely garden it would make if it was just cleaned up, shown a bit of care. She had it mapped out in her head, exactly where she would put everything. In her mind's eye, right now, the garden would be waiting for summer, tiny buds on trees, some early flowers still blooming while summer plants were waiting for their own special moment. That's why she loved gardens – everything had its time, nothing was ever denied its chance.

No opportunity to blossom ever passed a flower by.

CHAPTER 6

Zoe sat in Lily's room and wondered how much longer she should give it. June had asked her to keep an eye on Lily because the woman had become very agitated that morning and was refusing to get out of bed. 'The doctor examined her and she's fine,' June had said, 'and I don't want to worry her family, not just yet. She's only been here four days so maybe she just needs to adjust.' And as Lily had taken a shine to Zoe, referring to her as 'the girl who reads', June thought Zoe would be ideal to stay with her. Zoe had had the brainwave of asking her dad to drop Lee over to her after school. Lily had been enchanted with a visitor's little girl yesterday, so hopefully Lee would work his charm on her, pull her out of wherever she was.

At three, from Lily's room, Zoe saw her father pull up outside the clinic. 'Back in a second, Lily,' she said, touching the woman briefly on the arm.

Lily muttered something and stirred, her eyes on Zoe's face, trying hard to communicate.

It was kind of worrying, Zoe thought. Whatever Lily was saying, it was the same thing over and over. At first, she'd pressed her ear close to Lily's mouth in order to understand but Lily had just become more restless.

When Zoe arrived at reception, Lee was kicking his schoolbag around the foyer while her dad, oblivious to the destruction, was chatting avidly to Carrie. He seemed to be explaining to her what was in his shopping bag.

'It's just a few bits,' he said, hauling some enormous metal things from his euro bag. 'I looked up the make of our washing machine on the internet and apparently, from what I can conclude, the drum is gone. Now when the man comes to repair it, I'll have the necessary equipment and he won't charge us a fortune for it.'

Carrie gave the requisite wide-eyed look of approval. 'Wow! That is so clever. Why don't you just fix it yourself?'

'No time,' her father said hastily. 'Lee is quite a handful, you know.'

'I bet he is,' Carrie nodded in agreement, her red curls bouncing enthusiastically. 'But I'd say you're brilliant with him.' She cupped her chin in her hand and looked at Zoe's dad in admiration.

Zoe stood back for a second, amused by her Dad's preening.

'I was always fantastic with children,' her dad confided. 'Monica now, my wife, she can be a bit short.'

'I'm bored,' Lee moaned as gave his bag one last kick that sent it flying into the reception desk.

'Stop it, Lee!' Mr Killeen said shortly.

'You're so fantastic with him,' Zoe teased as she crossed towards them.

Her dad laughed good-naturedly.

Lee smiled at Zoe before asking, 'Why do I have to be here?'

'Just to help Mammy for a bit.' Zoe steeled herself for Lee's reaction. He loved going to his grandparents after school because they spoiled him rotten. Being stuck with her was not going to go down well.

His sunny smile dipped. 'Aw—'

'I have a lollipop behind here,' Carrie said in a sing-song voice as, magician-like, she produced a bright blue lollipop which she handed to a slightly mollified Lee.

'What do you say?' Zoe asked.

'Thank you,' Lee chimed.

'Thanks for bringing him, Dad,' Zoe said.

'Not at all.'

'I don't want to be here,' Lee complained as he shoved the lollipop into his mouth. 'It's all old people who smell.'

'Lee!' Zoe was mortified.

Carrie snorted back a laugh.

'Well it's either that or come to Lucy Lane's house with your old granddad,' Zoe's dad said. 'She's asked me to have a look on her upper levels for dry rot.' He nodded smugly. 'At least someone trusts me to know what I'm doing.'

'I'll go to Lucy Lane's upper levels,' Lee said, which caused Carrie to explode in giggles.

Oh, God, Zoe sighed inwardly, Lee was in a strop.

'Next time, Lee,' her dad said, holding back a laugh. 'Oh and by the way,' he directed this to Zoe, 'I almost forgot, Greg has invited us to dinner on Sunday in his place. He said to ask you and Abe to come along.'

'Oh, great.' That'd be fun, though Greg was not known for his cooking abilities. Then she frowned, 'What about Lee?'

Her father whispered. 'Apparently, no. He doesn't want Lee there. You'll have to get Audrey to babysit.'

'What?'

'Why doesn't he want me there?' Lee took his lollipop from his mouth.

'Oh, wow, your tongue is blue,' Carrie squealed in mock horror.

'Yeah?' Lee stuck out his tongue and attempted to have a look.

'Want to see? I have a mirror here.'

Lee trotted in behind the desk as Zoe grinned gratefully at Carrie.

'Is there something wrong?' she asked her dad in an undertone.

He shrugged, 'We don't know. I think there is something he'd like to tell us, he really hasn't been himself lately. He's told us that he's not dying, so that's good. We'll just have to wait and see, I suppose.'

'I did think he looked a little stressed the other day,' Zoe said, remembering his pale face at Lee's party.

'Your mother is up the wall. She thinks she might be becoming a grandma again, but as I said, it happened to us once before, and wasn't it the best thing ever?' He smiled at her.

Zoe smiled back. They hadn't acted like that at the time.

He paused and said wryly, 'At least it's taken her mind off the flipping washing machine.'

Zoe laughed.

'Look at my tongue,' Lee said, bouncing back into the centre of them, tongue shoved out. 'Carrie says it's the bluest tongue she ever seen.'

'She ever *saw*,' Zoe corrected, taking him by the hand. She inspected his tongue and nodded, 'I think Carrie is right. It is the bluest one ever.'

'Well, I'll be on my way,' her dad said. 'See you Sunday. Bye now, Carrie, congratulations again on your engagement.'

'Thanks,' Carrie giggled. 'And you enjoy Lucy Lane's upper levels.'

'Now, now!' He dumped his nuts and bolts back into his bag and, chuckling away to himself, he left.

Lee, crunching his lollipop, obediently followed Zoe along the corridor, peering into room after room with childish curiosity. It wasn't that he had never been in the home before, but it had been months ago and he'd forgotten what the rooms were like.

Ronnie was in the day room, pulling coins from the ears of the other residents. He waved at them as they passed. It seemed the magic hat had given him an interest in things again. Lee bounced beside Zoe all the way to Lily's room and then, when he saw his final destination, he hissed, 'I don't want to go into an old lady's bedroom. That's gross.'

'Just for . . .' Zoe looked at her watch – she had half an hour left before dinner in the canteen, '. . . thirty minutes. Then you can have dinner. This lady likes to talk to little boys.'

'OK,' Lee slouched into the room, hands jammed into the pockets of his school trousers, his eyes narrowed.

Lily turned around at the interruption and as Zoe had predicted, her eyes brightened. 'There's a great lad,' she said, her voice as clear as a bell, as if the sight of a child had unlocked the chains on her brain.

'Thank you,' Lee said. To give him credit, he attempted a smile. 'I'm five.'

Lily smiled. 'Big boy,' she blinked. Then a puzzled look crossed her face. 'Who are you? Not mine.' She seemed to be getting agitated again.

Zoe put her arm around Lee. 'No, Lily, he's my little boy. You have a girl, Deirdre.'

'Deirdre. Yes.' Lily blinked. Then sighed. Then began gesturing with her hand. Fluttering motions. And mumbling the words she'd been mumbling all morning.

'Is she sick?' Lee asked curiously, creeping closer to her bed.

'She's just tired,' Zoe explained. 'And a little old too, maybe.'

Lee was on tip-toe now, his head sideways. 'She's saying something.'

'Careful,' Zoe crossed to him, remembering how her proximity had upset Lily earlier, 'she doesn't like it when you come too close.'

'She wants something down there,' Lee hopped down off the bed and looked at the ground.

All at once, Zoe knew what it was. How stupid could she have been! Lily must have dropped her diary. Since she'd come here, she'd held on to that diary, only letting it go when she could see exactly where it was. It must have fallen onto the floor. Or maybe Lily thought it had been stolen.

'Is it your diary you want, Lily?' Zoe asked.

Lily blinked, still confused. Zoe got down on her knees and saw it splayed just out of sight under the bed. She pulled it out and couldn't help noticing that every page bar the last had been filled in with the neatest writing. Closing it over and brushing it down, she placed it between the woman's hands. 'Here you go.'

Lily blinked again. Then turned her gaze to the book. She sighed as if she'd been reunited with a long-lost friend. Her whole body relaxed, her shoulders softening under the bedcovers, her tiny hands seemed to squeeze the book and then, quite suddenly, she looked at Zoe again. Zoe smiled uncertainly under an unexpectedly penetrating gaze. To her surprise, Lily held out the diary and nodded.

'No, it's yours,' Zoe said.

Lily swallowed hard, tried to form words with her mouth but nothing came out. She held out the diary, pushing it towards Zoe with surprising vigour.

'Do you want me to have it?' Zoe asked. But as Lily's eyes dulled a little in despair, she knew that that wasn't it. She tried again, 'Do you want me to, I dunno, read it?'

Lily seemed to hesitate.

'Maybe like a story book,' Lee said. 'I like things to be read to me when I'm in bed, Mammy, don't I?'

Zoe looked at him, then looked at Lily. Maybe Lee was right. Maybe that's what Lily wanted. She loved the newspapers being read in the morning room each day. But would she want Zoe reading her private diary? Only one way to find out. Slowly she took the book from the woman's hands and opened it on the first page. It seemed to have been inserted afterwards, but there was an instruction at the top. *To be read first.*

CHAPTER 7

Today, 9 September 2009, I walked to the local shops and bought all the things I thought I needed. Balloons, cakes, a ballerina tutu, I bought a card that said 'Happy Birthday, you are five'. The woman serving me asked if I had a granddaughter who was having a birthday. No, I told her, this is for my little girl. And as I said the words, I realised that my little girl was fifty and that while it was indeed her birthday, she certainly wasn't five. It was as if time folded over on itself for just a moment, and I forgot all those other years. But, in embarrassment, I ignored the puzzled look of the woman on the till and just paid over my money. 'I hope your daughter likes her tutu,' she called after me.

I don't think anyone I knew was in the shop. I don't think so. I hope not. That would have been humiliating.

Up to now, I've largely ignored the symptoms. The forgetting where I lived for a whole hour, so that I found myself wandering around and around looking for my house – my old childhood home – before – snap – back to myself again. As if someone in my head shook out a creased-up old rug and there was my life, all straight and orderly once again.

The symptoms are small, yet the smaller they are, the more monstrous they become. One time I couldn't figure out how to put a button in a buttonhole. I looked from one to the other for ages, knowing I should know what to do, but totally unable to remember. It's not like forgetting something you know you've learned and searching your brain for it, it's like knowing that you can do it, knowing that you shouldn't have to search, and that if you can't do it then there is something wrong.

I came home and put the tutu away in the spare room, hanging it in a wardrobe. And it was then that I rang him. Then that I thought about the diary, how I'd once, up until the day of Deirdre's birth, recorded everything as if I was in a movie or something. I'd written sporadically in the following years but time had passed since then – and that time needed to be recorded too. So I wrote the last few pages then. I hope that, at some point in the future, when I can no longer remember, someone might read this to me and maybe, somehow, I'll connect with the person I am. I'll feel my memories slowly sliding down into me like milk in a glass and making me whole again. So whoever you are, dear reader, please don't judge me on what I've done or what I failed to do, just know that I never set out to have the life I did, that no one ever sets out to have the life they do. All the choices I made, I did for the best of reasons. But it was a different time. A different country. But I have

81

loved and been loved and surely that is the greatest thing a person can do. In the end, that is all they can do.

Please contact Deirdre and have her present when this is read. She knows most of it anyway, but knowing is not the same as understanding and she needs to understand before she is told the whole truth and can forgive . . .

'Dinner, Lily.' One of the young nurses bustled in, startling Zoe from her reading. 'Oh, sorry, have I disturbed you? It's just that June said to give you a break. I'm going to give Lily something to eat, isn't that right, darling?' She brushed some hair from Lily's face and then eyed the diary in Zoe's hands. 'Is that Lily's diary?'

Zoe nodded, 'Yes, I think she wants it read to her. So that she can remember.'

'Oh,' the nurse blinked away sudden tears. 'How sad.'

'No, it's boring,' Lee made a face. He was lying on the floor trying to do tumbles. Hopping up, and dusting himself down, he asked, 'Can we have dinner now?'

'Yes, come on.' Zoe closed the diary and placed it in Lily's hands. 'I'll talk to Deirdre, Lily, and when she comes next, I'll read you the next entry, OK? I'll look forward to it.'

Lily turned to look at her and smiled.

'Now,' the nurse settled in, 'you had us all worried, Lil, so Dominic made your favourite, potatoes, carrots and a little bit of ham. He says you like it boiled best, is that right?'

Zoe closed the door and pretended not to hear Lee moaning that he didn't like carrots and he hated ham.

The dining room was almost full but Lee's face fell as he saw the dinner on offer. 'Yeuch!' he said loudly and folded his arms.

Zoe bit her lip to stop herself from being cross with him. Lee was a great lad most of the time, but when he was feeling hard done by, as he certainly was at this moment in time, he was liable to go off on one. 'I'll get you chips later,' Zoe promised.

'No!' he glowered at her. 'I want to go home. Dad might be home now.'

'And if he's not, you'll have to stay with Marty from next door, how about that?'

Lee glowered. He knew when he was beaten.

'Whey hey, is that Lee I see?' Dominic, going by with two plates, grinned at them. 'I believe you had a birthday the other day?'

'Yeah,' Lee said glumly.

'What age are you now?' Dominic deposited dinner in front of two of the residents and, turning back to Lee, he said, 'No. Let me guess, you're, eh, twenty-seven?'

'No!' Lee snorted out a laugh. 'I'm too small for twenty-seven.'

'Forty?'

'Nooo!'

'So what age are you then?' Dominic asked, pretending to be completely baffled.

'Five.'

'Wow, five is a cool age.'

'It's not so cool when I have to eat crappy dinners,' Lee glowered.

'Lee!' Zoe snapped.

Dominic shook his head, trying to look wounded. 'Well, the old give out about my culinary skills and now the young. What hope have I?'

'Jesus, Dominic, I'm sorry. I swear—'

Dominic laughed and hunkered down to Lee's level. 'So, what would you like to eat, big fella?'

'Chips and a burger.'

'Hmmm,' Dominic cocked his head to one side, 'I guess we could rustle up something for you. But there is a catch.'

'What?'

'You'll have to try cooking it yourself.'

'All by myself?'

'I'll help you. And, anyway, you're five now.'

'OK,' Lee was smiling again. 'I never done that before.'

'It's *did*, Lee,' Zoe corrected. She smiled at Dominic. 'You don't have to, you know. He's just being . . .' she mouthed the word 'difficult' at him.

'He's grand,' Dominic stood back up, unfolding his long lean body and stretched. 'You can hand out the rest of the dinners, Zoe, if you don't mind, and I'll get some chips on for this lad.' He thumbed towards the kitchen, 'Come on, my man, let's get an apron for you.'

'Only girls wear aprons,' Lee scoffed.

'Nope, not true. I wear one so my clothes don't get wrecked and you should too.'

Zoe followed them and was delighted to see Lee so animated, hopping up and down, chatting to Dominic with more enthusiasm than he showed her. But a promise of burger and chips tended to do that to Lee.

Twenty minutes later, Lee was sitting in the dining room with June, shovelling chips into his mouth as he told her how he'd made them. Because Dominic had been so good, Zoe felt obliged to help him clear the finished dinner plates and prepare the desserts.

'Successful dinner today,' she said as she stocked the empty plates in the dishwasher. 'Not even Ronnie complained.'

'Yup, that's cause it was a boring dinner,' Dominic grinned wryly. 'I only cooked it because I found out from June that it's Lily's favourite. Why they can't like more exotic food, I dunno.' He pulled a tub of ice-cream from the freezer and began to scoop it onto plates. This he topped with some fresh fruit. 'More of the boringness,' he declared.

'Yes, but such delicious boringness,' she smiled, leaning up against the counter and, plucking a piece of apple from a plate, she popped it in her mouth. When she looked up, Dominic was looking at her. Zoe laughed and asked, 'What?'

He shook his head and turned away. Then, picking up a kitchen knife, he began to furiously slice some more fruit. He was faster than any chef she'd seen on TV. The guy was so at home in a kitchen, Zoe realised as she watched him. In fact, he was so at home and so confident that he was actually quite sexy looking. The way his broad back moved under his T-shirt, the way he scooped the fruit into the big serving bowl. The way he plated it all up. Not even the white apron could emasculate him. She wondered in amusement if she was drooling at the gorgeous dessert or the gorgeous man.

'You ever afraid that you'll chop your finger off?' she asked, as he began tossing syrup onto the fruit.

'Nope. Used to it now. I've been cooking since I was a kid.' He spoke matter of factly, without turning around. His hands deft and sure.

'Really?'

'Yep.'

'And did you use sharp knives like that as a kid?'

He nodded, 'Uh-huh, at ten, I was cooking every-thing in our house. Still am, to be honest.'

'D'you still live at home then?' She couldn't help the surprised tone in her voice, because Dominic had to be at least thirty. His sex-o-meter rating plunged. It was no wonder he never talked about his private life.

Dominic paused momentarily before pouring

some cream into a mixing bowl. 'Well,' he answered carefully, 'I lived out of home for a while, but four years ago I moved back in.'

'Run out of money did you?' she teased.

He turned around then and quirked an eyebrow. 'With the wages I get here, yep.'

Zoe laughed, though she was thinking how awful it would be to still be living with her parents. Maybe his were pretty cool and didn't give him the Spanish Inquisition whenever he came home late. But still . . . 'Well, they're lucky to have you cooking for them,' she said diplomatically as she plucked a syrup-covered piece of fruit from a bowl.

'Stop it,' he ordered. 'You'll spoil your dinner.'

'But it's yum.'

'Like it, yeah?' he looked pleased. 'Let's hope the critics do too.'

He finished up by doling out the cream and together they served everyone. Dominic gave Lee an extra big helping, whispering to him not to let on to anyone else. Lee promised solemnly that he'd never tell.

Then Zoe and Dominic sat down together to eat. 'Thanks for the help,' Dominic grinned. 'The lad that usually preps left last week. Got a job in Langton's. June is looking for someone else but in the meantime, I'm doing it all.'

'Wow, impressive,' Zoe said through a mouthful of ham. According to all the papers, Langton's was the newest and best restaurant in Dublin. 'You must have trained him well.'

'He was good,' Dominic nodded. 'I gave him all the tips and off he went.'

'Would you not like to do something like that yourself? Don't get me wrong, I'm not saying here isn't good; I mean, this ham is great, but surely cooking the food in Langton's would be more challenging?'

Dominic looked down at the table and seemed to take a second before he answered. 'Here has normal hours, no one screaming at me, I'm my own boss and, yeah, I wish it was a bit more interesting cooking-wise, but it's steady, you know.' He met her gaze like it was a challenge.

Zoe backed off. It was obvious that he wasn't happy admitting to liking a steady job and, in truth, she felt a little disappointed in him. He had never struck her as a steady Eddie type of guy. He'd travelled loads for one thing, backpacking across the world for about two years, in an unplanned, haphazard way. She'd seen pictures of him smoking dope and hanging around with the weirdest-looking individuals, a big sloppy grin on his face. Plus, if he loved cooking as much as he said, surely the main thing was to make exciting food, not have steady hours. If Zoe had spotted Dominic at a club, she'd have had him pinned down as a bad boy. Even the way he dressed in denims and T-shirts with the name of rock bands she'd never heard of emblazoned across them made him look sort of cool. His retro docs and his ear piercings gave him a 'don't mess with me' vibe but it was sadly misleading. Zoe was thinking that a v-neck jumper and slippers might have suited his personality better.

'The steady hours are handy,' she conceded. 'It suits me because of Lee, but when he gets bigger, I'd love to be programming pop concerts and stuff like that. Bringing a magician to an old folks' home wasn't exactly high on my to-do list.' She grinned at him.

'But you made them happy,' he said simply. 'And thanks to you, Ronnie is now more demanding and obnoxious than ever.'

Zoe laughed. Then said, 'Don't get me wrong, I love the job, but sometimes it's nice to be challenged, you know?'

Dominic nodded but didn't smile back or even reply. 'Dessert?' he asked.

'Yeah. That was gorgeous Dominic.' She handed him her plate.

He took it with a small smile. 'Pleasure.'

CHAPTER 8

Even though he was almost eighty, Rick moved with the ease of a much younger man, Deirdre thought, as she followed Rick into her mother's kitchen. He dressed young, too, wearing a pair of jeans and an open-necked shirt. Denims suited him. Deirdre supposed Rick's commitment-free lifestyle contributed to his youth and energy.

'I hope you don't mind me calling in like this,' Deirdre said. 'I've to pick some clothes up for Mammy and drop them into her on Wednesday.'

'Call in whenever you like,' Rick smiled. 'It's great to see you. I could have brought the clothes in though. Saved you a journey.'

Yes, Deirdre thought, he could have, but then she wouldn't have had an excuse to call and keep an eye on him, would she?

'Sit down,' Rick motioned her to a seat. 'Have a cuppa.'

'Oh, well, thank you.' Deirdre sat down and began flicking through a *Daily Mail* that was lying on the table, flouting it's lurid headlines. Her attention was drawn to a piece about two gay men who were photographed proudly showing off the baby they'd had with two lesbian women. It was a lovely baby. Everyone looked so happy.

'Great paper that,' Rick pronounced, 'gives me a great laugh.' He rinsed out a cloth and began wiping the table down. 'I had a few people over for a coffee,' he went on. 'Some of the lads from the bookies and one or two from the Alzheimer's coffee mornings. They all got on great together.'

The oven pinged. Rick abandoned the table and rushed to the oven. Opening the door and waving away a blast of heat, he pulled out a batch of perfectly shaped scones. 'Ta-dah!'

Deirdre was very impressed. She watched as Rick placed them on a wire rack on the table to cool. 'No wonder my mother wanted you to care for her. I'd never be able to cook anything like this.' She'd never had cause to either, she thought suddenly. What would she do with twelve scones?

'I used to be hopeless,' Rick took some cream and a pot of jam from the fridge and placed them in front of her. This was followed by a plate and a knife. 'Then when my marriage broke up, I had to fend for myself. I took a cooking course, bought a few recipe books and, hey presto.' He sat down. 'Eat up.' Cutting into a scone, he spread it with jam.

'You were married?' In the nine months since she'd met him, he'd never mentioned a wife or family. Even now, he didn't look like the sort of man who would marry. There was a certain twinkle in his eye that was probably lethal fifty years ago.

'Oh, it was a long time ago,' Rick waved his knife in the air. 'We broke up. It was incredibly painful and it horrified people. I lost friends over it. In those days, marriage was for life – or a life sentence, I'm not sure which.' He smiled wickedly.

Deirdre had to smile back. 'Must have been hard,' she remarked.

'Yes, but if something's not working, you have to change it. Hard at the time but better in the end.'

Deirdre had no idea how he sounded so matter of fact. If something wasn't working, it was hard to change things. She knew that much. Sometimes things dragged on until they came to a stop and died and other times they were killed before they went wrong. That was her and John. Like a still-born child, a perfect painful memory. Deirdre's brain hurt suddenly so she took a bite of scone. The taste of sweetness and spice took her by surprise. 'Gorgeous,' she exclaimed as Rick smiled in pleasure. 'I'd bet if you cooked these for your wife she would never have let you go.'

Rick rolled his eyes and said wryly, 'I seriously doubt that.'

'So what happened, or do you want to say?'

'I was a bit too fond of going out and having a drink. I spent money like water.'

'My goodness, really?'

'Yes. I liked my freedom.'

'So why get married?'

'Because she was mad about me and, saddo that

I was, I wanted someone to be mad about me. And I loved her for that. She told me I was exciting. So I became more exciting and then, once we were married, she wanted me to be less exciting.' He sounded baffled.

Deirdre didn't blame his wife. Exciting men were all very well but you wouldn't want to marry one.

'Still,' Rick continued, 'I was who I was. I changed a lot when we split up.' He took a bit of scone and said, 'Break-ups do that. You either learn from them or you go under. Isn't it true?'

Deirdre shrugged. She wondered what she'd learned from her own break-up all those years ago. It must be going on for fifteen years now. 'I never thought of it like that,' she hedged.

'Well, I did. I realised that the way I lived my life was hurting too many people.'

'It's good that you saw it that way.' Rick was full of surprises. She'd never have had him down as the reflective type. Men who dyed their hair just weren't, she'd always assumed.

'It was,' he smiled.

'And did you have children? How did they cope?'

There was silence for just a fraction too long and she knew she'd put her foot in it. She always seemed to say the wrong thing in conversations. The curse of living alone. The smile died on his face and a look of intense hurt crept over it. He stood up abruptly. 'No.'

'I'm sorry.' Deirdre was horrified, the scone was like a stone in her mouth. 'None of my business.'

She unbuttoned her top button and blew some air up onto her face, pieces of scone spraying out all over the table. Obviously childlessness had been the real cause of the break-up. What a fool she was to ask. Deirdre knew how hard that was to live with. She would have loved a little boy or girl in her life but she was too old now and she felt the loss keenly.

'No need to be sorry,' Rick turned to face her, his smile back in place. 'It's a natural question. No children. But we were so incredibly wrong for each other that it was a blessing.' He turned to fill the kettle just as Deirdre's phone rang.

She pulled it from her bag, glad of the distraction, but gasped when she saw the caller ID. 'It's Lakelands.' She stared at the phone, a little afraid to answer it. Finally she held the phone towards Rick. 'Could you?'

Rick abandoned the kettle and took the phone from her. He'd paled. Pressing the 'answer' button, he said, 'Hello?'

It was with relief that Deirdre saw his anxious expression break into a smile.

'Zoe is on the phone,' Rick relayed, putting his hand over the receiver, 'she's the girl who reads the papers to your mother.'

'Yes?' Deirdre nodded. 'And?'

'She wants to know when you're going in to visit your mother as Lily wants her diary read aloud and she wants you to be there to listen.'

'Mammy wants her diary read aloud?'

'Yes.'

'And Zoe wants me there?'

'No. Lily wants you there.'

'What?'

Rick patiently explained again but Deirdre, still confused, took the phone from him. 'Hello? This is Deirdre.'

A cheerful bubbly voice that she didn't recognise said, 'Hi, Deirdre, this is Zoe. Your mother has a diary in with her?'

'Yes. She won't let it out of her sight.'

'Well, she handed it to me today and I read the first page to her. It's basically a request to have the diary read aloud whenever you're visiting. Is that OK? You can see the diary if you like and where she's written it.'

'She wants me to *hear* her diary?' Deirdre asked feeling disorientated, shooting a puzzled look at Rick, who shrugged. 'Can I not just read it? I know most of her story anyway.' Though there was a part of her mother's story that she'd refused to listen to once. A part that she really did not want to find out. It was just like her mother to do this to her.

Zoe hesitated. 'Well, of course it's your choice, it's just that this is what Lily seems to want. She wrote that you need to understand before you know the whole truth.'

The whole truth. Deirdre closed her eyes. How bad would it look if she ignored her mother's wishes, she thought? She could never do that. And she already knew the truth. The whole truth was unimportant, it barely mattered. That's what she'd told Lily once, though maybe Lily had forgotten. And for her to have to listen to it being read by this girl could be painful and embarrassing . . . still, it was what her mother wanted and this was a chance to make her mother happy after all this time. And perhaps she'd airbrushed her diary. Perhaps she'd censored what would be read. Deirdre knew that she certainly would have. 'OK,' she agreed, feeling totally at sea. 'That's no problem.'

'So when do you think you could come? June, the manager, says a routine is best, so, say, once a week on a certain day?'

'Tomorrow, Wednesday is my half-day from work,' Deirdre said. 'I'll be there for two.

'Perfect,' Zoe said. 'See you then.'

Deirdre hung up. What a week this was turning into. Her mother's diary on Wednesday and the new producer coming to change her show on Thursday.

Fantastic!

THE FIRST WEDNESDAY

Lily was sitting in a wheelchair, her hair scooped up into a neat bun. A skinny woman who looked like she could do with a good feed took a seat beside her. 'Hi, Mammy.' The woman pecked her on the cheek. Then a man, looking apprehensive, came in and did the same. Lily pulled away from him. It was one thing being kissed by a strange woman but she drew the line at men.

The man sat down too and Lily was glad to see that he looked a little chastened.

'Hey,' a girl poked her head in and spoke to the two people sitting there. 'Aw, great, you're here.' She shoved out a hand to the woman. 'Hi, I'm Zoe.'

Zoe. That's right. Lily knew Zoe. Tall and busty, clothes always a little too tight, big wide smile and kind brown eyes. And my, what a lovely voice, she read the papers in the morning and always made them come alive. She was the one Lily had picked. Lily pushed her diary towards Zoe. She wanted to listen again. To relive those times. To have little Deirdre understand. Most of all that.

'Is Rick OK to be here?' the skinny woman asked.

'For sure,' the girl with the too-tight clothes nodded. 'Hey, Rick, no magician today!'

The man laughed.

Lily knew that laugh. From somewhere.

October 1955

My name is Lily Flynn. I am fifteen. I live in Cavan. I have one brother – he's older than me – Sean. After she'd had me, my mother almost died and though such things aren't talked of, I think she was unable to bear any more children after that. It's probably just as well because our house is small, with a fireplace in the kitchen that takes up most of the room. Sean has a tiny bedroom downstairs whilst mine and my parents' are upstairs. My room is about the size of a cupboard, but it holds a bed and my collection of dolls. We have a small farm, chickens and a goat and a few cows and we all help out on it. I hate it. My dad calls me Lazy Lily but it's a joke. My main job is to take the eggs from the chickens in the morning and deliver them to McCabe's, the shop in town, to be sold. It takes ninety minutes to walk there and the same back. I cycle most days so it's not so bad, plus it's on the way to school so I have to go into town anyway. I drop the eggs off before school and collect the money for them on the way home.

Today, Eddie, the owner of the shop I go to with the eggs, offered me a job working there. His son

Patrick, who is nineteen, has gone to Dublin to see how the big shops run their business and Eddie has fallen into bad health and so he asked me if I'd like a job. I said I would, it's better than school and who knows where it may lead. By the time Patrick comes back, I told Eddie, I'd have his shop running like clockwork. I have a gift for organising things, for seeing where problems lie and ironing them out.

'There's a piece of paper taped to this page,' Zoe said, and read:

Footnote. To be read. ***It was the day Patrick arrived back in the shop that my life changed. Not immediately changed, nothing like a loud thunderclap happened or any sort of significant thing, but thinking back, as I often do, I can pinpoint that exact moment – eleven o'clock September 15th 1957 – I can remember the weather and various smells and even exact conversations. And though many people through the years have tried to tell me that what I remember is incorrect or exaggerated, I know I'm right.***

I've torn out the preceding two years because they are not important to my story.

September 1957

Patrick arrived back today. My seventeenth birthday and what a present! Twenty-one and as fine a man as any in Cavan. He was wearing a suit and shiny shoes and his hair was brushed to the side and it flopped over one of his eyes in a very cheeky kind of way.

'Hi.' I smiled, for I didn't recognise him. 'Can I help you?'

He stood in the centre of the shop, hands on hips, and surveyed it like a king his kingdom. I had just cleaned the place that morning. I had the tins all neatly stacked, displaying their labels. Fresh vegetables were positioned in such a way that any bruises didn't show. The sweets looked colourful in their jars and I'd polished the windows so that the sunlight poured in and made everything glint. 'Well, well,' Patrick said and he gave a low whistle, 'this place is looking grand.'

'Thank you,' I pushed my hair back behind my ear. My mother had said my left-side profile was the best and I turned a little left so that I wasn't looking at him directly, much as I wanted to! 'I cleaned it myself.'

'Well Lily, you've done a fine job.' His voice was like coarse brown sugar. Manly yet sweet.

I couldn't understand how this fellow knew my name. Maybe he'd asked about me in the village? But why would he do that? 'You know my name?'

'I do indeed, sure haven't you been working for my father for the past two years and doing a fine job,' he says.

I blinked. 'Patrick? Is it you?'

'The very one.' And he bowed in front of me and held out his hand for me to shake.

100

And when I touched it, just a lick of fingertip, I zinged. It was like electricity. I'd never felt that way before about anyone, not even Jimmy, who I'm sort of seeing from time to time. Jimmy isn't a bit like this fellow at all. Jimmy never wears a suit or polishes his shoes. Well, only if he's bringing me to a dance and we don't go to them very often, it wasn't like there were many dances to be had in Cavan. It's as dead a place as the soul of hell. Jimmy's nice though, he makes me smile. He picks me wildflowers and presents them to me with a sort of flourish but that's the height of it.

Patrick is a whole different animal completely. His walk is different, for a start. In fact, he doesn't walk, he glides along as if he's on wheels. Sometimes I even expect God and his holy angels to serenade him as he passes. And his hair has a style. He is the first man I ever met with a hairstyle and it impresses me a lot. Plus he's clean, with a good fresh smell off him. In fact, I think he imports special soap down from Dublin especially. His nails shine as if he polishes them every day. The minute I noticed that I tried to keep my hands out of sight. It's hard to keep fingernails clean when you're mucking out hens to fetch their eggs all the time anyway. And Patrick's smile is powerful enough to light a city. In my opinion anyhow. It sort of fills his whole face and when he shook my hand, he pressed it gently in his and he looked straight into my eyes and smiled. I felt like I would explode.

Then just as quickly as it happened, he let my hand

go and I was bounced back to earth. 'So, Lily,' he said, and even the way he said my name, sort of delicate like the flower I'm named after, made my head whirl. 'So, Lily,' he said, 'where's himself?'

He meant his father.

'Inside. He's not been too well this week.'

'I know, that's why I'm here, to cheer him up.'

As I watched him disappear into the family quarters behind the shop, I couldn't help but hear the exclamations of delight from his father. His mother had been dead this long time and I know Eddie missed her. Maybe Patrick being in the shop would cheer him up. I knew, right at that minute that it would certainly cheer me up.

Zoe laughed. She wondered if she imagined the smile Lily gave her back. Then Lily pressed her hand on Zoe's arm before reaching over and taking her diary away. That was enough for now. Zoe watched as she closed her eyes and smiled.

'You OK?' Rick asked Deirdre as they drove home in the car an hour later. Deirdre nodded, feeling a little upset. Maybe it was the offhand way her mother talked of her dad like that. OK, so it was written when she was young, but still . . .

'Do you remember that shop?' she asked Rick, hoping to divert her thoughts from the hurt she was feeling.

Rick nodded. 'Yes, I do actually, and your mother behind the counter. It was a tiny shop,' he went on, his face screwed up as he remembered, 'there was a small window, crammed with all sorts of things. Lily told me once she loved nothing better than polishing the tins. You must remember it,' he said then, 'it was called something different in your time though. New people bought it over. It was on the centre of the main street, squashed in beside two other shops.'

She didn't remember it. 'Maybe later on we'll take a trip down and you can point it out to me,' she said. 'And we could drive by my old house and call into Uncle Danny.'

'Oh, I'm not sure,' Rick shrugged. 'To be honest, Deirdre, I don't have great memories of the place.'

'Well, think about it. It only has to be a day trip.'

Rick had looked even more uncomfortable, so she hadn't pushed it. But whether he went or not, she was determined to go. Maybe this diary would be good. Maybe she would understand her mother better. She still had nightmares about that trip to Dublin when she was about five. The memory of it floated about her head, making no sense, and yet she knew there was sense in it somewhere if only she'd been old enough to understand. Sometimes she wasn't even sure if the memory was a real one.

CHAPTER 10

Zoe had met Abe at a charity event for mental illness that she'd programmed. It had been her first big gig working for Golden Eye PR and though it was barely a blip on the social calendar of Dublin, it had caused Zoe a lot of sleepless nights. She'd needed to prove herself and she would only do that if she got the right speakers, the right entertainment, the crowd in and made sure that the press covered it.

She'd convinced her mother and father to buy tickets and then she'd put them at a table with the most boring people in the room so that no one else would have to endure them – the boring people, not her parents. It had been a bit mean, but she had warned them in advance and her mother had said that if it helped her daughter's career, she would do anything.

At that stage, they'd all been convinced that she'd be the next Harry Crosbie.

On the night, things had been a bit of a blur. Some parts stood out though, the MC had got drunk in the toilets and had taken to the stage, slurring his words. Even the English-speaking people in the audience had a job understanding him. And there had been a tense situation between her mother and father when the boring man at her mother's table had started to chat her up. Things had reached crisis point for her when her dad had confronted her, just as she was attempting to sober up the MC.

'I am going to lose my mind completely if your mother insists on flirting with that man,' her dad had said loudly, and a woman nearby burst into tears.

'Dad, this event is to raise money for mental health,' she hissed. 'Stop talking like that.'

'She is driving me nuts.' He folded his arms and glared over at his wife, who seemed to be giggling.

'Not a good expression either, Dad,' Zoe said crossly. 'Now excuse me if I have more important things on my mind than someone flirting with my mother.' She gave the celebrity MC a shake. He muttered something incoherent, though it sounded like 'piss off'. No wonder he'd been cheap and available, she thought. 'Wake up, you idiot,' she hissed.

'I hosted *University Challenge* once on a guest spot. I'm not an idiot,' the MC garbled indignantly.

'I saw you on that,' her dad said, 'and I thought you were better than that Pacman chap. No dignity in having a computer game named after you.'

'Really? You thought that?' The MC looked at her dad with such gratitude in his eyes that Zoe felt sorry for him – fleetingly.

'I did. You were on top of your game. Then you vanished.'

'My world collapsed about me.'

'You were in an earthquake, were you? Shocking.' At this point, Mr Killeen sat on the floor beside the man and shook his head.

'No. My wife ran off with my son-in-law and my son ran off with his mother-in-law. And I went on the white stuff.'

'You're joking!' Mr Killeen was agog. 'That's like a plot straight out of *Fair City*.'

'That's the story of my life,' the MC said dolefully, shaking his head then clutching it and moaning. 'Fairly shitty.'

'Not at all,' her dad consoled.

The MC seemed to be listening to her dad, Zoe thought, a little flair of hope expanding in her chest, though most people tended to like her dad. 'Can you try and sober this fella up, Dad? He won't listen to me.'

'Where are you going?' her father asked, looking panicked.

'Just outside. I need a breather.'

'Go on so,' her dad whooshed her away. 'I'll abandon your mother for the evening, have a chat with the celebs, see how she likes that!' In triumph, he moved closer to the MC and Zoe loved the way he valiantly tried to ignore the other man's stinking breath.

Stepping outside the front door, onto the wide sweeping steps of the Georgian building, Zoe was immediately soothed by the silence. A guy was sitting on the steps a few feet in front of her, his

106

back against the railings. He was blissfully puffing on a cigarette, sparkling white shirt sleeves rolled up to the elbow, a jacket beside him. He looked like the most contented person she had ever seen. She sat behind him, carefully arranging her dress so that it wouldn't crease it and inhaled a long deep breath – that felt good.

'Bit of a shit night,' the guy said out of the blue. 'How are you enjoying it?'

She was so taken aback, she couldn't answer immediately. When she did manage to huff something out, it made no sense.

'Was that a yes or a no?' the guy turned around and she was struck by the sheer wickedness of his eyes. They were dancing provocatively in what was an average-looking face, transforming it into something quite special.

'It was a yes, I am enjoying it,' Zoe lied.

'So you can understand Gary Sims, yeah? The guy has a major drug problem. He's off his head tonight.'

'He has?' Zoe hadn't known that about her MC.

'Everybody knows that,' the guy took another drag on his cigarette. 'When I saw him, right, I thought genius.' He flicked some ash onto the steps. 'I thought, this guy has been off his head on drugs, has had psychotic episodes, he's the right person to be talking about mental health.'

'Psychotic episodes?' Visions of him stabbing her dad *Psycho*-style assailed her. Even the dingy cinema music played in her ears.

'Oh, yeah, everyone knows that.'

'I didn't.'

'OK,' he smiled at her, revealing a row of cute crooked teeth. 'Everyone except you.'

She basked in the smile like a cat in the sun. Then she remembered he was criticising her event. 'So, why do you not think it's genius now?' she asked.

''Cause he's just a name. I thought he was here to give some insight into mental health.'

Now *that* was genius. In fact, she should have got a few speakers. How stupid could she have been, thinking that a celeb was all that was needed to draw in the crowds? 'Excuse me a sec,' she hopped up from the step and rushed back inside. Maybe she would be able to convince Gary Sims to talk about his issues. He mightn't want to but maybe he would and—

Her dad and Gary were still talking together. Gary seemed to have perked up a little, or maybe he was just getting really high. Her dad wouldn't know the difference, thankfully.

'Gary, hello,' she sat beside him, 'I was wondering, as this event is for mental health, if you would share some of your experiences with our guests? I could put you on for ten minutes after dinner.'

Gary blinked slowly. 'Share what?'

'You were ill for a time, weren't you?'

'I was. In hospital for months.'

'Well, I think our audience would like to hear about that. In your own words, as honestly as you can.' She moved nearer him. 'What do you think?'

'I think it's a fantastic idea,' her dad nodded.

108

'He's been telling me all about his stay in a psychiatric facility.'

Gary shifted about, suddenly seeming more alert, more normal. 'I can tell you, Liam,' he'd said, 'because you're a nice man.'

Her dad beamed with pleasure.

'But some people here seem like assholes.' He said the 'assholes' quite loudly and Zoe winced.

'In fairness now,' her dad said, 'when I saw you up on the stage there, I thought you seemed a little odd yourself but now I know you, you're a top man. A top man.'

Gary Sims flushed, seeming pleased. 'My agent said nothing about this.'

'I know. I just thought of it now,' Zoe admitted. 'And it's only if you want to.'

Gary sucked in his fleshy cheeks and seemed to think for a second. Exhaling noisily, he nodded, 'Well, all right then, I'll tell them what it's like when your world crashes in. I will.'

Zoe smiled and patted his arm. 'Thank you.'

And after dinner, Gary stood up, swaying only slightly, and, microphone in hand, began to speak. Initially there was a lot of talking in the audience, but Gary's voice, with all the loudness and abrasiveness of a lawnmower, assailed the general hubbub easily and eventually silence descended. By the time he finished, people were wiping tears from their eyes, others were standing and applauding and the journalists, who'd been very reluctant to come, started writing notes. Gary Sims was all over the papers the next day, being praised for his honest and frank confession. He got radio slots and TV interviews. He even had his own radio show on Dublin Live.

He became a star again. Now he was promoting his new book entitled, *I Am a Celebrity: How Did I Get Here – Again?*

And at the end of that first night, Zoe found the guy with the cigarette and the great eyes, sitting on the same step outside the door. She was glad to leave the noise of the dining room – her mother was tipsy and her father had gone to rescue her from the clutches of what was once a boring man. Mr Boring had morphed into a bit of a letch in the space of a few hours. Her mother, grateful to be rescued but not allowing it to show, had accused her husband of not caring about her. He was tolerating it with good grace because her flirting had allowed him to befriend a celebrity.

Zoe sat down beside 'great eyes'. 'Thanks,' she said.

He looked up. His eyes had lost some of their sparkle. 'Huh?'

'For putting me on the right path about this event. Of course there should have been a speaker. I was so stupid.'

That smile again. It filled up his whole face. 'You were in charge, eh? No wonder you went haring off.'

'No wonder,' she agreed with a roll of her eyes.

'Sorry for saying it was shit.'

'Aw, don't be. Can I have a fag?'

He passed her one and lit it for her. 'I don't normally smoke,' she said, 'but I need this.'

'Yeah, well, stay well away if you can help it.' Then he took a long drag himself which struck Zoe as funny and she laughed. So he laughed too.

'Abe,' he stuck out his hand.

'Zoe.' She shook his hand. His grip was firm.

'Space-agey name.' He sounded impressed.

'Biblical name,' she said in response.

He grinned. 'Yep. My mother has a thing for the prophets.'

'Well my folks just thought it sounded like an American soap star. They thought if I was ever to be famous that Zoe Killeen would have a ring to it.'

'No way!' His laughter sounded gorgeous. In fact, even though he wasn't gorgeous gorgeous, there was a pleasing easiness about him that was so attractive.

They smoked for another while in companionable silence. Then Zoe heard the unmistakable voices of her parents bickering.

'Well.' Reluctantly, Zoe stood up and stubbed out her cigarette with her shoe. 'That's me off. Nice to meet you, Abe.'

'Yeah.' He nodded.

And she walked away, feeling a little let down that he hadn't even asked for her number or email or anything.

But two days later, she got a phone call in work and Abe asked her out.

It was probably one of the highlights of her life.

CHAPTER 11

Reversing into her space in the car park behind the station, Deirdre took a deep breath as she switched off the engine. She took a last look at herself in her mirror. She'd have liked to think that she didn't care what she looked like today, but of course she did. If nothing else, she wanted to show this new hot-shot producer that she was no radio host in need of a makeover. She had even invested in some new pink lipstick to match the pink flowers on her blouse. Along with the pink flowery blouse that had cost twenty euro in Marks, she had a black skirt and sensible black shoes. Businesslike was the look she was going for. That and efficient. She applied a little more lipstick, quite liking the pinkness of it, took a deep calming breath and left her car.

She always made a point of getting in early so she could go through the running order of her show for the day. Suzi always laid it out on her desk for her. Then, later, Suzi, Matt and Emma arrived in and over coffee and cakes, they'd have a final chat before the show aired just after midday.

Deirdre climbed the stairs to the small staff office

on the first floor. She waved in at Roger Ryan, the early-morning DJ who was in studio and on air, and he blew her a kiss. She loved the calm in the place before the hustle and bustle of the day really began. Huffing and puffing from the stairs, she pushed open the door to the office and let out a yelp as she saw the figure of a tall man, leaning against her office window and staring out into the back yard.

The man turned and though she knew who he was she was still shocked to see him standing uninvited in what was her space. He looked thinner than his online picture and about fifteen years older too. She deftly calculated his age from Wikipedia and realised that he must be in his early fifties, at least. He wore a sharp suit of charcoal grey and a tie so thin that it could be mistaken for a stripe. His shirt was a dazzling bright white. He was handsome, if you liked the loutish look, which she didn't, though it suited his boyish frame, she supposed. His eyes were large and grey and had an errant expression, as did his slightly upturned grin. His hair was shaved tight to his head, but he had the eyebrows to carry it off. Hands sunk into pockets gave him a sexily casual air that unnerved Deirdre and had her tugging on the buttons of her blouse, which resulted in the top button popping open. She had to fumble to close it.

There was a moment of silence before he broke it. 'Deirdre,' he said, and she had a searing mental image of seduction in a dark room with a lot of steam, 'I recognise you from your picture. Hi, I'm Paul.'

She felt a little asthmatic all of a sudden. Paul held out a large hand. She clasped it in her small one and immediately felt a crushing pain as his shake rattled her bones. She had to suppress a cry though her eyes widened and, wincing, he dropped her hand like one of his many ex-girlfriends. 'Sorry, did I shake too hard? I do that a lot. Sorry.'

Deirdre made a big deal of flexing her hand as he looked on. He said nothing more, obviously feeling that because he'd apologised, it was fine. And it wasn't fine, her hand ached and she felt breathless and hot.

'I take it this is where you sit.' He nodded to the prints of flowers she'd hung on the walls and the picture of her mother and herself in a silver frame on her desk. Deirdre wished she'd thought to load the desk with pictures of herself meeting various other famous radio people, but it was too late now.

'Yes,' she said. Her voice shook a little and it wasn't just because of her sore hand. This was too much. Seeing him here ready to take over her show was too much. Already she could feel her stress levels rising. She consciously relaxed her shoulders. There was no way a person like this could improve her show. Not in the way she would have liked, that was for sure.

Paul pulled up a chair and sat down behind her

desk. 'It was a pity you weren't here yesterday when I came.'

Was that said in a faintly reproving tone? Deirdre gritted her teeth. She remained standing. 'Yes,' she agreed, reining in her annoyance like a great fish on a line. 'But it was my half day.'

He smiled up at her, disarming her with a charming grin. He had a dimple. The unexpectedness of it shocked her like a bee sting.

'Well, as you are here, perhaps we can go over today's show? Your production staff seemed to suffer from collective amnesia yesterday.' He raised his eyebrows questioningly.

'Really?' Deirdre's mouth twitched. 'I'm sure they'll be fine today. Wednesdays can be like that.'

There followed a silence as Paul let the ridiculousness of her words sink in around them.

'Busy, you know.' Deirdre refused to be intimidated by him and his tactics.

She watched as Paul did a swivel in her chair. With big hands he loosened his tie and she saw his Adam's apple move as he opened the top button on his shirt. 'So, will we get down to it?' His long legs poked out from under the desk, big shoes encasing big feet.

'Pardon?' Her mouth was dry. Really big feet . . . 'The show?'

She blinked, feeling a little dazed, as if she had just stepped from shadow to sunlight. But she recovered admirably. 'I will. At nine o'clock. Excuse me until then. I'm going to have a coffee and a smoke first.' She left the room on shaky legs, grabbing a coffee from the machine in the canteen. Then, cup in hand, she headed out to the smoking bench. Sometimes in the early morning, she broke the 'no smoking' rule by opening the window in her office and puffing out into the air, but with Paul here, that was on hold.

It was only when she had cleaned and sat down on the wooden bench that she allowed herself to feel the shakiness inside. Her heart was jumping about in her chest like a small puppy and she felt sick. The thing that upset her most was that he was here at all. She didn't know what she'd expected – a crash on the way or something, not that she wished for it – she just hadn't actually believed that this would really happen. Taking a long drag of her cigarette, she exhaled deeply and closed her eyes.

'I take it you met him?' Suzi startled her as she opened the canteen door and joined her outside. Squishing in beside her, she added, 'I thought I'd come in early and give you the lowdown on yesterday.'

'Oh, thank you,' Deirdre smiled. 'I appreciate it. So, tell me. I believe there was amnesia involved?'

Suzi laughed. 'Did he say that? Well, he arrived at four and, you know us, by four we're finishing up for the day.'

'Uh-huh.'

'And to be honest, I didn't want him seeing today's show without your say so. So I told him I didn't know exactly where it was. Or where it was stored on the file.' She made a face. 'Was he really mad with us, cause that wouldn't be a good start?'

Deirdre grinned, 'He didn't seem to be.' She held out her cigarette box and Suzi took one.

They sat and smoked for a bit in silence.

'He's dead sexy though, isn't he?'

Deirdre started to cough, the cigarette making her choke. 'Sexy?' She made a 'pft' sound. 'I thought he was a bit obvious. A bit cheap.'

Suzi cackled with laughter, 'You knew who I was talking about all the same.'

Deirdre flushed, remembering the feet. 'Well, yes,' she conceded. 'There is a certain,' she thought for a second, 'maleness about him, but, honestly, he's the sort of man that you wouldn't know where he's been.'

'Well, if the answer was my bed, I wouldn't complain.'

Deirdre tittered, always a little shocked at Suzi's frankness. She'd never been one for girly confidences, much as she'd longed to be. The whole dating scene had always baffled her, the one time she'd got a lovely man, it had been by accident. She certainly hadn't set out to seduce her gardener co-worker, but as they'd pruned rose bushes and cared for exotic plants and experimented with grasses and heathers, they'd come to understand each other's awkwardness. They didn't have to talk, their whole romance was conducted like a bizarre silent movie, their desire for each other being communicated in the quiet of a garden as they breathed in each other's air. And then just as things got really serious, she'd cut and run. In fact, she'd run so far away from him that she'd never been able to find her way back to that easy intimacy with anyone else. If she had any regrets, that might be one of them.

'I don't think I'd have a chance with him.' Suzi broke into her reverie as she flicked some ash onto the ground, 'I'd say he likes twenty-year-old blondes.'

'All men like twenty-year-old blondes,' Deirdre said.

She hadn't meant to be funny, but Suzi laughed.

Paul was still behind her desk when they got back and his feet still sprawled out the end. He'd opened another button on his shirt and his chest looked smooth and tanned. He didn't appear to be doing a whole lot. 'Mammy save me,' Suzi whispered.

'If you'll just let me sit in my seat,' Deirdre ignored Suzi as she walked towards Paul and eyeballed the top of his scalped head.

Paul dropped another damning smile before he hopped up and with a flourish offered Deirdre her own seat.

Feeling a little petty, Deirdre sat down, fixing herself comfortably behind her desk as she did so. She adjusted her blouse and slicked her hair back behind her ear, before deliberately straightening

118

her ornamental ashtray that he'd moved. 'Suzi, can you pull up a chair?' she said.

Suzi did.

There followed a moment of hesitation on Paul's part before he too located a chair and sat in beside Deirdre. She could smell his aftershave, musky. And a clean, washed smell from his skin. And something else. Nice but unidentifiable. She shot him a look. 'You're sitting a little too close.'

Suzi snorted back what might have been a laugh.

'Well, have you any other suggestion about how we all go over the show?' Paul asked sweetly, widening his eyes so he looked communion-day innocent. 'I am a man of many talents but even I can't see through a computer from the other side of the desk.'

'It's on a printout,' Deirdre picked up a file titled 'Show' and waved it about. 'And you can examine it when I've studied it and asked Suzi any questions I need to.'

Paul nodded, leaned back in his chair and folded his arms as if to get the measure of her. His foot tipped her leg and she pulled away sharply. 'Oops,' he said, not sounding too bothered. Then nodding at the file, he said, 'Fire away.' He looked at them expectantly. 'I'll observe for a week, if that suits.'

Deirdre resisted the urge to glare at him.

By four o'clock, Deirdre was frazzled. It might not have been so bad if Paul had asked numerous questions of her and her team, but he hadn't.

Instead, he'd sat back, listened and jotted down mysterious notes in a green notebook. It had freaked them all out. Though when Paul had asked Emma to get him a coffee, the young girl hadn't hesitated. She'd smiled at him and asked around a hundred breathless questions about what way he liked it. Deirdre had thought that potentially dangerous.

To top it all, Deirdre knew that her show had been a little all over the place that day, which wasn't like her. She was normally quite controlled, everything she needed was always to hand, but today it felt as if part of her brain had gone AWOL. Then, at the planning meeting, Paul had introduced himself formally to them all and told them that he would be in charge from now on but that he would let them work as they were for the next week. Then he'd sat in the room and contributed nothing to the rest of the meeting, just scribbled away in a disconcerting manner. His presence had frozen any creativity Deirdre might have had.

Deirdre, hands clenched tightly on the steering wheel, negotiated the traffic. Right now she couldn't think of anything more pleasurable than buying the *Daily Mail* and reading it while sinking into a bubble bath. That'd ease the stress that was currently making her neck and shoulders ache. And after that—

Her phone jangled. 'Hello?'

'Deirdre, it's Rick.' He sounds in need of a

bubble bath himself, she thought. 'Any chance of a favour?'

Her heart sank. The only day that she really wanted to go home. 'What is it?' she asked, trying to sound enthusiastic.

'I hate to bother you, but I need a lift to the Alzheimer carer get-together this evening. Normally it wouldn't matter, but I promised I'd do the teas and coffees and I've just missed the bloody bus.'

Deirdre sighed inwardly but, really, Rick had been lovely to her this past week, making her scones whenever she found an excuse to call over. 'Where are you now?' She tried not to let the weariness show in her voice.

'I'm at the bus stop on Dobson's Road. There's no more buses for an hour. Sorry about this.'

'Not at all. I'll swing by and pick you up.' If she was home by six, that'd give her plenty of time to have a nice relaxed evening before tackling tomorrow.

Fifteen minutes later, she pulled up at the bus stop and a man that she hadn't recognised as Rick at first, due to the horrendous Parka jacket he was wearing, hopped into the car.

'Thanks so much. I really appreciate this.' Glancing at her, his face dropped. 'Oh, were you on your way out? Did I spoil it for you?'

'What gives you that idea?'

'You look different,' he screwed up his face and peered closely at her. 'I can't quite—'

'Lipstick,' Deirdre said. 'I have a new producer

on my show and today was his first day so I wanted to look the part.'

'Well,' Rick said as he divested himself of his jacket, which smelled of mothballs, and clicked on his seatbelt, 'it's very nice. I hope the producer was suitably impressed. Carys Lane Community Centre,' he directed.

Deirdre drove towards the centre.

'So what does a producer do exactly?' He turned up the heat and began to warm his hands. A blast of it hit Deirdre in the face and she angled it back towards Rick, who basked in the heat.

'Decides the format of the show basically,' Deirdre explained. 'He decides what guests to run with, who to call, what jingles to use, all that stuff. Basically he's all about upping the listenership.'

'I thought your show was very popular.'

Deirdre gave a toss of her shoulders. 'They want to make it more popular.'

'And a good thing too,' Rick nodded approvingly. 'I love your show.' He adjusted his seat to accommodate his long legs. 'I really appreciate this.' Then he flipped down the passenger mirror and carefully examined his hair, patting it into place. 'I'd feel bad if I let them down and, believe me, they're scraping the bottom of the barrel asking me to serve tea, I always make it too hot.'

'How can you make tea too hot?' Deirdre asked, amused at the comment and at his preening. 'Boiling water is always the same temperature.'

'I mean, smarty pants, that I put too little milk

122

in it for them.' Satisfied with how he looked, Rick flicked the mirror back up. 'Last time I did this stint, Mary Madison burned her mouth on my tea. But as I told her at the time, give her ten minutes and she'll have forgotten all about it. That's the beauty of Alzheimer's.'

'You did not say that!'

Rick winked at her.

She laughed loudly and it was then she realised that it was the first time since she'd heard about her mother being ill that she'd allowed herself to laugh about it. Rather than making her feel guilty, she felt liberated, and the knot in her neck eased for just a second.

Twenty minutes later, Deirdre pulled up outside the front door of the centre. Rick climbed out, hauling his coat with him. It was a relief as the warmth in the car was beginning to seriously bring out the smell of mothballs. Just as he was about to slam the door, Rick asked, 'D'you fancy coming in to say hello?'

'No, thanks.' Deirdre cringed inside. She might be fifty-five but she did not need an elderly man to arrange her social life for her. And besides, she wanted to go home.

'They'd love to meet you,' Rick persisted. 'Lily never stopped telling everyone about you.'

The words caught her short. 'She did?' Then trying to deflect the emotion she felt, she added, 'That's worrying.'

Rick laughed gently and looked at her keenly, 'Have you got any other plans for tonight?'

'Well, I was going to have a bath.'

Rick blinked. 'That's not plans.'

She had no idea why he looked so appalled. 'It's to de-stress me,' she explained. Rick couldn't have looked more puzzled if she'd broken into Mandarin.

'Lily loved it here, you should come in, meet her buddies.' A smile. 'Lily used to joke that you could have the same conversation five times in a row with the same person and each time it was just as funny and entertaining.'

'Rick!' Deirdre was a little shocked at his irreverence.

'You gotta laugh, honey. If you don't laugh, you'll cry. Come on.'

It was his sparkly eyes that persuaded her. 'OK.'

'Atta girl.'

His approval made her feel a little more interesting and quite daring doing this unexpected thing in the middle of the week. She could have a bath any old time. 'You go in, I'll park the car,' she said with sudden confidence.

At the top of the room, Rick was behind a table pouring cups of tea while another lady, with a massive chest and a low top, arranged biscuits onto plates. There was a happy hum of conversation in the air. The hall wasn't large, it was just the right size for the number of people there. There were tables scattered about the room that would easily accommodate four to five people each. Deirdre joined the queue for the tea and when she got to the top, Rick pointed her to a table and told her he'd be down soon.

Feeling a little self-conscious, Deirdre sat down with her tea and biscuit.

'Can we join you?'

It was a couple in their forties.

'Sure, sit down.' Deirdre smiled brightly. She wasn't good at talking to strangers, but a smile went a long way. It put people at ease. But if she smiled too much, it freaked them out. It was all about balance.

'Now, Elle, sit here, OK?' The man pulled the chair out and the woman did as she was told.

Such a gentleman, Deirdre thought. There weren't many men who would do that nowadays. No, it was all women doing it for themselves now. Next the man handed the woman a biscuit and told her to eat up.

It was the way the woman looked at the biscuit that floored Deirdre. As if she had no clue what to do with it. The man gently pushed it towards her mouth. The woman remained mute. Finally the man turned, ran his hand through his hair and sighed.

'She's terribly young,' Deirdre found herself saying.

'Forty-eight,' he nodded. Then as if remembering his manners he said, 'I'm Adam, by the way. This is Elle. Haven't seen you before?'

Deirdre was still reeling from hearing Elle's age. 'Lily,' she blurted out, 'she was my mother. I'm here with Rick.'

'You're the radio show presenter,' Adam seemed delighted. 'Oh, we heard all about you. This is the radio show presenter, Elle,' he said to the woman. Then back to Deirdre, 'We all listen to you.'

'Oh, God,' Deirdre felt embarrassed. Trust her mother. 'I hope you don't.'

'Of course we do,' Adam laughed, 'Lily was a character. Her and Rick, they were such a double act.' He paused. 'She's missed.'

The simple statement got her in the gut. Even though Lily was there, she was gone. That was the horrible thing about Alzheimer's. 'Thanks,' Deirdre said, swallowing hard.

Adam was about to say something else but was interrupted when a tall, scattered-looking woman with a harried expression joined them. She nodded a greeting to Adam before quickly divesting herself of a florid red jacket and clashing scarf. 'Now, Pete,' she said, sounding efficient, 'sit here.'

Deirdre flinched. There was no one with the woman.

'He's gone on you, Mona,' Adam said cheerfully.

The woman turned around and tisked in exasperation. 'Jesus, look at him. Look at him up there.' She raised her voice to a holler, 'Pete, over here! For God's sake, can't you see where I am?'

A large man turned around slowly, like a

126

juggernaut on the M50. Then he blinked. 'Are you talking to me?' he asked, sounding haughty.

'Yes,' the woman said. 'I'm your wife, so sit here.'

'My wife is beautiful,' he declared with authority, 'not old like you.'

'In your dreams,' the woman snorted. 'OK, go and look for her and when you don't find her, come back here, you eejit.'

Deirdre felt embarrassed to have witnessed this exchange. Adam however laughed easily.

The woman turned back to them and shook her head. 'Every bloody time we come here he does this,' she said to Deirdre without rancour. She lowered her voice, 'We met here see, years ago. It used to be a dance hall in the fifties and it hasn't changed too much. I think that's what he remembers.'

Deirdre opened her mouth to reply, but found no words to say how sad that was.

The woman flapped a hand, obviously sensing Deirdre's upset. 'Sometimes with Alzheimer's you find out long-ago things that you never knew,' she confided. 'When we married I was,' she lowered her voice, 'pregnant. In those days it was a terrible thing so I always thought that's why he took me on. It's only since he got sick that I've found out he thought I was beautiful.' She smiled. 'He wasn't one for saying things like that.' She held out her hand. 'I'm Mona, by the way.'

'Deirdre.'

They shook hands.

'The radio presenter,' Adam chimed in. 'Lily's daughter.'

Mona made a big impressed 'oh' with her mouth, drawing away from Deirdre and looking her up and down. Then with emphasis on every word, she added, 'Wait. Until. I. Tell. Everyone. I. Met. You.'

Lily must really have built her up, Deirdre thought, feeling like a big fraud.

'Now, here we are,' Rick interrupted the conversation. He had Pete by the arm. 'There she is, Pete, your beautiful wife.'

Pete nodded, 'Thank you. Yes, indeed.' And without hesitation, he plonked down beside Mona, who smiled like a teenager before kissing his cheek.

Rick winked at Deirdre and bounded back up the room again. On the way, he stopped to chat and laugh with people.

'Such a lovely man,' Mona said, looking after Rick. She leaned across to Pete and helped him off with his coat. 'So, Adam,' she said, as she patted her husband down and straightened his tie, 'how has Elle been?'

Elle registered interest at the sound of her name but seemed content to let Adam talk for her. 'It's been rapid,' Adam shook his head. 'I have to be with her twenty-four-seven now, you just don't know what she's going to do. It's hard on the kids.'

'It must be,' Mona shook her head. 'Our children are older and have their own lives, so it's not as devastating as it is for yours.'

Adam rubbed the heel of his hands over his eye and quite unexpectedly Pete reached out a hand and patted his shoulder. 'Thanks, Pete,' Adam said. He swallowed a little before asking Deirdre, 'And Lil, how is she? I'm sure Rick misses her.'

Deirdre jerked as the attention turned to her. She really wasn't used to chatting with strangers about her mother. In fact, she hadn't talked to anyone bar Rick and Suzi about her. It was far better to keep a work–home balance, and not go stirring and mixing them all up. Hesitantly, she began, describing Lakelands and the room her mother was in and because they'd been so frank with her, she felt she had no option but to return the honesty. It was a relief to talk about it to people who understood. She found herself telling them about Lily's diary and of how she was having it read aloud to her.

'That's lovely,' Mona said. 'I think I might write down stories for Pete and read them to him.'

'Spare me, woman,' Pete said, his voice a rumble. 'You'd write things like how I forgot to put out the bins or complain that my collection of . . . of . . .' he paused and frowned. 'My collection, you know?' he said. He gestured with his hands.

'Your comic collection,' Mona prompted gently.

'Yes, you'd complain how it was taking over the house.'

'It *is* taking over the house.' She turned to Deirdre, 'He collects *The Beano*. Can you imagine?

He goes online on talks to *Beano* fans around the world.'

'I'm sure it's a relief to have Alzheimer's to try to forget that, mate,' Adam joked, and Pete laughed.

As Deirdre soaked in her bath two hours later, she found herself thinking about the people she'd met that evening. Of how lovely they'd been, of how they had all started out with such hope for a happy future and of how it was now crumbling in their hands. Deirdre felt more certain now than ever that it was better to be alone than to lose a loved one bit by bit, day by day, like liquid leaking from a glass.

But thinking about the love between Adam and Elle she began to wonder, were the good times worth the pain that came afterwards?

If you could know the end of a relationship, would you begin it?

Her neck felt sore again.

CHAPTER 12

On Sunday, Zoe and Abe, having dropped off Lee at June's, pulled up outside Greg's apartment block. 'Ready?' Abe asked.

With a sense of dread, Zoe climbed out of the car. Greg was not a man for throwing dinner parties, he could barely cook as far as she knew and when he'd first moved out he'd made a habit of collecting casseroles from their mother. Lately, he'd been looking stressed and, thinking back on it, Zoe realised that he'd avoided a lot of family occasions. There'd been a wedding which he'd not gone to and the subsequent christening of the couple's first child two weeks later. The only thing he had turned up at recently was Lee's birthday and that was probably because he was Lee's godfather. What had he to tell them? Zoe was good at speculation and the very worst thing she could think of was that he had murdered someone or had run over them in his car one night and left the scene of the crime. Now his guilt had got to him and he had to confess to the police, but he was confessing to his family first. If she held this scenario in her head, Zoe thought, nothing else

131

would seem as bad. Unless of course he had run over two people.

'What do you think he has to tell us?' Zoe asked.

Abe shrugged. 'I dunno. Maybe he's decided to become a man of the cloth.'

'A priest? You think so?'

'No, a tailor,' Abe said and laughed.

Zoe belted him, annoyed that he could laugh about it. 'It's not funny, Abe. Stop!'

'I know,' he tweaked her hair affectionately, 'sorry.'

He wasn't a bit sorry, Zoe knew. Abe just didn't 'get' family. He wouldn't think it at all odd if Zoe never called her mother and had no contact with her brother. For a guy that went about saving the world, he had remarkably few people he cared about. As far as Abe was concerned, if people in your family weren't people you'd befriend ordinarily, there was no point in being with them. It was an oddly sad thing that used to make Zoe love him all the more, in a effort, she supposed, to make up for those that didn't. But lately his unapologetic aloofness was beginning to rankle.

'Have you got the chocolates?' she asked. She'd bought some chocolates knowing that if dinner was bad, at least they'd have the sweets to fall back on.

Abe nodded, plucking them from his jacket.

'Oh, good,' her mother said, 'chocolates, something to look forward to at least.' She lowered her voice, as if Greg could somehow hear her from the top floor. 'I asked Greg what he was cooking and he said chicken. A word of warning, just check that it's not pink before you eat it.'

'I will.' Zoe didn't need the warning. The last time Greg had cooked chicken it was so pink it had almost clucked and walked off the plate. She pressed the doorbell.

'Hello, Abe,' her mother said, turning to Abe and adopting the unnaturally polite voice she used whenever she talked to him. 'Nice to see you.'

'You too,' Abe nodded.

'Hello, son,' her father said to him, and Zoe couldn't help noticing the way Abe flinched on the word 'son'.

At that moment, the buzzer sounded and, pushing open the enormous glass doors, they entered the foyer. Greg occupied a penthouse that sported panoramic views all across Dublin Bay. As a top advertising executive, Greg earned a serious amount of money working with large companies to promote their products and though things weren't as good as they used to be, he still had the means to live in this gorgeous part of Dublin.

'I do so love Greg's apartment,' Mrs Killeen declared as they stepped into the lift and pressed the button.

'Yes, I know,' Zoe said. 'You've said it before. But we're not all loaded.'

'Well Abe must be – he works all the time.'

Beside her, Zoe saw Abe flinch. Again.

'He doesn't earn a lot,' Zoe defended him. 'His wages are crap actually.' Then as Abe gawked in disbelief at her, she amended, 'But we don't care, we like where we live. Don't we, Abe?'

He looked at her in disbelief.

Zoe didn't blame him – just that morning she had again given him an earful on the state of the kitchen ceiling. It had got burned a year ago when a chip pan had caught fire and still hadn't been repaired. The landlord had refused to take responsibility for it and Zoe had rejected her dad's offer of help because Abe had promised to do it. Only he hadn't.

The lift pinged open. Zoe, her mood dampened, clumped behind her parents towards Greg's super shiny front door. Everything about this place showed up hers, she knew that, but did her mother have to keep reminding her of it every time they came?

'Hey, come in,' Greg, smiling a little too widely, opened his door before they knocked. He was dressed casually, in jeans and a blue hoodie. His angular face was unshaven and his green eyes, the same shade as Zoe's, looked a little stressed. He looked beyond Zoe, 'Hey, Abe, you came.'

'Of course he came,' Zoe said. 'You invited him, didn't you?'

'Well, yeah, I didn't mean—'

'Oh, ignore her,' Mrs Killeen waved a hand and sat down on Greg's brilliant orange sofa. 'She's in a strop.'

'I am not,' Zoe scoffed. 'You started it. You said—'

'Thanks for inviting me,' Abe interrupted. Then spotting a newspaper on the chair, he picked it up and disappeared behind it.

They all looked at one another. Abe made them uneasy, Zoe knew. His reluctance to engage freaked them out a little, but, damn it, she wasn't going to make it easy for them now. They deserved to be frozen out by him, criticising his wages and their apartment.

'I was just looking at the wall,' her dad said then, all jovial, 'and, eh, wondering what the hell that painting is all about.'

'It a copy of *Guernica* dad,' Greg said. 'End of the world.'

'I'd say now the fella that painted that had a few pints on him.' Mr Killeen sat down beside his wife. 'Our Lee would paint that with his eyes closed, wouldn't he, Zoe?' He smiled at his daughter, a peace offering.

'Yes,' she said, taking it. This was Greg's day after all.

'I was just saying,' her dad raised his voice as if Abe was deaf, 'that your Lee would paint that horrible auld picture with his eyes closed.'

Abe looked over the pages of the paper at the picture. He seemed unsure. 'That's *Guernica*,' he said. 'It's a masterpiece.'

Could he not just get the joke, Zoe wondered as her dad blustered, 'Yes, and I was just saying that Lee—'

'Greg, what is that you have cooking?' Mrs Killeen interrupted, sniffing. 'It smells, well, quite *nice*.'

'It's chicken with a sauce on it and some roast potatoes and carrots and parsnips and some other things that I don't quite know what they are.'

'—would paint it. It's a total mish-mash of stuff.' Mr Killeen paused and sniffed the air too. 'That does smell nice, Greg,' he said, sounding surprised.

'You don't know what the vegetables *are*?' Mrs Killeen wrinkled up her nose. 'Did you buy them in a shop?'

'I got a friend to make this food, all I have to do is heat it up,' Greg gave a shrug. 'You all know how crap I am in the kitchen and anyway, like I said, I have something to tell you all and I wanted to tell you all together so that I wouldn't have to repeat it. I just couldn't seem to concentrate on cooking anything.' He swallowed hard and jammed his fists into his pockets. 'And I think you should eat the food before I tell you,' Greg hopped from foot to foot. 'You know, so that what I have to say doesn't put you off your food.'

There was a brief silence. Abe put down his paper and shot an uneasy look at Zoe. She shot him one back.

'I think I'd like to know now,' Mrs Killeen said firmly. 'I haven't been able to eat for the past few days for worrying, Gregory. And your father has been eating more than he usually does because he's worried.'

'Eh, no, I'd say it's all the work I'm doing in Lucy Lane's attic,' Mr Killeen piped up. 'I'm there all day every day.'

'Work?' Mrs Killeen quirked her eyebrows. 'Chatting up Lucy Lane is work?'

'I am not chatting her up. She has dry rot in her attic.'

'You're worried too, admit it,' Mrs Killeen snapped at him. Then before he could reply, she stood up and walked towards her son, 'Look, Greg, whatever it is, we are your parents and we love you and we'll always be there for you.'

Abe made to get up, then, glancing at Zoe, he sat down again.

Greg dipped his head, 'Thanks, Mam.'

'Now, have you got some girl pregnant?'

Startled, Greg's head shot up again and he spluttered out a laugh. 'Oh, Jesus!'

'Oh, God,' Zoe grinned.

'I'm glad you both think it's funny,' Mrs Killeen went on. Then added, 'Anyway, what I was about to say was if you have, Gregory, well, it's not a disaster. Is it, Liam? It happened to Zoe and it was great.'

'Great,' her husband agreed, winking at Zoe.

'Mam, you have no idea what you've just said,' Greg laughed again. He sounded slightly unhinged.

'You sound a bit mental there, son, if you don't mind me saying,' Mr Killeen stood up now. 'Like we're happy to have dinner here and everything but, if you had something to tell us, we don't need to be fed, we just need to be told. Now, have you lost your job for, I dunno, stealing money?'

'Eh, thanks, Dad,' Greg said and he laughed weirdly again.

Zoe watched in slight alarm as Greg wiped tears of mirth from his eyes. Then, as he did so, his body began to shake and he was suddenly sobbing. Big heaving heartbroken sobs.

The three of them looked at each other, appalled.

'Oh fuck,' Abe stood up abruptly and left the room.

'Abe!' Zoe shouted after him but he had gone. She ran to catch him up. He was just about to leave. 'Abe!'

'Stay there,' Abe said, 'I'll be in the car.'

'What's the matter?' He was hardly bailing on her, was he?

Abe gave a vague wave in the direction of the sitting room. 'This . . . that,' he stuttered. 'Whatever it is, it's not my business.'

Zoe blinked. 'Well, it is. My business is your business.'

From inside, Mrs Killeen was saying, 'Oh dear, Gregory, what is it? Nothing is that bad.'

Abe looked momentarily stricken. 'I'm useless in these situations,' he said, giving her an anguished look.

And he probably was, Zoe thought. 'Go then,' she felt so let down, so mortified by him. 'Go on.'

He hesitated, then mumbled, 'Sorry,' before leaving as if his life depended on it.

Zoe watched him go and something inside her shifted a little. She bit back tears and walked back in and saw her mother patting Greg reassuringly.

'Come on, son, just tell us,' her dad said.

'Have you killed someone?' Zoe asked apprehensively.

'He has not killed someone!' Mrs Killeen spluttered indignantly. Then, as Greg's sobs increased a little, she asked tentatively, 'You haven't, have you, Gregory?'

He shook his head.

'Even by accident?' her father went on, 'like maybe you dropped something on someone's head from the window here and maimed them?'

They all looked anxiously at him.

'Greg?' Zoe tipped his arm. 'Please. You have us all scared now.'

Greg took a deep shuddering breath and lifted up his head. His family moved a step back in anticipation. Zoe was startled to note that his eyes looked puffed as if he'd been crying earlier too. Her heart cracked a little. Her big brother who'd always been there for her through everything. The day she'd told her own parents she was pregnant, she'd told him first so he could be with her. And he had. She laced her arm through his and gave him a little playful shake, 'Come on, spill.'

'OK.' Greg sucked in his breath and, his Adam's apple bobbling, he said, in a half whisper, 'I'm gay.'

The silence that followed this statement was as loud as a thunderclap.

'Gay?' Mrs Killeen eventually spluttered out. 'Gay as in . . .' She let the sentence hang.

'As in homosexual,' Greg swallowed. His voice was a little louder now, as if he'd finally faced the executioner's axe and hadn't died. 'As in I could never get a girl pregnant, Mam.'

'Oh,' she gaped at him with wide eyes. 'That kind of gay?'

'Is there another kind?'

'But, but you did have girlfriends.' She frowned and wagged her finger, as if trying to convince herself of the truth of her statement. 'I defiantly remember one girl, Amanda something or other, she was fat and not good enough for you. I remember her.'

'I had a lot of girl friends, Mam,' Greg said. 'But that's all they were, friends. It never went anywhere.'

'But you never had, you know, a boyfriend,' Mrs Killeen went on, 'so how could you know?'

'I just,' Greg paused and looked at her hopelessly, 'well, I just know, Mam. The way you know when you fancy someone.'

'Oh,' she blanched. 'I . . . I see.'

'It's not something I chose,' Greg spoke again.

There was silence. Zoe was as shocked as her parents, there was no point in thinking otherwise. She had never, in all the time growing up, thought that her brother was gay. He liked boy things, sport and cars. He had been captain of the soccer team

140

in his school and never once had he expressed an interest in playing with her dolls or admiring her dress sense.

'But, but you can't cook,' Mr Killeen said, sounding a little dazed.

'No you can't,' his wife piped up. Hope sang in her voice.

'So?' Greg asked.

'All gay men can cook, everyone knows that,' Mr Killeen said with the desperation of a survivor trying to leave the *Titanic*. 'And they, you know, faff about in aprons.'

'Oh, Christ!' Greg rolled his eyes. 'I don't believe it. I don't believe you just said that, Dad.'

Mr Killeen looked at his son as if he'd never seen him before. 'I'm just trying to understand—'

'There is nothing to understand,' Greg said. 'I'm gay. That's it.'

'Yes, but how? How are you gay? We don't have any gayness in our family.'

Greg swallowed. 'Would you rather I had stolen money from work, then, or murdered someone?'

'No, no of course not.' Mr Killeen's shoulders slumped and he shook his head. Then he looked desperately at his wife.

Neither of them seemed capable of saying anything.

'It doesn't change who Greg is,' Zoe said then, thinking, actually, it does a little. He's not exactly who I thought he was.

Neither of her parents said anything to this.

'I think,' Mrs Killeen said slowly, 'that you're just feeling stressed, Gregory.'

'You got that right,' Greg mumbled under his breath.

'I think it's stress, love,' she said softly as she moved nearer her husband, who clasped her hand.

'It was stress,' Greg agreed. 'The stress of living a lie. I, just . . . well, I'm sorry.'

'You don't have to be sorry for being gay,' Zoe said softly, her shock tempering into sympathy for him and also a strange sense of loss for herself.

'I'm not sorry for that,' Greg swallowed, 'I'm just sorry for ruining things or for any hurt I've caused or for . . .' his voice trailed off.

Zoe touched his sleeve and was surprised when he grasped her hand in his and squeezed it so hard it hurt. Then he didn't let go.

Mr Killeen was the first to speak. 'Well, now,' he said as he rocked back and forth, 'thanks for telling us, Greg. Bit of shock all right, but I suppose if you had killed someone it'd be worse.'

Greg stared at his dad incredulously before nodding in agreement.

'That would be worse,' Mrs Killeen nodded, injecting her voice with a false positivity. 'Much worse. Having a little baby would have been all right by comparison though.'

'Mam!' Zoe said appalled as Greg flinched beside her.

'Oh, it's all right for you,' Mrs Killeen flapped

her hand dismissively. 'You're young and liberal and have this twenty-first-century attitude. I'm not like that. What am I supposed to do with the knowledge that my son is gay?'

'Live with it,' Zoe said simply. 'It's the same as knowing that your child is left-handed or has red hair, that's all.'

Her mother pursed her lips and didn't look convinced. 'No one was gay in my day,' she said.

'Oh, now, I think they were,' Mr Killeen said. 'D'you remember that lad that used to turn up at the dances when we were going out. He'd wear the pink shirt and the trousers with the fringes on them and—'

'That was my cousin and he's married now, thank you.'

'Oh, right, I see.'

More silence. Then Greg asked, 'So, dinner?'

Mr and Mrs Killeen looked stricken.

'I, eh, feel,' Mr Killeen said, 'that this news is enough to digest and a dinner might just be too much on top of it.'

Greg's shoulders slumped in defeat. 'Oh. OK.'

'I'll have some,' Zoe smiled.

'I think we'll just go,' Mrs Killeen said. 'And we do love you, Greg, we're just, well, shocked to our core.' She shivered as if her core was in meltdown.

'Yes, thanks anyway, son,' Mr Killeen nodded.

'OK, I'll see you both out,' Greg said.

They demurred, telling him to look after his

dinner and to enjoy it and thanks so much for asking them and for Zoe to say 'hi' to Lee for them and that they'd see him tomorrow after school.

Then they were gone, and silence descended.

'I thought that went well,' Zoe half-grinned. Then at Greg's crestfallen face she held out her arms, 'Come here, you.'

She enfolded him in a hug, which he returned with interest. Then he pulled away and his green eyes studied her. 'Thanks, Zoe,' he said. He walked into the kitchen and slumped into a chair, massaging his head with his hands. 'You've no idea how hard that was.'

'Look,' she sat down opposite him, 'they're shocked now but it will wear off and they'll see that it's no big deal. And it really isn't.'

'You're not shocked?'

'A bit,' she admitted. 'But you know, we'll all come around.'

'I wish I believed that.'

'Well I do.'

He said nothing, just turned off the oven and threw a packet of biscuits on the table. Zoe took one. So did he. Then, he looked around, 'Where's Abe?'

'He left when you started crying.'

'Oh, God,' Greg groaned. 'Tell him I'm sorry.'

'I will not,' Zoe said. 'You're entitled to cry if you want. Emotional stuff gets to Abe, he's weird like that.'

The way she said it made Greg look sharply at her. 'Is everything OK?' he asked.

'I don't know,' Zoe gave him a watery smile, then changed the subject, not wanting to talk about it. 'So,' she asked, 'when did you know you were gay?' It was a bit embarrassing asking her brother these things, but she guessed that was what she was supposed to do.

'Oh, long time ago. I never had an interest in girls, ever. Did you never suspect?'

'Nope.'

He looked sad at that. 'I hid it well then.'

'Were you hiding it?'

'Yeah.'

There was silence. 'So why now? Why did you decide to tell us now?'

He took a while to answer. 'A number of reasons.'

'Which are?'

'Well, I was tired of living this lie, you know? Of everyone thinking I was one thing and me knowing I wasn't – does that make sense?'

'Uh-huh.'

'But mainly,' Greg swallowed hard and coughed before admitting, 'it's because Louis told me he'd leave me if I didn't.'

'Louis?'

'My boyfriend.'

And despite all her declarations of being cool with it, Zoe started to choke on her biscuit.

THE SECOND WEDNESDAY

October 1957

Jimmy called to the shop today. I was behind the counter and Patrick was explaining to me about how in one of the shops he worked in all the staff wore uniforms. All I could think of was the army uniforms we used to see around about as children, but Patrick was explaining that these uniforms were black and white, like staff in a big house or something. And if he was in charge here, he'd probably get me to wear a black dress with a white apron over it. 'Nipped in at the waist,' Patrick said, placing his hands on my hips and I nodded to let him know I understood.

Jimmy walked in then and his eyes nearly popped out of his head when he saw that Patrick had his hands on me.

'Are you OK?' he asked, his bushy eyebrows drawing downwards in a frown. 'Is this fella taking liberties with you, Lily?'

'Oh, will you stop,' I rolled my eyes at Patrick to show him what an idiot Jimmy was. 'I'm capable of minding myself, thanks very much.'

Jimmy uncurled his fists. Honestly, that boy would fight with his own shadow sometimes.

'What do you want anyway?' I straightened up and glowered at Jimmy, mortified. 'I presume you haven't just come in for a fight.'

Patrick laughed behind me and I felt a bit ashamed of myself. Jimmy is a good man and I suppose he was only defending me, though he doesn't own me, like the way he owns his cows or his fields.

'It doesn't matter,' Jimmy said, 'forget about it.' And he stormed out, slamming the door.

I watched him walk by the window of the shop, all cross, stamping his feet really hard on the ground, little bits of dry muck flying everywhere. 'Jimmy!' I shouted. 'Jimmy!'

He pretended not to hear me.

'Go on,' Patrick said, 'though if you ask me, he's hardly worth it.'

I pushed up the counter and fled out through the shop. Flinging open the front door, I almost ran into Mrs Gibbons, who was not pleased, though when she saw Patrick, her face lit up. In the meantime, Jimmy must have run off like a hare because he was nowhere to be seen. I scurried up the street in the direction he'd gone, but even in the distance there was no sign of him. I turned to go back to the shop when he pounced at me from a laneway.

I gave a bit of a scream and people looked over and Jimmy coiled up laughing. I watched him crossly as he doubled over, clutching his stomach as if he would vomit.

'That's not funny,' I said.

'Ah, but it was,' he tweaked my cheek and I pulled away.

His eyes darkened. 'You didn't pull away when that boyo had his hands about your waist, did you?' he said.

'He was showing me a uniform,' I poked my head right into Jimmy's, 'while you were making a fool of me.'

'Showing you a uniform, is that what it's called now? I must remember that, so I must.'

'If you're capable of remembering anything, which I doubt, remember that I don't take kindly to almost being frightened to death.' Now it was my turn to stomp off.

'Why did you run after me if you're only going to go away?' Jimmy called, and I swear he was making a show of the two of us.

'Why did you call into the shop if you were going to walk off?' I said. 'Huh, tell me that now.' I was very proud of my comment.

Jimmy laughed. 'OK, well, there's a dance on Friday in Patsy's Hall. Patsy is playing. I was wondering if you wanted to come.'

Patsy's Hall is a small little place just outside the town. There's a stage and bands play there now and again. I was surprised I hadn't heard about it before now, I normally knew months in advance and spent the whole time living for it.

I tried not to show how delighted I was that it was on. 'Are you inviting me?' I asked.

'Well there'd be no point if you're not coming.' Jimmy shoved his hands in his pockets and smiled a little.

He's a stubborn man, but he makes me laugh.

'I'd go if someone invited me.'

'Well I am so. I'm inviting you.'

'Fine,' I turned on my heel, 'I'll let you know.' I walked a few steps, then turned back. 'OK. Thanks.'

He grinned and left.

There weren't many dances in our place and to be honest, it wasn't encouraged too much what with Fr Costello being in charge. He thought dances were a bad idea, he thought it made people get out of control. I think when people have nowhere to let off steam it makes people get out of control.

Her mother was asleep, and Deirdre nodded for Zoe to stop. It was very disconcerting having this girl read her mother's story. Rick hadn't been able to come that afternoon and listening to the diary without his support had been harder than she'd thought it would be. Quite an audience had gathered inside the room too and Deirdre hadn't the heart to object, particularly as they were all so kind to Lily.

The receptionist, a bubbly, plump girl with blazing red hair, whose name Deirdre had forgotten, sighed dreamily, 'Aww, isn't it lovely to think Lily was young once and had a fella ask her to a dance?' She leaned her head against the door frame, smiling hugely.

It was strange to think of her mother as a young woman all right. In fact, Deirdre realised that she'd never seen Lily as anything but her mother. She'd never seen her as young and vibrant, the way she came across in the diary. She knew her mother had worked once, but not the details. Lily had never spoken about it. She reached over and gently touched her mother's small hands, brittle as dry twigs as they rested on her lap. She marvelled that once upon a time they'd stacked shelves in a shop somewhere in Cavan. That this woman who couldn't remember anything had once flirted with a man in the middle of a street. Tears started up in her eyes and she brushed them away. It was funny, but since her mother had become sick, it had allowed Deirdre to be more affectionate with her, touching her and cuddling her.

'I think you could do with a coffee,' Zoe said to Deirdre as she placed the diary underneath Lily's hands, folding them across it gently as she did so.

'Totally,' Carrie said. 'It's very draining listening to that. I'm exhausted.'

'I actually meant *you*,' Zoe said quietly, rolling her eyes and grinning at Deirdre.

'And I would love a coffee,' Deirdre picked up her coat and bag, thinking it might be nice to chat to Zoe and get to know her better. Her mother had obviously taken a shine to her. 'I'm on a half day and have nothing else planned.'

She followed the two girls from the room.

★   ★   ★

150

The canteen was empty save for four old men playing cards, one of whom was in a wheelchair. They looked up and greeted Zoe before resuming their game. 'That's Ronnie, Len, Harry and Charlie,' Zoe told Deirdre. 'They play cards every afternoon. Ronnie cheats,' she confided, 'and I'm waiting on the day the others cop on.'

Deirdre gave a shocked giggle as Zoe turned to Dominic.

'Three scones, three coffees, Dom, please,' Zoe ordered.

'Coming right up.'

'How much do I owe?' Deirdre lobbed her handbag onto the counter and began a search for her purse. She pulled out a roll of bandages, a pair of scissors, three pens, a notebook, a pack of pins and—

'On the house,' Dominic hastily waved her away. 'Free to visitors. Enjoy.'

'Thank you.' Deirdre scooped everything back up and dumped it all in her bag. Carrying her tea and scone, she followed Carrie and Zoe down to a table. She noticed Carrie's ring immediately. That was a good conversation opener, she thought. 'When's the big day?' she asked.

Carrie looked blank.

'Your wedding? I love the ring.'

'Next June,' Carrie answered. She held her hand towards Deirdre to give her a proper look. 'My mother said to get a good ring from him, she said that it might be the only piece of jewellery he'll ever buy me.'

'That's a bit sceptical,' Zoe remarked.

'She did live with my dad,' Carrie made a face. 'She said the only jewellery she ever had from him was a ring through her nose.'

Deirdre didn't know how she was expected to react to such personal information, so she just took a large bite of her scone. That should save her having to say anything.

'Aw, well,' Zoe said, 'if Harry stops buying you nice things, his mother will fill the gap, eh? Her mother-in-law loves her,' Zoe said to Deirdre.

'She does love me,' Carrie agreed, moving her chair aside so that Dominic could fit in beside her. 'Maybe more than her son does.'

'Which is a lot,' Dominic confirmed, buttering his scone.

Deirdre got the impression they'd discussed this before. She liked the way they all seemed at ease with each other. She wasn't like that with anyone in work. It had been her choice of course but, sometimes, when she watched other people banter, she wondered what it felt like to be that comfortable with people.

'She called me again yesterday,' Carrie said, 'three times this week. She wanted me to go shopping with her. How do I say no? How do I tell her that I have my own life and my own friends?'

'You say, I have my own life and my own friends, now get lost and find your own,' Dominic offered.

Deirdre thought that that was quite witty and she giggled.

'Shut up!'

'Sorry,' Deirdre said.

'Not you,' Carrie flapped an arm. 'Him.' She glared at Dominic. 'She's all right. It's just she has three sons and she always wanted a daughter and I think I've drawn the short straw.' Chin in hand, Carrie looked despondent. 'Does Abe's mother bother you much?' she asked Zoe.

'They live in Toomevara,' Zoe said. 'It's in Tipperary.'

'What a funny name,' Carrie said. 'It's probably ages away from here.'

'About two hours,' Zoe said.

'And would you see her much? Would she help out? I mean with Abe away all the time, you'd think she would.'

Deirdre thought Zoe looked a little uneasy, but when she answered, saying it was too far away, her voice was bright, so maybe Deirdre had imagined it.

'It's only two hours,' Carrie exclaimed, as if she'd known that fact all along. 'It's not like outer space.'

Zoe shrugged.

'Maybe it's as well,' Carrie said. 'You don't want someone like Harry's mother in your life, that's for sure.'

'Does your boyfriend go away a lot?' Deirdre asked, diverting the conversation away from Zoe's long-distance, unhelpful mother-in-law. She'd always been good at knowing when people were uncomfortable talking about certain subjects. Intuition.

'Yeah, he's heading to Somalia for three months on Friday.'

'What does he do?'

'Aid worker,' Zoe answered.

'Oh, how wonderful.' Deirdre thought that Zoe looked like the sort of hippy person who would be married to an aid worker. Or not married as there was no ring. But that was OK. That's the way it was done now. She was OK with that. Totally.

'Isn't Somalia quite dangerous at the moment?' Dominic asked. 'Is there a war going on or something?'

Zoe shrugged. 'Abe likes to go to those places.'

There was a small silence.

'He *likes* it?' Deirdre found it hard to keep the incredulity from her voice.

'I think so, yeah,' Zoe gave a smile. 'Maybe it reminds him of home.'

They laughed.

'But three months,' Carrie shook her head. 'Harry would never leave me for three months. We'd miss each other too much.'

'Yeah, well, we're not all tied to the hip and foot and arm and soul with each other, are we Zoe?' Dominic hopped up and Deirdre saw him gently squeeze Zoe's shoulder.

'Well, who's the mysterious Rosie then?' Carrie asked triumphantly. 'You jumped pretty quick when she rang the night we were in the pub.'

'That is my mysterious sister,' Dominic answered, grinning.

'You never said you had a sister.' Carrie sounded as if she didn't believe it for a second.

'And a dad,' Dominic bopped her gently on the head with the plate, 'so now you know. No in-laws, no girlfriends, nothing. Just a dinner to make.' He left them.

'How can a guy like him not have a girlfriend?' Carrie scrunched up her face as she looked after him. 'I mean look at that ass. What a waste.'

Deirdre tittered. She'd actually been thinking the same thing. Not about the ass, of course.

'I'd better get back,' Carrie hopped up. 'Bye now.'

With Dominic and Carrie gone, Deirdre was left alone with Zoe. They smiled at each other.

'This was what I had in mind initially,' Zoe said, 'just the two of us. Sorry for the gatecrashers.'

'Not at all,' Deirdre said. 'It's lovely to meet you all. Everyone here seems nice. And you read really well.'

Zoe smiled at the compliment. 'Thanks. It's the first time I've read a diary though.' She paused, then asked delicately, 'You don't mind me reading it, do you? Like I know it's what your mother wants and—'

'I don't mind at all,' Deirdre said, not actually sure that it was true. 'It's my mother's story, not mine. Though I can't for the life of me think why she'd want me to listen to it. None of what I've heard so far is new.'

'She sounds as if she was a lot of fun to know.'

'She does, doesn't she?' Deirdre couldn't help

the slightly sad, embittered tone in her voice. 'Maybe she was. Maybe that's what she wants me to know.' She raised her eyes and heaved a sigh. 'She wasn't much fun as a mother, really. I'm not sure she was cut out for motherhood.' She didn't know what had made her say that and she wondered for a second if she'd been too honest – Zoe seemed a little stuck for words. 'But I loved her,' she added hastily.

'Of course you did,' Zoe said.

Deirdre knew she'd created an awkward moment. Only it wasn't a moment, it was stretching beyond that. She wiped sweaty palms along her skirt as her mind searched for something to say. In the kitchen, that nice chef began to chop vegetables. 'She's the only real family I have left,' Deirdre said haltingly. 'So it's important, isn't it? Family.'

'Yes.' Zoe felt as if Deirdre had dropped a stone into her stomach. 'Yes it is.'

There was more silence. Deirdre wondered what other clanger she'd dropped. Zoe looked as if she'd seen a ghost. Deirdre licked her lips.

'We love your show by the way, me and Abe,' Zoe said, blessedly breaking the awkwardness. She smiled a bit, said a little off-handedly, 'Him especially.'

She grabbed the compliment. 'Thank you.'

'Abe listens all the time and he plays back anything he thinks I might be interested in. I know Gary Sims in there in the station. He's a good friend of my dad.'

Gary was another DJ, a bombastic though funny and slightly rude talk-show host. 'I'll tell him I met you,' Deirdre said, knowing she wouldn't. Gary was liable to say anything and she knew she wouldn't be able to think of witty rejoinders. Zoe, with her cool look and aid-worker boyfriend, was exactly the sort of person Gary would know all right.

Zoe glanced at her watch, 'Well, I'd better go. Great to chat, and if you have any concerns about me reading the diary, just shout.' She nodded at Deirdre's half-drunk coffee, 'You stay and finish up.' She picked up the empty plates and mugs, 'I'll just drop this back. See you next Wednesday.'

'You will,' Deirdre smiled.

CHAPTER 14

Thursday, and Paul's week was up. It was the first thing he said to them as Deirdre thanked her listeners, reminding them sternly to prune those roses as she signed off.

'OK,' Paul said, ushering the team out of studio and into a conference room, 'now that I've been here a week, I'd like to make a few observations.'

Deirdre saw Suzi, Matt and Emma shoot anxious looks at each other. This was the moment they'd all been dreading. It was like waiting for a teacher's verdict on a test. For the past week, they had tried to make the show as good as it could be, but judging from Paul's copious note-taking, he hadn't been impressed. Even when Deirdre had spent half her programme talking about the leaf structure of the dandelion, no compliment had been forthcoming.

'Sit down,' Paul urged, 'find a seat. Get comfortable.'

Like animals being hoarded to the abattoir, they moved in the direction he pointed. Deirdre was aware that her shoulders were almost touching her ears and she tried to relax. She resented the fact that she was nervous of this man who had only been around for a week. And a week ago, he'd come dressed in a sharp suit with a skinny tie, now he was in faded jeans and a blue jumper, wearing blue Doc Marten's. Did they not merit any respect? Is that why he turned up in those clothes? In contrast, her make-up had got heavier and her clothes had got more elaborate. It was as if she was trying to shore up her flagging confidence by looking good. They were ensconced in the smallest meeting room, a dreary, off-white place with a tiny window. It was a permanently gloomy room, not the most creative of spaces and yet Paul fizzed with energy. He was like a firework waiting to go off.

'Don't all look so scared,' Paul grinned. 'I'm on your side.'

To Deirdre's dismay, out of the corner of her eye, she caught Matt and Emma smiling back at him. Where was their loyalty? She was on their side too. At least Suzi had the good grace not to look impressed. As for her, she folded her arms and crossed her legs.

'OK,' Paul began, 'overall you have a good show. What I see as the main problem is—'

The word 'problem' was a problem. 'I think I'd like some water before we start,' Deirdre said. 'Anyone else?'

Everyone seemed a little taken aback at her interruption. Everyone except Paul. 'I'd like one too,' he said.

She hadn't meant to turn into his gofer, but she had no choice now. With as much dignity as she could, she left the room. Once outside, she concentrated on taking deep calming breaths before going to the water cooler. It was empty, so, with a sort of desperation, she joined the slowest queue in the canteen and poured two glasses. Then she took her time walking back. Maybe he'd have talked about the problems by now.

'Thank you,' Paul said. Then added audaciously. 'Did you have to go outside and dig your own well?'

Matt tittered but Deirdre froze him with a look. Turning back to Paul she said, 'At least I'd know how to bore a well, what do you know about gardening and nature?'

His grin faded.

Deirdre sat down and pretended to adjust her chair so that she wouldn't have to look at anyone. She knew her remark was a bit out of order, but she couldn't help it. This show was hers. Hers. She noticed that the other three were looking quite uncomfortable, which made her feel uncomfortable. As a rule, she didn't like atmospheres. When she had finished adjusting her chair, she glanced up and saw with shock that Paul was eyeballing her.

He let the silence build until Deirdre's eyes were sore from holding his gaze.

'OK, what do I know about nature?' Paul said. His grey eyes raked her over and she could feel a slow flush starting on her cheeks and working its way like a virus over her face. Paul seemed to wait until she was redder than a forest fire before turning away. 'I know nothing. But I do know about programming,' he said, as his gaze came to rest on the other three. 'I know what makes a great show, I know how to get listeners, I know how to inject interest and humour into presentations. Suzi?'

Suzi jumped as if he'd tazed her. 'Yes!' she half shouted.

'I know I'm stepping on your toes, I'm not trying to, but I'd appreciate your support.'

Suzi swallowed and shot a look at Deirdre.

'Does she have a choice?' Deirdre asked.

'Did I ask you?' Paul snapped without looking at her.

'No, but I'm asking you,' Deirdre snapped back.

Paul had the cheek to ignore her. 'Suzi, you do have a choice. You can ask to be transferred to another show but I'd really like you on board here.'

Oh, he was dead clever, Deirdre thought crossly.

'I'll give it a go,' Suzi's voice was barely above a whisper. 'See how it pans out.'

'Good,' Paul bestowed a huge smile on her. She looks all chuffed with herself, Deirdre thought sourly.

'OK,' Paul continued. 'As I said, I know about programmes and, for the last while, I've been listening to yours both live and on podcasts. In my opinion, there are a few problems.'

There was that word again. Deirdre fished a hankie from her sleeve and began flapping it in front of her face as Paul pulled his big green notebook from his back pocket. She watched him flip page after page.

'Looks like a lot of problems,' she remarked. 'What do you think, Suzi?'

Suzi glanced at her, a deer in the sights of a gun.

'Mainly you,' Paul snapped.

The other three inhaled sharply. Deirdre let out an 'oh'.

Paul laid his hands flat on the desk and said sternly, 'I'm here to up the ratings for this show. If anyone doesn't want to achieve that, go now.' His look swept over them all, then landed with the subtlety of a missile on Deirdre.

Deirdre wondered if she could push him another little bit, but decided not to. There would be other times.

'Good,' Paul said, sounding a little sarcastic, 'you're all staying.'

'Yes, we'd love more listeners,' Emma piped up.

Deirdre glared in exasperation at the girl, who deftly avoided her eye.

Paul, notebook in hand, began to pace a little. 'From what I heard over the past week,' he said, 'your show is exactly the same show that aired over five years ago. I got Michael to send me the recording. Nothing has changed.'

'So you're saying that we haven't moved on? That our show is stale and uninteresting and boring.' Deirdre looked around at the other three. 'That's what he's saying,' she gasped.

The other three avoided eye contact.

'I think what I'm saying is that you haven't moved on. I don't throw insults about.' Paul turned back to his notebook. He tapped at a page. 'Where is the humour?' he asked them, 'Where is Joe Public in all this?'

There was a blank silence. Deirdre looked up at the ceiling.

'All I've got from the show this week are facts, statistics, dry shite reports. Where are the ordinary Joes? Why aren't they included?'

'We go out on meet and greets,' Deirdre felt compelled to defend herself if the rest of them wouldn't.

'Yeah, and that's fine. But how often does that happen?'

'Four times a year. Each season.'

'Exactly,' Paul pronounced, as if she'd just pulled a rabbit from a hat. 'Not often enough.'

'We don't have the budget,' Suzi said, with a little too much respect, in Deirdre's opinion.

'These are the days of Joe Public. The man on the street wants to see his concerns reflected in the shows he listens to. He doesn't want to hear a droany report on the . . . what was it?' Paul flicked some pages. 'Yeah,' he chortled. 'The dandelion leaf. I mean, come on.' He looked at them. 'You don't need a budget. All you need is the price of a phone call. I've jotted down some notes and I'd like you to listen. Can we do that?'

Everyone nodded except Deirdre. There *were* people who liked to hear about dandelions.

'Deirdre?'

She looked at him.

'Can we do that?'

She muttered something that could be taken as a yes.

Paul gave a tiny smile. 'What I propose is to change the format of the show bit by bit over the next six weeks. That way we'll hold on to as many listeners as we can while hopefully attracting new ones.'

'You're going to revamp the whole show?' Deirdre asked the question with as much doubt in her voice as she could. Nothing like a bit of under-mining. 'I happen to think most of the segments work well.'

'They work all right,' Paul conceded, with as much doubt in his voice as was in hers. 'But I can get them to work better.'

Oh, he was good, Deirdre thought resentfully. Her arms ached from her defensive folding and she had to unfold them and cross her legs in the opposite direction.

He was going to introduce a book segment, reviewing various wildlife publications. He was going to have some 'bonkers nature facts' alongside the proven ones. He was going to encourage people to ring up and discuss topics. Garden centres would feature. Their resident gardener, who was a decent-looking bloke, was going to be sexed up and sent onto the streets. When Deirdre objected, Paul said that Michael had already agreed to it. In fact, he couldn't wait. They were going to have a garden of the year competition with *X-Factor*-type knockout rounds.

'It sounds like the whole country will be tromping into the studio,' Deirdre said, trying to mask her horror.

'Let's hope so,' he replied. 'The whole show needs to loosen up. Nature is fun, you know?'

'Loosen up. I'm not sure what you mean by that.' She gave him a glare.

'I just want you to be the fun person I know you are,' he said with an easy grin. 'It'll give you a chance to be yourself.' A smile.

Emma giggled and tried to turn it into a cough.

Deirdre was wrong-footed. He'd actually succeeded in making his insult sound like a compliment. Her brain was playing catch-up now, so that by the time she thought of what to say, he had moved on, focusing his attention on Emma as he explained to her new items for the show that might involve some research.

The young girl was hanging on his every word. She had her mouth open, her gaze riveted on the movement of his lips and she was nodding so much, she was bound to do herself some sort of brain injury if she didn't stop. 'I can do that,' she said, sounding quite excited. 'It'll be fun. That'll be fun, won't it, Matt?'

Matt agreed that yes, researching the funniest facts of nature would be fun. Reading books would be fun. Searching through thousands of entries for the gardening competition would be brilliant. Putting them up on the website would be a doddle.

Yeah, right, Deirdre wanted to snort. He didn't have a clue.

In the following hour, though, Deirdre watched with the dismay of an army general as her troops deserted her. Suzi was still slightly onside, but Deirdre could feel her little bit of power sliding from her grasp, like a rope chaffing her hands. It was alarming. Not that she'd ever wielded power or made people do things they hadn't wanted to but she had been in charge and even Suzi always listened to her ideas and took them on board. Now, it was Paul who tossed his seemingly endless ideas around like sweets at a party.

Finally, he stopped and, rubbing a hand over his head, thanked them all for their attention. 'Go home,' Paul said. 'Have a think, come back to me with any suggestions. I propose next week that we'll run with the garden competition.' He grinned at Matt and Emma. 'You two, get on the phones tomorrow, get sponsorship and prizes for it. It shouldn't be too hard, most gardeners would welcome plants and most garden centres will oblige for a free plug.'

'Can't wait,' Emma said, then flushed as she

166

caught Deirdre's glare. She turned away as she pulled on her big puffa jacket and shook out her hair so that it flowed down over her shoulders. 'I'll be off so. Bye,' she chirruped as she fled out the door, followed closely by Matt. Suzi was slower, she pulled on her black coat as if she were adorning herself in the crown jewels.

'Drink?' Suzi asked her.

'Eh, Deirdre, can I have a word?' Paul said. 'We won't be long,' he added to Suzi.

Suzi nodded and scurried out, making 'phone me' motions to Deirdre behind Paul's back.

Deirdre grinned at her, feigning nonchalance, pretending not to care about what Paul had to say. She pulled her raincoat on and began to clip up the buttons. It was a nice raincoat, see-through. It worked well if you wore nice clothes underneath. 'Yes?' she asked.

Paul hesitated before finally sitting back down and motioning her to do the same. She considered refusing but finally sat as far away from him as she could. 'I sense some hostility,' he said.

My, he was very direct.

'I'd like to know why.'

His flinty eyes were unnerving so Deirdre looked down and saw those big feet again. 'This is my show, I happen to like it the way it is. It's as if you're asking me to change my baby.'

'Do you have a baby?'

The question cut like a knife. 'No.'

'If my baby was dying on its feet, I think I'd like

167

someone to make it better.' Paul stood up. He crossed towards her and dipped his head so he was looking into her face. Silkily, he said, 'I'm trying to make your baby better, Deirdre.'

His breath smelled of mint and warmth. She had to pull back.

'You can thank me some other time.' He cocked a well-defined eyebrow and sauntered from the room.

She didn't know why she was trembling so much.

CHAPTER 15

Zoe put the phone down on Greg, then turned to watch as Abe packed a small suitcase. He was going away for three months and yet his case was one of those carry-on ones. There was something weird about that, but she couldn't quite figure it out. That there was something a little off about Abe had always appealed to her. In the six years they'd been together, Abe was as mysterious as he'd always been, which she was now beginning to realise was not right. There was a part of him that he kept under wraps and, in order to do that, he had to readjust his whole personality. In the beginning, his moody mysteriousness had excited her, his passion had thrilled her. And, boy, was he good in bed, all his emotions bound up with sex. But now Zoe was sure that it wasn't normal to not have a clue about the man who shared her life. Carrie knew most things about Harry and the bits she didn't know weren't sufficient to leave a gaping hole in the middle of their relationship.

'All packed?' she asked. Her voice sounded sort of dead.

'Uh-huh.' Abe had his back to her as he zipped up the case.

Zoe waited but Abe continued to potter about. Eventually, she snapped at him. 'Greg is grand, thanks for asking.'

'Good.' Abe turned around, took one look at her expression and said, 'I've said it already, Zoe. In fact I've been saying it every bloody day this week, but I'll say it again if it makes you feel better, I'm sorry for leaving you on Sunday.' He paused. 'If I'd stayed you'd have been even madder, trust me.'

'I'm not mad,' Zoe said.

Abe looked at her in disbelief. 'You've been giving me grief all week.'

'I didn't say I was mad. I just realised, sadly, that I expected nothing else from you.'

Abe flinched, but rallied, 'Well, sorry if I don't surprise you anymore.' He attempted a smile, which she didn't return. He stood up, crossed over towards her. Standing in front of her, he looked skywards and shoved his hands deep into his pockets before sighing and saying, 'I tried that day, I really did. I went along with you even though I'd have been much better minding Lee.' He took the risk of touching her arms and she pulled away from him. 'I know your ma and da are important to you, Zoe, which is why I went with you.'

'But you didn't stay.' He didn't stay when the going got tough. That scared her.

'No, I couldn't.'

'Why? Was it the emotion, the news. What?'

'Dunno.' He turned away and, opening the bedside locker, started rifling through a pile of paper, looking for something.

Zoe desperately wanted to shake him, to rattle him, turn him upside down, like she did with Lee's piggy bank when she was short of cash. She wanted to get all there was inside out of him. She watched him for a few seconds, wondering if he'd say anything. When it looked unlikely, she said dully, 'We've been at this for the last five years, Abe, the same old argument.' He looked up, surprised by the way her voice had dipped, 'Every Christmas Day, every Easter, every birthday celebration, we have the same argument.'

'Yep.' He found what he was looking for and slipped it into the front pocket of his case. 'Passport,' he said as he hefted the case from the bed. He sounded resigned.

'I think it's time we stopped.'

A pause. Abe froze, the case still in his hand. 'What are you saying?' he asked warily.

Zoe swallowed, feeling hot and sweaty all of a sudden, as if she was about to tear away her safety harness. 'I'm saying that maybe you going away is the break we need to rethink where all this is heading.'

'What?' he half-laughed, in disbelief. 'You're breaking up with me?'

'No, but you're going away for three months, it's

the ideal thing for us to have a think about what we both want.' She could barely get the words out, she desperately wanted him to tell her she was being ridiculous, that he wanted her and Lee and that he would do whatever it took to keep them. But he didn't. Instead, his eyes narrowed and he glared at her. 'Basically you're saying that if after three months I don't decide to do things your way, we break up?'

'No.' Zoe shook her head, her voice catching. 'No, I'm just . . . well, Abe, I need to think about the way you carry on. I'm tired of pretending that it doesn't bother me that you don't do family, mine or yours. It does bother me, I hate having to defend you to my family all the time. I hate the way you won't give me anything to work with. You never think of how I feel, not ever.'

'I bloody well came with you on Sunday.' Abe was shouting. 'I didn't want to, but I went along like a bloody turkey at Christmas, waiting to be slaughtered.'

'No one slaughtered you. They were all nice to you!' she shouted back.

Abe held out his wrist to her. 'Do you want blood, is that it? How much more have I got to do to keep you happy, you keep pushing and pushing and pushing.' He gave his case a kick.

Zoe was taken aback at the violence of his reaction. 'I don't push, Abe,' she said, shocked. 'I just want a normal relationship. Even my family notice the way you go on.'

'Why do you care that they notice? Why does it matter to you so much?'

'Because I love them, I want them to love you like I do.'

'Stop fighting,' Lee's voice came clear as a bell from his bedroom. 'I'm trying to go asleep.'

Zoe winced. 'We're not fighting,' she called.

'Yes we are,' Abe eyeballed her, daring her to disagree. 'But we'll stop now if it's bothering you, Lee.'

'Yes it is. You're always fighting.'

'Sorry, bud,' Abe called again.

Lee didn't reply.

'OK,' Abe said to Zoe, his voice under control, though he was pale. 'Take your three months, figure out if you can live with me or not.'

'And if you can live with me,' she said, trying to be fair.

Abe shrugged.

'I do love you, Abe,' she said. If he reached out now and took her in his arms and nuzzled her neck, she'd probably tell him it was OK, that she hadn't meant it.

'Yeah. Not enough,' he muttered. Then he added, defensively, 'I'll be still Skyping every second night to talk to Lee, right?'

'Of course. Abe—'

'I wasn't asking permission, I was telling you,' he cut her off. 'Now, if you don't mind, I've packing to do.'

'If you'd just—'

'Look, let's just say that the three months start now, yeah? That way we won't start arguing again and upset Lee.'

It was as if he'd slapped her. She took a step back. 'OK.'

'Good, then can I pack?'

He'd already packed, his case was zipped up. Zoe left the bedroom and went to the sitting room. She flicked on the TV. Ten minutes later, she heard Abe climb into bed.

She wished she could cry, but it was as if she was frozen.

CHAPTER 16

Zoe hardly slept that night. When sleep finally came, she'd been woken about an hour later as Abe mooched about, getting ready to leave. Zoe kept her eyes shut, not sure if she should say goodbye. The word sounded so final, so she decided to just let him go without saying anything. She listened as he crept about, pulling on his uniform of jeans and T-shirt. She heard him making coffee and smelled the aroma of the burned toast that he liked to eat. Then, he came back into the bedroom and Zoe heard him pick his case from the floor. He seemed to pause in the doorway for a second or two, and she wondered if he'd kiss her but instead he left and went into Lee's room before leaving the apartment with a soft click of the door. She opened her eyes and lay in the semi-dark until it was time to get Lee up for school.

When she'd dropped Lee off, Zoe debated whether she should phone in sick. At the moment she felt fine, but numb. There was heaviness in her chest that she was sure would turn into tears, given enough time and provocation. She didn't need the indignity of sobbing her heart out in a room full of people. But she hadn't cried in front of Lee, in fact he'd been a distraction. If she went home, she'd spend the day worrying; at least if she was in work, she'd have things to do. There were acts to be confirmed, people to be paid, invoices to account for. She arrived with minutes to spare and the first thing she saw was a huge bunch of sunflowers sitting in vinyl wrapping, on the reception desk. A big yellow bow was tied around them and a card was taped to the front. They looked so vibrant and cheerful that Zoe felt suddenly bereft. Carrie was examining them proudly, standing back, cocking her head, before shifting their position slightly on the desk.

'Wow, lovely,' Zoe forced her voice to be as bright as the petals. 'Are they yours?'

Carrie smiled. 'Yes. From Harry.' A laugh bubbled up like champagne. 'Today is our one-year anniversary.'

Abe had only bought her flowers once, after she'd had Lee. He'd arrived into the hospital with seven roses. Seven, she thought now, who buys seven roses?

'Are you OK?' Carrie's pert little nose wrinkled in concern. 'You look . . .' she tried to find the right word.

'I'm just tired,' Zoe smiled. 'The flowers are gorgeous. You're so lucky.'

Then before Carrie could say anything else, Zoe bolted for the comfort and solitude of her office.

* * *

176

Deirdre's alarm woke her. Turning over in bed, she flicked it off and lay there, looking at her pristine white ceiling with its hopelessly dated lampshade. Florals, tassels and old stone were her big interior design loves. She had picked up the lampshade in a car boot sale for a fiver and after cleaning it up as best she could, had hung it in her bedroom.

Yellow sunlight was streaming through her thin pink and green flowery curtains. Deirdre allowed it bathe her face for a second before suddenly remembering, with a sickening whump, the confrontation with Paul yesterday. She felt weary, abruptly realising that she hadn't the energy to face him again so soon. She didn't know how she'd done it yesterday. It wasn't like her to be so . . . combative. It had been a little thrilling though, she had to admit, but it had sapped her energy so that now she felt like an odd shoe with a hole. All used up and good for nothing.

It was a sin, Deirdre thought, to have to suffer the indignity of him undermining all her work on a beautiful day like this. Serve him right if she took a sickie. But she couldn't. She'd never done anything like that before. She got up and showered – but the idea was like wisteria, twisting itself into her brain and not letting go. The very rebelliousness of it made her pulse race. Ring. In. Sick.

The plan tumbled over and over in her head like a brightly coloured sock amid grey washing. Could she do it? Dare she do it? Someone else could cover her show for one day. Deirdre sat up, her mouth dry, her heart thumping a little harder than necessary. Would she be able to pull it off? She attempted a sniff. Sounded good.

Before she lost her nerve, she picked up her mobile phone and dialled Suzi. A man answered and Deirdre almost hung up, convinced she'd dialled Paul by mistake. Of course that's who she should have dialled, he was her boss now, after all. But Suzi had been her boss, so technically . . .

'Is Suzi there?' she asked cautiously. In the background, the radio was playing an upbeat song. Her heart thumped in rhythm.

'Hey, Suz, it's for you,' the man called.

This was curious.

Suzi came to the phone. 'Hello?' She sounded all bright and chirpy. How could she sound like that when the show was changing?

'Who was that?' Deirdre asked, all trace of her practice cold gone.

'That's Robbie,' Suzi said as if Deirdre should know. 'Anyway, what's up? I waited to hear from you last night and you never rang. It looked like you and Paul were brewing for a row.'

Deirdre suddenly remembered why she was calling. But who was Robbie? She had a feeling that Suzi thought she should know so she didn't ask. 'Suzi, I've been sick all night.' Which was true actually. Sick of Paul.

There was silence from the other end of the phone.

'Suzi?'

'You're not coming in?' Suzi sounded shocked. 'Is this because of Paul? I know—'

'I'm sick.'

'Paul might think it's because of him. It won't look good for you, Dee.'

'It's not because of him.' She managed a cough. More silence.

'I've been sick all night.'

'I happen to think his ideas are good,' Suzi said. Her tone was defensive, as if she was expecting Deirdre to argue back. 'I think we should give him a chance.'

Now she really was sick. Suzi? Her friend and ally. 'I have to go,' Deirdre coughed a little to make it more authentic. 'Give my apologies to all. Thanks.'

Before Suzi could say any more, she hung up.

Zoe deleted the email from Marvello asking her if she had reconsidered his offer of a magic table and turned her attention to the next one, but a sharp rap on the door made her jump.

'Yes?'

'Well, you're going to have to open up for me, I'm in a wheelchair.'

Ronnie. The last thing she needed was him banging on complaining, not when she was feeling as raw as she was now. Still, she pulled open the door and Ronnie wheeled himself into her office. He spent a second or two gazing about, nodding

179

in approval. 'Some pad you have here,' he said, 'bigger than my bedroom.'

'It's not bigger than your bedroom,' Zoe said, a little crossly. 'Your bed is enormous, remember? You insisted on having it brought here? And you've piles of books all over the place and—'

'Oh, someone is in a bad mood.' Ronnie sounded amused at this turn of events. He smiled at her, 'So, what's happened?'

'Nothing. Now, what do you want?' Zoe took a seat behind her desk.

'Ouch!' Ronnie looked pained. Then his face cleared. 'Right, if you won't tell me, there's nothing I can do. So, down to business. I was wondering, seeing as you are the entertainments manager, if you'd let me entertain people some night.' At Zoe's lack of response, he carried on. 'I'd do a bit of magic, bit of singing, tell a few jokes. I used to do all the clubs in London way back before . . .' his voice dipped, and he dropped his gaze, '. . . well, before I had the car crash.'

As far as Zoe knew, Ronnie had never talked about how he'd ended up in a chair and it was just listed as 'an accident' on his files. 'And you had to give it up?' she said.

He shrugged, his expression darkening. 'In those days, there were no special arrangements for wheelchair users, I couldn't drive, I couldn't take a bus, nothing. I was shoved into this thing' – he indicated his chair – 'and told to get on with it.'

'And you did,' Zoe smiled.

180

'I did not. The wife left me, can't blame her, I was unbearable.' He gave a wry grin. 'Bit like I am now.'

Zoe didn't smile back. Instead she studied him. She'd discovered that the best way to deal with Ronnie was to shoot from the hip. 'So, if the discerning audience of Lakelands hate you, what will you do?'

'They won't hate me,' Ronnie said with enviable confidence. 'I'm brilliant. Trust me.' He offered her a smile. 'And I know all the old numbers, I'll have them all singing along. And I can do my tricks on the Alzheimer's patients, that way they'll be more impressive.'

'Stop!' Zoe had to laugh. 'You are a terrible man!'

Ronnie beamed at his terribleness. 'So?' he finally asked, sounding a little nervous. 'What do you think?'

Zoe considered. Ronnie was high risk. 'I don't know, Ronnie—'

'Please,' he said, and for the first time he sounded a little bit desperate. 'Please, Zoe. I'm going mad here. My daughter doesn't even visit any more, I used to look forward to her visits.'

'Yes, well, you shouldn't have accused her of parental abandonment then, should you? She did her best from what I can tell. You almost ruined her marriage.'

Ronnie dipped his head. 'I know.'

The sight of him, so down, melted her a little. 'OK. I'll give you a half an hour at first.'

His face dropped.

'Just at first, Ronnie. I need to see that you can keep your cool – if you can, I'll give you longer.'

He didn't answer immediately. 'OK.' He managed a small smile. 'But you'll wish you'd put me on longer, you will.'

'I hope I will,' Zoe said. 'There is, however, one condition.'

'I already said I won't insult anyone!' He was back to grumpy Ronnie mode.

'That's not it.'

'So what is it?' Then he nodded, sounding bored. 'OK, I give in, I will be your sugar daddy.'

She smiled. 'It's this – that you do not give out about Dominic's food ever again.'

Ronnie's eyes narrowed and glittered slyly. 'Oh, do you fancy him?'

'Eh, no, but he is a great chef and you keep undermining him.'

'Undermining him?' Ronnie snorted in derision. 'That guy knows how good he is. He might be quiet, but he'd never feel undermined, believe me.' He cackled a little as if the thought amused him.

'Nevertheless,' Zoe said, 'if I hear you complaining about the food one more time, there will be no shows.'

'I'm sure you can't do that,' Ronnie frowned. 'I pay good money to be in here, you can't bribe me.'

'I can,' Zoe nodded. 'I just have.'

Ronnie grinned slowly. 'OK. I will not complain

about the food ever again. Now, my dear, can we discuss a date for my show?'

Zoe took out her diary as Ronnie beamed.

Her roses were coming along nicely. Deirdre stood back to admire the one she'd just pruned and thought that with any luck, it'd be beautiful this year. When she'd first moved into the cottage, Deirdre had spent a long time cultivating the soil in her garden. Her motto, feed the soil and not the plant, was working brilliantly. If the flowers failed to thrive, there would be no excuse except her own bad management.

Just like her radio show.

The thought came unbidden, like a huge spot on the face of her day.

'Hello! I'm looking for Deirdre.'

She jumped at the voice calling out its welcome and her pruning shears clattered to the ground. It couldn't be Paul, could it? She wouldn't put it past him.

'Hello! Deirdre, is that you?'

It was Rick hailing her from the side gate. The relief that it wasn't Paul almost made her stomach heave. 'Hi' she called. 'I'm here, come around. Open the gate!'

Rick, looking very dapper in black trousers and a crisp white shirt, bounded towards her. 'I didn't recognise you at first,' he said, apprising her delightedly. 'You look nice.'

Deirdre laughed at the feeble joke. Look nice?

She was wearing old jeans and a man's shirt that she had picked up in a charity shop. 'What brings you here?'

'I didn't hear you on your show today and I got worried. I called the station and they said you were out sick. Then I called your house and couldn't get an answer, so I came over, just to check you were OK.'

'That's really nice.' She pulled off her gardening gloves and untied her blue bandana. 'As you can see, I'm not really that sick.'

'Thank God,' Rick smiled. 'So, any chance of a cuppa?'

'Every chance.' Deirdre dropped her gloves to the ground and led him to the house. 'I'm glad you called. It's not often I get visitors.' She pushed open the back door and pulled off her wellies. 'Come on in, I'll put on the kettle.'

Rick followed her into the kitchen.

'Tea? Coffee?'

There was no reply and Deirdre turned to find him standing at the door, peering around, looking quite surprised. 'Wow,' he finally uttered, a tad nervously.

Her kitchen tended to have that effect on visitors, Deirdre thought. In fact her whole house did. She wasn't quite sure why. Maybe it was just that she had so many things and she wanted to show them all off. Pictures, photographs, certificates, ornaments, furniture, objects of interest, presents from abroad. Old newspapers in boxes under the table. How did you choose what to exhibit and what not? 'Do you hate it?' she asked pleasantly.

'No, not at all,' Rick said unconvincingly, peering around him, 'I suppose I just prefer, well, more minimalist surroundings. I grew up in a kitchen like this, couldn't get away fast enough.'

Deirdre took it on the chin. She was used to people thinking that her house was a little quirky. 'I grew up in one too,' she said to Rick, 'and I loved it.'

'I'm glad,' he said, sounding a little strange.

Deirdre glanced at him and he looked away, he must have some painful memories of his own home, she thought. After a beat, she said, 'I suppose it's a blessing to love where you come from.'

'It is. Why did you leave? Your mother said you went to college? That you are a fantastic gardener.'

She flushed at the compliment. 'I don't know about fantastic, but I love it. I did horticulture and then I got a job pretty much straight out of college in the Botanic Gardens. And from there I advanced to the dizzying heights of radio.' She was a little taken aback at how bitter she sounded.

'Well, if you have time, I'd appreciate some advice on your mother's garden,' Rick said, either not noticing her tone or choosing to ignore it. 'I'm hopeless, I kill everything.'

There wasn't a lot in her mother's garden to save, Deirdre thought wryly. She'd bought plants for her mother in the early days and Lily had tried her best to look after them but her heart was never in it. And it only upset her mother when things died on her, so Deirdre had stopped. She had often thought that it could be a lovely garden. It faced south so the possibilities were endless. 'I might take you up on that,' she said, suddenly embracing the idea of a willing pupil.

'Great.' Rick clapped his hands together. 'I'll buy the wellies.'

They shared a laugh.

Then Rick swept his arm about the room with all its knick-knacks and photos and asked, 'D'you mind?'

'Not at all.' Deirdre got the cups together as Rick browsed.

'Are all these black and white photos of people you know?' he asked.

'Some of them.' Deirdre scalded the teapot and filled a little strainer with some leaves. Clipping it shut, she put it into the teapot, before pouring scalding water in on top. Leaving it to brew, she joined Rick at the picture rail. She took the photos down and handed them to him, one by one, explaining who everyone was, if she knew. The third was a picture of her dad in his teens. 'Dad.' Her voice caught on the word.

Rick stared at the picture. 'He was a fine man,' he said quietly.

'He was.' Deirdre touched the monochrome photo of the tall man with the piece of straw in his mouth. He was beaming into the camera, eyes dancing with fun, even after all the years. Though the camera didn't show it, his hair was a sandy brown, his eyes as blue as his wife's. His face was perhaps a little too long and his frame a little too narrow to be truly macho, but there was a decentness in his expression that negated everything. Or maybe it was just because she'd known how good he was that she saw it. Anytime she looked at this picture, she wished that she could be truly like this man, but she knew it would never be. She was who she was.

She passed another picture to Rick. 'That was my mother when she made front page in the local paper. I was mortified at the time but, then again' – she cracked a grin – 'I've spent a lot of my life being mortified by my mother.'

Rick studied the picture of Lily with her miniskirt and her halter-neck top and laughed. 'Oh, I'd say the good decent folk of the town didn't like that get up.' Lily had her hair up in ponytails and a swagger in the way she pouted for the camera. The caption underneath read, 'Lily Deegan, who supports the opening of the Fashion Emporium'.

'No, they didn't. And everyone talked about her. And she was upset so my dad made her wear it and they both marched through the town and my dad said he'd kill anyone that said anything.'

Rick chortled. 'Your mother was always a little bit ahead of her time.'

'Yep. She had all these ideas that were radical at the time but that no one bats an eyelid about

187

now. She was the reason I went to college. She told me on no account to ever leave my job if I got married.' Deirdre allowed herself a laugh. 'Chance would be a fine thing.'

'You were never tempted?'

Deirdre flushed, feeling she'd said too much. It wasn't like her. But Rick's interested look and keen gaze flattered her a little, so she said shyly, 'Once. He was a lovely man.' She reached up and took down another picture, handing it to Rick. Why she still had it hanging up, she didn't know. Maybe she liked the way she looked in it.

'Is that you?' Rick's voice registered surprise.

'Yep,' Deirdre nodded.

The photo had been taken on a beach in Dingle when the tide was out and the sand had become a shining brown mirror that stretched for miles upon miles. The sky was blue and cloudless and in the distance, the hills rose up, shade upon shade of blue. Deirdre's hair was long and dark, flowing over her shoulders like melted chocolate, her face was berry brown and she was laughing. She wore a T-shirt and Bermuda shorts. The man with her was in brightly patterned shorts and a white T-shirt. He was laughing too, his hand protectively loped around her.

'And this is the man?'

'Yes. For a month or two, he was my fiancé.'

There was something lovely about that picture, they both looked so happy. 'Then I got cold feet.'

Rick didn't seem to know what to say to that. He

spluttered out, 'Well, better not to make a mistake, eh?'

'I'm sure I wouldn't have made a mistake,' Deirdre said. She replaced the picture, running her finger over John's face. Over fifteen years ago and it was still a decision that haunted her.

She wondered where he was now. He had left the Botanic Gardens soon after and she'd never heard from him since.

Later that evening, Zoe pushed open the back door to the car park and breathed a sigh of relief that the day was over and she'd survived. She thought about returning home to the empty flat and her heart sank. Just then, she saw Dominic, bending over his motorbike. Yum, she thought, as she took in his fine ass in his motorbike leathers.

As she approached, Dominic gave the front wheel of his bike a kick and cursed, loud enough to be heard. Holding his hands to his head, he groaned.

'Something wrong?' Zoe called, bleeping her car open with the key fob.

'Damn thing is finished, I think.' He gave his bike another kick.

'Well you won't fix it like that,' Zoe said, amused.

'It's been playing up for a while, I thought I'd get longer out of it.' Picking up his helmet and his haversack, Dominic gave it a final frustrated kick and made to walk away.

'Where do you live?' Zoe jangled her car keys.

'I can drop you anywhere. My folks would take Lee all night if I let them, so I'm in no rush.'

Dominic hesitated slightly, then glanced down at his watch. 'Well, I'm not actually going home,' he said cagily, 'I was on my way to St Catherine's Hospital.'

'Oh, well, that's not far and it's the way I'm going anyway,' Zoe grinned. 'No problem. Hop in.'

'You sure?' At her nod, he grinned, relieved. 'That's great, Zoe. Ta.'

He dumped his gear on her back seat and hopped into the front. When he was strapped in, Zoe fired the engine and her car took off.

'No one too sick I hope,' she asked as she pulled out onto the road.

Dominic reacted as if she'd electrocuted him. 'What?'

'I, eh, said, I hope there's no one too sick?' Zoe flushed. 'You don't have to answer that, I was just making conversation.'

Dominic nodded and Zoe flipped on the radio. A news bulletin was just starting. As usual it began with a depressing piece on the economy. Zoe turned it down, waiting for the *Gary Sims Show* which always aired after the five o'clock news. She'd listened to it faithfully ever since it had first been broadcast. 'It's, eh, my dad,' Dominic said after a bit. 'He's in there.'

'Your dad?' Zoe glanced sideways at Dominic. He was staring at his hands. 'Oh, I'm sorry. Nothing too serious I hope?'

Dominic shrugged. 'He's been ill for the past three years. He's a paraplegic and any sort of infection is really serious for him. He got sick recently, that night we were in the pub?' As she nodded, he added, 'So my sister had to call an ambulance.'

'Oh, my God,' Zoe looked at Dominic in surprise. 'Oh, Dominic, I'm really sorry to hear that. I didn't know.'

He met her gaze. She noticed that his eyes, which she'd always thought quite soulful, were actually just sad.

'Yeah, well,' he muttered, 'I don't like to talk about it at work. It's nice to come in and start cooking and forget about it for a few hours. I like to keep it separate – I find it's better for me. Easier to cope with.'

Zoe knew all about that. 'Does June know?'

'Nah. The accident happened about a year before I went to work in the home and I didn't mention it in my interview because it never came up.'

'So you live at home to take care of him.'

'Uh-huh. I didn't always, at first he was in the hospital for a long time and then he came back to his home. I'd spend every second night there, but it didn't make sense and, besides, my sister was finding it too hard. It wasn't fair.'

'So she minds him when you're in work?'

'Yep. She gave up her job to do it. I take over when I get in from work, it gives her a break. It works.'

'Oh, Dominic, I'm so sorry.'

'Don't be. It's just the way things are.' He pointed out the window. 'You'd want to slow up, there's a car just there.'

Zoe planted her foot on the brake and slid to a halt. 'Thanks. I was so busy looking at you, I forgot I was driving.'

Dominic didn't look too reassured. 'Oh.'

'So, do you ever get out?' The traffic was moving again and she took off.

'Most Fridays either with you and Carrie or some other mates.'

'Holidays?'

'We did once, but we had to put him into a hospital.' A shrug as he turned his gaze to the window. 'He's our dad.' Those three words said a whole lot.

Zoe understood what he meant immediately. 'Yeah.' Without thinking, she gave his arm a reassuring squeeze. 'I guess it's the way people who put their parents into Lakelands must feel. They know they can't manage but they always feel guilty about it, as if they're abandoning their mother or father.'

'Yep.' A pause. 'It's funny how you just adapt,' he went on. He angled himself towards her. 'I hated it at the beginning, I was having a great old time, out every night, but now, well, it's just my life, you know?'

Zoe didn't feel that she did know. Imagine having that responsibility each evening. 'Well, if you ever need to talk about it at work, you can talk to me,' she said.

Dominic grinned, 'Thanks, but I'm grand.'

'And how is he? Is he really sick?'

His grin faded. 'Yep.' Then he added, 'I mean, when he gets sick, he does tend to get really sick, so . . .'

'Well, if there's anything I can do . . .' Her voice trailed off too. What on earth could she do for a paraplegic man?

'Well, until I get my bike fixed, giving me a lift after work would be great,' Dominic said.

'No problem. Anytime.'

They drove in silence for a little bit, then Dominic obviously feeling the need to make small talk, said, 'So how are you? How's Abe getting on?'

Now it was her turn to flinch, but Dominic had been honest with her so she really didn't feel she could lie to him. 'To be honest, Dominic, I don't know.'

'Oh.' He didn't seem to know what to say to that.

'We're on sort of a' – she thought how to phrase it – 'a kind of break.' She did her best to sound upbeat about it. 'It was actually my idea.'

'OK.' Dominic shrugged. 'And was it an idea you're, eh, happy with?'

'Well, *obviously* as it was my idea,' she said. Then she heaved a sigh. 'It's not much of a break though as it'll probably involve a lot of him not talking to me and me just going about my ordinary life.'

'Oh.'

The news ended and the *Gary Sims Show* began. Zoe turned up the volume. 'Tonight boys and girls,' Gary said chirpily, 'we're going to talk about getting over *that* person.'

Dominic and Zoe laughed at the serendipity.

'You should come for a drink or go out a bit more with your mates,' Dominic said. 'Then you'll see if you really miss him or not.'

Zoe smiled. 'Yeah, I might.' Though she would miss him, that much she knew.

'Eh, Zoe, you've just passed the hospital.'

She brought the car to a screeching halt, forgetting that she was in the middle of the road. Dominic was flung forward and about ten motorists blasted her with horns and the more expressive ones gave her the two fingers. 'Shit, sorry, Dominic.'

'No worries.' He looked a bit shaken.

She indicated to turn back.

'Jesus, Zoe,' he said, alarming her with his alarm. 'Don't try and do a u-turn in this traffic.'

'Someone will let me out.'

'Not if you get killed first,' he winced. 'Look, you can pull in there,' he pointed to a bus layby. 'I'll walk back.'

'OK.' Zoe pulled the car into the side of the road and Dominic hopped out. He grabbed his gear from the back. 'Thanks. See you tomorrow.' A pause. 'And sorry about Abe.'

He slammed the door shut and Zoe watched him walk away, understanding suddenly why

194

he wasn't interested in ever leaving Lakelands and wondering if he ever felt trapped. She knew without a doubt that as soon as Lee was older, she'd hunt down another, more high-profile job. But Dominic's dad wasn't ever going to get better and, as he aged, things would probably get worse for Dominic and his sister. Dominic was truly trapped in a web not of his making and, yet, he came into work and he made the best of it, by making great food and cheering up the residents.

So enough, she thought. Enough of bringing my problems into work.

After Rick had left, Deirdre tidied up and flicked on the television but her mind couldn't settle. The picture of her and John had raked up all the regrets she'd buried over her decision. It was as if she'd disturbed a shallow pool and sent little sea creatures scurrying for cover. Over the years she had been tempted to try to trace him, she didn't know why, maybe it was simple curiosity. It certainly wasn't love, well, not in the I-wish-I'd-married-you sense. Maybe it was guilt. She was good at guilt. Maybe she just wanted to see that he'd got on with his life and that what she had done hadn't hurt him too much.

She lifted herself from the sofa thinking that it couldn't do any harm to look.

And if he wasn't on Google, well, then she'd just leave it.

But even the smallest little tit-bit of information would help her. Just something to say he was OK. After he'd left the Botanic Gardens, three weeks after she'd called off the wedding, she'd asked him to keep in contact and he'd promised that he would, but they both knew that he didn't mean it. Instead, he'd sent her a letter. One in which he begged her for an explanation of what she'd done. If she wasn't willing to explain, well then he couldn't depend on her and he'd rather just not hang around. Deirdre remembered how she'd sat, pen in hand, thinking, puzzling, scribbling down inane sentences in an attempt to fill the blank space. But it was impossible. She couldn't put into words how her whole world had unexpectedly tipped sideways. Even Lily had asked her why but she couldn't tell her mother – her mother had been the cause of it, if only she'd known.

She flicked on her computer and made herself some tea and toast while it booted up. Like everything else in the house, it was ancient but, unlike everything else, she hated it's age. It grunted and groaned like a cranky old man as it loaded all its data.

After about ten minutes, she was able to access Google and typed in 'John Cant'. Fingers poised over the keyboard, she thought for a bit, before adding 'Botanic Gardens Dublin'. An old picture of John popped up onto her screen. He was standing in the Gardens in mucky boots, his hair plastered to his skull either with dirt or sweat. He had the most ridiculously happy grin on his face. In jeans and an old torn jumper, he looked like she remembered. Deirdre allowed herself a smile. John had been like her, intent on his work, and many afternoons they'd just potted and pruned and spliced and dug without exchanging a word.

Going into the article, she saw that it was one she'd read before. There wasn't much else on him, just bits and pieces from his time there. She deleted the 'Botanic Gardens Dublin' and searched under his name. But that produced way too many results. She tried adding a few gardening terms, but nothing.

In the end she gave up.

Maybe it was just as well. She might have embarrassed herself by contacting him, trying to explain herself.

And she wasn't able to. Not then. Not now.

Far better to let the past stay in the past.

Lee had been tired leaving his nana's and was now fast asleep. Zoe stood at the foot of his bed, her heart all tender and mushy as she admired his cute little arms and legs, which were sprawled in all directions. The top of his pyjamas had lifted up, exposing his soft little belly, and she was filled with such love for her child that tears welled in her eyes. He was the best thing ever to happen her and, despite everything, she had Abe to thank for him. Gently she pulled the duvet up over Lee before tip-toeing back into the sitting room.

She logged on to her computer and keyed into the Google maps website. She typed in 'Dodder Apartments Dundrum' and 'Toomevara' and immediately a list of directions popped up complete with map. According to the site, it would take only ninety minutes and the route was very straightforward. Her heart was thumping and her finger shook as she followed the map down the screen. But would she? No, she couldn't. It was none of her business. And yet . . . well, it was. If finding out could save her relationship with Abe, wasn't it worth it? As Deirdre had said, family was important. And Deirdre was alone in the world except for Lily and from what she could gather about Abe, all he had was his mother too. And even if his mother turned out to be awful, it might help her understand where he was coming from, metaphorically and literally. Plus, he would never find out. Or would he? Zoe felt she needed some wine. Pouring a large glass, she sat back and studied the screen. Even if she did go down, she thought, how would she go about getting to know his family? She could hardly walk up to the house and demand that they tell her all about themselves without telling them who she was. And if she did that, Abe would be bound to find out. Zoe sat and thought about it. She had three months before Abe came back. Three months before their relationship ended, because it would end if he kept on carrying on the way he was, of that she had no doubt.

It wasn't the fact that she didn't know that

bothered her. It was the fact that he wouldn't trust her enough to tell her. She needed to understand why that was.

The way she saw it, she really didn't have a choice.

What she needed was a plan.

THE THIRD WEDNESDAY

Lily stared at the woman with the awful clothes who was talking. She looked sedate and very beige. And so many buttons on everything. Little fiddly buttons. Buttons on her skirt, her blouse, her cardigan. Buttons on her coat and up the sides of her shoes. The sound of the woman's voice, husky, a little creamy, recalled images of small hands, cups of hot sweet tea and baked brown bread and a cream ceiling with peeling plaster, thick walls like a prison and the pattern of a bedspread, roses and butterflies, beauty that died so quick.

More people came in. A girl in tight clothes who read the papers. Bouncy hair, bouncy walk. Another girl, the flibbergibbit with the red curls. A woman dressed as a nurse. Another nurse.

Everybody saying hello. Everyone talking. Then all quiet as the bouncy girl with the tight clothes held out her hand.

Lily automatically handed her the diary.

Deirdre! That's who the voice belonged to. Lily grasped her daughter's hand and wondered where the years had gone.

October 1957

Jimmy called to pick me up for the dance. My mother was at the door to meet him. Both my parents think Jimmy is almost as good as the parish priest. It's embarrassing how welcome they make him feel, how they sit him down and give him tea and ask him all about his day. And Jimmy just loves it. When I eventually arrived down, having kept him waiting so he wouldn't think I was too eager, he was stretched out in a chair beside the fire, a cup of tea in his hands and both my parents hanging on his every word, and all he was yammering on about was the birth of a calf. Even Sean, my brother, was listening to him as he went about doing his work. Jimmy is an entertaining speaker but, honestly, there is no need to give him such a swelled head.

'You needn't think I'm as impressed with you as my parents are,' I said to him as he opened the door of his father's clapped-out car for me. 'Any man who can talk about birthing a calf when he's meant to be courting a girl is not someone that I'd like to encourage.'

'Aw, there's no pleasing you,' Jimmy laughed as he slammed – yes slammed! – the door really hard after me, almost making me deaf. 'Now, d'you like me new suit?'

I did, actually. It was the first thing I'd noticed about him when I'd come into the kitchen, though I wouldn't give him the satisfaction of telling him that. The suit made him look tall and almost handsome. 'It's all right,' I sniffed.

'Well, I like your new dress,' he said, sitting in beside me and starting the car. Big plumes of blackish smoke poured into the vehicle and made me cough.

'It's not new,' I said, choking. 'I didn't go out of my way to buy anything new. Sure it's just a dance.'

'Well, it is and you're right,' Jimmy said as he put his foot down really hard on the accelerator, making the car jump forward like a rabbit. I don't think he knows how to drive or else the car was on its last legs because it hopped like this all the way to the hall.

By the time we arrived, I had the window rolled right down and my head stuck out of it, gasping for air. The car was toxic. I knew I smelled of petrol and so did Jimmy and I knew that it'd never come out of my dress, which actually was quite new.

The smoke didn't seem to bother Jimmy. He drove up to the hall like he was in command of a big fancy car. Hopping out, he opened my door with a flourish. I stumbled from the seat and staggered away from the car, doubled over, coughing and spluttering.

'Oh dear, what have you done to her?'

It was Patrick of course, looking all supercilious. I wished I could dissolve into the air. His suit was even nicer than Jimmy's, his hair in the latest Teddy-boy style and he was with Ann Morrisey. She was hanging on to his arm like a limpet on a piece of rock. She looked like a limpet too, in a brown dress. I hate brown.

'The car is on its last legs,' Jimmy said cheerfully.

'And by the looks of it so is your date,' Patrick sounded amused. 'Big deep breaths, Lily.'

I could hardly catch my breath and I knew my face was all red and my hair was a big mess from having my head stuck out the window. I couldn't bear to look at him or Ann. But I had to.

'I'm fine,' I said, taking Jimmy's arm the way Ann had Patrick's. Jimmy looked delighted, so I loosened my grip a tiny bit as I didn't want him thinking I was that interested in him. 'Have a good night the two of you.'

'We will,' Ann said.

A photographer took our pictures as we went into the dance. First one with me and Jimmy and then one with all four of us. I got to stand beside Patrick.

'Save a dance for me,' Patrick said, and winked at me when the pictures were done. My legs went suddenly wobbly. Ann dragged him off and shot me a look as if to say, 'If you dance with him, I'll kill you.' Which of course made me determined to.

The hall is a big draughty barn at the top of which, on a badly constructed podium, was Patsy's band. Patsy is a farmer from about five miles away and he plays the uilleann pipes like you wouldn't believe. The music he can get out of such an ugly-looking instrument would make your heart soar. His band consisted of another few bedraggled fellows; all of them were great musicians. They could play anything you asked, mostly Irish stuff though and most of it pretty fast – the slower music leads folk into sin apparently.

Because there are not a lot of dances on around here, the hall was packed and there was a lovely atmosphere. I knew a lot of the people there, neighbours, friends, even my cousin Rick was there with his latest squeeze. And she was a squeeze. As my dad says, Rick likes the sturdier girls. He also likes to change girls the way he changes his socks, my mother says with a sniff. I like Rick.

A cheer went up and Rick, looking embarrassed, nodded around the room.

Next thing the music starts up and the fellows cross the floor and ask the girls to dance. Jimmy comes up to me and makes a big production of bowing low and offering his hand. I slapped it off and glared at him and he winked at me and pulled me into his arms. Jimmy has nice strong arms, which wind themselves right around my waist and pull me tight into him. I quite like that actually, but there's no point in giving Jimmy ideas about it because he'd be unbearable then.

'Do you mind,' I say, pulling a little away. 'I'm a lady.'

'And what a beautiful one you are too,' he said.

I was laughing when Fr Costello tipped Jimmy on the shoulder. Neither of us had noticed him circling the dance floor like some great winged vulture ready to pounce and devour anyone that looked as if they were enjoying themselves.

'You're dancing a bit too close there, Jimmy,' the priest said. His eyes were flat, emotionless. Half-dead, I would say. 'Keep your distance,' he said to me.

'So, Father, how far should I keep back?' I asked him.

Jimmy dug his finger into my back to make me shut up, but I couldn't.

'Have you a ruler so that I won't overstep the mark?'

'I think, Miss Flynn, that you just did overstep the mark,' he said in the same half-dead way. Then he nodded at both of us and swept off, his clothes billowing behind him.

'Jesus,' Jimmy looked shocked. 'What on earth did you say that to him for?'

'Because it's stupid, that's why.' I tossed my head, though I was feeling a little bit uneasy. I wondered what happened to people who overstepped the mark with Fr Costello. He'd probably read me from the altar tomorrow.

'Well, bravo!' From behind, Patrick gave a little clap. 'You tell him, Lily.' He lowered his voice, 'I mean, who does he think he is?'

'He thinks he's the parish priest,' Jimmy hissed. 'She shouldn't have said anything.'

Patrick dismissed Jimmy with a glance. 'Well, I like my girls with a bit of guts,' he grinned.

'Come on, Patrick,' Ann pulled him away. 'Let's go get something to drink.'

'Next dance is mine,' Patrick said to me. 'That's if Jimmy doesn't mind.'

'Jimmy has nothing to do with it,' I spluttered. I was annoyed with Jimmy. Who did he think he was? My father? 'I'd love to dance with you, thanks.'

It was comical to see Ann dragging him away.

I ignored Jimmy and his big sulky face through the rest of the dance.

Patrick was a smooth mover. His mother used to dance him around the kitchen when he was younger, he said. She'd twirl him about and he could still remember almost flying through the air as she'd spun him around and around.

'D'you miss your mother?' I asked. I took the opportunity of moving closer to him on this question. Not so close that it would annoy Fr Costello, who had sent a girl home in tears when he'd given out to her. Not that he'd make me cry, nothing could make me cry that night. I love being out, looking good, having fun. Being stuck in the back end of Cavan doesn't allow much opportunity for a bit of a laugh, so you have to make the most of them when they come along.

'I hardly remember her,' Patrick said, looking down on me. I swear I could've melted into those brown eyes. 'But I do remember her laugh, strangely enough.'

'That's a nice memory to have.'

'Yes.' He pushed a tendril of hair out of my face. Then tailed his finger down my cheek. How I shivered.

Then he took the risk of leaning his chin on top of my head and I breathed in the smell of him, all fresh and dewy. He started to cough and I realised that he too was breathing in my scent, all oily and fumy. I could have killed Jimmy and his father's car.

The music ended. Ann appeared beside him almost as if she'd popped up out of the floor. 'Your date is holding up the bar,' she said to me accusingly, as she took Patrick's hand in hers.

Patrick smiled at her and bid me goodbye.

I found Jimmy downing a pint of Guinness, leaning against the makeshift bar and not looking too happy. 'What's wrong with you?' I asked, leaning in beside him, though Fr Costello hated to see women in bars. But technically this wasn't a bar.

'Nothing. I'm having a great time.' He sounded cross.

'Well so am I. Are you dancing with me?'

'The man is meant to ask the woman,' Jimmy snapped.

'So ask me.'

'No.' And he took some more drink. 'Why don't you get St Patrick, the fecking saviour of Ireland, to ask you?'

'Because he's dancing with Ann,' I said back. 'And you're my date and you asked me here.'

'Oh, you remembered that, did you?'

'How could I forget it when I smell like a tractor?'

'Well, if it's any consolation, you look like the back end of one too.'

I was truly taken aback. No one had ever spoken to me like that before. I thought about lifting up his pint and pouring it over his head, only I knew one run-in with Fr Costello was enough. Plus some of the drink might have spilled on my dress and I didn't want to have to spend ages washing it out. Instead, I turned on my heel and, looking as dignified as I could, I left the hall. Tears stung the back of my eyes. I'd known Jimmy since we were small, we'd grown up just fields away from each other and from as far back as I can remember, we'd always sought each other out as playmates, except when he had other things to do with other boys, then he ignored me and pretended he didn't know me.

I'd walked up the road in my uncomfortable shoes for about three minutes when I heard running footsteps after me. For one tiny moment, I fantasised that it was Patrick, coming to see where I'd gone, but then I heard, 'For God's sake, you know I didn't mean it. Anyway, I happen to get very excited about tractors.'

I kept walking now, secure in the fact that I held the high ground.

'Lily, for God's sake. Talk to me. I'm sorry. I am.'

I whirled around, mentally checking that I looked regal enough. Head high, neck extended, disdainful look on face. 'Well, James,' I said. I always called him James when I was cross. 'I'm glad you're sorry. I accept your apology but you've ruined my night and I'm going home.'

'Aw don't.' He didn't come any closer, just stood in front of me, hands by his sides, looking quite forlorn. 'Nothing is any fun when you're not there.'

'Well, you gave out to me for questioning Fr Costello and you didn't want me dancing with Patrick—'

'I never said you couldn't dance with him. I just didn't see why you'd want to.'

'Well, I did want to as it happened because he wasn't a big-sour-faced-gloomy-afraid-of-the-priest type of man.'

'Thanks.' Then Jimmy turned away and walked off.

I felt a bit bad. A bit mean. And I realised that if I was walking home, it'd take me until the morning and my father would go mad. 'Can I have a lift home at least?' I called after him.

He pulled his keys out of his pocket and dangled them, without looking at me. I ran to catch up.

There was a collective sigh as Zoe closed the diary, as if everyone in the room was coming out of a dream. Deirdre gently loosened her hand from her mother's grip. What had seemed such a simple thing in the beginning, listening to a story she thought she knew, was more difficult than she'd thought it would be. There was this Patrick character, for instance. She really did not want to hear any more about him. Hearing about him made her feel ill. Pulling on her coat, as the others filed out, bidding her goodbye, Deirdre pictured her mother as the coolest girl in the class, the one everyone wanted to be friends with. The fun one.

And yet . . . She shook her head, not under-standing. Bending over, she kissed Lily's cheek. 'Bye, Mammy. See you next week again.'

Lily smiled and tried to say something. Deirdre waited, her heart hammering. But finally Lily gave up and turned away. Deirdre patted her hand.

After everyone had left, Zoe sat awhile with Lily. In the silence of her room, with the old lady staring unseeingly in front of her, there was a kind of peace. Zoe studied Lily and saw the young woman she must have been. 'Does it all work out in the end, Lily?' she asked suddenly. But she didn't know if she was asking the question about herself or Lily.

A pair of intense blue eyes fixed on her face. Lily shrugged. 'It's not the end until it's all over,' Lily said, with such clarity that Zoe gaped. 'And really,' the old woman added, with a wicked smile, 'who ever wants it to be over?'

'Yeah, you're right,' Zoe nodded. 'We have to keep going, eh?'

'We do, no matter how hard it gets,' Lily said. 'It's all we can do sometimes.'

The silence filled the room again. Zoe thought of all the things she had to do. Book a restaurant for Friday night so she could meet Greg and the mysterious Louis. Confirm an act for next month. Talk to June about expenses. And yet she couldn't make herself leave just yet. Something told her Lily had been through a lot in her life and yet, here she still was, battling on. That's what she wanted to do too, Zoe thought. So she stayed awhile.

CHAPTER 18

Zoe sat in the restaurant she'd booked for Greg and absently looked at her menu. She was nervous meeting her brother and his, well, boyfriend. It was akin to the first time she'd ever seen her dad in work. She'd been twelve and the way her dad had sat behind his big desk, making and taking telephone calls and asking his secretary to do stuff, had made her aware, for the first time, that her dad as a dad was a person only she knew. He was a whole other person to other people.

The waitress placed some olives in front of her and Zoe absent-mindedly began to eat. The words of the menu danced in front of her eyes.

'Hey, little sister, how's things?'

Greg's arrival sent her thoughts skittering all over the place. She didn't even bother trying to gather them back up, instead she grinned at her brother, determined to be the liberal sister he needed. Well, she was liberal, but when it was your brother, it was just a bit harder.

'You OK?'

Shit, she was drifting again. 'Yeah, good to see

you.' Zoe accepted a kiss on the cheek and Greg, looking quite cool in an arty T-shirt and black denims, settled into a seat beside her.

Her eyes scanned the restaurant. 'Where's Louis?' she asked, feeling a bit funny using his name when she'd never met him.

'He'll be here in five.'

'OK.' Zoe set the menu down. 'Any subjects I should avoid asking him about? Is he madly political, religious, does he have any strong views on anything?'

'Don't worry your head about it,' Greg grinned. 'You're so easy to get on with, it'll be fine.' He looked so much better than the last time she'd seen him, Zoe thought. She tried to pinpoint how and settled finally for the fact that he looked so happy. Incredibly, masterfully, blissfully happy. The realisation hit her, sudden sunshine on a patch of dark grass.

'Are you all right?' Greg was peering at her. 'You look a bit . . . upset.'

Zoe swallowed hard, fighting the weird urge to cry. 'I'm grand. Fine. Don't mind me.' She leaned on the table, cupping her chin in her hand and digging her nails into her skin to keep the tears at bay. 'I was just thinking how happy you look.'

'I am happy,' Greg said simply, and she had to turn away and busy herself flapping open her napkin and laying it on her lap.

'Hello.'

They both looked up and Zoe's breath caught

in her throat like a fish in a net. Standing before her was her ideal man, every woman's ideal man actually. In fact, *everybody's* ideal man because this had to be Louis. He was tall, over six foot, slim hipped and wide shouldered with neatly cut brown hair, gelled to perfection. His skin had a hint of a tan and his chiselled jaw line held a sexy hint of stubble. He was dressed like a model on a catwalk in cool baggy denims and a sloppy white T-shirt. The smile that he bestowed, and bestowed was the correct word, was all square white teeth and a sexy upcurl of lips.

If there was a God, he had a warped sense of humour.

'Oh Jesus.' It was out before she could catch it.

'Nope, that's Louis,' Greg said, and Louis giggled.

OK, illusion shattered. Ideal men do not giggle. They chortle, they guffaw, they laugh loudly, they do not cover their mouths and chuckle gently.

'Hi, Louis,' Zoe said, glad that this guy had a major fault; it would not do to start fancying her brother's boyfriend. Only people on *Jerry Springer* did those sorts of things. 'I'm Greg's sister, Zoe.' She held out her hand and Louis gripped it and shook her till her bones rattled.

'Hi,' he said and his voice was low and soft. She could imagine him doing an ad for bubble bath. 'Greg has told me so much about you. It's a pleasure.' He sat down and smiled. 'It's so great to meet some of Greg's family. I was beginning to think he'd made you all up.'

'Well, if he told you I was gorgeous and talented with a fantastic personality, then he didn't make anything up,' Zoe said.

Louis giggled again. Oh dear, Zoe thought, it was probably better not to make him laugh. 'So, tell me all about yourself,' she said.

'Wow, that's a big ask,' Louis grinned.

Greg took his hand and Zoe squirmed just a little. Yes, she was a twenty-first-century girl, she was hip, hop and happening, but her brother holding the hand of another man in a public place did make her a teeny bit self-conscious.

'Tell her how we met,' Greg said, smiling into Louis' eyes and Zoe's discomfort shot up a little more, though in fairness she kept a smile plastered determinedly to her face.

'We met at an advertising junket.' Louis focused on Zoe again. 'We got to talking about motorbikes—'

'No, it was cars,' Greg interrupted.

'Motorbikes.'

'Cars.'

Zoe smiled, they were like two kids, she thought. She tried to remember the last time she and Abe had acted like two kids – before they had one, that was for sure.

'OK, seeing as it's your sister,' Louis said, holding a hand up in a gesture of surrender, 'I'll say it was cars.'

'Because it was,' Greg insisted, and Louis giggled again.

Shit, she was going to cry. Their happiness together was like a warm blanket, covering them both and leaving her outside. She popped another olive into her mouth, hoping the slight kick from the chillies would distract her.

'Cars,' Louis went on. 'And it turned out that Greg's favourite car,' – he stressed the word 'car' as if it hadn't been a car at all – 'was the same as mine. And then his favourite ad was the same as mine, and his favourite film—'

'*Planes, Trains and Automobiles*,' they both said together.

'—was the same as mine,' Louis finished.

'That's Zoe's favourite film too,' Greg said.

'Aw, it's great, isn't it?' Louis said, obviously delighted that he had something in common with Greg's sister, 'John Candy and Steve Martin – classic pairing.'

'Zoe always cries at it,' Greg said teasingly.

And she did. And it wasn't the comedy that made it her favourite film, it was the idea of the two men trying to get home to be with their families against all the odds. 'Nothing wrong with that,' she flashed back at Greg, her voice wobbling a little.

He shot her a concerned look but then, blessedly, a waitress arrived. 'Are you ready to order?' she asked with a massive smile, which dropped when she saw the hand-holding between the two men. Then her professionalism reasserted itself and the mega beam returned.

'Pizza Caribbean,' both Louis and Greg said together. Then went 'Ahha' together.

The waitress smiled indulgently.

'I, eh . . .' Zoe hadn't even read the menu. 'Well, the same.'

'And a side order of chips,' Louis said.

'Garlic bread,' Greg chimed in.

'Nothing,' Zoe said. For some reason she just wanted this dinner to be over. She had been looking forward to it but now all she wanted to do was to go home and cuddle Lee really tightly.

'You OK?' Greg asked her.

'Yeah. Just thinking about, you know . . .' She fished about for something. 'Well, there's a woman in the home whose diary I'm reading. It's sad, you know, to think she was young once, like us.'

The two men looked mildly curious.

'And that she had a family and that now all she has left is one daughter . . .' Her voice trailed off. Better to ask questions than to answer them, she decided. 'So, Louis' she managed another smile, 'have your family met Greg yet?'

'They all have,' Louis said. 'I couldn't wait to introduce him. They're mad about him.'

'Oh.' Another lump materialised in her throat and though she tried to smile, she couldn't.

'They're lovely people,' Greg said.

'Well, they have surprised me.' Louis took a sip of water. 'You know when I told them I was gay, I thought they would react badly, but they didn't.'

'Was this recently?' Zoe asked, shoving two olives into her mouth.

'Nah, I was seventeen,' Louis said. 'I'd suspected it for years but, you know, I hadn't quite believed it. But after a while, I knew it and so I decided to tell them.'

'Were you nervous?' Zoe glanced at Greg. He must have known for years too. Greg's eyes were avidly focused on Louis' face.

Louis nodded. 'Oh, yeah, terrified. I mean, it's not just the telling, it's the embarrassment too, you know? It's like exposing yourself to judgement.'

Greg was nodding in recognition. 'And never being able to go back,' he said and turned to Zoe saying quietly, 'Knowing you're changing the view people have of you and maybe hurting them too.'

There was a second's silence before Zoe caught Greg's other hand. 'I never thought of that,' she said, squeezing it. She looked at Louis, 'Our parents haven't been exactly open-minded about it,' she explained. 'They're not bad people, they're lovely and all, but they—'

'I'm sure they are lovely,' Louis said. 'They'll come around eventually.' He smiled at her, and Zoe suddenly had an insight as to how plants felt in the sun.

She smiled back. The olives were working.

'It was the telling them that was the big step, that's what I said to Greg. Just tell your parents and if they care at all, they'll come around.'

Oh no, no, the olives *weren't* working. A big fat tear leaked out of her left eye. She grabbed up her napkin and frantically dabbed at it but it was soon followed by another one and then another one. She tried to turn away but Greg pulled her back.

'Hey, what's the matter?'

'I'm sorry, Louis. I'm not normally like this,' she gabbled, unable to stop the flow.

'I hope not,' Louis attempted an uneasy joke as he glanced worriedly at Greg. 'Was it something I said?'

'Yes,' she sobbed as she dissolved into tears.

'Three Pizza Caribbeans,' the waitress arrived back and looked dispassionately at Zoe before glancing at the men. 'Eh, where can I put them? Yez are leaning all over the table.'

They moved aside and she briskly laid out the food.

'What did I say?' Louis asked as the waitress disappeared back up the restaurant. 'I'm terribly sorry.'

Zoe flapped her hand at him and sniffed some more.

'Are you uncomfortable with, you know, us?' Greg asked softly.

'No. No. I'm so jealous.' Zoe's voice rose in a sort of wail that she couldn't control.

'Garlic bread and extra chips,' the waitress was back, sounding bored. 'Where can I put them?'

Again they moved aside and she laid them out. 'Enjoy,' she said, and left.

Greg spluttered out a laugh then turned back to Zoe. 'You're jealous? Why?' Then his face fell. 'You're not, well, gay too, are you?'

The ridiculousness of the question momentarily halted Zoe's tears. 'What?' She looked at him. 'No!'

'Will I leave?' Louis made to stand up.

'No,' both of them said together.

'That's what Abe would do. Just leave if someone started to cry!' And off she was again.

'OK,' Louis sat back down. 'Well, I'll make a start on the food, shall I?' Without waiting for an answer, he took up a huge slice of pizza and began to munch.

'Would it be insensitive if I ate mine too?' Greg asked. 'It's just that I haven't had any dinner and I'm starving.'

'Eat away,' Zoe's voice trembled. Greg took a slice from Louis' plate and she began to sniff again. 'You're both so happy,' she said miserably, 'and you seem to "get" each other and you are both doing your best to know one another's families—'

Greg put his pizza slice down. 'Oh, I know what this is all about. Abe hates our family, doesn't he?'

Zoe blinked. 'No, he doesn't hate you, he just doesn't want anything to do with you all.'

'My life might have been easier if Louis had had that attitude,' Greg half-smiled and Louis punched him in the arm.

'Family is important,' Louis said then. 'And honesty.'

'Yes,' Zoe swallowed and took the risk of taking a tiny bite of her own pizza. She scrubbed her eyes. 'But Abe, he's my . . .' She paused, not sure what to say. 'Well, partner I guess, and he's not big into families. He doesn't talk to his mother and she doesn't even know that I and Lee, that's our son, exist. We've gone down once since Lee was born and Abe left me sitting in the car for twenty minutes and then came back out and said we were never going back, that his mother wanted nothing to do with him.'

'Why?'

'I don't know. Abe won't talk about his family at all. I know nothing about them,' her voice rose. 'And I've begged him loads of times to go down with me, but he won't.'

Greg sighed. 'It's his choice, Zoe.'

'I know, but it's ruining our relationship. He's holding things back from me. And if it was just that, I could probably accept it, but he shuts you lot out too and makes me feel guilty for wanting to spend time with you. And look' – she had to swallow hard or she'd cry again – 'look what you did for Louis, you confronted us. For him.'

Louis and Greg looked at each other.

'But I wasn't estranged from you all before I did it,' Greg said softly. 'Abe didn't talk to his family when you met, Zoe. Maybe he feels they've no right to know.'

He had a point. Zoe sighed. 'I just feel, well, that he doesn't trust me. And if I could understand

220

why, I could accept his decision better. But what he does instead is to laugh at me for wanting to be with you.' She paused, 'We're reconsidering our relationship while he's away. He's got ten weeks left now.'

'Aw, Zoe,' Greg looked at her sadly.

'And don't tell Mam. I haven't said anything.'

Greg crossed his heart.

'He's away for ten weeks?' Louis almost choked on his pizza.

'Three months. He works for Aid for Africa.'

'Well, that's your problem right there.' Louis jabbed a droopy slice of pizza at her. 'He really isn't interested in family if he's prepared to spend three months away from the two of you.'

Beside him, Zoe saw Greg wince and aim a kick at Louis under the table.

There was a moment of absolute stillness in Zoe's mind, almost like shock after an accident, before the noise and colour and clamour of realisation hit her. Greg had thought this all along too, that's what his face said, plain as day. 'You think—'

'Forget it.' Louis shoved a few more chips into his mouth.

How could she not have known? That was it exactly. How had she been so blind? Three months. Abe wasn't only abandoning his mother, he was running away from her and Lee too. 'Do you think that too, Greg?' she asked suddenly and her brother jumped.

'Well, now I don't . . . wouldn't . . .' Greg coughed

slightly. 'This wouldn't be my, well, um, I guess . . .' He shuddered to a halt. 'Well, maybe,' he added. Then he nodded. 'Yes. Actually. Yes.'

Abe had never wanted a child. He'd sworn never to leave her. And in a way he hadn't. But in another way he had. Plus he didn't want another child, another reason to be tied to her. 'How long have you thought that it was odd that Abe went on all these trips?' she asked.

'Oh, not long,' Greg attempted to sound upbeat about it.

'How long?' Her voice was firm even if her eyes were watering again.

'Three years or so.'

'Well, that's . . . ages,' Zoe half-whispered. She pushed her pizza over to Louis, who seemed to have eaten all of his. 'Why did you never say anything?'

Greg looked a little shell-shocked, which wasn't surprising, he hadn't envisioned discussing his sister's turbulent private life on a first meet and greet. 'I suppose because you love him,' he answered, 'and well, at times, I do believe he loves you too.'

'At times?'

'Well, I don't see him that often, Zoe. He never bothers with us, you know?'

'Yeah, sorry. Of course.' She felt embarrassed now. What must Louis think of her? He was probably sorry Greg had ever brought his family into their lives. She made a herculean effort to pull her tattered ego together. 'Sorry, Louis,' she said. 'I'm usually lots of fun. Sorry Greg for ruining the meal.'

'Hey,' Greg loped an arm about her, 'don't be. It's made it interesting.'

She managed a weak grin.

'And it's all the more pizza for me,' Louis winked.

They were such a nice couple, she thought.

'OK,' Paul grinned, 'good news. The gardening competition has three hundred entries so far.'

Matt and Emma cheered. Deirdre wondered how much longer this meeting would continue. When she had been in charge, or rather when Suzi had been in charge, they'd never worked past four. It was now nearly seven. She supposed that all the changes would take time to implement, but honestly, seven o'clock on a Friday evening? Did the man have no life? Paul was saying something else and she was arrested by the sound of her name.

'Pardon?' she asked.

'I said,' Paul repeated, 'that when the shortlist is drawn up – it'll probably be a shortlist of five – that you will travel to meet the finalists. That'll start next week. One finalist a week.'

Her? Interview people? 'The budget,' she spluttered.

'It's fine, taken care of. We're being sponsored, thanks to this little beauty.' Paul smiled at Emma, who seemed to be standing tall and looking proud.

Or something. Deirdre couldn't put her finger on it. There was something different about Emma.

'Taken care of?' Deirdre spoke slowly. 'How so?' She pointedly looked at Emma, who swallowed nervously.

'Well, see, I rang up, eh, this place, see, and when I explained, see—' Emma shuffled from foot to foot as her voice got lower and lower. 'Well, they said, see—'

'She got Gardening Inc to sponsor the competition,' Paul cut Emma off. 'Which is very impressive, I'm sure you'll agree, Deirdre.'

Deirdre nodded curtly. It would be impressive if she'd actually *wanted* Emma to do it. This was her worst nightmare. The meet and greets were bad enough, but it was only four times a year and she normally spent about two weeks preparing. She was not good at that stuff. She liked the studio, with her headphones on and a list of questions all laid out in front of her. She liked being locked into the room, everyone else on the outside feeding her what to say, telling her when to wrap up. Members of the public, out in public, could and would say anything. And she had to do one a week! Deirdre opened her mouth to protest but Paul, obviously sensing her reluctance, clapped his hands together, really loudly, saying, 'If that's OK, we'll leave it at that. Thanks for all your hard work, folks. Anyone like to go for a drink? I'm buying.'

Deirdre was taken aback by the way everyone,

224

including Suzi, embraced this idea. Did they not want to go home? But then again, knowing them, a free drink was a free drink. She watched with mounting dismay as, chatting and laughing, they started to gather up their things. Paul was in the centre of everything. She watched as Suzi fished out her mobile and invited the mysterious Robbie along. She watched as Matt and Paul traded merry insults over soccer results. And Emma, shy little Emma, who wouldn't squeak at one stage, slagged them over their bad taste and elbowed Paul in the ribs. Was that any way to treat the boss? Deirdre felt a little outside it all, as if she didn't quite belong anymore. It was as if the show and the station were moving on without her. Oh she knew she could jump onboard if she wanted to, but she wasn't sure she did want to, not unless she was driving – but it was as if she'd been firmly relegated to the back seat. Paul was at the controls now, a coup d'état. She knew in her heart that she couldn't blame him, he was only doing what he was being paid to do, though she was coming to realise that what he was being paid to do was to obliterate the show the way she'd done it.

Unlike her, Paul had slotted into the station like a piece of jigsaw. At lunch, as she sat on the bench, smoking, in her imaginary garden, she'd often seen him in the canteen, sitting with Michael and all the other bigwigs of the station, eating lunch together. Paul was changing her whole world and he didn't even realise it. Just like Lily was changing her whole perception of her past. Deirdre clipped on her rain jacket. 'I think I'll go home,' she said.

No one reacted. No one turned around to ask why.

They just moved on.

Later that evening after leaving Greg and Louis, Zoe made her way back to the flat where Dominic was babysitting. He had offered to do it in return for all the lifts she was giving him. Zoe had been delighted by his offer as it meant that she wouldn't have to lie to her mother about where she'd been. So far her parents had been very silent on the topic of their son's sexuality, her mother's only statement being that Greg hadn't always been gay because Elton John was only gay sometimes.

'Hello,' she whispered to Dominic as she entered the dining room, 'how have things been?' He was watching a war film and muted it as she crossed towards him.

'Good,' he grinned at her, then his face fell. 'Rough evening?'

Zoe winced. She thought that she'd managed to get rid of her reddened eyes on the way home. 'Is it that obvious?' she asked as she flopped down beside him.

'What happened?' Dominic angled himself towards her.

'Oh nothing. It's just,' she managed a strangled laugh, 'well, they're so happy together.' She fingered a tassel on the ancient sofa. God, she had monopolised the whole meal with her problems. In the end, both men had advised her to try to talk to Abe again when he got back and if he still refused to open up, then she defiantly had to make a decision. But sod that. She was tired of that, she'd had five years of that; nope, Louis' words stuck in her head. Was Abe somehow running away from the little family they'd created too and if so, why?

'But that's good, isn't it?'

'It's great. I'm delighted. But looking at them, being so happy, makes me feel not so happy, you know?'

'You're missing Abe?'

Zoe shrugged, reluctant to get into it. 'I don't know, but yeah, it's lonely here at night.'

'It must be,' Dominic wrapped a companionable arm about her shoulder, 'three months is a long time.'

And it dawned on Zoe that everyone must think the same. Her whole family and now Dominic obviously thought that Abe wasn't totally committed to them. 'It is,' she said, her voice wobbling a little, before she pulled herself together. Hadn't she made a vow on Wednesday beside Lily's bed that she would battle on. That it wasn't over till it was over.

'Well, anytime you want to escape, and I'm free, I'll babysit,' Dominic gave her shoulder a squeeze. 'Or even better, I'll go for a pint with you. Maybe even push the boat out and get some curry chips as well.'

Zoe smiled. 'Curry chips, how could a girl refuse?'

Dominic laughed. 'Tea?'

'Go on.'

He hopped up and, without commenting on the state of her flat or the big burnt hole in the ceiling as her mother might have done, he made a pot of tea for them both.

For now, this was as good as it got.

Deirdre threw back a sherry as four elderly men studied her. She had never gone to the pub on a Friday night without careful planning before. But here she was, ever so slightly tipsy and it felt all right actually. Not half as decadent as the actual idea of it.

'This Paul guy is changing your show?' one of the men said. 'Is he making it better?'

She had called over to Rick with some plants for her mother's garden and she didn't know why, but for some reason she had ended up confiding in him her problems with Paul. She felt as if she needed an outsider's view, someone who wasn't connected to work. And it had occurred to her that she had no one like that. Other people might tell their mother, but she hadn't told Lily anything unpleasant in years. She guessed it was because she never liked to upset her mother, it was something she had learned a long time ago, though she could never remember when. It was just one of those unspoken things kids absorb.

She felt closer to Rick these days. Other people's positive opinion of him had helped her see what she sort of knew anyway, that he was a genuine man, that he wasn't about to take Lily for everything she had. He was lauded in the Alzheimer's society and he seemed to have made more friends in the two years with her mother than she had managed to make in a lifetime. That, plus his interest in her and her life and his keenness for gardening, had earned him huge brownie points.

'He says he is,' Deirdre shivered as the sherry slid down. It was Rick's idea that they go to the pub. He had to meet some friends there, he said, and besides, he ascertained, pubs were better for talking. A bit of drink loosens the tongue while a little dimness in the lighting is no harm either. Deirdre guessed he was right. The only downside was that Rick's friends had arrived before the conversation about Paul had run its course and instead of changing the subject, Rick had filled them in. She now had these four men hanging on her every word.

'But you don't think so?' one of the men leaned across the table to her. 'Is that the problem? Is he wrecking your show?' He sounded indignant for her, which was lovely.

'I think your show is a very good show,' another old man sporting a huge and very false hairpiece said, 'the gardening competition is great. I entered my garden. Would you like to see a picture of it?'

Deirdre winced. Validation of Paul was not what she was after. 'Well, eh . . .'

229

The other men told her that she had to see it. That it was worth seeing. That she'd never see the likes of it again. Beaming around at his comrades, the hairpiece man fished out a state-of-the-art phone. 'Just browsing my pictures folder,' he said importantly, before handing the phone to Deirdre seconds later with a triumphant, 'There now, what do you think of that? Will that get the prize?'

It was indeed a great garden. Deirdre told him that if she was judging it, he'd certainly be in with a shout. He smiled in delight before remembering her grievances, 'But you're not judging,' he muttered glumly. 'Aw, well, just have to wait and see what that Paul chap thinks.' He tucked the phone into his shirt pocket and said, his face brightening, 'Maybe if you keep on his good side, you could put in a word for me like? Isn't that how it works anyway, pull?'

Deirdre smiled weakly. 'Not quite, but I'll keep my fingers crossed for you.'

'Grand.' He wasn't too impressed with that.

'There was a young one presented your show last week now,' another old man said, 'very good she was.' Then as Deirdre flinched, he added, unconvincingly, 'Not as good as you mind, but now, she was very good.'

Deirdre wondered who that had been. She hadn't thought to ask. 'That show is my baby,' she stated, fumbling about in her bag for cigarettes and matches.

Everyone murmured that of course it was.

'They took me on because they liked what they heard. I gave them ideas and they implemented them. I made that show grow, I nurtured it, I was in charge of every segment.' She found her fags underneath her first aid kit. 'And now, after all that, they flipping well shove him in,' she finished.

Indignation followed that remark and Deirdre felt a little better.

'He sounds like an arsehole,' Rick patted her hand.

They all chorused that indeed he did.

Deirdre smiled. Another few sherries and a couple of smokes and she would feel a lot better.

THE FOURTH WEDNESDAY

October 1957

Sunday mass, and I had a lump the size of a spud lodged in my throat. Fr Costello was bound to say something about the dance. Whenever there was any sort of fun in the parish, he'd get up onto the altar the following Sunday and say that what we had actually thought of as fun, wasn't fun at all, instead it was 'an occasion of sin'. I tell you, I liked occasions of sin a lot better than occasions of mass.

On Saturday night, Mammy would lay out Daddy's Sunday suit and polish his shoes. Then she'd do the same for my brother. Of course, being a girl, I had to do my own, which annoyed me so much. On Sunday, when the four of us were dressed up, we wouldn't look like ourselves at all. We normally went to eight o'clock mass because that way when we came back we weren't too hungry for our breakfast. Sometimes, when Mammy wasn't looking I'd sneak a slice of bread and eat it really quickly. Of course, it put me in a dilemma when the time for communion came – did I go up or didn't I? To my shame, I normally did go up, mentally apologising to God as I did so, telling him that I'd say extra prayers that night if he didn't send me to hell.

The church was about a mile from our house and we normally walked, meeting others along the way. If it rained, Daddy would take the car but petrol was expensive so trips in it were strictly rationed.

Yesterday morning, I was extra nice to Mammy and Daddy so that they wouldn't be too hard on me if the priest read me, as I was sure he would. Just as we turned out our gate, we met up with Jimmy and his parents. The sets of parents got talking and Jimmy, wearing a grey suit which had seen way better days, fell into step with me. 'So, all set to be hung, drawn and quartered?' he asked, grinning.

'I don't care,' I lied as I tossed my head. 'You're the one who was dancing too close, not me.'

'Ah, but I didn't argue with him, did I? Nope, I was a good Catholic boy.'

'And that's why you'll never be exciting, Jimmy Deegan, because you're such a good boy.'

With that I stalked off. If he was going to enjoy Fr Costello making a holy show of me, then he could do it without me condoning it.

Loads of people were at eight o'clock mass that morning. We sat in our usual seat, which unfortunately was third from the front. My parents liked to see what was going on, which, as I told them once, was the same every week. It wasn't going to change. 'And thank God for that,' my mother had said piously.

The mass started. Fr Costello walked up the church followed by about ten altar boys all praying, heads bent devoutly. I'd wanted to be an altar boy at one stage and had begged my dad to have a word with the priest. I loved the idea of parading up to the altar in a costume with everyone looking at me. Only thing was, I was a girl so I couldn't. Anyway, Fr Costello began the mass in his low, droning voice. I think the way he spoke was a trick. It sounded like a swarm of bees in heavy summer as he intoned the mass in Latin, which no one could understand anyway. After a bit, you'd see people beginning to nod, their eyelids flickering, their heads falling forwards, before they were woken by a nudge from a more devout member of their family. But sometimes, people glazed over so much that when Fr Costello suddenly shouted aloud his sermon in English, they'd jump. Then everyone would wake up and Fr Costello would be on a roll, with parishioners hanging on his every word, the way you would to a runaway horse. Today was no different. He began the same as usual, looking us all over with his half-hooded eyes, almost as if he was bored himself. But I noticed, or maybe I was just paranoid, that his eyes kept flitting to gaze at me. So I sat up straight as I could, trying to appear demure, but my act didn't fool the wily Fr Costello. Right on cue, just when he was losing the whole congregation, his droning voice took on an awesome power as he boomed, 'And the dance last night in Patsy's barn was an occasion of sin.'

People love the word 'sin'. Immediately they all sat up. My mother shot me an anxious sideways glance.

'Sin is not just a nasty deed, or something done in secret that others can't see. It is not just a lie, or unlawful sexual congress or adultery. No,' he shouted.

Somewhere a little child started to cry.

'Sin thrives in the darkness of your heart,' he said dramatically. He paused so that we could take that in. The little child's cries had turned to whimpers. 'Sin occurs when you flout the rules, the rules God, yes God, Himself put down for our own good, so that we can remain pure until the day we meet Him again. You are from God, you shall go back to God, but only with the grace of God. Some people here have no grace, no hope of redemption unless they change their wicked ways.'

There was a hush in the church. Even the baby stopped crying. It was an expectant hush, the sort that is accompanied by a heartbeat of fluttering anxiety. Who here had no hope of redemption?

'The things I saw last night,' Fr Costello said as if he'd been to hell and back, 'would make our Lord Himself destroy this parish, for it is nothing better than a Sodom and Gomorrah.'

'I think we left the dance too early,' someone whispered in my ear. 'It must have been a lot of fun afterwards.' It was Patrick and he made me giggle. And my giggle filled the tense air of the church and my parents whipped around, horrified to see their daughter looking amused. Patrick was back in his place, all innocent, and I had to make the sound again and pretend I was coughing.

Fr Costello pointed a shaking finger at me. 'And here is one such sinner.'

A collective relieved 'aah' from most people. Then a craning of heads to see who the priest was pointing to.

I flushed, wondered what I should do. Brazen it out, look contrite, look puzzled. My mother had her mouth hanging open and my father glared at me, his eyebrows drawn together.

'For not only were she and her partner indulging in some shameful dancing,' the priest went on, wincing on the word 'shameful', 'when I intervened and tried to put a stop to it, to put her back on the path to the Lord, she questioned my authority.'

Shocked silence.

I have no idea what expression settled itself across my face, but I reckon it was brazen or cross because his next words were, 'And still she does not see the error of her ways. She—'

'Excuse me,' a voice shouted from a few seats back, 'I think I deserve some blame, too, it wasn't all Lily's doing.'

I smiled slightly to see Jimmy up on his feet, glaring at the priest. His mother tried frantically to yank him back down but he brushed her off.

'At least you are prepared to acknowledge your part in the sin,' Fr Costello said. 'There is hope for you.'

'Yes, but what I mean is—'

'James, sit down,' his mother hissed.

'Let us all pray for our sister Lily,' Fr Costello intoned, obviously deciding to ignore Jimmy. 'Let us pray that she will see the error of her ways and repent.'

The congregation rose to its feet, so Jimmy's standing up was now defunct. I couldn't look at my parents. I was sorry to bring that shame on them, but I was also livid. I knew I had done nothing wrong. I knew it in the same way I knew that I had curly hair and bright-blue eyes and a stick-thin figure. I was certain of it like I was certain that the sun would rise in the east and set in the west. I had done nothing wrong, so in my dark heart, I said, 'I reject your prayers, we meant nothing wrong and we did nothing wrong.'

'He just wants to spoil everyone's fun because he has none himself,' Patrick said, again leaning in towards me.

I ignored him but I had to agree.

Mammy and Daddy could barely meet people's eyes as they slid from their seats at the end of mass. 'Home,' Daddy said, grabbing my arm quite hard and propelling me along.

'Mr Flynn, Mr Flynn,' Jimmy ran to catch us up outside mass.

'Not now, Jimmy,' my mother said sternly.

'Yes, stay away,' my brother said, squaring up to him.

'But you can't just blame her,' Jimmy called after us.

I turned around and gave him a grateful smile but, really, I wasn't surprised. I should not have questioned Fr Costello last night, but for me, tying to keep my mouth shut was like trying to stop the earth from turning.

When I got in, Daddy threw me across the kitchen like a sack he was finished with. I fell into a chair and sat there. I told myself that I would not cry. I would not beg, I would not try and put my side forward. I had shamed them and I would take what was coming.

'Getting read from the altar.' My father approached me, the veins on his forehead bulging like ropes. I cowered back in my chair. 'Shaming us.'

'Now, Michael,' my mother said, 'you know what she's like. She never means any harm by it.'

'No harm? She just got us read from the altar, woman! What will people think?' I hadn't realised he was directing the question at me until he repeated it, looking hard into my face. 'What will people think?'

'I'm sorry,' I said then, because I was sorry for bringing it on them, but I still, honestly, could not get my head around what I had done wrong. It had been nice in Jimmy's arms, natural. His body had been firm and hard and he'd looked good for once. What was so wrong with that?

'There, she's sorry,' my mother said. 'In a week it'll have been forgotten, there'll be some other sinner to take her place.'

I looked up in surprise at my mother. She sounded a little bitter and my daddy, too, shot her a look.

'I'm sorry,' I said again. This time I really meant it.

My mother gave me a small smile. Daddy glared at me still, but after a few seconds his shoulders relaxed. 'It's not so much what you did,' he said then, gruffly, 'it's what it might have led to. The priest was only trying to help you.'

I was mortified. I muttered a sorry again and disappeared from the room. I spent the rest of the day lying on my bed, wondering if there was any escape from this small goldfish bowl of a place.

The following day I went into work. Never having been read from the altar before, I hadn't bargained on the looks I'd get from people I passed along the way. Still, I managed to hold my head high and ignore them, it was the best way to deal with people like that, that's what my mother had told me when she crept into my room to say goodnight last night. 'Just ignore it and it will pass,' she told me in a whisper.

And so I did.

I work most days in the shop now as Patrick has to care for his father more or less full time. Poor Mr McCabe is in a bad way, he can hardly get up out of bed and the days he does, he likes to sit on a chair in his living room and look out onto the shop. Maybe he feels that he's still a part of it then. I'm always terribly self-conscious when he's there, afraid to say anything to the customers in case it's wrong. So on those days, I just serve them as quickly as I can with a pleasant smile. The problem is we got a lot of customers in that morning, wanting I suppose to look at one who is doomed.

And then Ann Morrisey came in, prancing about in her polka-dot poodle skirt, her little pigtails springing out from either side of her head like a fungus.

'Hello,' she said, all snooty. 'Just these.' She put some biscuits down and I wrapped them in a brown paper bag. 'For the girls' tea break in work,' she explained, as if I cared. Ann Morrisey thinks she's something special just because she's in charge of a lot of knicker-makers. That's what Jimmy says.

I told her how much it was and held out my hand for the money.

Ann made a show of rooting about in her bag and finally she handed me the coins. 'Someone is not happy today,' she said, arching her eyebrows.

'Really? Who might that be?' I cursed myself as soon as I said it. I should have ignored her.

'You, of course,' she said. 'Still, if you must dance too close to your partner, you will pay the price.'

What a prissy, self-righteous little bitch, I thought.

A cough from behind stopped me from saying those words.

'And how is my fair dancing partner,' Patrick bounded out of the back room, full of cheer. Oh God, every time I see him, it's like seeing him for the first time. My heart just pings, like someone had flicked an elastic band in my chest.

Ann giggled.

'I do have a complaint to make, though,' Patrick

240

turned to me. 'What was wrong with me that you didn't dance close? That's unfair, I say.'

'Well, if you must choose Average Ann over Lovely Lily, that's what you get, I'm afraid,' I said. I turned about and went into the back room to try to recover from my flash of temper and left Patrick chatting to Ann, who didn't sound as chirpy now.

Mr McCabe managed a clap as I entered and a little feeble nod. 'Thought you were losing your spark there for a minute,' he rasped out.

I laughed and winked back at him. 'Never,' I said. Then I put the kettle on and made him a cup of tea.

Lily jumped at the sudden cheer that filled the room. A hand was holding hers. Lips on her cheek. For some reason she smiled, though what had made her smile flitted in like a butterfly and was gone.

Later that afternoon, as I was cleaning the windows outside the shop, Jimmy's mother came up to me and tipped me on the back. I turned and there she stood, black handbag clutched tightly in front of her like a shield. 'You keep away from my son,' she said. 'He's a good boy.'

I was a bit shocked at that. 'You tell him to keep away from me,' I said back, facing her full on and brandishing my window rag. 'Because let me tell you, he might be a good boy now but he really wants to be a bad one.'

Her mouth dropped open, I don't think she could believe her ears.

'And you'll catch flies if you don't close your mouth,' I said, turning back to polish the windows, my heart thumping and my hand shaking.

She made a sort of 'huh' sound and the next thing, I heard her little heels click-clacking away down the street.

Later Jimmy called over to see how I was after the day. I sneaked out the back door while Daddy was up in the top field and my mother washed clothes and pretended that she didn't see.

Jimmy pulled me into the shade of a tree and he was grinning a little as he said, 'I heard you gave my mother a right earful today.'

'Are you going to be keeping away from me then?'

'Keep away from you?' Jimmy laughed. 'You're the reason I get up in the morning. You're the sugar on the dry bread of my life.'

I do think that was very romantic, being compared to sugar. Jimmy has a way with words when he wants to. 'And what about your mother?'

'What about her? She'll just have to accept that you're my friend.'

And then my father arrived back and hollered when he saw me and shoved me back into the house making a right show of me.

Zoe couldn't read anymore. He voice trembled. She shut the book and coughed a little. 'Sorry, I'll leave it at that for now, my throat is a little sore.'

She was glad when no one protested and she

left the room as quickly as she could. She knew now what she had to do about Abe.

'That was curious, Zoe running out like that, wasn't it?' Rick said as he lit a cigarette on the way back to the car. 'She seemed to get quite upset.'

Deirdre unlocked her car and they both sat in. She'd noticed Zoe's reaction too but was more interested in what Lily had written about the dance. 'Do you remember that dance?' she asked Rick, careful not to sound too eager.

Rick nodded, smiling a little. 'There weren't that many so, yes, I do. Probably because of Lily getting read from the altar. It's not something I've thought about for a while.'

Deirdre shot a sideways look at him. He was concentrating on rolling the window down so that he could smoke. The handle was a bit stiff, the car didn't have electric windows, which were just a fad anyway. 'She makes herself sound like a lot of fun,' Deirdre remarked.

'But she was. She lit up a room.' Window down, he sucked on his cigarette and blew a thin stream of smoke out.

Deirdre watched as it caught and drifted away on the breeze.

'So what happened her?' Deirdre asked. 'It's like she disappeared. I could never make her as happy as she was then.'

Rick turned to face her. 'It wasn't up to you to

make her happy,' he said. 'She had to do that for herself.'

Deirdre blinked. She turned her gaze back to the road and tightened her hands on the steering wheel.

'All you could do was love her, and I'm sure you did that.'

It was as if someone had chipped away a stone she'd been carrying without even realising it.

CHAPTER 20

'And . . . go!' Paul said in her headphones.
It was Friday, the last show of the week.
Thank God was all Deirdre could think
as she swallowed hard and smiled awkwardly at
the young woman opposite. She felt like a goldfish
in a bowl, sitting as she was in the Dublin Live
van on the main street of Cavan Town. A crowd
had gathered around outside and the murmurings
of conversation could be heard through the window.
It was a bit off-putting, as was the knowledge that
she was back in the county of her birth. She felt
oddly disorientated.

'Welcome to the show, May,' Deirdre said to the
woman.

'April,' the woman spluttered out a laugh.

'April?' Deirdre blinked. In her headphones, Paul
said, 'Her name is April.' Then Deirdre saw him
say something to Suzi and they laughed.

Bastard.

'I'm sorry, April,' Deirdre grit her teeth and felt
herself blush. Outside people laughed. Deirdre's
only thought was that she had to do this well
because it was the only way she might have a say

in her show again. 'Congratulations on making it into the final of the gardening competition in association with Gardening Inc. Can you tell us about it?'

Deirdre smiled encouragingly and leaned back in her seat. The woman should go on for a while now.

'Well,' the woman looked as if she'd just been asked to translate Arabic. 'Eh, I have to say I don't know much about it.'

Deirdre bolted upright. Her headphones fell off. She had to readjust them. 'You don't?' She flashed a look at Paul, dabbed her forehead with a hankie. 'Why not?'

'I don't work there.'

'Work where?' This was awful. Deirdre unbuttoned the top two buttons of her blouse. My, she was warm.

'Gardening Inc.'

'I know you don't.'

'For fuck's sake,' Paul thundered. 'She thinks you want her to talk about Gardening Inc. Will you tell her it's her bloody garden we want to hear about?'

How dare he say 'For Fuck's Sake' to her? Now she had to take her cardigan off. 'May—'

'April.'

Oh, God, if it kept going like this she'd be naked by the end of the interview. 'April,' she corrected, 'can you tell me about your garden please? What have you planted? How have you planted? We all know Gardening Inc is the top garden centre in the country so no need to talk about that.' She gave a very false and desperate-sounding laugh and rolled up the sleeves of her blouse.

April shifted in her seat. 'Well, actually, my garden centre, Gardens Limited, is very good too,' she said.

'Jesus!' Paul moaned.

Deirdre flinched. Part of the deal with Gardening Inc was that no other garden centres got a mention. 'Just tell me about your garden,' Deirdre said a little sharply, making April blink. Deirdre smiled then, totally wrong-footing April and making her start to spout nervously on and on so that no one could understand a thing she said.

Deirdre nodded encouragingly, thinking how awful this must sound. She slipped her shoes off.

'Will you help her?' Paul said loudly, making Deirdre jump. She shot him a look and he gestured wildly.

'Looking at the photo of your garden,' Deirdre interrupted April mid-flow, 'I can see a variety of roses, among them my own personal favourite, the Pilgrim Rose.' Deirdre rattled out a long list of plants, and began to expound on the planting the woman must have done.

April just kept saying, 'That's right, that's right,' like a faulty talking toy.

Finally the segment ended, and to cheers from her friends, April exited the van. Deirdre went to a commercial break.

'You're going to have to loosen up in there,' Paul warned. 'You had that woman terrified. No wonder she sounded crap.'

'Me? What did I do?' Deirdre flung her headphones across her desk and barged into the production room. 'I did nothing. This was your bad idea, don't blame me if it didn't work.'

Suzi gasped. Matt and Emma looked away hastily.

'I will blame you,' Paul stood up and crossed towards her. His voice was calm. 'And don't ever come in here during a show. You're not in charge here, Deirdre. Now get out there, we've Andrew on the phone. He's reviewing a book we sent him called *Humongous Fungus*.'

'Like some I could mention,' Deirdre muttered, stomping back to her seat and pulling her blouse out of the waistband of her skirt.

Fifty minutes later, the show ended and, heaving a sigh of relief, Deirdre slumped back in her chair, washed out. These travelling shows caused her to sweat like a marathon runner. This one, no question, had been one of the worst. Not only had she interviewed April, but Paul had dragged in the local tidy towns committee and the people who cleaned the waterways. Local shop owners had had their five minutes of fame and if that hadn't been bad enough, she had messed up spectacularly when she'd announced that Gardening Inc, to celebrate local lady April making it to the final, had donated five hundred euro worth of plants to beautify her local area. Only Deirdre had said fifty thousand, thinking to herself what a humongous amount that was and how on earth could Gardening Inc afford it. But, of course, the decimal point was practically invisible and it should have been five hundred and so Gardening Inc, instead of looking generous, only looked miserable.

Paul barely flicked a glance at her as she staggered into the production room after the show. Instead he was concentrating a little too hard on packing up.

'Not bad,' Suzi said with false cheer, her smile barely creeping upwards. Then she too turned away.

'It's not my forte,' Deirdre said into a moment of silence. 'I wasn't ever employed to do this sort of thing. I'm not Joe Duffy you know.'

No one responded. Emma squeezed by her and left carrying a cup of coffee.

There was a sudden tap on the window of the van. Turning, they saw an elderly woman with fluffy brown hair and a wide smile, waving in at them. They all waved back.

The woman waved again and mouthed something, gesturing with her hands.

'What is she saying?' Suzi asked, striding to the door. 'Hello?' she said to the woman.

'Oh, hello,' Deirdre heard the woman say breathlessly. 'I was wondering if I could talk to Deirdre please.'

'Sure. Deirdre, someone to see you.'

Suzi came back in and Deirdre, her heart sinking like an Irish Eurovision entry, crossed to the door. The last thing she needed was to make an idiot of herself with another member of the public.

The woman was tall, well padded and with a bright eager face that encouraged smiles from those in her company. Deirdre found herself reluctantly smiling back. 'I'm Deirdre,' she said.

The woman held out her hand. 'I'm sure you don't know who I am, but I know who you are. I mean *really* know. Not just from the show. I used to live in Moanavale when you were small.'

Moanavale? Her home town. 'What's your name?'

The woman laughed, breathlessly. 'Oh, yes, how silly of me. I'm Ann. Ann Roche. I knew your mother. We grew up together.'

Deirdre smiled.

'I thought I'd ask after her. I heard she wasn't well.'

The last thing Deirdre wanted was for her co-workers to start asking about her mother. She liked to keep her work and private life separate, thank you very much. The only one she'd told was Suzi. 'I'll just get my cardigan,' she said, 'and my shoes and we'll grab a coffee.'

Without waiting for Ann to say any more, Deirdre fetched her cardigan and shoes from the studio, buttoned herself up, tucked herself in and joined Ann outside on the street.

Five minutes later they were in a coffee shop,

where Deirdre ordered a cheese sandwich and tea and Ann a latte.

Ann sighed contentedly. 'I love my cup of coffee,' she said. 'Growing up, there was tea or milk, nothing else. When Patsy Junior died, he was my husband, the first thing I went out and bought was a state-of-the-art coffee machine.' She took another sip before asking, 'Tell me, how's Lily?'

'Not so good,' Deirdre wrapped her hands about her mug for comfort. 'She's got Alzheimer's. She barely remembers anyone.'

'That's terrible.' Ann shook her head, upset. 'She was such a personality. In fact, when we were young, I was pure jealous of her a lot of the time.'

'Really?' Deirdre smiled. 'She's written a diary and she does sound as if she was a bit wild.'

'I'm probably in that,' Ann sounded delighted. 'Sure, we hated each other. Ann Morrisey I used to be.'

Deirdre sat back in her chair. So this was Ann Morrisey! Somehow, she'd pictured her a little like Nellie Oleson in *Little House on the Prairie*, not this homely, warm-looking woman. She couldn't help smiling. 'Oh, *you're* there. You sound as if you gave as good as you got.'

'I tried,' Ann said, 'but I was no match for her. We both fancied the same chaps and your mother was better at getting them than I was. I fancied your dad from afar for a long time. He was a lovely man.'

'He was,' Deirdre agreed.

251

'And when you were small, you'd follow him about like a little sheep,' Ann remembered.

'I did.'

'Well, Lily deserved a good man if anyone did. Her father was not the best, if rumour were to be believed.'

'Really?' Deirdre had never met her grandfather. Her grandmother had called over from time to time, she'd even stayed with them for a few weeks once, but her grandfather had been totally absent. Deirdre had thought he was dead until she'd gone to his funeral when she was around ten.

'Black and blue some days your mother used to be when we were in school. She'd tell us some story about falling off her bicycle, but we all knew. Is it any wonder she wanted to leave the place?'

Deirdre said nothing. This was all news to her. 'Well, she left it in the end,' she said, not wanting to think of her mother being hurt like that.

'Oh, she did,' Ann smiled. 'That's something to be grateful for at least. She never liked Moanavale but your father tamed her for a while. She was happy with him.'

Deirdre said nothing. Lily's 'episodes' of lying in bed were the family secret it seemed, if this Ann Roche didn't know.

She decided to deflect the conversation back to Ann. 'Tell me about yourself so I can tell Mammy when I see her next. She seems to remember long ago a lot better than the present.'

Ann sighed. 'Well, I was an awful fool, as your

mother used to so rightly point out. If there was a disastrous man in a population of a million, I'd pick him out blindfolded. After your mother married the only decent chap in the place, I married the son of the man who ran the local dance hall.'

'Patsy?'

'That's right. He had two sons and I married the eldest. Honestly,' Ann tossed her head, fluffy hair billowing for a second before settling back, 'the meanest, most miserable man he turned out to be. But his meanness got him in the end,' she said, with a hint of glee, 'he grew sick and was too miserable to pay a doctor and didn't he have a massive heart attack.'

Deirdre was unsure whether to sympathise or congratulate her.

'Of course,' Ann went on, before Deirdre had a chance to do either, 'he left me with six children, but they've turned out well, thank God.' She paused. 'Which brings me to the reason I came to meet you.' She pulled a brown bag onto her lap and pulled out an envelope. 'I owe your mother this.'

'What is it?' Deirdre asked, not wanting to open it as it had her mother's name on it.

'Some money that she gave me once to tide me over. I never promised to pay it back because, to be honest, I didn't know that I ever would be able to, but here it is. It's not a lot, but it was at the time.'

Deirdre tried to push the envelope back across the table. 'My mother won't even remember,' she said.

'Well I do.' Ann was firm. 'She was very good to me.' She paused, caught up in a memory. 'I met your mother, oh, it must have been just after my youngest was born, forty-odd years ago now, when my bastard husband was still alive. You don't mind me saying that word do you?'

Deirdre shook her head.

'I was standing by the lake contemplating God knows what, crying, really upset and your mother passed. We weren't the best of friends and she walked by, then something must have made her stop, maybe because I didn't snort or make a comment about her. So she stopped and asked if I was all right. I told her I was fine, to mind her own business. But she always did the opposite of what I said so she sat down and wouldn't move on. If I'd wanted to throw myself in, I couldn't now. So, we had a bit of a staring competition. Then she said, "Is Patsy Junior treating you bad?" And I told her to get lost. And she said that he was a bastard and I was a fool to have married him and that I should pack up and leave. I just started to cry. I told her I was desperate. I had no money. I asked her where I could go. I said the kids had no schoolbooks or shoes and that Patsy Junior was refusing to give me anything. Well,' Ann swallowed hard, 'didn't she pat my hand and tell me not to worry, that she had money and that I

254

was welcome to it. I'd never have taken it for myself but for my kids, well, I swallowed my pride and took it. I thought she might lord it over me or tell the town about me, but she never did. Your mother was a kind lady, it was the first time I knew that.' She slid the envelope across again.

Deirdre took it, the emotion she felt was betrayed in her voice as she croaked out, 'Thank you.'

Ann stood up. 'And thank you for accepting it, it means a lot. I know now I paid for my children myself.'

Deirdre nodded.

'And I'll say a prayer for Lily.' Ann patted Deirdre's hand before walking away.

Deirdre stared after Ann for a long time, envelope held like a prayer book in her hands, thinking about her mother, her mind flitting to the various small, unacknowledged kindnesses people do for each other. That time in the Botanic Gardens when one of the apprentices had inadvertently killed a rare plant, how John had taken responsibility for it. How Suzi always bought her the first coffee of the day. How Rick always brought the biscuits that Elle liked to the Alzheimer's carer get-togethers. That Lily had remained silent on this thing stunned Deirdre a little. Maybe she didn't know her mother all the way through.

Before she left Cavan that evening, she drove down to Moanavale, just to see if she could spot the shop her mother had worked in. It would have been brilliant if Rick had come too, but he had been adamant that he didn't want to go down and, besides, he had some bets to place that couldn't wait.

In the end, Deirdre was glad he hadn't come. She hadn't been home since her mother had moved to Dublin, there being no point in seeing what she could never have any more. It was just as poignant as she thought it would be, different yet the same. There were more houses and better roads but the heart of the town was unchanged. Squished shops and a narrow main street. She drove down the main street, looking for the shop Rick had described. According to him, it was third past the corner of St Ronan's Street on the left. And there suddenly was St Ronan's Street and then, there was the shop. A blue building, squashed in between two larger ones. A picture of a cake on the blue-and-white sign. Deirdre pulled in and hopped out of her car. Through the window, she could see an array of cakes arranged on shelves. Entering, she was assailed with the delicious aroma of bread and spices.

The woman behind the counter was carefully icing a cupcake. They were all the rage now. An overrated bun, Deirdre thought.

'Hi, can I help you?' the woman said.

'I'll have a cupcake,' Deirdre said. Then ventured, 'My mother worked here years ago when she was, I dunno, in her late teens, early twenties.'

The woman looked mildly interested. 'Would she be in those pictures there?' She pointed to a number of black-and-white framed photos that were to the side of the counter, arranged lengthways on a wall. 'We found these when we bought the place ten years ago and thought it might be nice to hang them up. Preserve history and all that, you know.'

Deirdre scanned the photos. Most of them seemed to be more modern than Lily's time, but there was one that looked as if it was taken way back. A man, woman and a small boy of around eight. Probably too early for Lily. The man had a familiar look about him, Deirdre thought. Or maybe it was just the black-and-white picture, most people tended to look the same.

'They were the original owners as far as I know,' the woman said, joining Deirdre. 'Or maybe not, no one could tell us but the picture was taken in 1927 because there's a date on the back so we figure that it's a fair bet.'

If that was the case, the little boy was Patrick, most likely. Deirdre smiled a little.

'Here is your cake.' The woman handed Deirdre a prettily wrapped box. 'That's three euro please.'

Good God. Deirdre handed over the money and the woman headed back behind the counter and pressed buttons on the rather old-fashioned till. 'Enjoy.'

She had no option at that price.

She ate her cake sitting in her car wondering what to do next. Maybe as she was down, she should take a trip past her old home. One of her cousins had the farm now, but it wouldn't do any harm to have a look, would it? And maybe, if she was brave enough, she could call in? Maybe.

Before she could chicken out, she carefully pulled out into the traffic. Hoping she remembered the way, she drove along the main street and took the turn off for her old home. It was about seven miles from the town and, as she drove, she marvelled at the array of fancy new houses that had been built on the road. Large palatial structures that wouldn't have looked out of place in an episode of *Dallas*. Then, quite abruptly, the road narrowed even more, the houses vanished and she found herself crawling up and up until just over the crest of a very steep hill, there was the place where her old house would be. It had sat among fields of green and Deirdre fantasised about how it would be tucked into the landscape as if ashamed of being seen by the newer, fancier abodes. But instead, she saw a new house with stark white walls and a big sunroom and, from her vantage point, Deirdre thought she made out decking. They'd knocked down the old cottage, obliterated it, uninterested in how long it had been there or what it had represented. Instead a newer version of it had been created and while Deirdre could see that it had its plusses, something in her – she didn't know what – mourned the change. She parked her car at the top of the hill, reluctant now to venture any farther and stood, looking down, remembering how she'd loved running from the school bus down the hill, her bag flying, dying to get to her dad so that they could herd the cows or feed the chickens or whatever he was doing that day.

The last bit of her connection to her dad was gone, she realised with a jolt.

Deirdre leaned against the wall that boarded the road. All around was still. It was more silence than she'd had in thirty years.

CHAPTER 21

The next day dawned bright and sunny, the Dublin mountains a fabulous backdrop, as Zoe indicated and pulled away from her mother's house.

'Bye, Mammy, bye, Audrey,' Lee called, waving madly.

'Bye, have a good time, girls!' Zoe's mother called.

Audrey, who was sitting in the passenger seat, rolled down the window and exhaled a stream of cigarette smoke. 'God, it must be crap being a kid,' she remarked, as she blew a kiss to Lee. 'Imagine being so excited about staying in your granny's.'

Zoe laughed. 'He likes my mother!'

'My granny smelt of wee and my granddad coughed all the time. I hated their house.' Audrey closed her eyes and sighed deeply. 'I'm still in shock, you know,' she said wearily, as she lifted her cigarette to her lips.

'Me and Abe haven't split yet,' Zoe said, 'so don't go telling people, especially your mother. If she went and told mine, my mother would kill me for not telling her.'

'Yeah, what you just said makes sooo much sense,' Audrey deadpanned. 'And, anyway, I wasn't talking about you and Abe.'

'Oh,' Zoe was surprised, but her friend always had the ability to ambush her. 'So what *do* you mean?'

'I'm talking about Greg.' Audrey said it as if it was obvious. 'Like when did he just go and decide to be gay? I always had a thing for him, you know.'

'Eh, yeah, I noticed.' Zoe indicated and moved onto the M50 motorway. 'I sometimes used to think you were my friend only so you could hang out with him.'

'That's not true.' Audrey grinned before shrugging out, 'Well, not entirely.' She laughed loudly as Zoe squealed.

Just as Google promised, they reached County Tipperary about eighty minutes later. It was only then that the full impact of what she was doing sank in and Zoe suddenly felt sick. Her mind began tumbling like washing in a dryer and she couldn't concentrate on what Audrey was saying. It was all Lily's fault. It had been the moment when she'd read Lily's diary about Jimmy's mother having no option but to accept Lily that she'd finally made up her mind to come here. Audrey, upon hearing the story, had agreed to go with her.

'And so I said,' Audrey seemed to be building to a narrative climax, 'all this talk of cancer just makes me sick!'

She waited a second and Zoe realised that she had been meant to laugh. She smiled weakly.

Sensing that her punchline didn't have the desired effect, Audrey asked, 'D'you not think that was funny?'

'Yeah.' She sounded unconvincing.

'You weren't even listening, were you?'

'Sorry.'

'It's OK, I forgive you.' Audrey gave her a sympathetic smile. 'It can't be easy tracking down your boyfriend's parents to see if they are loopers.'

'Sensitively put as always.' Still, she smiled and added, 'That's not what I'm doing.'

'Hmmm,' Audrey stubbed out her cigarette. 'OK. I'll shut up, shall I, and see if I can spot the sign for, what's the name of this place?'

'Toomevara.'

'Right. I'll do that.'

'Good plan.'

Audrey mimed zipping her mouth closed.

Ten minutes later, Audrey spotted the small road sign announcing that they had arrived. It was an anticlimax somehow. In Zoe's mind, the last time she'd been here, everything had been so much bigger, the road through the village had seemed longer, but that was probably because she'd been nervous and Abe had driven quite slowly as well, as if he'd been really reluctant to bring her. It had been dark too, not the bright brash day it was now.

In less than a minute, Zoe spotted the house, a small bungalow just on the bend of the road to Limerick. 'Here we are,' she said, about to pull off the road and up the drive. Her voice shook.

Audrey laid a hand on her arm and told her to stop. Right there.

Zoe, startled, took her foot off the accelerator and the car juddered to a halt. 'What?'

'I'm only going to ask this once,' Audrey said, sounding more serious than she had all day, 'but are you sure about this? Abe will kill you if he finds out.'

Zoe shrugged, 'All I'm really sure of is that things can't keep going the way they are. This is all I can think of to try and save us.'

'There is no going back. Once we knock on that door, you can't ever go back.'

It was as if Audrey had plunged her hand into Zoe's throat and pulled her heart right up into it. 'I know,' she managed to say. 'I know.'

'And you're sure about this for Lee? It'll be his dad that'll either stay or leave.'

'Look,' Zoe said firmly, 'Abe can make his own decision, I'm not responsible for that. If he leaves,' her voice wobbled, knowing that it would hurt her, 'well, he leaves.'

'Oh, come here.' Audrey enveloped her in a brief hug, warning, 'Now don't stain my shirt.'

Zoe hiccupped out something between a laugh and a sob.

'If I'd known there was a chance of tears, I'd have worn something else.' Audrey hugged her for a second more before pushing her away and chucking her under the chin like a baby. 'That's my girl. Now, I was thinking that it might be better to let me do the talking because that way his family mightn't remember your face as clearly if they do meet you again.'

'Good idea,' Zoe nodded. 'I never thought of that.'

'Yes, well,' Audrey grinned, 'it's down to years of practice tracking down men that never ring back, so I should be good at this. Now start the car.' Audrey closed her eyes and rested her head against the seat as if gathering herself for a performance.

Starting the car again, Zoe drove slowly up the driveway. It was like stepping back in time. She could remember the night Abe and she had driven down, Lee in his baby seat in the back. Abe had parked the car opposite the house, in a layby, not wanting to get too near for some reason. Then he had told her to stay there, that he'd be back for her. After a few seconds staring straight ahead, his face conveying emotions that Zoe hadn't fully understood, he'd got out, slamming the door. The noise had woken Lee so she'd spent a few minutes comforting him and when she turned back, Abe had gone inside and the next thing she saw, through the gathering darkness, was him exiting the house alone and striding back down the drive. He'd looked cross and when he got back in the car, his only words were, 'Don't ask me to do that again.' Then he'd driven like a mad thing all the way back to Dublin.

This time, Zoe was determined to drive as near

to the house as she could; she wanted to see the place for herself, she was not going to be left behind again. The ground was pitted with giant potholes and, weirdly, there was a child's bike in the garden. Someone had attempted to plant some flowers and they were beginning to bloom just in time for spring. The place looked cheerful enough, not the oppressive home she'd been expecting.

A fairly new car was parked outside the front door and Zoe pulled up behind it.

'Ready?' Audrey asked.

'Yup.'

They smiled at each other, like soldiers going to war, and together they climbed out of the car and, with Audrey leading, made their way to the front door.

Zoe was transfixed by the pink Barbie bike. 'I wasn't expecting a kid's bike.'

'Maybe there's another grandchild,' Audrey mused as she pressed the bell.

'He never said he had any other family.' Zoe felt uneasy. This place was wrong, somehow. And yet it was the house she remembered. She was convinced of it.

'Someone's coming,' Audrey hissed and her voice rose up in a squeak.

A woman poked her head out the door and gave a bit of a start when she saw Zoe and Audrey. 'Hello?' she looked puzzled. 'What can I do for you?'

If it was a sister, she didn't look like Abe, Zoe thought. This woman was plump and blue eyed with a double chin that wobbled. She couldn't be more than forty and yet she dressed like, well, like a womanly woman. A patterned mid-length skirt and a white blouse. Large Winnie-the-Pooh slippers were the only surprising thing about her.

'We're actually looking for Abe,' Audrey said pleasantly, smiling widely and unthreateningly. 'We're old college friends, he told us to look him up if we were ever down.'

'Abe?' the woman looked blank. 'There's no Abe here.'

Zoe bristled. Had they just written him off? 'Abe Kane?' she said.

The woman frowned, 'I'm afraid you must have the wrong house,' she said. 'I honestly don't know—'

'Have you always lived here?' Audrey asked, interrupting her.

'For the past ten years we have,' the woman nodded. 'Did this man live here before that?'

Zoe shook her head. This was the house. She knew it was. It was burned into her memory as the place where she might introduce a tiny Lee to his other granny and have Abe finally relax. When Lee had been born, Abe's naturally hyper nature had worsened. Zoe had put it down to new fatherhood and him suddenly realising that family mattered after all. His edginess had been most apparent whenever her parents visited; Abe had either monopolised Lee, making it impossible for them to hold him, or just abandoned the whole scene, citing work. He'd improved over the years, especially with Lee, whom he adored, but there was still something wrong. And this was the house where her hopes had rested five years ago and where they rested now.

'Well, I'm afraid I can't help you then,' the woman made to close the door when a man appeared beside her.

'What's up?' he asked.

If this was her husband, they were well suited. He was small and fat and comfortable looking. 'We're looking for Abe Kane,' Zoe blurted out as Audrey shot her a warning look.

'Abe Kane,' the man frowned and rubbed a hand over his thinning hair. 'Why are you looking for him here?'

'Do you know him?' Zoe ignored Audrey. 'I thought he lived here.'

'Who is he?' his wife asked.

'Lived here?' the man shook his head. 'Whatever made you think that?'

'Who is he?' his wife asked again.

'Well, I haven't seen him in years, not since I changed jobs.'

Audrey shot Zoe a puzzled look.

'You worked with Abe?' Zoe asked. 'I'm sorry, I don't—'

'Yeah, if it's the same guy,' the man shrugged. 'I mean he didn't live here, we were great friends,

did a few stints in Africa, we'd go for a pint whenever we could, then I got married, moved down
here. I left the job about four years ago. I thought
he'd keep in contact but he didn't.'

Each word was like a slap. 'You were a work-
mate?' Zoe whispered.

'Yep. Top guy, Abe, young, enthusiastic, very
dedicated. I haven't seen him in years.'

'I never knew him,' the man's wife said.

'Aw, he called here once, ages ago, d'you
remember? I was meant to go to Africa and I
was sick and he volunteered to go instead. Great
guy. He came down, collected all the details,
d'you remember, Marie, it saved you having to
post them?'

'Oh, yes,' Marie nodded. 'That's right, I'd
forgotten his name.' She turned to Audrey. 'He
never even spent the night under the roof, though
I did offer but he was in a hurry back to Dublin.
Apparently his girlfriend had had a baby.'

Zoe couldn't take it anymore. She turned on her
heel and stumbled back to the car; if she didn't
sit down, she'd faint. It was too hard to believe.
And what made her feel worse was that on the
journey to this fabricated home all those years ago,
Lee had cried most of the way down. She'd been
unable to pick him up or cuddle him, instead she'd
sat in the back with him until he'd fallen into a
fretful sleep. And despite the fact that she was in
a state of near exhaustion, she'd made the effort
to dress up, to look nice so that she wouldn't let

Abe down. And he had let her do those things knowing that he was going to lie to her. She was a fool.

She'd been so full of hope.

Zoe was shaking as she sat into the driver's seat. She rested her head on the steering wheel and hoped that she was sufficiently hidden from view behind the other car. Meanwhile Audrey continued to chat to the couple, Zoe could hear their voices drifting in on the breeze.

A few minutes later, Audrey startled her by knocking on the car window. 'Move over, sit in the passenger seat. You're in no state to drive,' Audrey said.

If Zoe hadn't been so shocked, she would have replied that she was fine rather than let Audrey take the wheel. Audrey had the unnerving habit of speeding up until she met a car whereupon she slammed on the brakes, letting off a stream of expletives. Abe called her driving style 'Up close and curse and all', which used to make Zoe laugh. Thinking of Abe made Zoe obligingly shuffle across to the passenger seat as Audrey slid in behind the wheel. Without another word, Audrey started the car and with a wave to the couple they'd been talking to, drove away at speed. Zoe welcomed the way the bumps and ruts of the driveway caused her head to bang off the window; the pain mirrored the pain she felt inside and couldn't properly articulate.

Finally, when they were on the road and going

way over the speed limit, Audrey said softly, 'I don't know what to say, Zoe.'

'Try "Abe is a fucking bastard."'

'Abe is a fucking bastard,' Audrey repeated.

'I would have to say that that is a fair assessment of the situation,' Zoe said dully.

There was a pause. 'Joe, that was the man's name, he gave me a picture of him and Abe in Africa, if you want to see it.'

'Why didn't he just lie to me and say his mother was dead?'

'I dunno.' Audrey took one hand off the steering wheel and pulled the picture from the pocket of her jeans. 'Maybe he couldn't bring himself to lie quite that much.'

Yeah but he could bring me on a wild goose chase across the country, Zoe thought bitterly as she picked up the photo. It was an old one, taken just after she'd met Abe, when his hair had been in that slightly long, unkempt style. She'd liked his hair that way, there was a carefree air about it. And the picture mirrored that. And the way Abe was grinning in the slightly out-of-focus shot made Zoe's heart catch. He had his arm slung about Joe's neck and the two men were laughing. Abe's head was slightly back and his posture exuded a lot more happiness than she'd ever seen in him before.

A slow ache worked its way up through her. 'I think I've been kidding myself, Audrey,' she said softly.

'What?'

'I don't think he really loves me. I don't think he ever did.'

'No,' Audrey said, her indignation making her press more firmly on the accelerator. 'No, he does love you.'

'There's no need to try and make me feel better—'

'I'm not, I just think, well, that he loves you as much as he can.' And slam, she braked just in time to avoid rear-ending another car. 'Fuck,' she made a face. 'Sorry.'

'As much as he can? Great.'

'No,' Audrey struggled to explain, 'all I'm saying is how could anyone love someone fully when they're keeping such a large part of themselves hidden? What you've got, it seems, is not the real Abe, just the part he wants you to see.'

Zoe looked at the picture again and said nothing. She supposed it was true. Then another thought hit her, almost winding her. 'You weren't shocked when I told you we were on a break, were you?'

'Nope,' Audrey said bluntly. 'I've never been a big fan of Abe's. No matter how many lives he saves in Africa, wherever he is—'

'Somalia.'

'Somalia. But I think he loves you.' She swung the car suddenly to the right, making Zoe yelp and clutch onto the seat. 'Drink,' she said. 'You need a drink.' With a flourish, she pulled up to the steps of a small pub. 'Get out and order a whiskey for you and an orange for me. I'll park the car.'

Zoe didn't argue and five minutes later, they were huddled in a snug, both drinking whiskeys.

'I really shouldn't,' Audrey said as she lifted it to her lips.

'But you will,' Zoe gave a faint smile, which disappeared once she looked at the photo again. There was no denying it, Abe was incredibly happy in that picture.

'He looks quite good-looking in that,' Audrey remarked.

'He *is* good-looking.'

'Hum, well, maybe if you go for that sort of look.' She sounded as if she was saying, 'Well maybe if you go for the really ugly look', with emphasis on the 'really'.

'So you never liked him.'

'I did,' Audrey said, 'until I got to know him.'

'Stop!' Zoe half-laughed, but stupidly she felt incredibly hurt for Abe too. Of all her friends, he liked Audrey the most.

Audrey took a huge slug of whiskey. 'I'm only joking. I suppose I never took to him because, well, there *is* a huge chunk of him missing.'

And that was it, Zoe thought, that was what she'd always felt though never properly acknowledged. More than Abe actually being there, she'd been more aware of the part of him that wasn't. 'When he calls Lee tomorrow night, I'm going to talk to him,' Zoe declared.

'Would it be better to wait until he gets back?'

'Wait that long?' Zoe was appalled. 'I don't think so. I can't make my mind up about him when I don't have all the facts.' She drained her whiskey glass. 'Another one?'

'I'm driving.'

'Sod the driving. Let's gets drunk, there's a hotel across the way.'

'I like your style,' Audrey clinked her glass against Zoe's empty one. 'But then again, that's why I'm your best friend.'

THE FIFTH WEDNESDAY

November 1957

My father didn't talk to me for a whole week after the mass. If I came into a room, he'd walk out. If I tried to talk to him, he'd flick me a look that told me I should keep silent. My mother kept telling me that he'd get over it, to leave him alone, but as the week went on, I began to get annoyed so by the time the following Sunday came around, I had stopped bothering with him.

And I wouldn't have minded only he still bothered with Jimmy. Jimmy could call whenever he liked and get a warm welcome and a slap on the back. That maddened me even more. So that by the time Sunday came, I could barely look at Jimmy either.

'You're in bad form,' Jimmy said the following Monday when I met him after work. He'd taken to coming into town to meet me and driving me back home in his smelly car, throwing my bike into the boot.

'And are you surprised?' I made a face at him. 'My father treats me like a criminal and you like a god. Are you surprised that I'm annoyed?'

'Well,' Jimmy dug his hands into his pockets and shrugged, 'I'm surprised you're annoyed at me, it's hardly my fault.'

'Well it is,' I said. I was carrying a basket of eggs that Patrick's father had given me to bring home. Even though we had loads of eggs, I could hardly refuse them. The poor man was going downhill fast and I think he sometimes forgot who I was. I moved the basket to the handle of my bicycle which I was wheeling along. They were very heavy.

'Can I wheel that for you?' Jimmy asked.

'No you cannot,' I said. 'Despite what men think, women are well able to do these things for themselves.'

We walked for a little in silence, the only sound being the click click of my bicycle chain. Jimmy broke the silence with an exasperated, 'You are so unfair, Lil. If your father wants to be nice to me, I can't stop him.'

'You could tell him that he has to be nice to me too.' I gave him a little shove. 'You are spineless, Jimmy.'

I walked a little ahead of him then, but not too far because if I did, he'd drive off without me and I'd have a long cycle home, especially with the eggs.

'But if I had a row with your father,' Jimmy called after me, 'he might not let me marry you.'

I stopped, dead still in the middle of the street, spine crawling, toes tingling, stomach heaving. Marry? Jimmy?

He caught up with me and stood in front of me.

'That's why I'm being nice to him. God knows I'd like to plant him into next week but it's because I plan to ask him. If he treated you like that and you were my wife, I'd put him in his place.'

I barely heard him. Marry? Jimmy? The boy I'd grown up with, half a mile away. If I married him, I'd never escape Cavan or see anywhere else.

'My dad is signing the farm over to me and we'll have a good life.'

He said it like he was giving me a present, but his words were just birds, flapping their wings, brushing across my face and moving on. I studied Jimmy, his lanky frame, his thin face and crooked nose. He was kind and good, I knew that. He'd be a great husband, dependable and honest. And boring.

'No,' I shook my head. 'No.'

For a second he looked a little startled. 'No? What?' he asked.

'I can't marry you,' I spluttered. I don't know what way I said it, I'm sure it was frantic, panicky. If I married Jimmy, my life would follow a predictable pattern, all straight lines and flat land. I would be able to see old age coming way in advance. 'No, I really can't.'

'Why?' Jimmy looked at me. 'What's wrong with me? I thought—' But he stopped and swallowed hard. 'Why?' he asked again, bending down and whispering, so the people passing wouldn't hear. How could I tell him that I'd drown in his sort of life, that I could never come up for air, that from morning to night I'd be milking cows or having babies. The idea made my skin crawl. 'I just don't think it's a good idea,' I said. I started to walk again, pushing by him.

'You're just scared.' He ran to catch up. Putting a hand on my arm, he swung me to face him. 'I'll be so good to you, Lil. I swear. I don't even mind that your soul is damned.' He gave a grin.

'No!' I wrenched my arm away from his. 'Please. No.'

I left him there, standing in the middle of the street.

'You're just scared,' he called after me. 'Come on, the car is this way.'

But I hopped on my bicycle and wobbled away from him.

A few minutes later, he pulled up beside me and bipped the horn. I turned to look at him. He mouthed the words 'get in' and I did because it was hard to keep balance with the basket of eggs. Also, I'd worn my brand-new shoes into work that morning – they'd cost most of my wages, but my legs looked great in them.

'I can hold off asking your dad until you're comfortable with the idea,' Jimmy said, once he'd put my bike in the back and sat in beside me.

'I don't want to marry you, Jimmy,' I told him.

The look of naked hurt in his eyes made me feel like crying. I did love the man, I really did, but sometimes, you just can't accept the man.

Zoe swallowed hard and fought to get herself under control, knowing exactly what Lily meant, though, in Zoe's case, her man was a little too unpredictable to be acceptable. She tried to continue, but blessedly she didn't have to. Lily raised her hand in the air, which was always her signal for Zoe to stop reading and, feeling relieved, Zoe closed the book and handed it back to Lily.

'Thank you,' Lily said, turning a watery blue-eyed gaze on her. 'I remember that moment.'

There was a stunned silence in the room.

'Mammy?' Deirdre said. 'Did you say something?'

But Lily was barely listening. She was looking at something as if it was a distance away.

'I hate to say it, Lily,' Carrie piped up after a bit, 'just in case you didn't marry Jimmy, but he sounds like a top guy.'

Lily's eyes unexpectedly filled with tears.

'Did you dump Jimmy for good?' Carrie was appalled. 'That was the end of him?'

Lily swallowed and repeated softly, 'The end of him,' then as she rubbed her hand up and down the spine of the old diary, 'maybe it was.'

Deirdre waited until everyone had left. Was she more like her mother than she thought? Both of them had rejected decent lovely men for no good reasons at all.

'Mammy,' she asked, and was gratified to see Lily turn towards her, like a flower opening up to the sun. 'Why are you making me listen to this?'

Lily looked blankly at her.

'It's not fair on Dad,' Deirdre continued, wondering

if she was wasting her time. If Lily would even understand her. 'You should have written nice things about him. Things about how you loved him.'

Lily's eyes widened as she struggled to say something. 'You're making him look like a fool,' Deirdre went on. 'He wasn't a fool.' A tear spurted out of her eye. 'I have always tried to do what you wanted, but this' – she gestured with her hand – 'this is too hard.' She stood up. 'I'm not sure I can come anymore.'

Lily reached out to her but Deirdre didn't notice.

Full of resolve, Deirdre knocked on Zoe's office door. She was glad that Rick hadn't come in with her that day. Perhaps lunch with the 'boys' was his way of avoiding the readings too?

'Come in,' Zoe called.

Zoe's office was untidy, yet cheerful and arty, Deirdre thought as she took a seat. Bright yellow walls, wooden floors and a large window which flooded the room with light. Photographs in vibrantly coloured frames adorned Zoe's desk. There was a charming one of a little boy with dark hair and a cheeky smile. Another of the same little boy with a man who was holding him upside-down by the ankle. Then one of a smaller version of the boy with two older people, who had to be Zoe's parents.

'Long time no see,' Zoe joked, smiling. It was a sad little smile though, Deirdre thought, as she tore her eyes away from the happy faces in the pictures.

'You're probably wondering why I'm here,' she began. Oh God, that sounded ridiculous. Did she honestly expect the girl to answer that? 'Well,' she went on hastily, 'it's that, well, I've decided, that, well' – big breath – 'I'm not coming to the diary readings anymore. If my mother still wants the diary to be read on Wednesdays, I'll wait until it's over before going into her room.'

Zoe gaped, not having expected that.

'She barely knows I'm there anyway,' Deirdre said a little defensively.

'You're not coming?' Zoe sounded more upset than surprised. 'Can I ask why? Am I reading it badly?'

'Oh, no,' Deirdre reassured her quickly. 'It's just that,' she sought a way of phrasing it, 'I'm uncomfortable with all this. I find it hard to listen to.' She swallowed hard and fussed with a button on her blouse before confessing, 'My mother and I, well, we've a complicated relationship, she does things I don't understand and I really don't like how she's writing about my dad.'

Another silence, this one very different to the first, though Deirdre couldn't have said why. She wondered if she should leave. Just as she'd decided to go, Zoe said, 'Jimmy?'

'Of course, Jimmy,' Deirdre said a little more sharply than she'd intended.

'What's wrong with how she's writing about him?'

'Well, I—'

'Was he horrible in real life?' Zoe asked. Then before Deirdre answered, she added, 'Oh, please don't say he was.'

'No, he was not,' Deirdre spoke indignantly. 'He was,' she paused, 'well, he was wonderful, a wonderful man.'

'But that's how he sounds,' Zoe said.

'No he doesn't. My mother is making out that she led him a merry dance.'

'She's making out that he's brilliant though.'

This was not where this conversation was meant to go.

'He sounds so good humoured and honest and witty and in love . . .' Zoe's voice trailed off. 'And loyal,' she added, sounding a little tearful. 'I loved when he came to see her after his mother had a go at her in the street, I loved that.'

'Yes, well, that's what he was like,' Deirdre admitted.

'And the bit,' Zoe's voice dipped alarmingly, then swept upwards in a sob, 'where he stood up in mass and told the priest it wasn't just her fault. I loved that too.'

'Yes, that was good,' Deirdre said, sounding a little tearful herself.

'And the sugar on the dry bread of his life, that was great.'

'I know,' Deirdre wiped her eyes with the frilly bit of her sleeve. 'Stop, please.'

'Sorry, Deirdre, but honestly, what's wrong with

all that?' Before Deirdre could answer, Zoe went on, 'I'll tell you something, I wish I had a man like Jimmy in my life.'

Zoe's tone was bitter and Deirdre looked at her in surprise. 'I thought you were with someone. The aid worker.'

'Yes, whenever he feels like it.' Zoe's eyes flitted away, down to the photograph on her desk.

'Oh,' Deirdre squirmed. She was unsure how to react so she nodded to the picture of the boy and the man. Weakly, she murmured, 'He looks like a lot of fun.'

'Oh, he is. He's a great dad.' Zoe said 'dad' quite pointedly, meaning obviously that he wasn't such a great partner.

'Oh,' Deirdre said again.

'I'm sorry, I'm being very unprofessional,' Zoe flushed.

'No you're not.' Deirdre took a chance and, reaching across the desk, she managed to pat Zoe's fingertips, the desk being too wide to make it all the way to her hand. Deirdre was a little embarrassed that her spontaneous gesture of comfort had been amputated in this way, but gamely went on, 'You've been great pointing all this out to me. You're right. I wasn't looking at the whole picture, just a tiny piece of it. My mother wrote about my dad as he was.'

'And as *she* was,' Zoe said.

'Yes.' Deirdre mercifully pulled away and sat back up straight in her seat. Then there was a pause as they both looked at each other. Finally Deirdre said, 'Thanks, Zoe.'

'So you'll be back next week?'

'Yes. I feel rather foolish now.'

'Don't be silly. You're very brave. God, if my mother ever released a diary, I'd leave the country.'

It made them laugh. Just as she turned to leave, Deirdre said, 'Good dads are important, but take it from me, happy mothers are important too.' A moment of silence before she added, 'Maybe more important.'

'Thanks,' Zoe nodded.

'Look after yourself.'

'I will.' And she would, Zoe thought.

CHAPTER 23

'Is Lee there?' Abe's tanned face appeared on her computer screen. The reception was a bit brutal and kept fuzzing in and out.

'No,' Zoe replied curtly.

'Why not? Is he OK?' Abe's face clouded with anxiety.

'He's fine. I just want to talk to you myself.'

Abe looked momentarily hopeful, but then, obviously reading her body language, settled for wariness. 'I thought we were on a break. You don't talk when you're on a break.'

'Oh, who died and made you in charge?'

'I'm only going by your rules. You haven't talked to me since I left, what do you expect me to think?'

He had a point, damn him. 'Yes, well, I'm talking now.'

He muttered a sarcastic 'obviously' and Zoe was suddenly flooded with hopelessness. Would they ever make it back from where they were? And would he ever forgive her for what she was about to say? It was a risk she had to take, though.

'I have a confession to make.'

His eyes flickered nervously.

'I called in to see your mother yesterday.'

His mouth opened. Then closed. Then opened again.

'Yeah,' Zoe said, sounding way more casual than she felt, 'I know what you're thinking. How could I go see your mother when I don't know where she lives? Isn't that right?'

Abe stared mutinously at her.

'But whose fault is that? I went to that house, you know the one you brought me and Lee to five years ago? But, guess what?' Zoe knew she sounded sarcastic but she couldn't help it, 'She must have moved!'

'You had no right,' Abe said softly.

'But guess what again? *She never lived there.*' Zoe poked her face into the computer screen, 'Why would you do that, Abe? Why would you pretend that we were visiting your mother?'

'You had no right,' he said again.

'I had every right to know if I was being lied to.'

'I only lied because you are so fucking insistent that the whole world has to be like you!' His voice was unlike anything she had ever heard before. He sounded like a cornered dog on the attack. Zoe flinched. 'Well, newsflash, Zoe, not everyone has the perfect family you seem to think you have. Not everyone else wants what you have either.'

'That's not—'

'I told you and told you but, no, you want to bulldoze your way into my life. You want to fix me so I can be as stupidly happy as you. Get it into

285

your head that I *was* happy. Not everyone else needs their family or wants their family or is tied to Mammy's apron strings like you.'

'I am not tied—'

'You are!'

'You're . . . you're jealous of my family.' How could she have never seen it before?

Abe faltered slightly, but then recovered. 'D'you know something? I always knew Greg was gay. So much for living in one another's pockets and being so close!'

He disconnected and Zoe was left staring at a blank screen. But realistically, what had she expected? He was hardly going to be overjoyed that she had found out about his fake home. He was never going to explain after all this time. It suddenly dawned on her, in a wave of what felt like nausea, that nothing was likely to change. Abe certainly wasn't and neither was she. They were stuck unless one of them did something. And she didn't expect everyone to be like her, she thought, growing a little indignant, all she'd wanted was for Abe to be able to talk to her about things. Talk to her so they could build a future together. Was that asking too much? Maybe it was. A small tear trickled its way down her face. But Deirdre's words came back to her – 'look after yourself'.

Had Abe ever needed her? Had he ever really confided in her? The thoughts were like thieves stealing away the foundation she had built her life on. Had he ever really loved her? Wanted to spend time with her? Zoe swallowed and forced herself to look around at her small flat. It was as if she was seeing it with new eyes. The pictures on the walls, the CDs in the rack, the throws covering the tattered sofa, the ornaments, the colours chosen for the walls. All hers. Abe had nothing of himself here. She thought back to the day he'd gone on this Somalia trip, his small suitcase carrying every stitch of summer clothing he owned, and she realised that that's what had bothered her. One small suitcase and yet it had held everything he needed. Abe was ready to run at any time, ready to head to Africa or out of her life at a moment's notice. Even his reluctance to fix the burned ceiling in the kitchen took on a new significance. Why bother when he didn't plan to hang around?

After weeks of trying to avoid it, Zoe finally knew that whatever they had had was over.

Maybe she'd known all along.

But acknowledging it hurt like hell. She was glad Lee wasn't there so she could cry.

CHAPTER 24

'What are you doing?'

Deirdre jumped, startled, her lunch-time coffee sloshing out of her Styrofoam cup and all over her new tweed skirt. It was a little shorter than previous skirts, skimming her knees. Deirdre had thought that if her wardrobe reflected adventure, maybe she could absorb it somehow. It wasn't working.

Paul was lounging against the old stone wall, hands sunk into the pockets of his baggy jeans. Baggy jeans on a middle-aged man! If he wasn't so self-assured, he'd look ridiculous, Deirdre thought. Paul had that amused expression he wore sometimes when she tried to make a contribution on the format for the show. How had he pulled the rug so firmly from under her, she wondered? Once upon a time, she'd been in charge. It seemed an age ago.

'Well? Whatcha doing?' Paul walked towards her, casual, easy, like Clint Eastwood in the *Dirty Harry* movies, all sexy and menacing. A shiver shot up her spine.

'Nothing,' her voice quivered. She made an effort

to brush the coffee from her skirt. But luckily enough, it was plaid and the stain didn't show.

'What's all the pacing for?' Paul asked, sitting on the smoking bench without even inspecting it first.

'Nothing.'

'You do it all the time. Every lunchtime you're out here, pacing. Are you measuring something?'

Deirdre felt a little indignant, a little . . . invaded. He'd been watching her? 'I've the measure of you anyway,' she told him archly.

Paul threw back his head and laughed. 'You're just so old-fashioned, I love it.'

'I am not.'

'You are.'

'I am not.'

'So? What are you doing?' He took out a pack of cigarettes and offered her one.

It'd be rude to refuse, particularly after the show today when Emma had told her about a million times not to ask the man she was interviewing about his wife who had helped him grown the biggest cucumber in the world. And the first question she'd asked was, 'I believe your wife helped you?' Whereupon followed a tear-sodden rant about his cheating wife. Apparently she'd left him for a man with no interest in gardening whatsoever. Deirdre took a cigarette and lit it.

'Sorry about the interview today,' she muttered. 'I get nervous.'

Paul exhaled. 'So I noticed.'

'My mother—' Deirdre began, then stopped. Lily, despite her diary and all its uncomfortable revelations, was not the cause of her car-crash programme. 'I'm just more comfortable talking about gardens,' she said.

Paul shrugged and made no comment. His long legs sprawled outwards in a very ungainly yet manly manner.

Deirdre tore her eyes away from them and, because she was unable to think of anything else, she gestured at the derelict site and confessed, 'I *was* pacing it out. I think it would be a good site for a garden.'

'Yeah, I thought that's what you were doing. And for the record, you're right. It'd be great.'

Deirdre was pleasantly surprised that he agreed. 'So what are you going to do about it?'

'Me!?' she laughed nervously, 'Me?'

Paul nodded. 'You.' He flicked some ash.

'Well . . . nothing.'

'It'd make a great segment for the show,' Paul said, eyeing her up like a piece of meat and making her legs wobble. 'You could describe how you'd build a garden from scratch. People with gardens to make over might listen in. You'd like that.'

She would too, but she was wary of his enthusiasm. 'Yes, I suppose.'

'So how about, we both go to Michael and pitch it to him? It'd mean a few bob for plants and stuff. Do you have a gardening plan you could show him?'

'Now?'

'Yeah.' He said it as if it was obvious.

Deirdre felt as though she was being blown along in a particularly powerful storm. For years she'd plotted and planned this garden, now in the space of two minutes, he had her at pitching stage. 'Here?'

'No time like the present.' Paul glanced in through the window. 'He's in there now having lunch, how about we ambush him?' He tossed his cigarette away and looked at her expectantly.

'Oh no, no, that's not my style.' She took a long draw on her cigarette. But there was a little quickening of her heart at the thought that she could work from scratch building a new garden and as for the plan, she'd had it in her head for about four years.

'Well, lucky for you ambush is my style. Do you have a plan or not?'

'In here.' She tapped her head.

'Right.' Paul bounced up from the seat. Then he hesitated. 'Now don't fuck up, Deirdre.'

'Stop saying the word "fuck",' Deirdre bristled.

'You're hilarious!'

Deirdre glared at his back as she followed him inside the canteen and over to Michael Allen's table, the one she'd never dared to sit at in all her years in radio.

Ten minutes later, Deirdre's head was reeling at the speed at which Paul worked. Michael loved the idea, thought Paul was a genius, fired some kind of a look Deirdre's way and then excused himself.

'Brilliant,' Paul sighed, leaning back in the chair. 'I knew he'd love it.'

He'd only loved it because it was Paul's idea, Deirdre thought. He lent it an air of cool that she'd never have managed.

Paul angled himself towards her. 'So, next week we'll get the rotavators in and begin.'

'I'll rotavate,' Deirdre said. 'When I garden, I like to do it all myself.'

Paul looked at her in surprise. 'OK,' he said doubtfully, 'if you insist. We might record that segment though, so that you can talk about what you did.'

'Fine by me,' Deirdre stood up from the table. Then just as she turned to go, she paused. 'Thanks, by the way.'

'No need,' Paul waved her away. 'I'm sure you would have asked him at some stage yourself.'

Deirdre nodded a 'probably', though she doubted that Paul believed her.

'But I'm sure you'll agree it's nice to make things happen,' Paul went on, ruining the goodwill she felt towards him.

Huh, Deirdre thought, the things she wanted to happen might not be too good for Paul. 'Yes,' she smiled tightly.

Paul laughed for some reason.

THE SIXTH WEDNESDAY

So much for her Wednesday visit, Deirdre thought, as she pushed Lily towards the day room, hoping that the music she could hear being played would calm down her mother. Lily had grown quite agitated when Carrie had tried to take the diary from her a few minutes earlier and, as a result, Deirdre had been forced to bring her mother for a walk. Lily hadn't wanted to go, she'd actually cried out. She was getting worse; each time Deirdre visited, her mother seemed to grow smaller and more childlike. Her hands fluttered like birds and then lay still in her lap. Her eyes seemed locked in, peering out at a world that made no sense, like a child in a prison. Deirdre pushed her mother up the white corridor, the music pulling them along, an invisible pied piper. As they approached the door of the day room, Deirdre saw that the piano player was the man in the wheelchair, Ronnie. He didn't see them as his long fingers caressed the piano keys like an old lover and his body swayed to the music he made.

'Oh,' Lily said really clearly, clapping her hands together, 'how lovely.'

With relief, Deirdre brought the wheelchair to a stop and they stood, just inside the door, listening to Ronnie as he played. Ronnie's voice as he sang along to the tunes from the fifties was strangely melodious in comparison to his normal rasp. When he finished, Lily clapped delightedly and Ronnie, aware that he had company, gave a little inclination of his head before he launched into a selection of tunes from the showband era. Lily silently mouthed the words to some of the songs, looking at the man in delight.

'"From the candy store on the corner . . .",' Ronnie turned around and sang to Lily.

Lily's eyes filled with sudden tears and she gestured in a vague shrugging way that Deirdre should bring her nearer to Ronnie. He moved his wheelchair up so that she could be beside the piano too. 'What else would you like, Lil?' he asked. 'Do you like The Miami Showband? How about 'Just For Old Times' Sake'?' Without waiting for an answer he began to sing.

Lily clapped along, out of rhythm but Ronnie didn't seem to mind.

'She likes that.' Deirdre swallowed hard, touched at his kindness.

'So do I,' Ronnie said cheerfully.

There was something beautiful seeing this man and her mother, people who'd come from the same era, sharing a moment that only individuals of that vintage could truly appreciate. They weren't only sharing the songs, Deirdre thought, they were sharing their youth.

Zoe knew she'd got off lightly. June had come to tell her about Lily's mini-meltdown at the diary reading that afternoon. It wasn't on, June said, to let the old lady down like that. On top of which, Carrie felt terribly guilty for upsetting Lily. The old woman had almost walloped the poor girl, June said with a twitch of the lips. Then she'd asked Zoe rather sternly what on earth was the matter with her.

Unable to control it any longer, Zoe had had a mini-meltdown of her own and told June about Abe and his deceit for the past five years. Like everyone else, June wasn't surprised, which was crushing each time it happened. June also said that Zoe could take a few days off but that if she wasn't going to, she had to read to Lily whether she liked it or not. Patients were their first priority. Zoe had agreed and promised that she'd read to Lily after she'd grabbed a cuppa. But reading about other people's love lives while her own was falling apart was like baking a cake and being forced to eat vinegar. Still, Zoe knew that she had to get it together not only to read the diary but for poor Lee as well. The child spent his time anxiously studying her face because he knew she was upset. She had to be strong, which was why she was now sitting in the canteen, with big red blotchy eyes, trying to decide if she wanted tea or not.

'Hey,' Dominic startled her. 'Hello stranger.' He put a plate of fragrant curry in front of her. 'Saved from lunchtime just for you. Nice to see you.'

Might as well get those apologies rolling out. 'Dominic, I'm sorry about the lifts this week—'

'You were sick, for feck's sake.' He grinned at her. 'Glad you're back.'

He had such a lovely grin, she thought. She sniffed the air. 'Smells good.'

'Me or the food?' he asked.

'The food,' she smiled.

'Aw,' he feigned disappointment.

'Will you get me a cuppa and stop chatting up the staff,' Ronnie called out amid a few laughs. He was playing cards with his comrades in the corner of the room. Then at Zoe's warning look, he shrugged innocently. 'What, O Red-Eyed One? I'm not giving out about the grub, just the service.'

Zoe flushed. Fecker. Trust him to draw attention to her eyes.

'He hasn't moaned about the food in ages,' Dominic whispered to Zoe. 'At first I thought he was sick, but now, instead, he's developed a fixation with how long it takes me to serve.' Raising his voice, he added, 'If he keeps moaning, I'm letting him go thirsty.'

'I pay good money to be here,' Ronnie shouted back belligerently. 'And you are paid good money to be here *and* serve me.'

'If I was paid all the money in the banks,' Dominic said, 'it still wouldn't be enough to cope with you.'

'Don't you read the papers?' Ronnie scoffed, 'there is no money in the banks.'

His comment was met with cheers and Zoe laughed as Dominic grinned. 'Touché.' Then he turned back to Zoe and said in an undertone, 'Look at him, he loves it.'

And Ronnie did, Zoe realised. He was grinning around like a king having vanquished a hated enemy and she knew right then that sparring with Dominic was what kept him sane. And Dominic knew it too, treating the elderly man exactly as he deserved instead of some fragile object to be mollycoddled and smothered in pity.

Ronnie, she saw, wasn't ready to give up the fight just yet.

And, she thought, neither am I.

Deirdre marvelled at the ease with which Lily handed over her diary to Zoe an hour later. The girl looked dreadful, as if she'd been crying, and Deirdre hoped it was nothing too serious. Of course she couldn't ask, it was none of her business, but she wondered if it was anything to do with the aid worker. When Zoe's voice shook a little on the opening lines, Deirdre awkwardly reached out and patted her arm. 'Take your time,' she said gently.

Zoe gave her a wobbly smile and began again.

I didn't see Jimmy for the next couple of weeks, he stayed out of my way and I stayed out of his. But I was on tenterhooks in case my father told me that Jimmy had been to see him, but after a fortnight of having to walk home each night, I began to feel hopeful that that would be an end to it.

Eventually, Patrick noticed. 'Where's lover boy these days?'

My folks have been asking the same thing and while I didn't tell them the truth, for reasons that weren't totally clear to me at the time, I told Patrick. 'I think he's sulking because I said I didn't want to marry him.' I was busy cleaning down the counter so I didn't have to look at Patrick as I answered.

'Well, well, well,' Patrick sounded amused. Most things had that effect on him. He came around the other side of the counter and I was forced to stop my work and meet his gaze. He stood, feet planted firmly apart, hands flat on the counter top and as he leaned in towards me, I could smell mint on his breath. 'So he wants to marry you, does he?'

'That's what I said,' I resumed cleaning, not liking at all the effect his closeness was having on me.

'And you said no?'

'Well, I led him to believe that it wasn't something I wanted.' Admitting to saying no just sounded a bit brutal, I thought. I turned my back on Patrick and began rearranging the shelves, which I had only done yesterday.

'So you said no,' Patrick stated. He sounded as if he was smiling.

I didn't answer. There was silence for a few seconds and I'd begun to think he'd left when he asked, 'Why?'

I shrugged, not wanting to say it out loud, not wanting to belittle Jimmy in front of anyone.

'He's a good catch,' Patrick said. 'He'll have a farm, a house. You'll be well off, Lily.'

He sounded like my father. 'Will I?' It came out all hard and bitter.

'You will. You can give up here for a start.'

'And what makes you think I want to give up here?' I whirled around, startling him I think. 'I like it here. I like earning my own money and mixing with people. I don't want a safe life with Jimmy, I want to see things, like, like' – I flapped my arm – 'like you did. In Dublin and London and everywhere.' I stopped and swallowed. 'Not every woman wants babies, you know.'

A slow smile lit Patrick's face, dazzling me with its charm. That man could hypnotise the bugs on the street into marching in straight lines. 'Well, good for you.'

I wasn't sure if he was laughing at me or not, so I dipped my gaze and shrugged.

'There's nothing stopping you from moving away,' he said then, leaning further in across the counter. 'You could catch a bus to Dublin and find work.'

It was like a dazzling star dangling just out of reach. 'I know no one up there, I won't have enough money.'

'You could come with me. I'll introduce you to people.'

I couldn't move for sheer disbelief. I must have

looked like a fool, my mouth hanging open. Eventually I managed to stammer out, 'You would do that for me?'

Patrick reached out a finger and tipped my chin up, his gaze pinned on my face. I was powerless to resist, like a butterfly in a display. 'Of course I would,' he said softly. 'I'm crazy about you.'

My mouth went dry. Crazy? About me? This was not real. I was dreaming. I had to be. I swallowed and I felt my world tip sideways and slowly open up, a flower in the bright light of the sun, brimming with possibility, ready to attract life.

'You were with Jimmy, I couldn't get in the way of that,' Patrick said, and he looked a tiny bit uncomfortable, 'but now, if you turned him down, I'm not going to miss my chance and if you want to go to Dublin and work, then I'll help you.'

'But Ann? I thought you were with her?'

'No.' He shrugged, 'I invited her to the dance but only because I knew I'd be able to ask you to dance at some stage.'

I pulled away, overwhelmed.

'You feel it too, don't you?' Patrick asked.

Oh, the attraction I felt for him was akin to jumping on a rollercoaster in Disneyland, while Jimmy was the local kiddie roundabout with the cute animals. I knew, for my own sanity, that I couldn't stay here, not on a farm anyway, where I'd be worked to the bone like my mother was. No, I had to get out, see the bigger picture. And Patrick was giving me that.

'I'm sorry,' Patrick said softly, misinterpreting my silence. 'I shouldn't have—'

I held up my hand. I was still holding the duster, in a scrunched up ball. Dizzy thoughts popped in my brain like champagne corks. 'I'm so glad you did,' I said.

We gazed at each other for a moment and I felt the world right itself, with everything in it changed. This was where I was meant to be. Jimmy had always felt wrong for me. Patrick's eyes glimmered, so dark I felt as if I could drown in them. We met halfway, stood facing each other for an endless second, then he reached out and his hands slowly caressed their way up my arms. My bones seemed to melt as he pulled me forward and, as his lips met mine, fireworks went off in my brain.

'Oh God,' Carrie groaned. 'I feel turned on, that's not right!'

The room erupted in giggles. Even Deirdre smiled a little, though inside she was mortified but it was an honest recounting and, though it hurt her to hear that her mother had done this, she now knew, thanks to Zoe, that it was no reflection on the man Jimmy had been.

'Keep going,' Lily ordered as if she hadn't heard.

'Can you remember it yourself, Lily?' Zoe asked. 'Can you tell us instead of me reading it out?'

Lily looked surprised at the question, then she smiled, shyly. 'I can remember it all right,' she said, glorying in her audience. 'Would you like me to tell you all instead?'

A chorus of 'oh yes' echoed in the room. Deirdre

tried to look comfortable with the idea, by arranging her face into a semblance of curiosity.

'Deirdre?' Zoe asked. 'You don't look happy.'

'No, I'm fine. Sounds fantastic. Brilliant even.' Had she over-egged it? One or two of the nurses looked at her warily. Was this it? The thing she'd been afraid to ask her mother all those years ago. It was as if she was balanced on a cliff edge. Behind her a cave, where she could hide and be safe and live without seeing the sun. In front, the jump that would launch her into she knew not where. She wished she had some water or a cup of tea – something to hold on to. She always knew that one day she would ask her mother, but then Lily got Alzheimer's and the chance seemed to have slipped away, and a tiny part of Deirdre had felt relieved at that. But here it was, like a great ugly beast that had camouflaged itself, waiting to jump up when she least expected it. 'I'm fine, I know it all anyway,' she lied.

'Great.' Zoe closed the diary, marking the page. While it was good for Lily to talk, it was good for her to stop too. While Carrie was getting turned on, she was feeling increasingly saddened. The beginning of a relationship was always such a happy time. She'd been besotted with Abe, loving his quirky nature, his casual attitude to everyday life, the fact that he didn't seem to have any roots. Yes, one time she had actually liked that about him, seeing in him the adventurer she had aspired but never managed to be because by some miracle she'd got a good job straight out of college, a job way too prestigious to turn down. And what had she done then? Got pregnant and scuppered her chances anyway. Not that she would swap Lee for anything. Zoe mentally shook herself and tuned back in. Lily was talking, softly, her audience of seven straining to hear her. Lily used her hands a lot as she described things and she seemed younger than she had only a few minutes before. And her words flowed, making sense, strung together like glittering jewels.

'—every day after that, we'd go into the little tiny stock room at the back of the shop and kiss. For any of you,' Lily looked around, meaningfully, 'that have fallen in love or lust for the first time, kissing is just like throwing dry twigs on a raging fire, it fails to satisfy completely.'

There was a pause. Then a collective intake of breath. Someone went 'aw'.

And that was it. Deirdre felt as if her head had smashed off a rock on the dive down.

'Sorry?' Carrie said, confused. 'I don't get that about the whole fire thing.'

The others looked incredulously at her.

'I think she means that, you know,' Olive, one of the nurses, said. 'Her and Patrick' – she lowered her voice – 'did it.'

Carrie's mouth opened wide enough to swallow a bristling hedgehog with ease. 'No way!' She gasped out a laugh. 'You didn't! You slept with Patrick!'

'She hardly slept,' Olive snorted.

More laughter.

'Can we not talk about my mother like that,' Deirdre gasped out.

There was instant uncomfortable silence.

'Oh, Deirdre,' Lily smiled over at her. 'I'm sorry, pet. I'm sorry.' She sounded it too.

Deirdre gulped. Her mother had recognised her. It was so brilliant that it almost made up for the sadness she felt. So now she knew. Jimmy had been a dad but this awful Patrick was her father. She hadn't wanted to know his name when she'd first found out, then she thought she'd never know because Lily had Alzheimer's. 'It's OK, Mammy,' she found herself saying, thought it wasn't OK at all, 'I just . . .' She floundered. 'It hurts, you know.'

'I was young,' Lily said. 'I was young, darling.'

The problem, Deirdre thought, was that *she* had never been young. All her life, she had felt middle-aged. She didn't understand how people used youth as an excuse for silly mistakes. And that's what she saw herself as. 'So Patrick is my biological dad,' she said. She was startled by the gasps that she received. She had forgotten that everyone else was in the room. 'Jimmy was never my dad,' she told them, even now, the truth of it cutting like a knife. She'd wanted to be his daughter way more than she'd ever wanted to be Lily's. 'She told me once only I didn't want to know who my real father was.'

She dashed away a tear. Zoe crossed over and put her arm about her.

'If Jimmy had been my dad, I wouldn't have

wanted to know about another dad either,' Olive smiled over at her.

'Thank you,' Deirdre said quietly.

'Was sex before marriage not a big sin in your day, Lily?' Carrie piped up.

'Oh yes,' Lily made a face, 'a terrible sin but neither Patrick nor I cared about that really.' She paused and said, after consideration, 'I think we were both born before our time, you know. The only thing that truly intimidated me was my father and to give him credit, he didn't get angry very often.'

'But the Church? I thought everyone was scared of the Church in those days.'

Lily looked keenly at Carrie. 'Yes, I underestimated the Church.' Her mouth twisted slightly. 'My life changed utterly because of the Church.'

'Because you got pregnant?' Carrie said.

'Yes.' Lily nodded. 'First time.'

'And then what happened?' Carrie asked, agog.

'Carrie, reception!' June had appeared in the doorway.

The rest of the nurses scattered like dust in a breeze. June shook her head and 'tsked'. Then looking at Deirdre, she asked, 'Are you OK?'

'Yes,' Deirdre heaved a sigh and realised that it was true. She knew who her dad was and the sky hadn't fallen in. And the chasm that had been created between her and her mother eased a tiny bit.

CHAPTER 26

When Zoe went to pick up Lee from her parents' house the following evening, her mother met her at the door, hissing, 'He has a boyfriend!' Then she pulled Zoe swiftly into the kitchen.

Momentarily disoriented, Zoe uttered, 'What?'

'I rang him today.' Her mother lowered her voice and closed the door while simultaneously looking furtively over her shoulder. 'I know it's taken me a few weeks but, anyway, I rang him today to tell him that I was sorry for all the, well you know, confusion that day in his flat when he told us, you know, that he had' – her voice lowered again – 'other inclinations.' She closed the kitchen door. 'I don't want your father to know, he's playing with Lee inside. Now, I rang him—'

'I think I know where this is going—'

'And when I did,' her mother overrode her, 'a man answered. And it wasn't Greg. And when I asked who it was he said—'

'Louis, yes, I know.' Zoe threw her coat across a chair and asked calmly, 'Any chance of a tea before I bring Lee home?'

'No, the man said, "I'm Greg's partner, what can I do for you?"' Then she paused, Zoe's comment seemingly registering, 'Louis? Is that his name?'

'Yes.' Seeing as her mother wasn't going to offer her tea, Zoe put on the kettle herself. Honestly, when she'd told her mother about Abe, she hadn't been as upset as she was now. In fact, her mother and father had been remarkably calm about it, telling her that it would all work out.

'Oh my God,' her mother went on, flapping her hand in front of her face in a vain attempt at cooling her flushed face down, 'I'm so embarrassed.'

'Embarrassed? Why should you be embarrassed?'

'Well, I said to him, I wasn't aware that Greg had gone into business.'

'Business?'

'That's what he said,' her mother went on. 'He said, "Business?", all puzzled. Then he asked who I was and I said that I was Greg's mother and he got all flustered. And that's when I copped on. He's Greg's *boyfriend*.'

Zoe nodded. 'Yes, I've met him. He's very nice.'

'You've *met* him?'

'I went for dinner with Greg and met him.'

Her mother didn't seem to know what to say.

'Hello, Zoe, how's things?' Her dad walked into the room. 'Lee has just gone up the road to Brian's house, I'll—' He stopped and looked at both women. 'Is there something wrong?'

'No.'

'Yes.' That was Zoe.

'Oh, anything I should worry about?' He looked from one to the other.

'No.'

'Yes.' Zoe again.

'Zoe?' her dad said.

Zoe looked at her mother with raised eyebrows. Her mother sighed and muttered, 'Well, I suppose you'll find out sooner or later—'

'Sooner,' Zoe interrupted.

'Your son has a boyfriend.'

There was a second's silence. 'Is this Greg we're talking about?' Mr Killeen asked.

'Well, do you have any other surprise sons out there?' his wife asked crossly. 'Yes, it's Greg. And he has a boyfriend.'

'Oh,' Mr Killeen looked at both women. 'Well, I suppose that's only to be expected – him being, you know, gay and everything.'

'Yes,' Zoe nodded. 'So maybe it would be a good idea for the two of you to call on him or something before you lose him altogether.'

'We're not going to lose him,' her father said. 'What he told us takes time to absorb. He knows that.' He crossed to his wife and wrapped an arm about her shoulder, announcing, 'Your mother is traumatised.'

'Well, I am now,' she said. 'Him having a boyfriend and his sister not having one. It just doesn't sit right with me.'

Zoe gritted her teeth. 'Thank you, mother.'

'Plus,' she went on, ignoring Zoe's sarcasm, 'we won't know what to say to him. Congratulations on your boyfriend seems, well, trite.'

Just then the phone rang. Mrs Killeen answered. 'Oh, Greg,' she said, her expression caught between surprise and horror, 'Oh, we were just talking about you. Yes, yes, it was me who called today. Yes, well, I was a little shocked. Why?' She gave Zoe a panicky glance. 'Well, I was shocked because, well' – she licked her lips – 'well, because you have a, eh, boyfriend and you, well, never told us. It's something we'd have liked to know. We'd, eh' – the words stuck but she got them out – 'we'd like to meet him.'

Zoe gave her mother the thumbs up.

Her dad rolled his eyes.

'Well, yes, that suits us fine. Fantastic. Dinner. OK. Great.' Her voice had grown fainter with each word uttered. 'Bye now, love.' She put down the phone and winced. 'He's invited us for Sunday lunch some Sunday soon.'

'Marvellous,' Mr Killeen said. 'Now what do we do?'

'You go,' Zoe said firmly, 'and you pretend to be happy for him.'

'I pretended to be happy for you long enough and look where it's got you,' her dad said, surprising her with his bitterness. 'If I'd been honest with my feelings, you might have left that waster long ago. My days of pretending are over.' And with that, he stomped out of the kitchen.

'Liam!' his wife called. Then when his only response was a slam of the front door, she turned to Zoe, 'Don't mind him, he's upset.'

'And I'm not, I suppose,' Zoe swallowed hard. 'I'm going up to collect Lee. See you tomorrow.'

'Have you told Lee yet?' Abe barked at her down the Skype line.

He looked tanned and fit, if a little tired. His hair had grown and was streaked with shades of blond. Her heart ached just looking at him. 'Tonight.' She strove for a neutral expression.

'Then I'll ring back tomorrow so and talk to him. I can't go about pretending that everything is normal when it's not.'

'Well, you've been doing it for five years, what's another few days?' Damn, she'd just neutralised her neutral-ness.

He opened his mouth to reply, but instead opted to disconnect.

'Bastard,' Zoe hissed, wishing she could throw something at the screen.

'Was that Daddy?' Lee asked, startling her.

He had changed into his pyjamas and looked as cute as a puppy with his floppy brown hair sticking out all over the place, his thumb stuck firmly in his mouth. He gazed at her with the same colour eyes as his dad. 'Were you there all along, honey?' Zoe asked, pasting on a smile.

Lee nodded.

Still smiling, Zoe patted her knee. 'D'you want

to sit up? We can play a game on the computer before you go to bed?'

Lee looked at her silently, which was pretty unnerving. Then he stopped sucking his thumb and asked, 'Do grown-ups always fight?'

'What?' Her smile vanished like smoke in the wind. 'What makes you think that?'

'You and Daddy fight all the time.'

'No we don't.' Stupid answer, Zoe.

'OK, not all the time.' Lee still hadn't moved any closer to her. 'But lots of the time. You fight about Nana and Granddad and—'

'OK,' Zoe nodded. 'You're right, we do fight.'

Lee said nothing.

'Can you sit up on my knee so I can cuddle you?'

Lee looked unsure. 'I'm getting a bit big for cuddles. Tom says only babies get cuddles.'

'Yes, but Tom won't know, will he?'

'OK,' Lee agreed quickly and, grinning for real, Zoe scooped him up and held him tight and kissed his mussed-up hair. For a second neither of them said anything. Then Zoe asked carefully, 'If Mammy and Daddy moved into a house each, would you be sad?'

'A house?' He sounded impressed.

'Well, maybe an apartment each, I'm not sure about a house.'

'And I won't have to live here anymore?' He gazed up at her and Zoe's heart flipped.

'Well, if Mammy got another apartment, no you wouldn't.'

'Cool.'

Momentarily taken aback, Zoe asked, 'Do you not like it here?'

'No,' Lee said as if she was mad. 'The ceiling is black in the kitchen. I can't open any presses because all stuff falls out. The old man next door is weird.'

'He's not weird, he's just old and likes to complain.'

'Granddad is old and he doesn't complain.'

Zoe grinned despite the revelation that her son hated his house. 'OK, so I live in a new place and Daddy does too, or maybe Daddy stays here, would that be OK with you?'

'Daddy lives somewhere else most of the time anyway,' Lee said logically.

She felt as if Lee had just punched the air out of her. So even he thought that – at five. Why had she been so blind? Or made herself so blind, more like. Still, all the books said not to criticise each other in front of the children, so she said, 'Yes, that's because he helps people, Lee.' 'He didn't help me when it was fathers' day in school. Granddad had to come in instead and no one was interested in hearing him talk about his old job of working in a pencil factory.'

'Well that's not very grateful.'

Lee looked mutinously at her.

Zoe sighed. 'Look, your daddy and me, we've decided that it's very hard to live together.' Her voice caught. 'And, well, we decided to live in two new places but you'll be able to see us all the time. 'And' – a sniff – 'we still love you very much.'

'OK,' Lee nodded. 'Can I have some toast before I go to bed?' He wriggled out of her too-tight embrace and looked expectantly at her.

She didn't know whether to be happy or devastated that it had been so easy.

CHAPTER 27

'Surprise!'

The voice was familiar. Deirdre, who was preparing for her next guest, another garden show finalist, glanced up. At first she couldn't place the man with the sideways toupee who was taking a seat opposite her. Then she remembered. This was Rick's friend from the pub. Deirdre relaxed, she'd found that knowing someone made it easier to talk to them. Though she didn't know too many people, which was a distinct disadvantage. Maybe this might be one interview that would go her way because, so far, the 'Friday Finalist Show' had been as successful as austerity. Most of the finalists, it seemed, were happier talking to plants than doing radio interviews. Of course, if she were a decent interviewer, she would have been able to draw them out with careful questioning; instead her prodding and poking was akin to treating a minor wound with a sledgehammer, as guest after guest morphed into a jabbering wreck. And she wouldn't mind, but she'd been sleeping better than she had in years, at least five hours solid now. It was hearing who her father was that had done it.

She had heard his name, heard all about him and it hadn't tilted her world the way she'd been expecting. Though Deirdre wondered if there was more to come. How would her mother explain for instance the time she'd thrown Deirdre off the bed? Picked her up and thrown her, so that she'd hit her head off the wall? Or the time—'

'Deirdre, focus.' Paul's irritating voice sounded in her headphones. He was right though, she had to focus.

The Nielsen listenership figures were due in a month's time and, for the first time ever, she was apprehensive about them. 'Remember me?' the man was asking.

Deirdre grinned. 'I do. Well done.'

'So this is where it all happens, is it?' The man gazed around in awe. He waved in at Paul and the others who were watching through the glass. They waved back and Emma gave him the thumbs up.

'Yes.' Deirdre pressed a few buttons on her computer. 'We're going to you after the ad break. Just enjoy the interview, don't worry about it.'

'I'm not worried,' he scoffed. 'Sure aren't we old friends!'

'Aren't we?' Deirdre smiled back. This was going to be great. She glanced down at the page to see what his name was. Bert. OK. 'The microphone is set up so just talk to me from there.'

Bert nodded, looking excited.

'Go,' Paul said in Deirdre's headphones as the last ad faded out.

'Thanks for tuning back in,' Deirdre said, 'we've got another Friday finalist here for our gardening competition. Bert, welcome.'

'Thanks, Deirdre.' Bert's voice had changed for some reason. He was making it deeper. 'And can I just say that I love this show.'

'Thank you. Now tell me all—'

'I think it's changed a little, but not for the better. I think your ideas for the show are great.' He gave her a wink.

Deirdre opened her mouth to say something but Bert ploughed on. 'Mind you, the gardening competition is fantastic. I'd like to win that now. Was that your idea?'

'Eh, no,' Deirdre said weakly. 'Our new producer thought of that. And it's been a great success. He's a marvellous man. Now your garden—'

'Not as marvellous as you, my dear,' Bert said loyally. 'You've been around a long time. He's only a wet week in the job.' Then he mouthed something.

'Pardon?' Deirdre was sweating. She mopped her neck with a cool cloth she'd started keeping beside her for that purpose.

'Rick,' Bert said and gave her the thumbs up.

'Can you tell us about your garden?' Deirdre gasped out. 'The listeners would like to know.'

'Of course I can,' Bert said, and off he went.

Five elderly men, including Rick, were waiting for her in the canteen. Deirdre groaned inwardly. After

Bert's interview, Deirdre had escaped as quickly as she could, not wishing to have to talk with Paul about what he'd said. She was hoping to convince him that Bert was some random man who happened to admire her, but there wasn't a chance in hell of that now, what with the cheer the five men gave her as she walked in.

A lot of people, including Michael Allen, glanced around and Deirdre flushed to the tips of her neatly cut hair. 'Hello,' she smiled at the men, wishing to God they'd just leave. Her team would be in soon and they'd think she had put Bert up to it.

'We thought we'd stay and have lunch with you,' Rick said jovially. 'It's not every day you get to hobnob with the stars.'

'That's Gary Sims over there,' one of the men said in suppressed excitement, pointing to a large man slurping on a bowl of soup. 'I love his show. It's full of scandal.'

There was a chorus of agreement among the men and Deirdre, seizing her opportunity, said, 'Go on over, tell him. Gary loves meeting fans.'

They all looked at each other, faces almost bursting with a mixture of disbelief, awe, hope and excitement. The stampede that ensued was a little insulting.

'I'll stay with you,' Rick offered generously.

'Thanks.' Deirdre sat down and unwrapped her foil-covered sandwiches.

'Are you not getting something from the canteen?' Rick asked.

'No, I always make my own lunch and, besides, all they do are curries and pastas. I prefer plainer things.' Deirdre pushed a sandwich over. 'Have one.'

Rick declined. 'I'll grab a dinner, back in a sec.'

He left, and Deirdre turned to see how the others were getting along. Gary was talking, and the lads seemed to alternate between bursts of laughter and draping themselves across the table in rapt attention to whatever the man was saying. That guy was talk-show host gold, Deirdre thought, taking a desolate bite from her egg and onion sandwich. She'd never be like that.

Rick arrived back with an exotic-looking dish that smelled hot and spicy. Her sandwich looked very uninspired indeed. 'Did you like what Bert said?' Rick asked, tasting the food before nodding in appreciation and eating some more. 'I told him to make some comment about how good you are on the show. Wasn't he brilliant?'

'Fantastic,' Deirdre said, hoping she wouldn't sound ungrateful, 'but I reckon my producer might think I put him up to it.'

Rick's mouth dropped open. Then clamped shut again. 'Not at all. Bert is just a big fan, that's all you tell him. He was going to thank you for putting in the good word for him, so count yourself lucky that I stopped him from doing that.'

Jesus. Deirdre hoped Bert didn't win now. God knows what he'd say. She stiffened as she spotted Paul out of the corner of her eye. She smiled weakly at him and raised a hand. To her horror he took it as an invite to come over. 'Hi,' he said, flicking a glance at Rick, 'I'm Paul, producer of *Wild*, Deirdre's show.'

'I know who you are,' Rick said, sounding a little menacing.

Deirdre cringed.

Paul turned back to Deirdre. 'Your friend is to be commended for his loyalty this morning.'

'I didn't—'

'See you later,' he said, before striding off and taking his place at the hobnob table.

'Ohhh.' Rick made a face. 'I see what you mean. Maybe Bert was a little heavy-handed.'

Heavy-handed? He was more heavy handed than King Kong on the rampage of New York. 'It'll be fine, don't worry about it.' Deirdre didn't want Rick to fret, he'd only tried to help. 'Just keep Bert away from me and I might be able to lie my way out of it.'

Some hope.

At four, Deirdre changed into jeans and a baggy sweatshirt. She pulled on a pair of bright-blue wellies and tied a bandana on her head. As she walked down the corridor, some people did a double take. It was probably because she was normally so well turned out, so neat and clean. It was faintly embarrassing to be wading around work in clothes like this, but she could hardly garden in her heavy tweed, could she? There was a certain freedom in wearing jeans though, a sort of letting go.

The rotavator was on site and Deirdre checked that it had sufficient diesel before spending a couple of hours clearing off the heavy stones and litter from the patch. When she was satisfied, she fired up the rotavator and began to churn up the soil. She loved doing this, the noise was almost like silence in that it was so all-encompassing that it surrounded her. The vibration of the machine took over her whole body so that it was just her, working away, and all the worry about her mother and her job was banished temporarily. In a small corner of her mind, Deirdre took note of everything she was doing, so that she wouldn't miss a thing in her report that Paul was due to record in the morning.

'Are all your friends really old?' Paul whispered into her ear, his voice startling her so that she lost control of the rotavator. The machine toppled over and Deirdre fell with it. For a second, as she lay flat on her back in the mulch, the noise of the machine roaring in her ear, Deirdre didn't know what the red fountain was and when she did, she wondered whose it was.

'Shit! Shit!' Paul slid backwards, pulling at the belt on his jeans.

'What are you doing?' Deirdre attempted to hop up but a sudden wave of dizziness hit her and she fell back again. 'Put your clothes back on!'

Paul yanked his belt free.

Deirdre gaped at him. Talk about taking advantage.

Suddenly he had it wrapped around her upper

arm, pulling it tight. His crotch was level with her eyes and Deirdre had to make herself not look. He smelled all spicy, though he looked stressed. She wondered if it was the show. 'Hang on,' he said, before sprinting over to the glass wall of the canteen and hammering on it, gesturing wildly. Deirdre looked at him in a strange detachment. What on earth was going on?

The red fountain seemed to splutter a little less now. That was a pity, it had been so unusual.

Deirdre woke with a monstrous headache. Squinting, she saw that the ceiling above was white with a bright light. Curtains were drawn around her bed. Deirdre turned her head and saw Paul slumped in a chair. He perked up when he saw her and came towards her.

'Hey,' he smiled, and his dimple flashed. 'How are you?'

This was alarming. What was he doing in her room? Only it wasn't her room, it was somewhere else. Was it *his* room? Oh my. She remembered the belt. She could have him for sexual harassment. Heat suffused her face.

'You're in hospital,' Paul said as if sensing her confusion. He sounded kind, worried. There was no cockiness in his expression. 'You cut your arm pretty badly on a piece of glass.'

Deirdre lifted her arm; it was so heavy, so sore. A huge bandage was wrapped around it. 'I did?' That information was strangely deflating.

Paul swallowed. 'It was my fault, I sneaked up on you and gave you a fright, I think. You dropped the rotavator and there was glass and you fell on it.'

It floated back to her. She'd been gardening. He'd come up from behind and whispered in her ear. 'You fecking eejit,' she said. It felt good, so she said it again. 'Fecking eejit.'

'I know,' he bowed his head. 'And the worst thing is I wanted to give you a fright. I was bloody cross with you.'

'Well, you've landed me in hospital so I hope you're happy.' Her voice was weak, though she had to admit, she was impressed with his honesty. It made her like him a little better.

'Of course I'm not happy,' he hissed, looking around, making sure he couldn't be heard. 'But, honestly, you are a very difficult woman to work with.'

'I've never had any complaints before.'

Paul snorted.

'And what's that supposed to mean?' Even though she felt weak, she wasn't letting him away with snorting at her.

'Nothing.' He seemed to be holding himself back by sheer force of will.

'You snorted. I'd like to know why.'

'OK,' he moved towards her. His voice was low. 'The reason no one ever complained before is that they're all too bloody terrified of you.'

Now she snorted.

'It's true. Matt and Emma, two great young kids and what have you got them doing? Running around for tea and coffee while you beat Suzi senseless with your rubbish ideas.'

'Nonsense.' She turned away.

'It's not.' He walked around the bed so she had to look at him again. Or rather at the bulging crotch in his jeans. 'You scared them all. It was either your way or the highway.'

'Bollox.' She was feeling a little woozy and it was the only word that came to mind. It wasn't a word she normally would have said.

'It's not. Now, Deirdre, you can—' He stopped, bit his lip and growled out, 'Maybe now's not the time.'

'Go on, keep going. We might as well have it out. It's been brewing since the beginning.'

'Right.' He sat on her bed, which was a bit intimate, she thought. 'OK, I'll spell it out. You will not get your friends to diss me on the show. You will—'

She blacked out.

She came to a few minutes later. Paul was hovering anxiously over her and a nurse was tapping her gently on the face.

'OK.' The nurse was smiling. 'You're still a little weak but you'll be fine. You'll need a lift home.' She looked expectantly at Paul.

He nodded.

'I can get a taxi,' Deirdre murmured.

'I'll bring you home,' Paul said with such gritty annoyance that the nurse looked startled before giving a nervous laugh.

Deirdre folded her arms and looked in the opposite direction.

Two hours later, Deirdre was wheeled out of the hospital and into Paul's car. It was a luxurious affair, the insides all wood and cream leather. 'Just give me directions,' Paul muttered as he drove out of the car park.

In a clipped voice, Deirdre told him where to go and without speaking he drove her to her cottage. Pulling up outside the front door, he told Deirdre to stay put while he ran around and opened the passenger door for her. If she hadn't been so weak she would have shrugged his arm off as it caressed her elbow, but she was glad of it. His touch was nice, she thought unexpectedly. She allowed him to lead her to her front door, before she handed him her keys.

'Are you on your own?' he snapped.

'And what's wrong with that?' she snapped.

'Well, you might conk out and die, it might be handy to have someone around.'

'I won't die, no thanks to you.'

Paul groaned loudly and rubbed a hand over his head. His hair had grown since he'd arrived at the station but not much. 'Please, Deirdre, can I call someone to come over – otherwise I'll have to stay.' He made it sound like a threat.

Deirdre wondered whom she could call. It was embarrassing but there weren't too many options. At one time she'd have rung Suzi, but Paul's arrival had definitely put a wedge between them. Maybe Suzi was glad, part of her mind spoke up, maybe she is scared of you and— Deirdre switched the voice off. 'I'll call Rick,' she said.

'I'll stay until he arrives.'

'You don't—'

'I do.' He stepped into the hall after her and shut the door firmly.

Deirdre rang Rick as Paul made them both tea. They sat opposite each other in the kitchen, Paul amusing her by continually gawking about. The silence stretched long between them. She heard him sigh and something in it made her look at him. He caught her eye and without even thinking, she blurted out, 'Thanks.'

'For what?' he asked, sounding glum. 'For putting you in hospital?'

'Well, no, but for being honest enough to admit you kind of wanted to.'

Paul smiled, embarrassed.

'And for bringing me home and waiting for Rick. Normally, I'd be really grateful to anyone who did that but with you, well, anyway . . .' She let her voice trail off.

'With me you hate my guts and wish I'd never come.' He said it jokingly.

'I don't hate you.'

Paul stared into his tea, then back up at her. 'I really want to make this work,' he said sincerely. 'I really want a show I can be proud of.'

'Like *Porn Unleashed*?'

'No, *not* like that.' He sounded a little frustrated. 'I'm sick of that.'

His frustration, his intensity, turned her insides to liquid. 'Oh.' Only it came out sounding all wobbly, as if she was cold.

He gave her an odd look.

'I'll try harder.' She meant it too. It was the eyes. The way he looked at her. It was terrible. It made her quiver inside.

'I was thinking,' Paul released his gaze, and said all businesslike, 'that you'll be too weak to do a show for a bit, so, to make it up to you, I'll get someone else to do the garden for you.'

Deirdre realised that with an injured hand, she couldn't create her dream garden at the studio. It would have been the one bloody thing she'd have been good at in all this change. She felt a lump grow in her throat.

'Are you OK?'

She looked at him, forced the stupid tears back and said with as much firmness as she could, 'It's my project, I wanted to do it. I have it in here.' She tapped her head.

Paul looked stricken. 'But you can't. And we have a slot to fill.'

'I can come in and tell the gardeners what to do.'

'How'll you get in? You can't drive.'

She had no answer to that. She must have looked a little forlorn because Paul said hastily, 'I'll come and collect you. Your house is on my way to work anyway. Please don't get upset, I feel shit enough as it is. I'll bring you over after the show airs each day. It's the least I can do.'

And Deirdre suddenly had an idea. It was for the good of the show of course. Not for any perverse satisfaction on her part because that would be unprofessional. 'The slot is aimed at beginner gardeners, isn't it?' she said.

'Yes, that's the idea.'

'And you know nothing about gardening, you said it yourself, so why don't you be the gardener and I'll tell you what to do?'

If he'd blabbed on about the fact that he was the producer and he couldn't possibly do anything like that, she would have backed down. But he didn't. His eyes lit up. 'Great idea,' he said. 'Well done. That'll make great radio. Get us some publicity too.'

'Thanks.' Oh, she couldn't wait to work him hard. She felt quite dizzy thinking about it.

'This could really work.'

They smiled delightedly at each other. A rap on the door broke the moment. Paul hopped up. 'That's probably Rick, so I'll head. Take care. I'll pick you up tomorrow.' He gave her the thumbs up.

Roll on tomorrow, she thought.

Rick arrived in then, complete with a suitcase. 'I'm moving in until you're better,' he declared.

It felt good to have him say that.

THE SEVENTH WEDNESDAY

Though Deirdre hadn't expected Lily to notice her arm, she was incredibly moved when her mother reached out to touch her bandage, her eyes expressing concern instead of their usual confusion.

'It's fine.' Deirdre clasped her mother's hand in hers. Looking her in the eye in what she hoped was a reassuring manner she added, 'I slipped onto some glass.' She told her mother about the past few days, how good Rick had been and of how Paul, the man in charge of her show, had called around with some flowers to apologise yet again. 'The best thing is the guilt,' she grinned. 'It's pouring from him in waves. And the rest of the gang have sent me a lovely bunch of flowers too.'

Just then Zoe arrived, accompanied by a posse of staff, and Lily's attention wandered from Deirdre to Zoe. She handed over her diary without a word.

Zoe noticed Deirdre's bandaged arm, 'Jesus, what happened you?'

Deirdre explained and more time was taken up with everyone chiming in and the nurses telling her how lucky it was that Paul was so quick-thinking.

That he'd probably saved her life. Their concern felt quite lovely, Deirdre thought.

A photograph fell out of the diary when Zoe opened it. It must have been lodged in the little flap at the back.

'A picture.' Carrie, who was in her usual position at the foot of Lily's bed, picked it up off the floor and handed it to Deirdre before she and a few others crowded around to have a look.

It was black and white and showed a woman and a little girl to the foreground. 'That's in Dublin,' Zoe said, jabbing it. 'Look, that's O'Connell Bridge.'

A chorus of 'oh yes' greeted her.

Deirdre inhaled sharply. That was the day she had nightmares about. It had to be. Her memory of it was kind of jumbled up in her head, she'd been so young. But it had started out so happily and ended so confusingly. She'd never known if it was true or not, but this confirmed it. The picture showed her mother and herself. Lily wore a white skirt and dark frilly blouse. Her good clothes. Her jet-black hair was set in the style of the time. Despite the fact that the picture was taken so long ago, Lily looked quite modern. She had the poise of a Hollywood starlet, small, full lips, tiny nose and the monochrome of the picture made her skin appear as pale and as flawless as porcelain. Her eyes, though, belied whatever chic-girl-about-town image she was trying to create, they were inde-scribably large and there was a sadness in them. She was holding Deirdre's hand. Deirdre was beaming at the camera, wearing a little summer dress with a big white bow in her dark hair.

'Is that you? Carrie asked Deirdre. Then without waiting for an answer, she went on, 'And doesn't Lily look great, not at all like I imagined. I thought you'd be more' – she frowned, looking at Lily – 'I dunno,' she finally said, shaking her head. 'Just different.'

Lily plucked the picture from Deirdre's hands and studied it. Her finger trembled as she traced the line of the girl's face. She said nothing.

'That was taken the day she brought me to Dublin, when I was very little,' Deirdre said. 'I can barely remember it.'

'Oh, there's another picture here,' Zoe found another picture tucked away in the back of the diary. It showed a tall man, lanky, with the biggest, widest smile, his arm about a stunning Lily, who was pouting for the camera.

'That was taken the night of the dance she wrote about,' Deirdre volunteered, taking the picture up. 'She used to look at that a lot.'

'Read,' Lily ordered suddenly, making them laugh.

'OK.' Zoe rapidly flicked through the pages and found the ones detailing Lily and Patrick's budding romance. 'OK, I'll go from here.'

December 1957

Patrick has promised me that he will bring me to Dublin and introduce me to people up there. He thinks that when he tells them how good and efficient I am that they will give me a job. We have decided to go next week under pretence of locating new stock for the shop. Patrick has said that he will close the shop for the day to bring me up and I only hope that I feel a little better for the long trip on the bus. I've been sick the past five mornings in a row and not able to eat until lunchtime.

My mother must have told Jimmy because last night he came in to see how I was. I told him that I was fine and not to be bothering about me. 'But I **am** bothered,' he said. Then he asked, 'Have you thought any more about my proposal?'

'Jimmy Deegan,' I said, jumping up off the stone wall that runs around our small farm – the sudden motion made me feel sick again, 'is that all you ever think about? Yourself? Here am I, sick, and all you can do is go banging on and on about weddings. I already told you, I have to think properly about it.'

And then, and I can't believe this, he leaned in and kissed me. I was taken completely by surprise. Of course, I pushed him off and slapped him right across the face for good measure. I was so tempted to tell him about Patrick, but I was afraid that it might hurt his feelings. Patrick and I have decided that when the time comes for me to go to Dublin, Patrick will come and visit me and that we'd be a couple then. That way, Jimmy won't feel too bad about it all. 'How dare you,' I said.

Jimmy laughed and rubbed his face, which was a bit red, I saw to my satisfaction. 'I've kissed you

331

before and you never objected,' he said. 'What's the problem now?'

'The problem is that we have no future together, Jimmy, now there's your answer!'

That seemed to do the trick. He pulled away, a little shocked I think. 'You've never told me that before.'

I felt a bit bad about the look on his face, but I'd done it now. I'd shattered his dream. 'I'm telling you now so,' I said and I made my voice hard. 'We will never be together.'

He stood up and looked at me as if he was seeing me for the first time. 'But we've always been together,' he said like a bewildered little boy. 'I can't imagine not being with you, Lil.'

I tuned my face away, not wanting to witness his pain.

'Lil?'

I shrugged, and when I turned back, he was stomping off across the fields towards his own place.

I'm beginning to get worried and that's something because not a lot worries me. However, I think I could be pregnant. The facts of life are all a bit hazy – they've never actually been explained to me, but June Carter brought a book into school once. She smuggled it out of her bag during lunch break and we all had a look. I remember that one of the signs of pregnancy is being sick in the mornings along with swollen breasts. The swollen breasts part stuck in my mind because I remember joking that if it took getting pregnant for my breasts to grow a bit bigger,

I'd sooner forget it. That had made everyone laugh really hard. But my breasts are sore and way bigger and I've been vomiting every day for two weeks now. My mother still thinks I have a bug and I haven't told Patrick yet, but the day we go to Dublin, I will. Things will be a lot easier up there; when I get work I can pretend that I'm already married, and I'm sure Patrick will stand by me, he says he loves me every time we kiss.

If he doesn't though, I can't even begin to imagine what will happen. It's bad enough being read from the altar, which wasn't actually that bad, but being pregnant and not married in our town will be intolerable. All sorts of stories go around about what happens to single pregnant girls. They are disgraced for life, tainted and no one wants them. Some go off and have their babies and then come back and pretend that they were visiting relatives, but everyone knows and the girl is treated like a plague. Some girls are put away into the laundries by their families and can only come out if their families agree to have them released. I don't know what happens there, but I've seen these women on the way to mass, walking side by side, their heads down as if they're no longer worthy of looking the world in the eye. They don't look happy. I've heard the whispers that accompany them.

They have their babies taken from them too and, if I am pregnant, I don't want that to happen. I've never been really maternal, but no one is taking away anything that is mine, that I have a right to. I will not let that happen. I had enough of the nuns in school with their canes and their religion – from when I was about ten and one of the nuns beat a girl because she couldn't read, I made up my mind that I would not let a nun decide the rest of my life for me.

I am counting down the days until I can tell Patrick. I've decided to tell him when we're in Dublin because if I do it here, people will notice his reaction and will comment if he acts a bit odd, and he is bound to. It'll be a shock for him, just like it is for me. I know he says he loves me, but I doubt very much that he had fatherhood factored into it.

A father! And me a mother! I don't feel old enough. I'm sure married women feel happy and maybe if Patrick and me get married, I will too. I hope so. Anything rather than this terror.

Zoe looked up. Lily waved her on.

Today, which is the day before our Dublin trip, I got sick in work. Patrick was tending to his father, who had taken a bad turn and was unable to get out of bed. The poor man, he's always been so good to me. I made him tea and sent it upstairs with Patrick. He says that his dad doesn't want me up there and I can understand that. Who wants others to see them helpless?

My sickness had been abating little by little but today a customer arrived in and whatever perfume she was wearing had a terrible effect on me. It was so pungent that I could taste it. My stomach clenched and I ran right out of the shop to the toilet, barging into Patrick on the way. I ignored the startled look on his face as I wrenched open the door and vomited up my lunch.

As I sat there on the floor, sweating and mortified, I could hear Patrick out in the shop dealing with the customer and assuring them that I was fine. A few minutes later, he tapped softly on the door.

'Lily, are you OK in there?'

'Fine,' I called out, mopping my forehead with my sleeve. 'I've just been a little sick recently.'

'Lily, come out and let me have a look at you.'

'No, I'm fine, leave me.' I just couldn't bear to see him, to have to look him in the eye and lie.

'Now, Lily.' It was an order.

'OK,' I called out rattily and stood up slowly. My legs were shaking, my body coated in sweat. My dress, which was my favourite, was creased and wisps of hair were stuck to my damp face. I took a deep fortifying breath and managed to assemble something resembling a smile before I opened the door. 'See,' I held my arms out, 'I'm fine.'

Patrick's beautiful dark eyes narrowed. I'm not sure if it was the shaft of morning light slanting through the dusty window that made him look suddenly pale. 'You don't look well,' he said. 'You haven't seemed well for the past couple of weeks now.'

'I'm grand.' Even to me, my voice sounded forced. I couldn't look at him.

Patrick leaned one hand against the door frame and his head dipped so his eyes met mine. 'Are you . . .' – he swallowed – 'Are you, well, pregnant, Lily?'

I was that shocked that I opened my mouth to speak but couldn't think of what to say. I think my silence spoke more than any words. His question was like a balloon floating above us. Now that it was there, I couldn't burst it by denying it.

Patrick exhaled very slowly as if he was only keeping it together by sheer force of will. 'You are?' he breathed.

I shrugged, tried to make a joke out of it. 'Well, never having been pregnant before I find it's hard to tell.'

'Oh, God,' Patrick groaned and it seemed to come from the very pit of his stomach. 'Oh, Jesus.'

I said nothing, taken aback by his dismay. I hadn't actually thought about how he would react, though I had definitely flirted with the idea of him scooping me up in his arms and telling me things would work out.

'How far gone are you?' he asked.

'I don't know,' my voice was small and scared. 'A month maybe.'

Patrick rubbed an agitated hand across his face and walked away from me. Then he came back. 'What are you going to do?' he asked. Then, seeming to think better of it, he said, 'Well, we, I suppose. What are we going to do?'

'If I am pregnant,' I said, 'I'm having it.'

He said nothing for a second, then asked, 'And?'

'And what?' I didn't know what he was talking about.

'You can't keep it,' he said.

I paused, steeled myself and said firmly, 'If you stand by me, I can. We can.'

He took a step back. 'What? Marry you?'

'You said you loved me.' I had an eerie sensation that I'd been transported into Jimmy's shoes, that I was looking at the world through his eyes.

'I know. I did. Do.' Patrick actually looked as if he could cry. 'I just never . . .' he paused. 'You have to give me time, Lily. I need to think. It's a lot to take in.'

'You don't have much time. People will start to notice soon and I'll end up in the laundry or somewhere.' I couldn't help the note of desperation in my voice. I wanted to add that if he loved me, it shouldn't be such a big issue for him.

'Tomorrow,' he said. 'When we are in Dublin, we'll discuss it. We'll figure something out. OK?' He looked at me, his brown eyes so deep and imploring and disbelieving and I nodded.

'OK.'

'Remember what we arranged,' he went on. 'Half eight at the bus stop. I've business in the morning in Allentown, so get off there and I'll pick you up in the car and we'll drive to Dublin. OK?'

'OK.'

He took my hand and I fizzed at his touch. Taking a step closer, he enfolded me in a gentle hug. 'Is this OK? I don't want to hurt you.'

'I'm not breakable,' I laughed a little, my world righting again. 'You can hug me harder.'

And he did. And as I inhaled the scent of him, as I rubbed my hand through his freshly washed hair and felt the skin of his face rub against my neck, I just knew that things would work out.

I caught the bus from down the road as arranged but Patrick was not waiting for me when I got off. Thinking he must have been delayed on his business, I settled down to wait. Two hours later, heart sore, soaked through and lacking the courage to go to Dublin on my own, I hopped back on the bus and was deposited right where I had begun with such happiness only three hours earlier.

Was this it? I wondered as I took the road for home. Had he abandoned me? Had he run out of town the night before? I'd find out for sure tomorrow. But the fact that he hadn't turned up told me all I had to know about his commitment.

It took me about ten minutes to get to the foot of our laneway and by the time I got there, the rain had abated and the sun had re-emerged, making my clothes steam in the heat. As my house came into view, I veered to the right, not thinking consciously about what I was doing. All I knew was that I had to keep my baby. All I knew was that in another couple of months it might become too obvious to everyone. And so, I did something I'm ashamed of and yet something that I was privileged to be able to do – I sought out Jimmy. I saw him in the distance, breaking stones in one of his father's fields, his strong arms smashing and smashing, bits of rocks flying all over the place. That's what I felt like in that moment. Bits of me were scattering and I was trying desperately to reform the course my life was taking. I walked up to him and placed a hand on his back. He hadn't seen or heard me approach and he jumped, startled before turning around. He made to smile at me, then stopped. 'What?' he asked instead.

For one heart-stopping moment, I thought that maybe he wouldn't want me. 'Sorry,' I said, my throat dry. 'I've missed you, Jimmy. I was scared. I will marry you.'

His smile was like the sun breaking free from the clouds. 'You will?'

'I will.' I reached for him, this had to be now. I pulled his head down to mine. There was no one around, the only sounds the soft swish of the grass and the call of the corncrake. 'I love you, Jimmy.'

His hands pulled me to him, his lips sought out mine and though I hated myself for what I was doing to this man, I heaved a sigh of relief. 'I love you, Jimmy,' I said again. If I kept saying it, maybe I'd believe it.

'And I adore you,' he said raggedly, pushing me away from him and looking at me as he'd never done before. His hand shook as he ran it over my face, his body trembled as he came closer and I encouraged him. I fingered a nipple as he gasped. I pulled him closer still and ran my fingers through his tangle of hair. He pulled me down into the grass and lay beside me.

'I have to stop,' he groaned, about to roll away.

I pulled him back. 'Don't. I've missed you, Jimmy, and we're getting married and all.'

'The priest?'

'Is a nosy old goat.'

He laughed loudly, his happiness in direct proportion to my misery. 'You are a bad influence,' he said. 'You've been a bad influence my whole life. My mother said you'd lead me astray.'

'And aren't you lucky she was right,' I said.

And that was it. Jimmy and me. Together.

There was silence after Zoe finished. Deirdre was glad Rick hadn't come with her. Glad that he didn't know what Lily had done. But at least Lily had been honest, she hadn't tried to airbrush her actions, though, really, how would it have been possible anyway?

The bell rang for lunch and broke the shocked mood.

'Lily, you should write a Mills & Boon,' Carrie said, lightening the atmosphere. 'Honestly, this is way better than some stuff I've read.'

'Carrie, this is Lily's life,' Zoe gently reminded her.

'Oh, yeah,' Carrie flushed. 'Sorry,' she muttered to Deirdre.

Lily had her gaze fixed on Deirdre and slowly she held out the black and white pictures.

Deirdre took them, not sure what else to do. 'Why did you do that to him, Mammy?' she found herself asking, as she looked at Jimmy's youthful face, so full of hope.

Lily's answer was a blank stare, though she started to fuss agitatedly with her clothing.

'She did it to keep her baby,' Zoe spoke gently. 'I would have done the same.'

Lily stilled and fixed Deirdre with a gaze.

At that, Deirdre's eyes filled with tears. She'd always been under the impression that her mother had stayed with her dad to save face, but Deirdre wondered if maybe Zoe was right. Did her mother do it to keep her? And if she had, maybe her mother had really, really loved her.

Maybe.

'We're a much luckier generation,' Zoe went on. 'We're not judged anymore.' And as Zoe said it, she realised how true it was. She might not have her man, but at least she had her child.

CHAPTER 29

At five, feeling better than she had in a while, Zoe left work. She'd spent most of the afternoon designing a poster for Ronnie's concert. He was due to perform in two weeks and Zoe decided that it'd be a laugh to make him feel like a real entertainer, the man he probably was in the fifties and sixties, before his accident. She'd googled and found old playbills of the time and designed a replica on her computer. After printing it, she'd put it up in the corridor hoping that Ronnie would spot it later on.

Pushing open the back door to the car park, she saw Dominic waiting for her. She enjoyed her trips to the hospital with him. Despite the fact that his life was terrible, he was such an upbeat guy that he made her feel better about herself just by being around. Zoe had caught glimpses of his sister now and again because she was sometimes waiting for Dominic when he arrived. She'd taken to waving at Zoe. She looked like her brother, tall and dark, with his smile.

She opened the car and Dominic sat in. 'You fully recovered now?' he asked her.

She flinched. She guessed she might as well tell him. June knew, and though she wouldn't say anything, it was only a matter of time before the others copped on that Abe was not much mentioned anymore. 'I was just heartsick,' she tried to make a joke out of it but it fell flat. Dominic looked appalled.

'You've heart trouble?'

'No,' she actually laughed then and said, 'I've split with Abe.' Only a tiny wobble in her voice. 'For good.'

'Oh.' Dominic coughed uncomfortably. 'Wish I hadn't asked now.'

'Aw, no worries, I think it's for the best.'

'Really?' he seemed surprised but she gave him her brightest smile. 'Well, that's good. I guess it's easier to get over because he wasn't around much. How's Lee with it?'

'Fine, we're both fine.' Her voice was getting higher in an attempt to keep it under control. If one more person pointed out the fact that Abe had never been there, she was going to crawl away and die. In order to distract herself she asked her usual, 'How's your dad, now?'

'Not good.'

His blunt answer surprised her. 'Oh, I'm sorry.'

He nodded. 'Yeah.' After a pause he added, 'I don't think he'll be leaving the hospital, put it like that.'

'Dominic, I'm so sorry.' With her free hand she touched his hand briefly.

To her surprise he clasped hers. 'Ta.' He smiled sadly at her and she was disgusted with herself when her heart pinged. How could she think that he was gorgeous when he was obviously suffering? When she was suffering? When her relationship had just ended? Maybe she was just a rebound girl. She tried to extract her hand and he flushed and let it go before turning his gaze straight ahead.

'If there's anything I can do—'

'The lifts are great,' he cut her short.

'Good.'

There was silence and Zoe fiddled with her radio in an attempt to find some music to fill the awkward gap in conversation. Just as she tuned into Gary Sims, Dominic's phone rang. Fishing it out of his pocket, he looked at caller ID and an anxious look flashed across his features. 'Hi, what's up?' he asked. 'Yeah, you have? Well, I'm in the car with Zoe.' He shot a sidelong glance at Zoe, then the person at the other end said something and he winced. 'OK, OK,' he said, sounding a little frazzled, 'I'll ask.' He turned to Zoe, 'Hate to ask but is there any chance you could swing by my house? My sister has left a book behind, she reads to dad every day and couldn't today. She wants me to do it tonight instead.'

'Sure,' Zoe nodded, 'Where do you live?'

'Opposite direction,' Dominic said. 'No don't—'

'It's fine,' Zoe swung the car around in an arc, 'the road is clear.' She laughed at his pale face, at the way his hands grabbed the dashboard. 'Don't you trust me?'

He shook his head, an amused look in his eyes. 'We've just done a u-turn on a busy main road,' he said back into the phone. 'See you in about half an hour. Oh, right, well maybe I'll grab a cuppa then. Where's the book?' She told him and he hung up. 'She says hi,' he grinned.

'Tell her hi back. Now what's your address?'

His house was in a quiet area about six miles from the city centre. It was a small, semi-detached bungalow. 'We moved here after the accident,' Dominic explained, as they pulled up in front of one of the houses. 'A bungalow was the best option for Dad.' He hopped out. 'Come on in.'

Zoe thought it would be rude to refuse, so she followed him up the unkempt driveway which was bordered by a garden full of daisies and dandelions. It looked quite colourful and cheerful.

'Hi, Dominic love,' a neighbour called. 'How's Matthew?'

'Not so good,' Dominic crossed over to talk to her. 'I'm on my way in now.'

'Well, give him our best. I did ring about visiting him but I believe it's only close family?'

'Yeah. And I will. Thanks.' He loped back to Zoe. 'Lovely woman,' he said, 'she's done so much for us over the years.' He unlocked the door and Zoe stepped into a hallway done in light green and cream. It was bright and airy, though underlying the cheeriness of the decor was the definite smell of disinfectant. 'I know,' Dominic made a face, 'it reeks like a hospital.' He walked towards a door, 'Now, to find this book.'

He disappeared into a room off the hallway and Zoe got a glimpse of a hospital-type bedroom with a special bed and machines alongside it. Dominic emerged a few seconds later holding the book. Looking questioningly at her, he asked, 'D'you want a cuppa while we're here? Rosie told me there was no rush as they'd brought Dad off for some tests.' He looked at her hopefully, 'I'm starving.'

'Go on then,' Zoe flapped a hand at him, curious now to see the rest of the house. She followed him down the hall and into the kitchen and gasped as she took in the tall glass sliding door that ran the length of the room. 'This is gorgeous. Oh, wow, I wish my place looked like this.' Sunlight bathed her face and pooled the length of the floor.

Dominic grinned, 'We bought the place because of the light in here. It's important, don't you think? Makes you feel good.'

'I wouldn't know much about light.' Zoe sat on a chair facing the sun and watched as he put the kettle on and ducked his head into the fridge freezer. 'My apartment is darker than an episode of *EastEnders*.'

He laughed. Then he asked, 'What do you fancy? Curry? Stew?—'

'Oh no, don't cook for me.' Zoe waved him away.

'It's already cooked. I do big batches of food and freeze it. Saves a lot of time. The yellow curry is nice, I make my own paste?' He waved a Tupperware carton in front of her.

'Oh, go on so.'

'I'll boil up a bit of rice and we're set,' he said.

As he prepared the dinner, Zoe stood up and examined the rest of the fabulous kitchen. There was no reason for this house to be horrible just because there was an invalid in it, same way there was no reason for her flat to be so mangy just because Abe couldn't be arsed to do anything. Things were going to change, she vowed. First thing tomorrow she was getting her dad over to fix the ceiling. Decision made. Zoe examined some photos hanging on the wall. They seemed to be arranged in chronological order and she was going back in time. Dominic holding a degree. A girl, Rosie obviously, holding back her dark hair and sticking her tongue out, Dominic in shorts on the beach, Rosie in a summer dress eating a lollipop, two baby pictures in black and white, a woman holding a baby and smiling.

A man holding another baby and smiling. He looked uncannily like Dominic. 'Your dad?' she asked.

'Uh-huh,' Dominic gave the rice a stir, 'and that's my mother holding Rosie.'

'She looks lovely.'

'She was,' Dominic nodded. 'She died in the crash that paralysed Da.'

Zoe winced in pity for him. 'That must have been' – she struggled to find a suitable word and could only think of 'awful' – 'awful,' she said.

'It was, of course it was,' Dominic said. 'It's scary how life can just change overnight, I never thought of it much before, but it makes you learn never to take anything for granted.'

'True,' Zoe nodded and sat back down again, watching him work. A few minutes later he handed her a plate of rice and a carton of heated-up curry sauce. Pouring the sauce over her rice, she dug in. The flavours were like an explosion of sunshine in her mouth. 'Yum.' She heaped more onto her fork, 'What did you put in that?'

'Chef's secret,' Dominic grinned.

They ate in silence for a bit but it wasn't the sort of silence that Zoe felt she had to fill with chatter. 'I'll come here more often,' she said as she finished up. 'That, hands down, was the nicest food I've had in ages.'

Dominic seemed pleased by the compliment. 'Yeah, well, cooking for me and Rosie keeps my hand in with the more exotic stuff. The stuff I get to make in work is turning my skills to mush, but at the same time, I get a great kick out of being there. They make me laugh.'

'They love you,' Zoe said.

'Glad someone does.' Dominic winked at her and, picking her plate from the table, rinsed it out in the sink.

The wink made her melt in some very neglected places.

Jesus, what was she like?

CHAPTER 30

'OK, there will be a pond here.' Deirdre ran a stick over the soil in a circular motion. 'So you'll need to dig to a depth of six feet.' At Paul's anguished expression, she added, 'Though you could get a little digger in if you're not up to it.'

'I'll give it a go,' Paul said.

Oh, he was so easy to wind up, Deirdre thought. Still, to give him credit, he had embraced the gardening life and had bought some wellies; she knew they were brand new because the sicker was still on the soles. He insisted on wearing expensive designer jeans teamed with an old jumper with a hole in the elbow. For the past few days, at her instruction, he had finished rotavating and clearing the site, which had resulted in calluses the size of onions on his hands and a distinct limp.

'Now! Flowerbeds!' Deirdre said. She walked around pointing out shady areas, sunny areas, a place for a little gazebo and where she thought some steps might be installed. When she finished, she became aware that Paul hadn't uttered a word. Turning around, she saw that he was staring at her as if she'd just landed from Mars. 'What?' she asked.

Paul actually went red. 'Nothing.' He hastily picked up a shovel. 'Flowerbeds, what do I have to do?'

She gave him instructions and sat back to watch. He was a crap gardener but a great worker. He listened to whatever she had to say and did it. Which was more than she had done for him, she thought with a worm of guilt. Every so often, Paul would stand back, one foot on his spade, and survey what he had done, before wiping sweat from his forehead and starting again. She liked watching him dig. His expensive jeans sold their wares well. A flare of longing started up inside her and she had to clamp her knees together. Good God, what was happening to her? No wonder the man had cast-offs everywhere if he had that effect on her.

'You're doing great,' she called, a little too loudly, to banish the lust from her brain. 'If you get that flowerbed dug tonight, we'll record it in the morning.' The she realised that it was his call and she flushed. 'If that's OK,' she tacked on.

'That is great,' Paul agreed. 'Provided I don't collapse beforehand.'

'Well, I can't take off my belt to rescue you,' Deirdre said back, tittering. 'It's an essential piece of my clothing.'

Paul's lips twitched before he shook his head and resumed digging.

⋆   ⋆   ⋆

350

He drove her home, the smell of his sweat filling up the car. Deirdre found it quite intoxicating. It mixed with the spice and the aftershave and as she inhaled, it travelled through her bloodstream, making her heart hammer a little harder than usual.

'Not used to heavy work as you've probably guessed,' Paul said ruefully. 'Jaysus, my back is murdering me.'

'I'll make a gardener of you yet.' She poked his arm and relished the contact.

He pulled up in front of her house and as usual Rick was there, door open before she even set a foot outside her car. 'That auld fella is great,' Paul remarked. 'What is he, your uncle or something?'

'He's a cousin of my mother's.' Deirdre took off her seatbelt and prepared to get out. Paul's car was very low slung and she lost a certain dignity trying to extract herself from the bucket seats. Last time her old gardening skirt had ridden right up. She'd caught Paul looking too, which gave her a secret thrill despite being mortifying. But she had stuck to jeans since.

'It's nice he cares so much,' Paul nodded. 'You're lucky. See you tomorrow.'

'Would you care for a tea?' The words were out before she could whip them back. But she wanted to discuss the next day's work with him and to do it now would save time later. And there was something in his voice, some sort of . . . she couldn't place it. 'Rick makes the nicest scones.'

Paul seemed a little taken aback at her invitation.

'Eh, OK,' he shrugged, as if he wasn't that keen on the idea. 'Sure.'

Now she wished she hadn't asked him. Paul was probably not a tea-and-scones person. 'We can discuss the garden, speed things up for tomorrow,' she said, wanting him to know that this was the reason for the invitation. It was nothing to do with prolonging the time with him in any way.

'Nope.' Paul held up his hands. 'Work is over.'

'It was just a suggestion,' she said as she clamoured out of the car, like a spider caught in its own web, arms and legs flailing.

'I hate most of your suggestions, you should know that by now,' Paul teased as he joined her on the path.

Rick met them at the door. 'I just invited Paul in for a tea,' Deirdre explained hastily, to divert Rick's glower. He hadn't been at all mollified by Paul's attempts to make things up to Deirdre.

'Grand,' Rick said, as if Deirdre had just told him she was selling herself on the streets. Then he added, 'Come, say hello to the gang from the Alzheimer's centre. They're in your kitchen and we're discussing the fundraiser for next year. All input welcome.'

Deirdre grimaced, not wanting Paul to know her business.

'You involved with that?' Paul asked Rick, ignoring his unfriendliness. 'Terrible disease. My father had it.'

The little confidence seemed to startle Rick.

'Deirdre's mother, Lily, has it too,' Rick said. 'That's how I'm involved.'

Paul shot a look at Deirdre. 'Really? How far gone is she?'

'She's quite bad,' Deirdre said. She hoped her tone conveyed her reluctance to talk about it.

'She's only in there a few months now.' Rick had no such qualms as he strode towards the kitchen. 'Traumatic on both of us having to put her in there.' Pointedly, he added, 'Poor Deirdre, she's had it so hard.'

Deirdre stiffened; Paul would think this was another set up if Rick kept going. Paul, though, flashed her a smile of understanding and she wondered why she had ever been so hostile to him.

'Everyone,' Rick announced, 'Deirdre's here.'

At once there were anxious enquiries about her arm and Deirdre had to show it to them all, secretly glad that Paul was witnessing just how many people she knew. She had a suspicion that he thought she was a bit of a loser in the friend stakes.

'And who's this fine young man?' Mona asked. 'Is he your partner?'

Paul laughed and Deirdre blushed as red as a communist.

'He's my boss, Paul,' Deirdre stammered out.

Oh shit! Too late, she realised that Rick had obviously told them about Paul because there was a stiffening of shoulders, a shifting of glances and lots of nudging.

If Paul noticed, he ignored it. Instead, he plonked

himself among them and told them exactly who he was and of how his dad had had the disease. 'The only way to get any sort of a reaction from him was to tell him we had kids and we weren't married,' he said. 'He'd hit the roof.'

Deirdre was surprised when they laughed.

'Jaysus, that's mean,' Adam grinned.

'Well, in my case it was true so it wasn't so mean,' Paul cracked a grin. 'I have a son, he's twenty.'

And just like that, the conversation started. Deirdre watched as he charmed everyone the way he'd done at work. He asked after all their relatives. She learned that Elle was going into a home the following week and poor Adam started to cry, right there in the kitchen. Mona fussed over him, consoling him by saying that at least his wife didn't go around dressed as Dennis the Menace. 'Do you know what Pete did last week?' she asked, handing Adam a copious amount of kitchen paper. 'Go on, guess.'

No one could.

'He got arrested for kidnapping a black dog. He thought it was Gnasher.' As they laughed, Mona shook her head, 'He was always mad. Now he has an excuse.'

There was more laughter and Paul caught Deirdre's eye. He held her gaze for a second before turning away. Deirdre couldn't take her eyes off him.

THE EIGHTH WEDNESDAY

December 1957–February 1958

The next day, after Jimmy and I had consummated our engagement and he'd asked my dad for my hand, I was dying to get into work to show Patrick that someone wanted me. That I could click my fingers and get a man.

I even let Jimmy drive me in and he kept smiling over at me and touching my hand and I had to smile back when really my heart was broken and I was trying very hard not to cry, wondering if it was all such a good idea. Maybe I should just live with the shame of being pregnant and go somewhere to have the baby, but they would have taken it off me. I wasn't letting my baby go out there to some stranger. Bad as I was, having committed a mortal sin, I knew I could sink no further by this deception. If I was damned, well there was only so much damned a person could be.

Jimmy parked outside the shop and it took a second to register. The place was closed. The blinds were drawn. There was a cream notice fringed with black in the window. 'Closed due to death in the family.'

My world spun and, feeling dizzy, I grasped on to

the door frame before I could fall. Just then the door opened and Patrick stood, all in black, his face as white as the shirt he wore underneath his suit. He must have been looking out for me.

'I tried to get word to you,' he said. 'I'm so glad you turned up today I was afraid—'

'He died?' I whispered.

'He did. Yesterday. That's why I couldn't meet you. I got a boy to run to the bus stop to let you know, but you had left. I'm sorry.'

'No one told me,' I barely whispered it. Oh, God, what had I done?

He leaned towards me and I think he was about to take my hands when Jimmy came up behind and placed his arm on my shoulder. 'I'm sorry for your loss,' he said to Patrick.

'Thanks,' Patrick said, pulling his hands away. His eyes darted between Jimmy's hand and my shoulder.

'Come on,' Jimmy said to me. 'I'll bring you back home.'

I turned with him, not able to speak. What had I done?

Patrick still had his eyes on Jimmy's hand, where it rested on my shoulder. 'Is there something I should know?'

Jimmy looked at me and me at him. Please don't tell him, I willed, but Jimmy shrugged, 'We got engaged yesterday, Patrick. I wouldn't have said it on account of your loss, but sure you were bound to find out anyway.'

I couldn't look at Patrick but I knew he was looking

at me. 'Well,' he spoke, and there was a funny note in his voice, 'that's fantastic news. Congratulations.'

'Like I said, I wouldn't have told you on account of—'

'No, no, I'm glad you did,' Patrick said, and I think he meant it. I glanced up and he was smiling a little. 'The shop will be closed for a week and then, well, we'll see.'

I let Jimmy lead me away. I wondered what 'we'll see' meant.

It meant that a week later, the shop was up for sale. I turned up for work, my heart beating like a trapped bird in my chest, to see a sign hammered into the wall above the lintel. When I pushed the door open, Patrick was sweeping the floor and he spun around as I came in. He looked wretched and I longed to flatten his hair and rub my hand on his pale cheek, but I couldn't anymore. He was out of bounds and the stark realisation of this was like my heart being wrung like a wet dishcloth. I'd seen him at the funeral of course but there had been no chance to talk to him. He always seemed to be with someone.

'You're selling up?' I asked.

'Well, here she is, the engaged woman,' he said by way of reply, leaning on his brush and looking at me.

I swallowed and blurted out, 'If I could take it back I would.'

'Take what back?' he said. 'Call off your engagement? Tell Jimmy you can't marry him?'

'Yes,' I felt a little guilty saying it, but at the same time, the possibility of doing it excited me. All of a sudden, my life seemed to spill out before me in glorious colour. 'Sell the shop and we'll leave here.' I crossed towards him and put my hand on his arm, and gave it a squeeze. 'We'll go where no one knows us. We can say we've been married for months.'

'It's not that easy,' he said as he pulled out of my grasp and turned away, pretending to sweep the floor.

'I know that!'

It meant that I'd never see my family again, they'd disown me. I could never come back to Cavan again, and even though I longed to leave, it was only on condition that I could come back. And I'd break Jimmy's heart and much as he annoyed me, he was a good man and I knew I'd like myself a little less by doing it, but overriding all that was the fact that I wanted Patrick. I loved him. I wanted the life he could give me and the baby. 'But we can do it.' I followed him up the shop. 'Come on, Patrick.'

'I can't,' he said, sounding desperate.

It was his voice that froze me where I stood, the sound of a man trapped. 'You can't,' I repeated softly, 'or you won't?'

There was a silence.

'I'm so sorry,' he muttered.

'For what?' I crossed in front of him. 'For getting me pregnant or abandoning me?'

'Aw, Lily—'

'Forget it.' I was gone, slamming the door hard. Tears blurred my eyes. And the life that I had seen only minutes before shrivelled up and grew dark and tattered. I was to be a farmer's wife. I was to live in

Cavan and work the land. I would have no shop job, no city life. The knowledge felt like a death.

A small glimmer of hope offered itself to me when I remembered who Jimmy actually was. I'd been happy with him until Patrick had come into my life.

I'd make myself happy again.

The next page was blank, something started then scribbled out.

'Read,' Lily commanded.

Zoe turned the page over.

Events up to September 1958

I haven't written because to write you have to be happy, to have a wish to record good things, or maybe that's just me. It's all been a blur anyway. Patrick sold the shop quite quickly, I don't know if he let it go for less than it was worth just to escape, but the night before he left, he called to my house and asked if I could go with him on a walk. My father, who was in right good humour, agreed.

I couldn't talk to him, the sight of him after so long was water in the desert of my life. My eyes drank him in as he strode ahead of me, the setting sun reddening his silhouette. Finally, when we'd gone far enough from the house, he turned to me, 'Here,' he said. He held out an envelope fat with cash. 'For the baby.'

I shook my head. We were in a field stripped bare. 'You can't buy forgiveness.'

'I'd like to help my baby,' he said.

'So stay here.'

He shoved the envelope in my direction. 'Take it.'

'No.'

'It's for the baby, you can't refuse to take it for the baby,' he said. Then he threw it at my feet and strode off and I fell to the ground and watched him grow smaller and smaller until he was just a dot on the road. How was I going to live the rest of my life without this man? How would I survive seeing Jimmy and his farmer face every day? I loved Patrick with a hot fire and hated him with a cold fury all at the one time. Tears fell and I buried my head in the lap of my dress.

A hand on my shoulder startled me.

'Are you OK?' It was my mother. She didn't wait for me to answer, instead she sat in beside me and wrapped an arm about my shoulder, cuddling me in the way she had when I was a girl. 'What's wrong?'

'Nothing,' I sniffed, obviously lying.

'What did Patrick want?'

'To give me this,' I held the envelope out and she took it, pulling out the money and fingering it.

'That's a lot of money.'

'I know. He wanted to give it to me as a wedding present. I tried to get him to take it back but he won't. He's leaving.'

My mother said nothing, just stared ahead, her profile proud and strong. I had her nose, people often said it, and while I thought it was too big for my face, it suited hers. Her lips were full and her eyes wide and bright. She was a beautiful woman, I realised.

'Your dad and I had a match marriage,' she said.

'I know.' And though she'd told me countless times, I'd never actually considered how awful it must have been for her. To marry a man she hadn't chosen.

'Time smoothes out all the bumps,' she said then, flattening my hair with gentle fingertips, her eyes searching my face. 'And you're lucky that Jimmy loves you,' she said. 'Sometimes the man we think we want is not the man we really want. In time, you'll love Jimmy back.'

'I do love him,' I said, flushing. 'What makes you say that?'

'Patrick,' she answered simply. Then as I opened my mouth to protest, she held up her hand. 'Patrick would not be good for you,' she said. 'I've seen him. I've seen the way he left his father when his father was ill. Rumour has it he only came back when there was an inheritance to claim. Patrick is for the good times. Jimmy will be there for all the times.' She caught my face between her hands and stared at me. I was so stunned, I couldn't protest or pull away. 'You remember that. You've chosen well. Trust your judgement.'

I managed to scramble to my feet. She too got up. 'I know you love him,' she said, and I wanted to cry, 'but stay away from him.' She nodded to the envelope. 'And put that money away for yourself. Jimmy never needs to know. A wife needs her secrets.'

With those words she strode off and even now I wonder if she guessed, if she knew that my supposedly premature baby who weighed in at eight pounds seven months later was really Patrick's.

And when my baby was born and Jimmy cradled both of us in his embrace, I didn't feel like a happy, proud mother, but like someone trapped, unable to find my way back out.

Zoe stopped reading, the image of Patrick's face blurring with Abe's. She was glad to see that Lily's eyes had closed and that no more reading was expected of her. Putting down the diary, she left the room before anyone could say anything, and wondered how Lily had had the strength to let Patrick go.

Deirdre watched Zoe leave and slowly picked up her own coat and bag. What a feckless eejit her real father had been.

She crossed over to her sleeping mother and looked down. Sleep had softened her features so that she almost looked young again. Deirdre wanted to touch her but was afraid she'd wake her. It was strange, feeling sick for her dad, anger at Patrick and so desperately sorry for her mother. Total mixed emotions. And listening to the story, from a point of view other than her own, made chunks of her childhood fall into place. Maybe she was finally after all this time beginning to understand.

CHAPTER 32

It was almost nine o'clock, Lee was sleeping and Zoe was watching the television, anxiously waiting for the news. According to her mother, there'd been an outbreak of violence in Somalia. Zoe had been shocked but her mother had muttered, 'Good enough for him.' Zoe bristled even thinking about what her mum had said.

'Here you go,' Audrey placed a huge glass of red wine and a bar of dark chocolate in front of her.

'Thanks,' Zoe smiled gratefully at Audrey and took a slug of wine. It slipped down smoothly but she barely tasted it. She was so nervous that her foot kept jiggling. 'I read on Google that they're pulling aid agencies out,' she said. 'And there are unconfirmed reports that people have been injured.'

'I know,' Audrey said softly as she sat in beside Zoe. 'And you won't learn much else looking at the news.'

Zoe groaned. 'I just have to hear it for myself.'

'So I take it you still care about him, even though he's lied shamelessly to you for five years?'

'Of course I care. I can't just switch my feelings off and, besides, he's Lee's dad.'

363

'I know that, but he's still a liar.' Audrey cracked her knuckles. 'God, when I think of him driving you down there that night and poor little Lee all bundled up in the back seat, I could smash his face for him.'

Zoe laughed. 'Stop. You'd hardly come up to his shoulder. Anyway, I wouldn't let you.'

'Your problem is you're too nice.'

'Eh, no, if there's any face smashing to be done, I want to do it myself.'

Audrey laughed. 'Nice one. I'll harden you up yet.'

But neither of them believed that. Zoe knew herself that she'd never do it, she was way too soft. Even in school, it was always the hopeless losers who had asked her out knowing that Zoe Killeen wouldn't have the heart to say no. She'd been out with the freaks, the geeks and the questionably crazy ones. And the normal guys, the ones she actually fancied, the un-desperate ones, had steered clear. Abe had been the most normal man she'd ever met. Only now she realised that he actually wasn't.

The news began. 'Somalia teeters on the brink of all-out war,' the newscaster said grimly before the title music played.

Zoe leaned forwards as if that would help her understand better. Audrey placed a reassuring hand on her arm.

'Somalia teeters on the brink of all-out war,' the newscaster repeated. 'Tonight its capital city lies

364

in ruins from a day of fighting. We'll turn now to our man at the scene, Tommy O'Reilly. Tommy, what's the situation there now?'

Tommy, looking morbidly excited to be in the middle of a warzone, spoke breathlessly into a big blue fluffy microphone. 'Well, it's gone quiet for the moment, but tensions are rising and those in the ruling faction are under pressure to resign. The people I've spoken to on the streets are in open revolt. Farther out in the countryside, make-shift armies are massing and it is thought that these will march onwards through the country, gathering people as they pass.'

'Any news on Irish citizens out there, Tommy?'

'We've a number of people living here and so far all are accounted for. We've no idea how many will leave in the coming days. Of course, there are a number of Irish aid agencies in the region too. Aid for Africa, which has about ten Irish workers, has announced that it will stay for the moment. It is working closely with a small town here, reroofing houses and installing clean water, and they have announced that they are reluctant to leave the people just yet.'

'Aren't they brave?' Zoe said, swallowing a lump as she thought of Abe out there.

'Hmm,' Audrey swilled the wine in her glass before swallowing it in one gulp. 'I hate to say it, Zoe, but how can Abe be responsible for reroofing houses when he left you with a kitchen ceiling about to cave it?'

Zoe said nothing. Audrey had warned her that there was no way she was going to come over if she had to listen to Zoe romanticising about Abe all night. Zoe had assured her that that would not be a problem. But she wasn't going to spend the night moaning about him either. How would that make her feel better?

Plus, she had to admit that what Audrey had said was true. Since Lee had expressed his desire to leave, it was as if Zoe's rose-tinted glasses had finally shattered. The apartment was a hovel, small and dark, with no storage space. A tiny kitchen with a table that rocked and three chairs that didn't match. She had loved it because Lee and Abe were with her, but now she saw it as everyone else did and her skin crawled with embarrassment. How had she not noticed? Was she truly stupid?

Zoe had made a decision that when Abe came home, no matter what happened, they were moving out.

The news item finished and Zoe heaved a sigh of relief. 'Well, it doesn't seem too bad,' she said.

'It's not.' Audrey seemed relieved at her reaction. 'Now,' she plucked a DVD from her bag, 'I picked this up on the way here, fancy watching it?'

Audrey's concern for Abe was very limited, Zoe thought in slight amusement. 'What's it called?'

'*Getting Over Oliver*,' Audrey said. 'I thought you could learn from it.'

'Is this a hint to stop feeling sorry for myself?'

'Yes,' Audrey said, her voice a little slurred from the wine. 'And the guy in the video shop said it was very good.'

'Go on so.'

Audrey stood up and swayed a bit. 'Whoops,' she chortled and put the DVD into the player.

The first scene was of a copulating couple.

'Oh, I vaguely remember that,' Audrey said, her head sideways as she studied them.

'Me too,' Zoe said, 'but it looks so much more fun than what I'm used to.'

Audrey laughed loudly. 'That's what I'm talking about,' she said, 'you're hardening up.'

'Eh, no,' Zoe pointed to the screen, 'I think he is. Again.'

More laughter.

Audrey and Zoe gawked in open-mouthed fascination as a succession of nubile young girls had frantic, erotic and weird sex with a willing, large-membered Oliver.

'Well, Audrey,' Zoe said as the panting reached a crescendo, 'this is so not what I was expecting.'

'No, it's a lot better, isn't it?' Audrey laughed. 'I've never seen a porn movie before, have you?'

'No.'

That struck them both as very funny and Zoe, pouring them both another glass of wine, realised that she hadn't enjoyed herself so much in ages. 'Is there a plot to this film?' she asked as Oliver abandoned one young woman in favour of another.

'Well if there is, it has a lot of holes,' Audrey sniggered.

And they both cracked up.

Deirdre had rarely stayed up beyond ten, but since Rick had come to stay, all that had changed. It was now eleven thirty and they were enjoying their night-time glass of wine. Again, Deirdre had rarely drunk at night, due to some acid reflux problems, but Rick was very fond of his night-time tipple and had persuaded Deirdre that she'd sleep a lot better if she just had 'the one'. He was right too. She was sleeping like a log, which surprised her, and had had no stomach issues so far. There was a documentary on the television about bees and it was fascinating. Once upon a time, Deirdre had flirted with the idea of beekeeping. Years earlier, when she'd decided that she'd like a pet. Something to lavish her affection on, given that her chances of having a baby had been diminishing because of her age and lack of a partner. She had decided that she might like a cat, before realising that she was a middle-aged lady, living alone and that a cat would only add to the batty stereotype. Beekeeping, however, didn't sound middle-aged or single or batty, only what with the show, she'd never got around to doing it.

'You OK?' Rick nudged her shoulder. 'You're very quiet tonight.'

The bee on the TV was managing the nursery, feeding all the babies on royal jelly. Deirdre swirled her wine about in her glass. 'Did you know about my father?' she asked Rick. There was no point hiding it now, sure the whole of Lakelands knew. 'That I wasn't his daughter?'

'Yes.' Rick was studying her keenly. 'That's what was in the diary, yes?'

'Yes. Did you know it was that eejit from the shop? Patrick?'

'I did. Though he wasn't all bad, I shouldn't think.'

'He was. He didn't hang around when the chips were down, did he? He just threw money at my mother and ran off.' She was getting angry now. 'And did he ever come to find me? No.' She took a huge gulp of wine.

'Would you have wanted him to?' Rick had angled his body towards her. Dressed in a western-style shirt and denims, all he needed was a cowboy hat and a horse.

'No, no way. But, you know, it might have shown he cared.'

Rick nodded and turned back to the television. They watched the battle for the hive. After a bit, Rick said, 'Imagine if he had turned up, especially when you were young, it might have messed things up at home with your parents.'

That was true, Deirdre supposed, but things at home had been a bit messed up anyway. 'She went a bit mad, my mother, I think,' she blurted out.

'What?'

'The diary, it's making me remember things I'd

forgotten. I mean, I remember her taking to her bed, and she wouldn't get up or talk or anything. Remember I told June that, but then there's other stuff. Stuff I didn't understand at the time so I kind of forgot it. She was taken off in an ambulance once.'

'Really?' Rick sounded surprised. 'Maybe she was ill.'

Deirdre scrunched up her face. 'Maybe. But she was fine just before. They took her in an ambulance. We'd just got back from Dublin. We went there for the day. Everyone cried.' She shrugged. 'I dunno. It's a long time ago. When she came home, no one ever talked about it.'

'Well, maybe the diary will clear it up for you.' Rick's arm found its way about her shoulder. 'My advice is: more wine and less worry. All I know is that Lily loved you and loved Jimmy. She told me that.'

Deirdre gave a wan smile.

'Now,' Rick teased, breaking the sombre mood, 'what is the story between you and your boss?'

'The story?' Deirdre coloured up. 'There's no story.' Her wine slopped onto her skirt. 'I don't know what you mean. He's gardening. I'm helping him. No story.'

'You bring him here for tea all the time now. You talk about your parents. He makes you blush.'

'He's my boss. He ruined my radio show. He told me I was a . . .' – Deirdre sought out the word – 'dictator before he came along. I—'

Rick held up his hand. 'If you say so. I'll tell you one thing though,' he said, looking serious all of a sudden, 'if you like him, don't let him go. Even if it ruins things, tell him how you feel.'

'Eh, I'd get fired,' Deirdre looked away and tried to make a joke. 'I can't stand the man and telling him that would be job suicide.'

'Just saying,' Rick sat back and took another glug of wine. 'You think you're old, wait until you get to my age. No regrets, Deirdre, that's the only way to be happy.'

She clinked her glass off his. 'No regrets.'

THE NINTH WEDNESDAY

Zoe took the diary and found that a number of scattered pages were Sellotaped together. They looked as if they'd been written at different times. She had just started when Carrie arrived in, flapping her hand and apologising for being late.

'If my mother-in-law comes looking for me, I'm not here,' she said, ducking behind the bed. 'Go on.'

Rick stood up. 'What does she look like? I'll bring her to the canteen.'

'Aw, Rick, would you? She's due here in five minutes and I want to hear this. You can't miss her, she's like Reese Witherspoon from *Legally Blonde* only way older.'

Rick looked impressed.

'Don't you want to hear this?' Deirdre asked him as he made to leave. 'You haven't been here in weeks.'

'You can fill me in,' Rick said and left.

Deirdre stared after him, feeling a little exasperated.

April 1961

The local doctor has said that if I write things down I might understand them. What he doesn't understand is that I've been writing things down all my life and still understand nothing.

Why was the doctor called? I don't know. I think Jimmy got worried because I can't get up. I try, I do, but the greyness is everywhere. It's a flat, dead colour and I wake up in the morning and it's seeping in through the windows and under the door, like a grey ghost coming for my mind. I have to stay really still and close my eyes so that it won't go into my eyeballs and through my brain because it will make me grey, like everyone else here. So I pull the covers up and close my eyes.

Deirdre came into the room today, tiny little thing, pushing the door open, letting the grey billow in and swallow her up and I had to save her. I screamed at her to get out, to leave. I pushed her off the bed and she hit her head and cried, and I told her to get out. To escape or the greyness would get her too. She'd be like me. Then they got the doctor. I think that's why.

June 1961

Deirdre loves Jimmy. Jimmy loves Deirdre. I stand in the kitchen and feel left out as I watch them on the bright days, when the sun scares the grey off. He holds out his hand, she takes his and his big hand swallows hers up. She's only three and a bit but already she plods around the farm after him, chattering away like a little duckling. I wish I could be them, so happy and content, but I can't. Sometimes, I damp down the scrabbling part of me and shut it closed like a big lid and I try to just be where I am. I try. I like it best when Deirdre wraps her arm around my neck and hugs me hard. Her hugs have power. They really do.

Jimmy brings me bunches of flowers from the fields to make me smile. He's been doing it since we were fifteen or so. I try to smile, but sometimes I can't. On those days, Jimmy puts the flowers in water himself.

September 1961

Deirdre is three today. She puts her hands on her hips and sticks out her tummy whenever anyone asks her. 'I'm three,' she says.

Jimmy made her a rocking horse. He spent ages in the shed carving it out and it's a beautiful thing. Deirdre says she will ride all over the world in it. Then she says that maybe she won't. She wants to stay at home. She wants to be with me and her daddy always. She wants to live in her house always.

Oh to be three.

December 1961

Today Deirdre asked me why I'm sad. She's getting big. She talks all the time now. Her face is bright and sunny and her voice high and singsongy.

'I'll make you happy, Mammy,' she said. 'I'll do whatever you want.'

I caught her face in mine. 'You just be you,' I said to her. 'That will make me happy.'

'So you **are** sad,' she said.

'When you make me happy, how can I be sad?'

May 1962

Ann Morrisey has married Patsy Junior. Apparently her wedding was the biggest wedding the town has ever seen. I saw a picture of them in the paper. She wore a long empire-line dress and her hair was piled up on top of her head like a pineapple. She looked happy. I haven't seen anyone smile so big in my life. My mother said that she's wearing Patsy's dead wife's ring. She drove through the town in an open-topped car and waved out at everyone like a queen. That's the sort of thing that'll keep this place in talk for a month.

Still, I hope she'll be happy. Patsy Junior is a fine-looking man.

September 1962

Deirdre caught a butterfly today. She put it in a jar for me to look at. Its bright wings beat against the glass, not able to understand why it couldn't get out. I started to cry and I shouted at Deirdre. I shook her shoulders hard. She's only just four. I took the jar off her and set the creature free. Then I hugged Deirdre. I think I scared her.

She said she will never make me sad again.

CHAPTER 34

On Friday, Zoe, her palms slick with nerves, her throat dry, tried to look stern. 'Now, Ronnie,' she said, 'no matter what happens, you keep your cool or this will be the last concert you ever do.'

'Do I look stupid to you?' Ronnie glared at her. 'You've told me that twenty-six times now. No, make that twenty-seven.'

'I know. Let's make it twenty-eight, shall we? Do *not* lose your cool.'

Ronnie snorted.

'You're brilliant, remember that. You'll win them over, even the rowdy ones.' The rowdy ones consisted of Ronnie's ex-pals who had shunned him ever since he'd been caught cheating at cards. These men had ensconced themselves at the front of the room, frowning in a most unsupportive way.

'Now, ye lot,' Zoe crossed to them, 'behave or I'll ban you from here.'

'Aw, reminds me of my twenties when I was banned from every pub in town,' Len said proudly. 'Best days of my life.'

The others chuckled.

'Hmm,' Zoe said. 'Did they kick you up the arse for good measure?'

'I wouldn't mind you kicking me up the arse,' Charlie, the oldest member of the group, said and the other two whooped as Charlie preened himself.

Zoe smirked and moved on. The place was really filling up. Her eyes scanned the room, wondering if . . . and there, right at the back, sinking into a chair and attempting to hide behind one of the other residents, could that be . . . yes, it was. Zoe grinned widely. Excellent. Now they could start.

She gave Ronnie a nod.

'Can yez all shut up!' Ronnie shouted loudly over the noise. Then even more loudly and aimed at his one-time friends in the front row. 'I said shut up! I'm starting.'

'Starting what?' Len asked. 'Entertaining us or cheating at cards?'

'Len!' Zoe snapped, moving up the room.

However, Ronnie ignored his ex-best friend and wheeled himself to the piano. 'These songs will be familiar to you all,' he roared, 'so sing along if you like.' Lifting up his hands, he composed himself before launching into a rousing rendition of 'Molly, My Irish Molly', the piano banging out the tune.

Those residents who could, began to sing along, though Zoe heard Len changing the lyrics to 'Lolly, where's my lolly? You cheating bastard dear . . .'

But Ronnie, thoroughly enjoying his audience, either didn't hear it or didn't care.

*　　*　　*

Deirdre's arm was almost healed and she wore only a light bandage as she climbed into Paul's car that afternoon. 'Give me a pair of gardening gloves and I'll be able to get down in the dirt with you today,' she said.

Paul grinned and winked at her.

Deirdre realised suddenly how her comment had sounded and she gave a little embarrassed laugh. 'You do know what I meant, of course.'

Paul glanced sideways at her. 'Yep.'

He sounded fed up as if he was in no doubt what she had meant. Deirdre squirmed. She wondered if he thought she was a . . . her mind stalled on the word before finally pushing it out, a *prude*. She knew she got uptight about things and yet, it was so not who she wanted to be. It was probably from years of living on her own and having no sex. Or, the thought crossed her mind, years of worrying about her mother, unable to properly relax, wondering what on earth Lily was going to do next. 'I'm not a prude,' she said suddenly, sitting up straight and eyeballing him. 'I can take a joke as good as anyone.'

Paul spluttered out a laugh. 'Where did that come from?'

'You. The way you look at me. The sarcastic way you said "Yep".'

He looked genuinely confused.

'Doesn't matter,' she said then. 'Forget it.'

★   ★   ★

Ronnie came to the end of his act. He beamed proudly around and ignored the booing that was coming from a certain section of the audience.

'Well, everyone,' Zoe said over the noise, 'thanks for coming. You'll be happy to know that Ronnie will be in residence in the hall every first Saturday of the month.'

There was more clapping. Ronnie looked thrilled. Zoe had kept it as a surprise for him. Then she bent down and said softly, into Ronnie's ear, 'Look down near the door, see who came.' She watched as Ronnie's eyes fixed on the red-headed woman who had just stood up. 'I wrote to her and told her you were performing and she came. Why don't you go and talk to her, and be civil for God's sake.'

'Veronica?' Ronnie said softly. 'She came to see me?'

'Yes, she did.' Zoe eyeballed him firmly.

Ronnie quickly squeezed Zoe's hand in a silent thanks before wheeling himself towards Veronica, banging into anyone who wasn't quick enough to get out of his way. Zoe watched as he caught up with his daughter and she smiled and gushingly told him how good he had been, or at least that's what it looked like from her vantage point. The next thing she saw was Veronica wheeling her dad in the direction of the canteen.

They worked in silence, Deirdre pointing out where she wanted him to dig, while she tenderly planted the flowers and shrubs she'd ordered from the garden centre. This was her favourite part of the process. Giving plants a home and a place they could grow.

The beds were taking shape and Deirdre instructed Paul on the best places to plant this season's flowers. With regular planting, there would be no part of the year when something would not be blossoming in this garden. As she dropped in some bedding plants for colour, she found herself explaining in detail to Paul about her vision for the future of the garden. She talked and talked, her hands gesturing as she explained how some things would grow, how tall they'd be, how they'd need pruning. Paul leaned on his shovel and watched her, his head to one side. He was so quiet and so attentive, that finally she became self-conscious and her enthusiasm waned and she shuddered to a grinding halt.

'Sorry for going on,' she apologised, fixing her bandana and hunkering down again to plant something else.

'You didn't,' he said. 'You're, I dunno, totally compelling when you talk about gardening. I love listening to you.'

Deirdre shrugged and moved some soil away with her hands, before planting a purple petunia. 'Yeah, well, it's why I got the job here, isn't it?'

'Is it?'

Deirdre looked up at him. The sun was behind him and she had to squint. She shaded her eyes. 'Yes, I used to work in the Botanic Gardens. I loved it. I did it for about twenty-five years. Then one day RTÉ came to interview me about some disease that was killing oak trees and next thing, every radio station in the country was on to me. I took the job here because it was less work and more pay. I was like this hot-shot star for a while.'

Paul was silent. He crossed towards her and hunkered down too. He began scooping out some earth. 'Why did you take this job if you loved your other one? You don't seem like a less work and more pay kind of girl.'

Deirdre paused, startled at his insight. Money had never motivated her, it was true. 'Well, everyone thought it was a great opportunity. My mother was proud as punch.' She handed him a petunia. 'And it was fun, I suppose.' She turned to him; he was closer than she'd thought, his face inches from hers. His lips were slightly parted, his eyes, sexily sleepy looking. His breath wafted across her cheeks. He reached out and fixed her bandana.

She wondered if he felt the 'zing' that she imagined was there. She definitely liked being near him. He made her feel alive, the way a patch of sun illuminates a dull spot.

'And is it fun now?' he asked. His hand lingered near her hair and she wanted to scream at him to touch her, just once. But he didn't. He did seem to be watching her intently though and Deirdre felt a lurch somewhere inside but, damn it, she was no good at reading signals, as she had proved so well in the car on the way over. So she just nodded and said that, yes, she was enjoying herself and would he mind handing her the trowel.

He seemed a little agitated as he hopped up. He didn't crouch down beside her again.

CHAPTER 35

'I believe the concert with Ronnie went well,' Dominic said as he hopped into Zoe's car that evening. 'That must be a relief for you.'

'You have no idea.' Zoe wiped mock sweat from her brow. 'I'm still shaking.'

Dominic grinned and peeled off his denim jacket, tossing it onto the back seat of her car. He was wearing a yellow T-shirt that showed off surprisingly muscular biceps.

Zoe caught her breath, then berated herself. Lack of Abe was causing her to think of Dominic in an unnervingly sexual way. Even today as he laid out the lunches, she had admired his long fingers and clean oval-shaped nails. And really, whoever heard of a set of fingernails turning someone on? But they had. Scarily they had. She blamed *Getting Over Oliver* with its loose sexual content. Oh dear, she had to force her gaze away from him and back onto the road as Dominic stretched, lay back in the seat, hands behind his head, his T-shirt riding up and giving her a glimpse of toned stomach.

'You OK?' Dominic asked. 'You look a bit hot.'

'I'm fine.' She pressed a bit too hard on the accelerator and the car shot forwards.

Dominic grabbed the door handle for support. When the car slowed again, he said, 'I was hoping to ask June for a few days off, to be with Dad. D'you think she'll be OK with that?'

'Oh, yeah,' Zoe was surprised at the question. 'June won't mind. She understands those things. How could she not, working at what she does?'

Dominic nodded. 'Yeah, good point. I'll ask the next time I'm in.'

'Do.' She turned on her radio and Gary Sims, talking about the state of the country in his uniquely comic way, made her smile. He was comparing the state of the banks to how he felt after a binge drinking session.

'He's the best radio presenter in the country,' Dominic grinned. 'No matter how crappy my life gets, I think of his and feel great.'

Zoe grinned at him. 'I know. Me too.'

They shared a laugh.

'I was wondering if you'd like to go out with me sometime,' Dominic said, startling her so much that she swerved, causing her car to bump up onto the kerb, wobble a little before bouncing back down onto the road. In the boot something rattled.

'Eh, if you don't want to come, just say so, there's no need to try and kill yourself.'

'Sorry.' Zoe smiled, 'You just surprised me.'

'Just as a thank you for the lifts,' Dominic said hastily. 'It's not like a date or anything.'

Her heart nosedived. So did her ego. It would have been nice if he'd asked her on a date. It would serve Abe right for one thing. 'It's off with Abe, so if it was a date it wouldn't be a problem.' She tried to make a joke, but it came out sounding a little twisted and bitter.

Dominic shifted about in his seat, looking a tad unconvinced. 'OK, if you're up to going out.' He elbowed her and said teasingly, 'I can be your rebound date.'

Zoe smiled. 'You don't have to. I like giving you lifts. I like the company.'

'Me too. But I'd like to say thanks. So, does tomorrow suit you or is that too short notice? Rosie is away on Sunday, so I'm in the hospital all that day which means I've tomorrow night off.'

'Tomorrow is great. I'd love to. My mum doesn't mind babysitting on Saturdays.'

'Great,' Dominic smiled. 'Now, I've no transport and I'm sure you'd like a drink, so let's say I meet you in the city centre, outside the Stephen's Green Centre, at about seven?'

'Perfect. Where are we going?'

'A surprise,' he tapped his nose. 'But you'll like it.'

A surprise. She loved surprises, Abe had surprised her a lot in the early days with quirky days out and CDs of music for her. But with Lee's arrival, which was ironically the biggest surprise of all, he'd stopped doing anything like that. Zoe smiled at Dominic, batting the sudden sadness away. 'I like it already,' she said.

CHAPTER 36

Zoe wished she knew exactly where Dominic was taking her. She was fairly certain that it wouldn't be a madly expensive place, so she had gone for a smart casual look. Her mother had told her she looked lovely, which made her seriously doubt her choice but it had been too late to change. She wore an asymmetrical, brightly coloured skirt and a white top.

She arrived outside the Stephen's Green Centre at five to seven and wondered if she should wander into a coffee shop and leave him waiting a few minutes. Was it a little too eager to arrive first? She knew her mother would certainly think so, but her mother didn't know Dominic. Zoe doubted that he'd read anything into the fact that she was early. He didn't seem the kind of guy to play those silly games. Sort of like Jimmy in Lily's diary. Zoe smiled at the thought. Reading the diary was having a weird effect on her. It was as if she was making Patrick–Jimmy connections all over the place. Abe had been very firmly placed in the Patrick camp now, since Patrick had defected on Lily when she needed him most. She was just

386

fishing out her mobile to ring her mother and check on Lee when Dominic joined her.

Oh *my*, she thought. Shaved, scrubbed and wearing a pair of black trousers, black leather jacket, a grey shirt and a matching grey tie, he looked sensational. Or might that just be an understatement? Zoe's heart fluttered like a piece of bunting in a strong breeze.

He smiled down at her. 'You look great.'

More heart fluttering only this time it was the thrill of the compliment. How long had it been since she had been told she looked great? How long had it been since a guy showed such open approval for her? Dominic was staring at her, with those seductive eyes, as if she was a new and coveted toy he'd been given to play with. Hmm, maybe not the best comparison, Zoe berated herself. 'You look good yourself,' she said lightly. 'You scrub up well.'

He held out his arm. 'I hope you're hungry,' he said as she linked her arm with his.

'Dinner? You're taking me to dinner?' The last time she'd been out for dinner she had blubbered all over the pizzas. This time it was highly unlikely she'd be able to eat anything having had chips and a burger before she left. 'Where are we going?'

'I told you,' he said, 'it's a surprise.'

They walked down Grafton Street, before cutting up Suffolk Street, heading towards the Powerscourt Centre. Just before they reached it, Dominic stopped outside a small green door. 'Here we are.'

They were standing outside Shandon's, one of the most expensive places to eat in Dublin. Zoe looked at Dominic, then gazed at the humble doorway. 'Shandon's?' she asked. Damn her burger and chips, she thought.

'Uh-huh. Great, eh? In you go.'

'This is, well,' she lowered her voice, 'really expensive.'

'No!' Dominic lowered his voice to match hers. 'You're joking.'

Zoe flushed.

'I've booked it,' he went on as if he was some sort of a millionaire. 'We have to go in now or I'll have to pay a cancellation fee.' He pushed open the door and a member of staff, better dressed than Zoe, came to greet them.

'Dominic Ryan,' Dominic said. 'I booked a table for half past.'

'Of course, Mr Ryan. Come this way please. The table is at the back of the restaurant as you requested.'

Dominic followed the man and Zoe, feeling as if she were dreaming, followed Dominic. She was so busy admiring his tight ass that she almost missed the Brad Pitt lookalike in the corner. Or, no, holy shit, was that *actually* him and Angelina? It was. She was certain of it. Would it be very uncool to yank at Dominic's jacket and point them out to him? She peered across the restaurant and Brad turned towards her. Zoe felt that if she were to die right then, she'd die happy. She had seen

Brad Pitt in the flesh. Dominic had walked on. Zoe scuttled to catch him up.

'And here we are.' The waiter was pulling out a chair for Zoe.

She thanked him and sat down. The waiter handed them their menus and the wine list. When he left, Zoe leaned across the table and hissed, 'Brad Pitt is over there.'

'Where?' Dominic swivelled on his chair and sucked in his breath. 'Oh, wow, so is Angelina. I could quite happily die now looking at that view.'

Zoe laughed loudly. 'That's what I was thinking!'

Dominic gave a final look at Angelina before turning back to Zoe. 'The view is not bad here either though,' he grinned.

'Hmm,' Zoe was unconvinced. 'I like your style, full points for effort.' Then lowering her voice again, she whispered, 'I don't mean to be rude Dominic, but how can you afford this? Look,' she pointed to her menu, 'they don't even have prices written down.'

'I do it all the time,' Dominic said back, 'book and run.'

'*Run?*' Zoe looked confused.

Dominic's grin widened. 'Book and run,' he repeated slowly. 'I book a table, we eat and then run away.'

Zoe's mouth almost hit the table. 'Sorry?'

He winked at her. 'Just don't eat too much because they tend to catch you then.'

'I can't, I mean, I just couldn't—' she was

hyperventilating. She fanned herself with the menu. 'Oh, I'm—'

'Dominic, my man,' a guy in chef's whites appeared at their table. Zoe jumped, wondering if he was going to throw them out.

He and Dominic did some sort of happy-clappy thing with hands before embracing and laughing. It was Craig Marshall from *Celebrity Chef*. He ran Shandon's.

'How are you doing?' He was still focused on Dominic, his accent a strange mix of US and European.

'Not as well as you, you jammy bastard,' Dominic pulled away and fisted Craig's arm. 'I see you're still fooling everyone with your fancy shit.'

Zoe gasped. Craig Marshall was notoriously temperamental, but not with Dominic it seemed. He threw back his bushy dark head and chortled with laugher. 'Jealously will get you nowhere, my friend. Green isn't your colour. So how you been? How's your dad?'

'In hospital,' Dominic said. 'Not so good. I'm taking some days off work to be with him. Oh, this is Zoe, by the way. Zoe, this is Craig. An old college pal.'

'So you're not—' Zoe asked Dominic as Craig pumped her arm up and down. Dominic's answer was a roll of eyes and she felt weak with relief. She was not a good runner. 'Hello, Craig,' she said, a little bit celebrity struck. 'I love you on *Celebrity Chef*.'

'You always had good taste in girlfriends,' Craig said. 'Great to meet you, Zoe.'

'Oh, I'm not—'

'Craig was the star in college,' Dominic interrupted her as he explained their connection. 'We all hated him.'

Craig laughed again. 'Dominic wasn't such a bad chef either,' he said. 'But, yeah, I was better.'

Zoe smiled.

'Anyway, sit down and enjoy. Delighted you could come. Dom, I'll talk to you when you're finished if that's OK?'

'No prob.'

'I'd recommend the crab starter and the lamb as a main.' He punched Dominic on the shoulder, 'Great to see you. Give your old man my best.'

'I will.'

As Craig left their table, Angelina waved him over to hers and Zoe's eyes boggled. 'You never told me you had famous friends,' she whispered, impressed.

'He's just Craig to me,' Dominic said. 'We hung out a lot together in college and he's always on at me to eat here, but when I do he never charges, so I hate taking advantage.' He smiled across the table at her. 'But I wanted to bring you somewhere special.'

His words were balm to her battered ego. And the sincere way he was looking at her filled her up. 'You did?' As he nodded, she reached across and touched his hand, 'Thanks.'

He squeezed her hand in response and his

half-grin made her breath catch in her throat. Her gaze was suddenly riveted to his Adam's apple, just above his shirt collar, and she couldn't look away. In the silence that followed, her heartbeat picked up pace and time zinged and stretched out with possibility.

'And before you go thinking this is a cheap date, well, first off it's not a date, is it?' Dominic's voice was like a hacksaw on a peaceful summer's day. He released her hand. 'And, second, I do fully intend to pay for the drinks and the wine we have here and the taxi home.'

'Right,' Zoe nodded, feeling as if he'd just thrown a bucket of icy water over her. 'Let's order the wine so.'

'Yes, let's.' Dominic hailed the waiter.

Suzi called over on Saturday brandishing a bottle of wine and a box of chocolates. She arrived just as Rick was heading out.

'Hi,' Rick smiled at her. 'Suzi, right?'

Deirdre was impressed. Rick had only met Suzi once before. Though as she was loud, bubbly and talkative, once met, Suzi was hard to forget.

'Rick, right?' Suzi bantered back, pulling off her coat and draping it over the banisters. 'How're the dogs?'

'Just heading out to them now,' Rick beamed. 'One of the lads has the inside track tonight. We're in for a couple of big wins we reckon.' He tapped his nose and winked.

'I'll let you take me out on your winnings,' Suzi cackled.

'Will that man of yours not get jealous?' Rick countered smartly. 'Most men find me a threat.'

Suzi laughed loudly and as Rick left, she turned to Deirdre saying, 'He's great. You're so lucky he was around to look after you.'

Rick had been great, Deirdre had to admit, even if he'd turned her quiet little cottage into Grand Central Station. It seemed that he knew the whole of Dublin and her little house had buzzed with life these past couple of weeks, from his betting cronies, to the Alzheimer's crowd to people he had met while shopping in Lidl. She'd miss the noise when he left.

'Open that, would you, I'm gasping.' Suzi handed her the wine before flopping on the sofa and making it groan. 'Just taking the weight off the floor,' she laughed.

Deirdre went in search of a corkscrew.

'I thought I'd call over and tell you all the gossip.'

'Gossip?' The bottle was screw top, Deirdre realised. She poured two glasses of wine, located a packet of nachos and a dip and brought it all in on a tray. 'What gossip?'

'Have you talked to Paul?' Suzi took her wine and sipped.

'Not since our recording yesterday afternoon.' Deirdre sat beside her. 'Did you see the job we did on the garden?'

'Well, he's resigned.'

'What?' Deirdre shot up in her seat. 'Why?' A few weeks ago, that would have made her happy. Now she felt a little bereft. 'Why has he gone?'

Suzi shrugged. 'Big row with Michael apparently. In the garden youse were making. No one is saying anything much. I thought you might know, everyone's talking about how he's spending so much time with you.'

'He's just doing a garden with me.'

Suzi shrugged. 'Well, apparently, Michael Allen is raging. Gary Sims said Michael was like a . . .' – she screwed up her face as she tried to paraphrase – 'like a mental patient in a straitjacket at lunch.'

Deirdre grinned before remembering that Paul was gone. 'That's terrible news,' she said.

'I thought you'd be glad,' Suzi elbowed her. 'It'll be your show again. Well, until they find some other pain in the hole,' she laughed.

That was a bit rough, Deirdre thought. She glanced sideways at Suzi, who sat there drinking contentedly. Some thought fluttered in the corner of her brain and she reached out to catch it. 'But I remember you said you thought his ideas were good,' she said.

Suzi shrugged.

'You liked him,' Deirdre pressed again.

'He was OK.' Suzi made a face and smiled at Deirdre. 'Not like us – we were hot.'

With a slight shock, like a camera flash going off unexpectedly, Deirdre saw the reality of the situation. 'We really weren't, Suzi.'

Suzi opened her mouth to say something but,

whatever it was, at Deirdre's expression, her smile died a little. A slow flush spread over her face.

'Tell me.' Deirdre laid her wine on the table and kept her voice calm, having to ask the question, yet dreading the response. 'Did I terrify you when I was in charge?'

'No!' Suzi flapped a hand and spluttered out a weak laugh. 'No way.'

Deirdre said nothing, just continued to stare at Suzi, knowing the woman was lying and horrified at the knowledge. 'Suzi,' she said as the silence stretched on, 'tell me the truth. Were people scared of me?'

'A little, I guess.' Suzi wriggled uncomfortably. 'You were pretty forceful sometimes. Matt and Emma were terrified.'

She had terrified two young kids. How awful was she? And she hadn't meant to. She'd just liked things done a certain way. 'So if I terrified you all so much, how come you're happy that I'll be back in charge?' Deirdre asked carefully.

Suzi flushed.

'You only came here tonight to save your skin, didn't you?' Deirdre said.

A hesitation before Suzi nodded. 'Yes, I did. And do you know why? Because if anyone knows about self-interest it's you.'

'Me?' This was terrible. It was as if Suzi was holding up a new mirror to the one she had of herself. Like the way Lily had done on certain aspects of her past.

'Yeah,' Suzi surprised her by sounding suddenly angry. 'All you ever talked about was you and the show. That day you rang me and Robbie answered the phone, you didn't know who he was, did you?'

'Well, not exactly—'

'Despite the fact that I told you about him a dozen times!'

Deirdre opened her mouth to defend herself and couldn't. It was true, she'd never really had any interest in other people's relationships. She'd always found the details too embarrassing and emotional. And Suzi was liable to get quite graphic.

'You never listened to any of my ideas for the show. And I wouldn't mind, but what would you even know? You are a gardener and you don't even have a life. I mean, what is this?' Suzi gestured around the room. 'It's like something from the nineteen fifties. You're stuck Deirdre, you're stuck in your life, you're stuck in your show. You don't want to hear of anyone else getting on, so you make them stick too.'

'That's not true!' Deirdre shouted, almost frightening herself. She'd never shouted in her life. 'I think you should go.'

'Pleasure.' Suzi flounced from the room and then flounced back in again, taking her wine this time. Then she slammed the front door so hard, the house shook.

Damn, Deirdre thought. 'Damn, damn, damn.'

*　　*　　*

396

The food was really weird, Zoe thought. It was beautifully presented but in teeny-tiny portions. The flavours were so condensed and strong, she thought she was going to gag. And what was the deal with the waiters in their white gloves with their French accents? She could barely understand a word they said. But she smiled gamely and ate everything, even though the burger seemed to be rumbling ominously in her stomach.

Dominic on the other hand was in heaven. He kept shaking his head over every bit of food that came his way, and playing 'guess-the-way-it's-been-cooked-and-the-ingredients-added' games with the waiters. 'He's a genius,' he mouthed on two occasions. 'I'd never have thought of putting star anise in the meat, but, wow, it really works.'

Zoe wondered what the hell star anise was, but Dominic's enthusiasm was endearing and Zoe found that she got more pleasure out of watching him eat than anything else.

'What you looking at?'

Zoe became suddenly aware that she was gazing at him across the table, chin cupped in the palm of her hand, a gloopy, sloppy grin plastered across her face. She gave herself a mental shake and sat up straight. 'You,' she answered. 'You're making me laugh. I never knew a plate of food could be so fascinating.'

'Oh, yeah,' Dominic nodded. 'But only in the right hands. Craig is amazing. He totally deserves this place.'

'I prefer your food,' Zoe said. 'At least when you serve it up, I don't feel that I have to find a picture frame for it.'

Dominic spluttered with laughter. 'Yeah, I know what you mean. Craig's food is like the clothes you see on a catwalk, a work of art. My stuff is the high-street version.'

'No it's—'

'And I don't mind that,' Dominic said, 'I do what I do well and I love what I do and that's all that matters. But I totally admire this stuff.' He held up a forkful of what to Zoe looked like suds and ate it. 'Fantastic.'

And that was what was so attractive about the man, Zoe realised. It wasn't his looks, it was way more than that. It was his ability to be so totally at home with himself. He didn't strive for brilliance; he didn't need the rat race. He seemed to delight in the success of his friends without feeling bad about his own hand in life. He had never been defensive about living in his parents' place or working in an old folks' home, which is what she'd thought he should be feeling, because that's how she felt. 'You are really happy, aren't you?' The question popped out of her mouth before she could stop it.

'Yeah,' he looked surprised, 'course I am. Why? Should I not be?'

She shook her head. 'No, it's really good. I really like that.' The admission made her feel sad. 'I really do.' She stood up and excused herself to go to the bathroom. She was not going to blubber at another meal. She just wasn't.

Deirdre sat for a long time in the silence of her front room, alternately thinking and then trying not to think about what Suzi had said. She wondered if she'd said it in anger, but thought not because it was bloody true. Deirdre was stuck. If she were honest, she'd known that for a while. She'd been stuck since she'd let John go. And that decision still eluded her. And maybe that had led to the blocking out of Suzi's happiness, she didn't know. Oh, God, she was a terrible person. And to think that she'd terrified Matt and Emma. How could she have done that? Because they had their youth and she was jealous? Deirdre felt tears slide down her face and didn't bother to wipe them away. Her youth was gone, her fertility withered like a dry leaf, she had nothing except happy memories of a father, who wasn't even her real dad, who had been dead years. Nothing except the memory of a house exactly like the one she was living in. Except the original had changed and was now bright and sunny and modern, while her little cottage was stuck too.

She jumped as the sitting room door was pushed open. She hadn't even heard Rick come in. At first, he didn't notice her attempts to wipe her tears away as he was on a high. 'We won on the last dog,' he said triumphantly. 'Oh, we were losing big up until then, it was like our dogs had three legs with no eyes. I swear Deirdre, it was shocking and—' He paused before taking a long look at her. 'What happened here?'

'Nothing.'

Concerned, he sat in beside her.

Deirdre glanced sideways at him. And realised that this hair-dyeing, Lidl-shopping gambler was her only friend in the world. 'I've been awful,' she began haltingly, before unleashing her story on him at a rate of knots.

If Rick got confused with all the names, he said nothing. 'Just do what you think is right,' he finally pronounced.

It seemed such a small sentence after her tirade. 'I would have thought that at eighty you'd have better advice than that.' Deirdre choked out a laugh.

'There is no better advice than that, kid,' Rick smiled.

An hour later, having consumed two bottles of wine, Zoe's head was spinning nicely and she had that lovely I'm-at-peace-with-the-world feeling. Dominic looked as if he felt the same. He was almost poured across the table as he told her a joke, his hand swaying, and she was laughing even before the punchline, though she'd forgotten what the beginning of the joke had been, which only made her laugh harder.

'Hey, how'd you enjoy the meal?' Craig slid into the seat between them.

'Lovely,' Zoe nodded. 'Pity I ate the burger and chips before I came though.'

'You didn't!' Dominic sounded a bit devastated. 'Why?'

'Because I didn't know we were going for dinner, did I?' Zoe said. 'You never told me. I didn't want my stomach rumbling when I was sitting beside you in a pub.'

'You'd have no objection from me,' Dominic said, shaking his head. 'You beside me would be enough.'

'Awww.' Zoe scrunched up her face. 'That is so nice.'

'And the food, Dom?' Craig interrupted, poking his face between them. 'Was that so nice?'

Craig sure knew how to ruin a moment, Zoe thought, drawing back and folding her arms.

'I loved it,' Dominic tore his gaze from Zoe and turned to his friend. 'You could have done with some sort of vanilla in the apple sauce though, might have made it less acidic.'

'And that is why I give you free food,' Craig pronounced grandly, plucking a notebook and pen from his pocket. 'Brilliant,' he said as he wrote it down. 'Anything else?'

Dominic looked at Zoe, who shrugged a 'go ahead'.

'OK,' Dominic scrunched up his face as he tried to think. 'Too much wine has deadened the brain,' he grinned. He winked at Zoe as he said it and she suddenly found it difficult to take her eyes off him as he and Craig got into a rather long discussion about the flavours and the reasons for adding this and that into bits of meat.

'There's a job here if ever you want it,' Craig said as the conversation wound down. He tucked his notebook away and turned to Zoe. 'I've offered him work loads of times, can you convince him to throw in his lot at the old folks' home and work with me?'

'I like my old folks' home,' Dominic said.

'And we like him at the old folks' home,' Zoe said.

Craig snorted and, pushing his chair back, he stood up. 'Right, well, I'll let the two of you alone now. Enjoy the rest of your night.'

'Might as well settle up,' Dominic said, signalling a waiter for the bill.

'No charge,' Craig waved him away.

'Yeah. But we had wine, I want to pay for that.'

Craig tapped his notebook. 'Hey, your ideas for improving the flavours are worth more than two bottles of wine, Dom.' Turning to Zoe, he said, 'Can you get him out of that habit? He totally underestimates himself. Safe home now.' He gave them a half-salute.

Dominic looked slightly annoyed. 'I'd like to pay. Zoe will think I'm a scabby shite if I don't pay.' He stood up, swaying slightly, as he attempted to dig some money from his trouser pockets.

'Well I'm sure he'll be able to pay for you the next time he brings you out, eh?' Craig asked Zoe, smiling.

'Put the money into a charity box,' Zoe evaded the question. 'Come on.' She linked Dominic's arm in hers. 'Let's go. Thanks, Craig.'

Dominic glowered. 'Last time I come here,' he said.

'Nah, you love the food too much,' Craig chortled as Dominic gave him the finger.

The night air was cool but not unpleasant. It was late and the pubs were closing. 'Can't even bring you for a drink,' Dominic said mournfully.

'It doesn't matter.' Zoe buttoned up her coat and sank her hands into the pockets. 'I had a lovely time.'

'Did you?' he sounded pleased. 'That's good.'

They walked side by side back up Grafton Street, Dominic's arm tipping off hers every now and again. There was a companionable silence between them. When they reached the top, Dominic gestured to a row of taxis. 'Over there.'

'Would you like to keep walking?' Zoe asked suddenly, not wanting the night to end. For the first time in weeks, she felt totally content. OK, it was probably the wine, but who cared? She just wanted to hold on to this small bit of peace she had unexpectedly found. In six weeks' time, Abe would be back and they'd have to sort through the mess of their relationship and she'd have to move out and look for a place for her and Lee.

'Yeah. Why not?' Dominic said, grinning. 'In fact, why don't you come back to my place, have a coffee and I can call you a taxi from there.'

'Sounds like a plan.' She looked up at him.

'Cool.' He looked down at her.

Then without thinking, Dominic held out his hand and she took it.

Well, she reasoned, it would have made things awkward between them if she didn't.

Ninety minutes later, they arrived at Dominic's. They'd barely exchanged a word since they'd taken each other's hands. All that had transpired since was that Dominic had rubbed his thumb along the outside of her thumb and she'd found it oddly erotic. She wasn't even sure he was aware that he was doing it, so of course she couldn't tell him to stop or he might get embarrassed.

'Eh, I have to let go of you now,' Dominic said. 'Can't get my key out of my pocket.'

'Oh, yeah, sure.' Zoe tried to sound blasé about it. Her heart was still hammering from the extra squeeze he gave her hand as he dropped it.

'Sorry,' he said.

She tried not to look as he plunged his hand deep into his trouser pocket to extract his house key.

'Don't be sorry.' She strove for coolness but her voice was a little squeaky. 'You have to get your key, right?'

'That's right.' Dominic inserted the key into the front door and it opened with a click.

'I mean, if you didn't find your key, we couldn't have coffee, right?'

'That is true,' Dominic agreed, not looking at her as he entered his hallway and flicked on the light. 'Come in, I'll put the kettle on.'

'Sure.' Zoe closed the front door and followed him into the gorgeous kitchen.

She slid into a seat at the table and watched as he filled the kettle. In fact, she watched every little thing he did from flicking the switch, to bending down to look for biscuits, to the way he walked, slightly unsteadily, towards the table to put down the unopened packet of biscuits. Then he sunk his hands into his pockets and with his tie hanging loosely, he nodded. 'I'll, eh, call you a cab. How long do you think you'll stay?'

Was that a loaded question?

'Eh, well, I suppose until I drink my coffee, which will be . . .' she shrugged, 'I don't know, about an hour?'

If he thought an hour was a long time to drink a mug of coffee, he didn't say. 'OK, I'll ring later, when you've finished your coffee. They're only around the corner anyway.'

'OK.'

The kettle clicked off.

'That's the kettle,' he said.

'It is indeed.'

Neither of them moved.

The silence stretched. Dominic moved towards her, about to say something. Then pulled back. 'Right,' he said, thumbing towards the press. 'Coffee coming up.'

'Coffee, biscuits, whatever you want,' Zoe said.

The words hung in the air. Dominic froze midway across the floor.

'Well, obviously,' Zoe blundered on, 'I don't mean—' Dominic turned around and the words died on her lips.

'I want you, actually,' he said.

Zoe's gulp could be heard right across the room. She was powerless to say anything.

He wanted her.

He *wanted* her.

He wanted *her.*

Oh shit.

'Me?' she squeaked.

'I'm a bit drunk,' he said, shrugging. 'But I know what I'm doing. I've always wanted you, I think everyone in work knows it, including Lily.'

Zoe giggled. 'She has Alzheimer's.'

'Exactly. And even she knows.'

Zoe laughed, a little shocked, a little thrilled. A lot drunk.

'Only you were with Abe—'

'I was.' It seemed important to confirm that.

'And we worked together.' He was coming closer.

'Yes. We still do.'

'But seeing as you're here and I'm here and you held my hand, I thought I might as well just say it. Well, initially I hadn't intended on saying anything, but well then you said—'

'That was just an expression.'

'Oh.' He dropped his gaze. 'I see.'

But he didn't see. 'Well, I mean—'

He waved a hand to stop her. 'It's OK. I'll blank out your rejection with copious amounts of drugs and alcohol.' He cracked a half-embarrassed grin.

Rejection? Who had said anything about rejection? And, really, how could she resist that grin? How could *anybody*? Zoe's thoughts were as scattered and as disorganised as the wardrobes in her flat. But her body knew what it wanted. And she was a free agent. 'I didn't actually say I wasn't interested,' she said carefully, only slurring her words a tiny bit. 'Just that what I said before was an expression.'

'Oh.' He blinked a little. 'So, eh' – he shook his head – 'I'm confused.'

'You're very sexy and good looking and you can cook. And you do a mean hand hold.'

'I do?' he sounded surprised. Then amended it. 'I do.'

'And it is all over with Abe so I'm a free woman.' Zoe tossed her hair back in what she hoped was a wanton sexy display. It made her feel a bit dizzy.

'You are a free woman.' Dominic came over and stood in front of her. Taking her hand, he pulled her up beside him. 'So,' he asked, his voice husky, 'do you still want that coffee?'

She could almost taste him he was that close. Her mind suddenly joined forces with her body. 'No,' she said, 'coffee is so not what I want right now.'

A small smile worked its way onto his face. He

reached out and ran his hand along her arm. Zoe felt as if every part of her body was screaming for contact. She moved nearer him.

'What do you want then?' he asked. His hand fingered one of her curls.

'You,' she said. God, her mother would call her a brazen hussy, tell her it was no wonder she ended up pregnant.

Dominic's hand moved to her face, he ran his thumb across her chin and she groaned, closing her eyes. And then his lips were on hers, kissing her slowly and exquisitely and he groaned, and suddenly his arms had pressed her to him, hard, and he was running his hands all over her.

CHAPTER 37

The following day, Sunday, Zoe, her head banging, felt trapped between her parents and her brother. With her mother on her left, holding Lee's hand and her father on her right, they'd arrived outside Greg's apartment. Her dad was not happy to be there and he made his feelings known by refusing to smile at Greg when he answered the door. Her mother, on the other hand, in a terrible attempt to compensate, was hyper enthusiastic in her eagerness to meet Louis.

Zoe wished she was at home in bed with some painkillers. Her hangover was not abating, though that might be something to do with the steamy images of the previous night that kept popping into her head. If she'd thought Abe was good in bed . . .

'Oh,' Mrs Killeen exclaimed as Louis walked into the room. This was followed by an even more high-pitched and honestly impressed 'Oh.'

Zoe's head banged and she closed her eyes briefly. Dominic had 'nuzzled' her. Oh God . . .

'You're, well' – Mrs Killeen gaped at Louis – 'you're . . .' She flapped an arm, unable to think of a word to describe his beauty.

'I'm Louis,' Louis said, proffering his hand.

'Well, *hello*,' she said back, shaking his hand and making her hello sound somehow flirtatious.

Mr Killeen snorted.

Louis, sensing that his handshake might not be reciprocated by Greg's dad, grinned at Zoe before turning his attention to Lee. 'Hey, you must be Lee. I've heard loads about you.'

'Shouldn't have the child here,' Mr Killeen hissed to Zoe in an undertone. He'd been saying it ever since they'd met on the doorstep. Zoe ignored him. All she could see was Dominic covered in a fine film of sweat, kissing her across her stomach. She wrenched her mind away and gave Lee a poke in the arm to answer Louis.

'Yep, I am,' Lee nodded a little shyly. 'And you're Greg's boyfriend, aren't you?'

Mrs Killeen inhaled enough air to float into space. Her husband coughed loudly. Greg flushed as Louis nodded, 'I am.'

'So are you in looove?' Lee asked, making the word 'love' sound all mushy.

'That's a personal question, Lee,' Zoe said, as her father huffed and puffed and coughed loudly.

'If they're boyfriend and boyfriend they must love each other,' Lee stated with the irrefutable logic of a child.

'We do,' Louis answered and as Lee made kissy sounds, he said, 'Well, enough about that. Come on, let's eat.'

He led them into Greg's dining room where the

beautifully set table was heaving under copious amounts of food.

'Oh, wow!' Lee almost choked on his awe. 'Oh, wow, I've never seen so much food in my entire life. Oh, wow!'

His spluttering delight made the adults smile and Mr Killeen said in a gentle tone that belied his stern exterior, 'Well, Lee, you sit down there now and eat your fill.'

Lee dutifully plonked into a seat at the top of the table and Zoe sat alongside him. The food made her feel sick.

'So you're the one who can cook,' Mrs Killeen stated. Then she pronounced in the wise tone of someone unmasking the third secret of Fatima, 'There's always one that can cook.'

'Pardon?' Louis said, carving knife in hand.

'You know with gay people, one can always cook,' Mrs Killeen settled into her seat. 'They're usually the feminine ones. Greg was never feminine.' She beamed proudly at her son.

Zoe wished she could dissolve into the water which her dad was currently pouring for them all. She should have stayed at home.

'That could be construed as a very homophobic remark,' Greg said, looking a bit pissed off with his mother.

'I'm not homophobic,' Mrs Killeen bristled, highly offended. 'I married a man.'

'No he means . . .' Her husband tried to think about how to explain the word 'homophobic' and decided instead not to. 'Your mother and I are not homophobic, Greg. Not at all.' He turned to his wife, 'If there was a gay person on a bus we'd gladly give him our seats.'

Holy Sweet Jesus, Zoe thought in despair.

'We play a gay game in our yard,' Lee piped up, his fork held aloft ready to eat. 'One boy runs around and when he catches you, he has to kiss your butt.' He gave a snort of laughter. 'It's fun.'

Zoe looked apologetically at Louis. She wished she felt better so she could help him out. This was terrible, his family had been so welcoming to Greg and look at the shambles Greg's family were creating. But Louis was smiling. 'Well, Lee, I don't think that game would be much fun if someone had smelly underpants.'

'Ugh!' Lee pretended to vomit. 'Can I have some of that chicken, please? I like the leg part.'

'You can have whatever you want,' Louis said. He turned around to Greg, who was looking murderously at his father. 'Can't he, Greg?'

Greg turned and marched out to the kitchen.

In the silence that followed, Zoe hopped up and went after him. 'I'll go.'

She found Greg standing with his back to her, his hands splayed each side of the sink, his head bent.

'They're doing their best,' she said from the doorway. 'Dad wasn't even going to come until I told him that you'd never forgive him if he didn't.'

'I might never forgive him after this,' Greg said

through gritted teeth. 'Honestly, they're like fecking aliens confronted with new and exotic life forms.'

Zoe giggled at the comparison and crossed towards him. 'Well, Lee is sure to explain to them how it all works.'

'Yeah,' Greg said glumly, turning around, 'he can get them used to the idea by playing the "gay game" with them.'

Zoe touched his sleeve and smiled, trying not to laugh. Greg gave a roll of his eyes and smiled back, before gently poking her in the shoulder with his finger. 'And what happened to you? You look like shit.'

'I might *look* like shit' – Zoe gave a dirty grin – 'but I feel—'

'Gregory!' Mrs Killeen interrupted as she floated into the kitchen, smiling widely, oblivious to the consternation she and her husband were causing. 'Are you not joining us, the food is divine. Louis is just telling us how he got the chicken so moist. And he says to bring in the wine.' With a toss of her head, she left.

'See?' Zoe grinned. 'He's working his magic already.'

'Tell me all later,' Greg said, before looping an arm about her shoulder. He picked up the wine and led her from the room.

Zoe was eating the most delicious chocolate thing, she couldn't remember what Louis had called it, but it oozed chocolate when you cut into it. She thought this morning that she might never eat again and, hey presto, she was cured.

'I don't think mine is cooked,' her dad said, looking in dismay as melted chocolate sluiced onto his plate.

'That is the way it's meant to be, Dad.' Zoe made a face at Louis.

'Oh, right.' Mr Killeen looked disbelieving. He gave the chocolate cake another poke before setting his fork down. 'I've eaten enough anyway. Not good for the heart. I've some hard work on later.'

'In Lucy Lane's house,' Mrs Killeen sniffed disapprovingly. 'His new friend.'

'Do you have a girlfriend, Granddad?' Lee asked.

'Not at all,' Mr Killeen looked a little pleased by the question, 'she's just a lady who needs work done.'

'Yes, on her face mostly,' Mrs Killeen said with a sniff.

Zoe's mobile rang for the fourth time since dessert. Everyone looked at her as she pressed 'ignore'. She was afraid it might be Dominic and she didn't want to talk to him in front of her family. Just thinking about last night got her all hot and bothered. The phone stopped but started up again immediately.

'You should answer that,' her dad said, 'it could be serious.'

They all looked at her.

'I'm sure it's nothing.'

With that the phone stopped and started up again.

They all looked at her again.

'OK.' Please don't be Dominic, she prayed.

'Zoe Killeen?' a voice said.

'Yes.' For some unexplainable reason she felt a flicker of alarm.

'This is Marty.'

For a second she didn't know who it was. 'Marty?'

'Yes. The man who has to listen to you and that long-haired man of yours bickering all night?' A pause. 'I had to give you my fire extinguisher to put out your fire in your kitchen.'

'Oh.' Zoe rubbed a hand over her face. 'Yes?'

'I never got that back by the way.'

Zoe winced. They'd meant to get him a new one and had forgotten. 'Well, sorry about that. I'll sort it.'

'Hmm,' he sniffed. 'I've had two policemen ringing here looking for you.'

'Policemen? Have we been broken into?' She couldn't help the note of hope in her voice. That'd be great, she could get new stuff from the insurance money.

'I don't think so,' Marty smashed her hopes. 'They just said to let you know that they want to speak to you. You've to call them as soon as possible. I suppose you haven't paid a fine or your child is in trouble. Fighting the way you do impacts on a child.'

'I'm sorry, what?' Zoe was vaguely aware that her mother was flirting with Louis.

'Policemen? It can't be good, can it?' Marty sounded positively thrilled.

'Are you OK, Mammy?' Lee asked, causing them all to look in her direction.

'I'm not in trouble, if that's what you're implying,' Zoe said to Marty, wondering if maybe she was. Had she neglected to pay some bill? Had someone reported her for storing her compost at the back of the communal garden so it didn't stink her house out? She did that whenever Abe went away.

'Well someone is,' Marty went on in a doom-laden tone. He recited the number and Zoe had to tell him to stop while she got a pen.

Zoe took down the number, thanked Marty and hung up. 'The police want to talk to me,' she said as she began to dial the number Marty had given her.

'What can it be?' Her mother sounded uncon-cerned as she fluttered her eyelashes at Louis.

'Probably someone complained about her dumping all that compost down the back of that garden,' her father said.

Zoe looked in a panic at him but it was too late, the phone had been picked up at the other end. 'Hello,' said a voice.

Compost matters were not a calling-out matter for the police, she thought. It had to be something far more serious, which, come to think of it, was not a good thing. Her heart skipped a beat. 'Hi, I'm Zoe Killeen, I believe someone from your station called out to me earlier.'

'That's right,' the man at the other end said. 'Did they not get you?'

'No.' Zoe wondered if the man was thick. 'That's why I'm calling.'

'Oh right, OK. Well, eh, where are you now? Are you at home?'

'No. I'm in Dún Laoghaire.'

'Any chance you'll be there for the next ten minutes. We can get a lad out to you from the police station there.'

Once more her heart skipped in alarm. 'Why?'

'Just procedure, that's the way it's done.'

'The way what is done?' she asked.

The policeman ignored her question and instead asked for her address.

Zoe gave it. 'What's wrong?'

'We'll have a man out there in ten minutes.'

And he hung up.

Zoe sat on the sofa chewing her nails as she waited for the policeman to arrive. The remains of dessert lay abandoned on the table as they all gathered around her.

'Stop that chewing, Zoe,' her mother berated her.

'Mam, I have police coming over here in ten minutes, can we forget about my nails?'

'Hmm, I suppose.'

Greg sat in beside Zoe and wrapped an arm about her. 'Calm down,' he said. 'Now, tell me honestly, you haven't got involved in any heavy stuff without telling us, have you? Drugs? Prostitution?'

'Gregory!' Mrs Killeen reprimanded.

'I'm only asking.'

'Can we please take this seriously,' Zoe stared at them all. 'I really have no idea what they want.'

Just then the buzzer sounded and Greg told them to come on up.

There was silence in the apartment as they waited for the policeman to enter. Zoe stood up as two men arrived in, an older man and a young lanky lad, barely out of nappies. They stood uncomfortably in the hallway. 'Zoe Killeen?' the older one asked and his voice was kind, his eyes soft.

She immediately relaxed. 'That's me.' She smiled, hoping to try a bit of charm in case she was being misled by the whole good-cop routine.

'I've a bit of news for you about Abel Kane?'

There was an instant moment of tension in the small hall. Abe! Zoe stared at the man, like a deer in the focus of a gun. 'Good news?'

'It's not really bad news.' The young cop rushed to reassure her and the older man glared at him. He immediately dipped his head and mumbled something that no one could catch.

'He's been injured in fighting in Somalia,' the older policeman said.

Zoe felt her dad's arm steady her as she swayed.

'He's been flown back today, they're bringing him to St Catherine's Hospital.'

'How bad?' Greg asked.

'Quite bad. They're running it on the news later tonight, so be prepared.'

'Oh, my God.' Zoe put her hand to her mouth as her legs seemed to go from under her. She had to clutch her dad so she wouldn't fall. It couldn't be true. Vibrant, daredevil Abe couldn't be injured. It was all her fault for sleeping with Dominic, she was sure of it.

'Mammy?' Lee tugged her arm.

Zoe turned and scooped him up, burying her face in his neck.

'Well, I'll leave ye to it,' the older policeman said. 'I am sorry to have had to tell you this. He is alive, however.'

'Thank you.' For some reason, Mr Killeen shook the policemen's hands heartily.

Zoe began to sob.

CHAPTER 38

Abe arrived at St Catherine's Hospital at eight o'clock that evening. Zoe was there as the stretcher carrying him was borne through the corridors. Her mother had taken Lee and it was her dad who sat beside her as Abe was rushed to an intensive care ward. Zoe and her dad watched through the small window set into the door as Abe was connected up to the hospital machines.

'Will they let me in, do you think?' Zoe asked.

'Oh, baby, I don't know.' Her dad rubbed her back. Then he tipped her chin up with his finger and looked her straight in the eye. 'I thought it was over with you both.'

Zoe squirmed away from his gaze. The guilt was like a steam train flattening her. And she'd compared him to Patrick too. He wasn't a Patrick. He'd stayed with her for Lee, hadn't he? 'It was, but he's Lee's dad and he needs me now. I can't just abandon him.' She didn't add that she thought she loved him still. Abe was her guy, no one else, and being with Dominic had been wrong. She should have known this would happen, this was her punishment for being unfaithful or whatever it was when you slept with someone before it was totally officially off with your partner. It was like an unfunny episode of *Friends*.

'Zoe, I don't want to upset you, but a week ago you were out to kill the guy.'

His choice of words was unfortunate, tears filled her eyes and seeing her distress, her dad cursed himself slightly before pulling her to him and telling her he was sorry. 'I didn't mean *kill*,' he stammered.

'Zoe Killeen?' a doctor asked softly.

Zoe lifted her face from her dad's chest and nodded, wiping her eyes furiously with the back of her hand. 'How is he?'

The doctor sat down beside them. 'To put it simply,' he said, 'Abel has had a head trauma which has caused his brain to swell. Now, if the brain swells too much it can start to push against the hard bone of the skull which can damage brain cells. So, we've opened up the skull to allow for this and, right now, Abel is in a medically induced coma. That means that we are using drugs to keep him asleep while his brain heals. He's on a ventilator, which will breathe for him. Over the next few days, we'll monitor him and if we're satisfied with his progress, we'll begin gradually reducing the drugs and the ventilator in an effort to wake him up.'

'And how will he be at that stage?' Mr Killeen asked.

'It's hard to say. Some people can be very confused; others are more lucid.'

Zoe nodded, not taking in half of it. 'Can I go in to him?'

'Yes.' He looked at Mr Killeen and added, 'Only one visitor I'm afraid. Make sure you put on a mask and wash your hands. Ten minutes.'

'Thank you. Thank you.' Zoe's hands shook as she frantically rubbed the alcohol wash into them and her dad helped her adjust her face mask. She was about to push open the door when it occurred to her that she didn't know what to do. 'Can I talk to him?' she asked.

The doctor nodded.

'OK.' Zoe felt slightly faint. She'd caught a brief glimpse of Abe as he was wheeled along and then again as she and her dad looked through the small window. But she hadn't seen the extent of his injuries and she wasn't good with blood. What if Abe looked like one of those people on *CSI* or *Grey's Anatomy*? How would she cope with that? She might puke. Oh, God, what if she puked? Zoe felt her heartbeat accelerate and mentally told herself to cop on. She was panicking over nothing. Well, not nothing, obviously. But she was being stupid. Beneath the bandages and the blood, he was still Abe. She had to remember that. Her dad was giving her the thumbs up and smiling at her in encouragement. He knew what she was like. She gave him a wobbly grin in return and, taking a deep breath, she pushed open the door and, as it closed with a soft click behind her, she felt almost as if she was suspended in another world where antiseptic was the only smell and the blips and hums from medical equipment were the only sounds. It was weirdly restful.

She steeled herself as she crossed towards Abe, her shoes clicking on the highly polished floor. Standing at the side of his bed, she was relieved to see that he didn't look so bad. OK, he didn't look so good either. His head had been shaved, she noticed with such a pang of sadness that she almost gasped aloud. Abe's lovely hair, with its streaks of blond and brown, all gone. A large bandage covered his head. His face looked the same though, tanned with laughter lines, though a line of ugly black stitches marched from his left ear down the side towards the neck. There was a tube in his mouth connected, she supposed, to the ventilator. His eyes were closed and his chest went up and down as the machine breathed for him.

Zoe reached out to touch him and then pulled back. She wasn't sure if she could. But he looked so small, so vulnerable just lying there. She wanted to run a finger along his face, touch his lips, kiss him softly on the cheek. But she didn't know if she should and so she stood, feeling useless, just staring at this man who had shared the past six years of her life. What could she say? They'd parted so badly.

'Abe,' she began, her voice trembling, 'it's me, Zoe.' She paused and swallowed suddenly, wishing for a large glass of water. 'I was told I could talk to you, but I don't know what to say.' She was silent for a second, taking in the room, knowing that this would be Abe's home for the next couple of weeks. 'Lee says hi,' she blurted out suddenly. And then it was as if the words tumbled like balls in the hands of a juggler from her mouth, they came so fast that even if Abe could hear, he might not have made them all out. She talked about when they'd met, the fun they'd had together, the time he'd bought her a hot-air balloon ride for her birthday and the balloon had taken off with the two of them in it and the instructor had been left on the ground. So many shared memories. 'Lee's worried and so am I. I love you, Abe. I do. When you get better, I promise that we'll get the ceiling fixed and I won't care if you hate my family and don't want to talk about yours. We'll have our own little family. I want that now. Please get better.'

She stopped abruptly, what she'd just said made her shiver a little.

'Well, anyway, just get better, we can sort everything out. But one thing I do know, I'm not going to fight with you anymore. Whatever happens will happen.' Without thinking, she reached out her hand and laid it on his. No alarms went off and so she bent down and very softly planted a kiss on his face. 'And I made a mistake last night, and I'm sorry. I'm so sorry.'

There was no response, just the in and out of the ventilator.

Zoe stood, tears trickling down her cheek, devouring his face with her eyes, beginning to pray silently, bargaining with any god who would listen. She would do whatever it took, she said in her mind, only please don't let him die, don't let him die. St Peter, don't let him die. St John, don't let him die. St Andrew, don't let him die. St— she stopped. She didn't know any more saints. Damn it anyway. Damn! Damn! Damn!

The ten minutes was over too fast.

'Go home now if you like,' the nurse on duty said when she came out. It was like resurfacing for air after a long time swimming. 'You won't be allowed back in tonight. You can't do anything here.'

'I can wait,' Zoe said, sitting on a chair. 'That's what I can do.'

'And I can too,' her dad said. He fumbled about in his pockets. 'Would you like a tea, Zoe?'

She shook her head and watched as he went off to get one for himself.

CHAPTER 39

As Deirdre made her way to her office on Monday morning, there was a definite tension in the air. It could be because the listenership figures were out that day, but a more likely cause of the strained anxious faces was the fact that Paul had gone. He'd been a popular member of staff and people were likely to be worrying about their own jobs now if someone so successful could go. No one had contacted Deirdre officially to let her know about Paul, and she hadn't heard from him either, but, over the weekend, Deirdre had decided that if it was her time to be fired, so be it. At least her garden was done and she had Paul to thank for that. Paul. Another reason she wouldn't miss this place. If he was gone, it'd seem a little colourless again. She'd never noticed how cheerless her world was until he'd come along and challenged her.

Deirdre pushed open the door to her office and found Matt and Emma deep in conversation. That was weird, they were normally in later than her. They jumped apart as she entered and looked at her guiltily.

'Oh, you're back,' Emma said in a high voice. 'Glad to see you're OK.' She looked stricken.

Emma had done the show for the two and a half weeks she was out and, listening on podcast, Deirdre had been really surprised at how good she was. She was cheerful and bubbly, not at all like the stammering wreck she appeared to be. Paul had chosen well, Deirdre had to admit that.

'I was glad to see my show was in such capable hands while I was gone,' Deirdre said, taking her seat.

There was a silence. From the corner of her eye, Deirdre saw Emma glance at Matt. He made an I-don't-know face. Did they always do that when she spoke to them? For the first time she noticed the tense set of their shoulders and their anxious expressions, and she felt stricken.

'You were really good, Emma,' Deirdre said again.

'Eh, thanks.' Emma blushed to her toes. 'It was nice of Paul to give me a chance. I didn't ask for it or anything, he just thought it'd be a good idea. I did broadcasting in college, you see and—'

'Well, he was right,' Deirdre interrupted. Then added, the words not coming out quite so smoothly, 'I'm a bit unadventurous, I'm afraid, and I'm finding it hard to embrace the whole new show idea. As you might have noticed, I like to control things. Maybe you could help me, Emma?'

Emma looked haunted, as if she was expecting some kind of evil trickery. 'Um, yeah. Sure.'

'Did you like the editing on the garden segments?' Matt butted in. 'I did them.'

Deirdre hadn't got as far as listening to that but a lie wouldn't go amiss. 'I was getting to that. Fantastic.'

'Well, in fairness, they were fantastic segments,' Matt said generously. 'You actually sounded good in them, Deirdre.' An audible gulp. 'Well, you know, you always sound good, as you know, it's just you sounded better.' He inflected the last part of the statement to make it sound like a question.

'Thanks,' Deirdre suppressed a grin. 'So what's the news here?'

'Paul is gone,' Emma spoke in a small voice. 'He left.' She sounded like she might cry.

Deirdre had been talking about the show but she nodded, 'I heard. Any reason?'

'No one knows,' she whispered.

By the tone of her voice, Deirdre had a vision of Paul been spirited off by fairies. 'Oh, I'm sure someone knows,' Deirdre said matter-of-factly. 'I'm sure we'll find out. Now the show?'

'Are we back to the original show?' Matt asked.

'We are not,' Suzi spoke from behind, startling them. She was scowling and was wearing a suit. It all looked very odd, especially as underneath the jacket of her suit, she had a T-shirt proclaiming 'Here Comes The Fun'. She scowled some more. 'Paul will have to work out his contract with the station, which runs until next year – I was just talking to Michael. Paul will be in from tomorrow.' She eyeballed Deirdre and said firmly and with more authority than Deirdre had ever seen before, 'We stick with what we know is going to work. Eventually.'

'That's fine by me,' Deirdre said. 'Are you producing again?'

'For today.'

'I'm glad it's you,' Deirdre said.

Suzi stiffened. 'Matt, Emma, take five,' she said.

They scurried out, whispering among themselves. Probably about Suzi's suit, Deirdre thought.

'You won't bulldoze me again,' Suzi snapped at Deirdre, picking up some pages and not even looking at her.

'I won't,' Deirdre agreed, making Suzi freeze. She swallowed. 'Everything you said was right, Suzi. I never knew it before. I really didn't. I'm just, well, I need the safety net of knowing everything and if that came across as terrifying, I'm sorry.' Before Suzi could respond, she went on, 'And if by any chance Michael Allen fires me today, I'll tell him you're brilliant.'

There was a silence. Suzi pursed her lips and looked up to the ceiling. 'Coming from you, that just might wreck my career,' she said, sort of jokingly.

Deirdre saw that her eyes were bright with tears. 'I'll say whatever you want. I've been desperate, Suzi. I've done a ton of thinking over the weekend and while your bum-licking routine hurt me, cause

I thought we liked each other, I realise that I wasn't a marvellous friend anyway. I'm sorry.'

There was silence. 'I did a pile of thinking too,' Suzi said, swallowing hard and sniffing. 'And I realised that I was so far up the arses of the important people in this place that they'd all need suppositories to get me out. Everyone probably laughs at me in here.'

'No one laughs at you. They laugh at me.'

'Only the public.'

Deirdre squirmed. 'Yes, I have become a bit of a laughing stock.'

'We'll fix it,' Suzi promised. 'Paul's ideas are good and I'm not just saying that because he'll be back.'

'Aw, you are a bit,' Deirdre teased, smiling.

'I'm not.'

'Truce,' Deirdre held out her hand.

Suzi shook it before embracing Deirdre, who felt a little uncomfortable with the closeness at first, but found it might be something she could get used to.

They followed Paul's plan for the show that afternoon. It involved one book review, a tome of a thing entitled *The Dangerous Garden*, which was an account of all the diseases that could be found in the average garden. The reviewer had obviously enjoyed it and recounted gory and graphic accounts of people catching gangrene through contact with various innocuous flowers.

430

'It sounds like your average garden is like an episode of *CSI*,' Deirdre bantered.

The man laughed. Actually laughed. And her team laughed.

'And to think the aim of our show is to encourage gardening,' Deirdre joked again.

There was a deafening silence from the other end. 'Youse gave me the book,' the man snapped. 'I can't help it if that's what it says.'

One joke too far, Deirdre thought glumly and she rapidly went to the next piece. A nature quiz. The two contestants, who had rung in and professed themselves keen gardeners in order to win a garden makeover, had lied. One of them, who had got everything wrong, even answered the door while she was on air and had a conversation with the caller. The other person was speaking from the bathroom in his work so the boss wouldn't catch him. A lot of toilet flushing was going on in the background.

This piece was followed by the gardening queries. And finally, the slot she and Paul had recorded from the garden on Friday, before he'd walked. And it was so damn good, she had to admit. Matt had done a great job but not only that, she was good. In fact, she had a hard time believing that the lively woman speaking was her. Her voice was fun, interesting, she narrated facts about the flowers she was planting effortlessly, like a guest throwing confetti at a wedding. The passion she had for the garden seemed to wrap the listener up in it. Deirdre sat back in her chair and listened to this other version of herself. At least it was one shining moment of radio among the dross of the past five years.

The call had come and Deirdre stood outside Michael's office and braced herself. Every time the listenership figures were announced, Michael called each of the presenters in for a meeting with their teams. Today it was just Deirdre. This was it, he was firing her. At least he wasn't going to humiliate her in front of everyone. She told herself that she had to stay calm, be dignified, she had done her best but it was obvious that she wasn't cut out for the direction the show was going in. It wasn't her fault. It was no one's fault, and Michael was only doing his job.

Feeling a tad overheated, she pulled a hankie from her sleeve and mopped her brow. Maybe she shouldn't have worn her thermal vest?

'Go on in,' Michael's secretary said.

As she opened the door, Michael hopped up from behind his desk, his unnaturally white smile seeming to go before him. 'Deirdre, sit down. Tea? Coffee?'

He'd never offered her a drink before. Was this how people got fired? 'I'd rather you got straight to the point,' she said, brown shoes pointed forwards, hands on her lap. Straight-backed, ready to take what was coming.

Michael gave a belly laugh, which was rather

inappropriate and insensitive, she thought. 'Well, well,' he said, 'aren't you the dark horse?'

That was strange. Deirdre had the presence of mind to bite the inside of her cheek to make sure she wasn't dreaming. She suffered from vivid dreams, but in her dreams she never thought to do that, which meant she must be awake. 'I don't follow,' she said instead.

'Your show. It's rocketed.' Michael clapped his hands together and nodded. 'Biggest jump in the country.'

Deirdre bit her cheek harder.

'Your car crash of a programme is causing quite a stir. Apparently the general public are finding it all rather hilarious. Probably an anecdote to the doom and gloom.'

Deirdre squirmed. If she had *meant* to be funny, that'd be good.

'So, well done. We'll be renewing your contract at the end of the year.' He leaned over. 'And you can expect a nice little bonus too. Now,' he reached for his jacket, 'let's go get your team and have some nosh. I'll buy.'

This was all very unexpected. And Deirdre had the feeling that she should be delighted, over the moon. She'd often seen Michael wining and dining other presenters, Gary Sims was a particular favourite. And now it was happening to her and all she could think was *shit, I haven't been fired*, which was strange. As Michael chatted on, she sat very still so she could catch her thoughts. And it became clear to her that if she had been fired, the pressure would be off. She would never have had to chat to strange members of the public ever again – but now, because of her success, the possibility of that life stretched out before her like a corpse. In fact, she realised that the possibility of being fired had offered her a glimpse of colour in her grey life. She stood up and tried to smile.

'So where to?' Michael asked.

'I don't know, anywhere.' She tried to muster enthusiasm, to return his delighted smile. 'Somewhere with big steaks.'

'Done,' Michael held the door open for her and prepared to usher her out.

It was a flash of insight. A moment of clarity. The thought 'What am I doing?' seared into her mind. What she was doing was making this man happy! This man who had never bothered with her before, who had sighed and grunted and moaned whenever she met with him. You've got to do what feels right, Rick had said. This didn't feel right. This wasn't her. But the alternative, actually leaving, was a little bit proactive. A little bit like throwing herself to the mercy of the universe. But flip it, she'd never be happy here. Not while the whole country was laughing at her. She felt like a ridiculous contestant on *Big Brother*.

And she had the feeling that Lily, who had lived a life of grey, would not want the same for her daughter.

'Actually, Michael,' she said, 'there's something I have to say.'

'Fire ahead,' he smiled.

'If you'd just close the door.'

Puzzled, he did as he was told, and the fact that he'd obeyed her made her feel a little more powerful.

'I quit.'

'What?' He cocked his ear like a man in a cartoon, as if his hearing had somehow let him down. 'What did you say?'

She could still back out. Pretend she had said something else. But that would be a betrayal of the woman she'd heard on the radio. 'I quit. I don't want to do the show any more.'

'You can't quit,' Michael looked like a kid who'd been bitten by his pet dog. 'That's ridiculous. Did you not hear me?' He spoke slowly to her, as if to an imbecile. 'Your show is one of the highest in the country. From zero to hero. Practically overnight.'

'Sorry about that.'

'Paul is coming back, you know?' Michael blustered. 'If he's put you up to this . . . I know how close you both are.'

'I haven't seen Paul and we're not close.'

He ignored that. 'I was going to ring him anyway. He obviously knew what he was doing when he said he'd walk if I fired you. He was right. I'll tell him that.'

'You *were* going to fire me?' Deirdre's voice rose. 'What?'

Michael realised he'd said too much. 'That's all water under the canal now,' he said. 'We'll get him back, it'll be great.'

'It's bridge, Michael,' Deirdre said coldly. 'And to save anyone the bother of firing me, like I said, I quit.'

'You'll have to work out your contract,' he snarled after her.

She didn't reply.

She found out Paul's address from personnel and rang him to say she was on her way over. Then before he could protest, she hung up.

Paul lived in a crappy-looking house, with a charming wilderness of a garden. His door was unpainted and his windows needed to be replaced. Deirdre delicately tiptoed up the cracked and broken driveway. The bell didn't work so she rapped on the door.

'It's open!' he called. He sounded a little drunk.

Deirdre stepped inside the hallway, which was done up in brown and beige, or maybe it was just dirty. 'Christ,' she exclaimed before realising that Paul was framed in the kitchen doorway. And he'd had the nerve to hate her house.

'It has potential,' he said. He held aloft a bottle of wine. 'Great news for you, eh? I bet Michael was all over you.' He got a glass and poured her some.

Deirdre shrugged. 'He was – until I quit.'

'What?' Paul gawked at her, seeming to sober up. 'Why?'

'Because I realised that when the show wasn't doing well, I didn't much care. And now that it is, I don't care either.'

'Jesus!' Paul laughed. 'I bet he loved that.'

'He wasn't happy,' Deirdre said, lips curving upwards, 'but it made me feel great.' She studied him for a second. 'You shouldn't have walked because Michael was going to fire me.'

'Well, I know that *now*,' Paul half-joked.

She followed him into a beige sitting room. 'I thought you'd have been dying for me to go. Emma is great.'

Paul didn't reply, just stared at her as if she was missing something crucial. He certainly didn't look like a man that had helped create a number-one show.

'Aren't you happy the show did so well?' she asked.

'Should I be?' He laughed a little. It sounded bitter.

'Well, yes, I would have thought so.'

He turned away as if she disappointed him and poured some more wine.

She got it suddenly. 'You didn't want it to turn into a comedy, did you?' A pause as she said softly, 'You wanted it to be a really good show.'

'I wanted it to be a really good show,' he repeated, slumping down on the sofa.

'I'm sorry.' She sat beside him and took the risk of touching his arm. His very muscular arm. Probably from all the digging in the garden. 'It's all my fault.'

He turned to face her. 'You did your best. It's my fault too. I didn't listen to my head.' Again that look.

'You need Emma.' She said it with no bitterness.

Paul gazed at her until she was sure she might combust with physical longing. Those eyes of his, drowsy, dreamy, sexy. She had to turn away or she'd do something she could regret. 'You'll have another crack when Michael offers you your job back,' she said brightly.

'He already did, I told him to stuff it up his hole.'

'You didn't!'

'I did,' Paul said, 'And you have no idea how good it was.'

'But what will you do?'

'Right now? I'm going to have another glass of wine. You?'

'I'll stick with this one, thanks.'

'I'll probably go back to England,' Paul said, as he poured, 'my son is there.' Then he added, 'Not that I ever see him.'

'You don't see your son?'

'Nope.' He nudged her with his elbow, 'Come on, don't pretend you know nothing about it.'

'I might have read something,' Deirdre blushed, thinking of the copious online stuff she'd perused. 'And if you don't mind me saying, you don't seem like that man at all.'

'Thank you,' Paul inclined his head. 'I probably

was a bit of an arsehole when I was younger, but who isn't?'

She'd never been an arsehole. Well, not the swilling-drink-and-sleeping-around kind.

'Except for you, of course,' Paul went on with a small smile and an affectionate bumping of her arm. 'Anyway, my wife wasn't an angel either and she's fed my son so many lies about me that now he won't have anything to do with me. I took the job here just to get away, but you can't, you know.'

Deirdre didn't actually know. She'd got away to Dublin and spent her life wishing she was at home. 'You have to keep trying though,' she said. 'Keep knocking on his door. Send him birthday cards, that sort of thing. Who knows? Maybe one day.'

'That's the hope,' Paul smiled glumly. 'Anyway, that's what I'll probably do. And you?'

'I might just garden and feed the birds and go on walks.'

'That makes you sound like a batty old woman,' Paul said delicately.

'Maybe I am a batty old woman.'

'A pretty good-looking batty old woman, it has to be said.'

Deirdre inhaled rather sharply. Did he just say she was good-looking? 'Thank you.' She took a large swallow of wine.

'The show became a farce because I didn't want to be looking at Emma every day for an hour, I wanted to be looking at you.' Paul spoke so quietly, she was sure she'd misheard.

'Pardon?'

He gave a small smile. 'You were so prim and then when you got agitated with the guests, you'd unbutton your blouse, fan your face and start hyperventilating. You'd mop your brow with a big flowery piece of material—'

'It's called a handkerchief.' She didn't know how to feel about this.

'It was all very, well . . .' he thought for a second, 'like Marilyn Monroe with a conservative twist. Oh.' The 'Oh' was said as if a lightbulb had popped inside his head.

'What?'

'Well, if I loved it, it must be why the public did too.' He groaned. 'I should have known.'

No one had ever compared her to Marilyn Monroe before.

'You dazzled me.' He met her gaze.

'I dazzled you?' Deirdre laughed uneasily. 'I'm hardly a magician.'

'You are so . . .' Paul cocked his head to the side, 'restricted on the outside, yet passionate on the inside.'

He was making her sound like an ad for a bottle of perfume. And he was looking at her in a most peculiar manner.

'I mean,' he leaned towards her, 'how many buttons are on that blouse?'

He was looking at her breasts, encased as they were in her good frilly blouse. Fear and longing coursed through her veins. She thought she'd faint. 'I don't know,' she stammered out, 'maybe twenty.'

'Hmm. Can I count them?'

He was moving in on her. His hand was reaching for the fabric of her blouse. It was like a door opening inside her and she was suddenly feeling quite overwhelmed by what might be on the other side. 'I have to go.' Out the words popped.

'Now?'

'Yes.' She stumbled up from the sofa, upending her drink. 'Bye now.'

She didn't look back. All she heard was, 'Jesus!'

CHAPTER 40

Lily was watching a programme when a woman came over and crouched down by her chair. It wasn't anyone she recognised, though there were so few people that she recognised anymore. She wondered if people were leaving her or something. She hadn't seen little Deirdre or Jimmy in ages. The show on the TV was something called *I'm Not the Father*, a brash American thing where men did rap dances when DNA testing cleared them of any false accusations of parentage. The men were good dancers, she thought. Patrick had been a good dancer, smooth and easy like his personality.

The woman said something about Zoe. The unusual name penetrated. 'Zoe,' Lily said.

The woman said Zoe was out sick.

The girl? she wanted to say. *Who reads?* But the words floated off, so she tapped her diary.

The woman nodded.

Lily wanted to ask what was wrong, how Zoe was, but she couldn't. The woman was talking again. Something about getting someone else to read the diary. Maybe Deirdre herself?

That wouldn't work at all. Lily shook her head. No. No, Deirdre had to hear it. Lily had done a most underhand thing and Lily needed Deirdre to understand. It wasn't just that she had waited until Deirdre was in her late thirties to tell her about Jimmy, it was worse than that. And Deirdre had to hear it.

'Fli— Fli—' She tried to get the word out.

The woman looked puzzled.

'Flibbergibbit.'

The woman smiled, 'Carrie? You'd like Carrie to do it?'

Lily sighed. Any port in a storm.

Her dad was drinking tea like it was going out of fashion. He was also buying scones and sandwiches and cakes every half hour. Food seemed to be all he could think of. Now he was trying to encourage her to come and get some lunch in the hospital canteen.

Zoe sighed. There was nothing she could do here anyway, so she might as well, she decided. It's a marathon, the nurse had explained that morning. Being in the hospital was going to be a marathon, not a sprint, and they had to take it easy because it could go on for a long time. It had already been two long days and it felt like weeks.

'The canteen is down here,' her dad said, leading the way. He knew the place inside out at this stage, with all his forays to the tea machines and the toilets. He'd gone to the hospital shop and bought her some facial washes and a face cloth first thing that morning. Another trip had resulted in news-papers. Abe had made a column on page three. Zoe couldn't read it. 'They look like they do a lovely meat pie,' her father confided as they descended in the lift. 'And a special Tuesday price too.'

'Great,' Zoe said, wishing he would go home and leave her to wallow in her misery.

The lift pinged to a stop and they got out.

Zoe froze, her stomach somersaulting, her heart flip flopping, her weak desire for some cheap meat pie ebbing away like sand through fingers.

'This way,' her dad said. Then at her lack of response, he turned around. 'Zoe, come on. What's the matter?'

But she couldn't move because Dominic was coming towards her, carrying two coffees. He paused when he saw her too. He looked puzzled, then the most beautiful smile she had ever seen crossed his face.

'Hey,' he said, when he drew level. 'What brings you here?' his smile grew a little broader. 'Couldn't stay away, eh?'

Zoe flushed. Her dad was gazing from her to Dominic in some confusion. She couldn't look at him. She made hasty introductions. 'Eh, Dad, this is Dominic, a guy I work with. His father is in here. Dominic, this is my dad.'

'I'm sorry to hear about your father, son. Is he very bad?'

'Yes,' Dominic shifted from foot to foot, uneasy, as usual, talking about his father.

444

'Oh, that's terrible, terrible,' Mr Killeen shook his head. 'We're in here with Zoe's boyfriend, Abe.'

Dominic flinched, causing coffee to slop out all over his hands. 'Abe?' he said faintly.

'He was shot at in Somalia,' Zoe said, her voice cracking. 'He's pretty bad.'

'Aw, Zoe, that's awful,' Dominic's expression conveyed nothing but empathy. 'You need anything, I'm up on the third floor. I've got food up there and cakes and everything.'

'Well, thank you, Dominic,' her dad answered in her stead. 'That's really nice of you and you with your own troubles.'

'Me and Rosie,' Dominic half-smiled, 'we're institutionalised at this stage, got it all worked out to a T. In fact, I can send you down some curry if you like. The food here is terrible. And Zoe likes my curry, don't you?' He gave Zoe a smile.

Her dad looked hopeful. 'Well, now—'

'No.' Zoe shook her head. 'We couldn't. You look after Rosie and your dad. Thanks anyway.'

Dominic looked crushed and she felt bad, but Abe mattered now. 'Come on, Dad. See you, Dominic.'

He barely nodded a goodbye.

It had been such a long day. Zoe's eyes were like sandpaper as she fought to keep them open. Her dad was sipping a coffee and munching on a packet of biscuits that he'd brought from home. 'Your mother will be in tomorrow to stay with you,' he

445

said. When she made no response, he said, 'That's assuming you are staying in for tomorrow night?'

'Of course I am,' Zoe was cross. 'Why wouldn't I?'

'Well, Lee for one thing. He's a little scared over all this and he needs his mother.'

'I know,' Zoe dropped her gaze and groaned, rubbing her eyes. 'Sorry, Dad, I'm a bit on edge.' She knew she looked a state even though she'd managed to shower in the hospital that morning. 'I'll talk to him tomorrow. I'll pick him up from school and we'll have tea together and I'll bring him in here for a few minutes and let him look in through the window at Abe.'

Her dad made no response.

'What?' Zoe asked, irritated by his silence.

'You'll wear yourself out,' he said.

'I'll be fine.'

'Zoe, you were leaving him. Lee told us you were looking for a house.'

'Stop!' Her shout made people look towards them. She lowered her voice. 'Stop, OK?'

'No,' her father shook his head. 'No, I'm going to say this. That man in there might have gone about saving the world, but he wasn't too interested in saving his relationship with you and Lee. And I despise him for that, Zoe. And while I know you have feelings for him and while I admire the way you've stayed in here, I can't understand it, honey, I just can't. And—'

'Dad,' Zoe said, eyeballing him sternly, 'you

446

know the way you try to fix every appliance at home and you tinker away at it and tinker away at it and it always ends up worse than before?'

'Well, I wouldn't say worse, that's a bit harsh, but, yes, I take your point.'

'Well don't do it to me, OK? You cannot try and fix me.'

'I'm not trying to do that, you're great as you are.'

And because she felt she was going to cry, she got up and walked away, a huge lump in her throat.

THE TENTH WEDNESDAY

'Where's Zoe?' Deirdre asked as she walked into Lily's room on Wednesday afternoon. She was wound up like a spring. Work had become unbearable. Because she and Paul had to work out their contracts, they were still thrown together. And she was mortified and he was out-of-proportion cross and now there were more undercurrents running through their relationship than in the whole of the Atlantic Ocean. And worst of all, she still found him sexy as hell and despised herself for her cowardice.

She became aware that the red-headed girl had said something. 'Sorry? I was miles away.' She wished she was.

'Zoe's boyfriend is in hospital,' Carrie said. 'He got shot.'

Deirdre's self-pity dissolved instantly. 'The poor thing. What hospital? Is this the aid worker?' Maybe it wasn't all over with him then.

'St Catherine's and yes, it is Abe, the aid worker.' Carrie held up the diary. 'Anyway, your mother said I could read this. I don't think there's a lot left.'

Lily sniffed in what sounded like loud disapproval.

'OK. Hey, Mammy,' Deirdre kissed her mother. 'How are you?'

Lily reached a hand up to caress the cheek of this lady. The woman closed her eyes and pressed Lily's hand harder. She looked a bit like Deirdre.

I'm writing this now as a seventy-three-year-old woman. One who is forgetting things that *are* happening to her but not the things that **did** happen. Things that I regret, things that at the time I felt I had no control over. Firstly, being married to Jimmy was like suddenly being buried alive. Oh, he was a good man, the best man really, but in those days I didn't want the best man. I wanted a man full of excitement, full of derring-do. The type of man I thought Patrick was. I did my best on the farm. I did my best as a mother, but there were times, especially in the early years, when I had to go to bed, cover my head and sleep. I suppose if alcohol had been more available to me, I would have tried that. Anything to blot out my reality, blot out my thoughts. But because there was no drink, I slept. Deirdre, bless her, would come up to me and climb onto the bed and cuddle in and when she did, feeling her soft warm body beside mine, I was swamped with love and despair in such a rush that I thought I would drown. I couldn't bear to live my own life and, yet, there was no other life I could have.

On the bad days, my mother would call up and

prepare Jimmy's dinner and do my chores. She'd look at me and shake her head and tell me things would be fine. But then, one bright-blue August day, when Deirdre was nearly five, there was a piece in the local paper.

'Oh, it's here,' Carrie squealed making them jump, as she uncovered a fragile tissue-like piece of paper.

'Read it,' Deirdre urged. She was four in her dream when her mother had gone in the ambulance.

Carrie took her time unfolding the page, taking care not to tear it. 'Oh, it's about a wedding,' she said, having finally smoothed it out. 'It's dated 24th July 1963. "Local Boy Marries A Dame",' she read. '"Local boy Patrick McCabe, formerly of McCabe's on the Main Street, married Dame Louise Eversham in London yesterday. Dame Louise Eversham, one of the most eligible ladies of the London social scene, is the heiress to the Eversham cigarette company, reputedly worth millions. The couple are honeymooning in Las Vegas before moving into their new residence in Kensington. We wish them all the best for their future life together."'

There was a silence. Lily stared ahead, saying nothing.

Carrie began to read again.

I told Jimmy I wanted a day out. He said the silage had to be brought in. I put my foot down. I told him in the throng, as people pushed this way and that way past us.

I could smell the River Liffey and chips and the whiff of alcohol. I heard cars and bustle and ringing-singing voices. I pulled Deirdre along with one hand and held our case in the other as I strutted towards O'Connell Street Bridge. There was a photographer there and he asked me if I'd like a picture of me and Deirdre. I thought it'd be nice to send to Jimmy, so I agreed and, snap, he took it for us. I give him the address to post it out and I paid him. He told me I should be a model and I laughed. The day was beautiful, bight and fresh, the sun a white ball in a blue sky. Deirdre and I went into Clery's and then on to Henry Street and into more shops. Finally, at six, I took Deirdre into a nice tea shop and bought her an ice-cream. I told her to make it last for ages. The boat wasn't leaving until late that night and I needed to kill time. At eight, I was going to call Jimmy and say that I'd missed the bus and that Deirdre and I would spend the night in Dublin and be home the next day; that way we'd be well gone by the time he realised that we weren't coming back.

'So,' I said to Deirdre, 'do you like Dublin?'

She spooned some ice-cream into her mouth and nodded.

'Would you like to go on a holiday to a place bigger than Dublin?'

She licked her spoon and looked at me. 'Is Daddy going?'

'No. He has to do the silage.'

I was tired of working on his farm. I was tired of being a farmer's wife and I wanted a day out. Was a day out too much to ask for? For me and Deirdre? Were we not worth it? I think I was crying as I asked him. Now that we were married, we never went anywhere. I remember he put his arms around me and told me that of course I could go anywhere I wanted. Wasn't I a free person? Didn't he want me to be happy? I held him and ignored the guilt eating me up.

On the Tuesday, he got up early, having to do my work as well as his, and when he was gone, I pulled my little case out from under the bed. It was full of my things and Deirdre's and if Jimmy asked I was going to tell him that it was my shopping case. That I was going to Dublin and I would buy something if I liked it. I dressed Deirdre and she looked like a little doll in her skirt and jumper, with a red ribbon holding back her curls.

We walked to the bus because Jimmy was too busy to bring us, but I didn't care. If he'd brought me, it would only be another layer of guilt on top of what was already an unbearable quilt of it. I felt like I was suffocating in it but, at the same time, my head was poking out the top and I was breathing the smell of freedom. Of the big city. Of choices. My heart was hammering and I think I almost squeezed the hand off Deirdre. The bus arrived in Dublin at five past twelve and left us in Westmoreland Street. We got off and stood there, I was holding on to Deirdre, both of us invisible and anonymous prepare Jimmy's dinner and do my chores. She'd look at me and shake her head and tell me things would be fine. But then, one bright-blue August day, when Deirdre was nearly five, there was a piece in the local paper.

'Oh, it's here,' Carrie squealed making them jump, as she uncovered a fragile tissue-like piece of paper.

'Read it,' Deirdre urged. She was four in her dream when her mother had gone in the ambulance.

Carrie took her time unfolding the page, taking care not to tear it. 'Oh, it's about a wedding,' she said, having finally smoothed it out. 'It's dated 24th July 1963. "Local Boy Marries A Dame",' she read. '"Local boy Patrick McCabe, formerly of McCabe's on the Main Street, married Dame Louise Eversham in London yesterday. Dame Louise Eversham, one of the most eligible ladies of the London social scene, is the heiress to the Eversham cigarette company, reputedly worth millions. The couple are honeymooning in Las Vegas before moving into their new residence in Kensington. We wish them all the best for their future life together."'

There was a silence. Lily stared ahead, saying nothing.

Carrie began to read again.

I told Jimmy I wanted a day out. He said the silage had to be brought in. I put my foot down. I told him

450

Lily sniffed in what sounded like loud disapproval.

'OK. Hey, Mammy,' Deirdre kissed her mother. 'How are you?'

Lily reached a hand up to caress the cheek of this lady. The woman closed her eyes and pressed Lily's hand harder. She looked a bit like Deirdre.

I'm writing this now as a seventy-three-year-old woman. One who is forgetting things that *are* happening to her but not the things that **did** happen. Things that I regret, things that at the time I felt I had no control over. Firstly, being married to Jimmy was like suddenly being buried alive. Oh, he was a good man, the best man really, but in those days I didn't want the best man. I wanted a man full of excitement, full of derring-do. The type of man I thought Patrick was. I did my best on the farm. I did my best as a mother, but there were times, especially in the early years, when I had to go to bed, cover my head and sleep. I suppose if alcohol had been more available to me, I would have tried that. Anything to blot out my reality, blot out my thoughts. But because there was no drink, I slept. Deirdre, bless her, would come up to me and climb onto the bed and cuddle in and when she did, feeling her soft warm body beside mine, I was swamped with love and despair in such a rush that I thought I would drown. I couldn't bear to live my own life and, yet, there was no other life I could have.

On the bad days, my mother would call up and

'I want to do the silage with Daddy.'

'But what about going on a holiday with Mammy?'

'I want to do the silage with Daddy,' she said, and she sounded very definite.

I took a deep breath and said as calmly as I could, 'No, you can't, we're going on a holiday.'

'But I want Daddy.'

And it was her big, trusting, brown eyes, the way she knew that I would never hurt her that hurt me. With trembling fingers, I reached out and smoothed her tousled hair, her ribbon had gone all astray. I felt, deep inside, the escape hatch that I had briefly but falsely created slam closed. I had a child, I was a mother. 'You want Daddy,' I repeated, my voice wobbling like a one-year-old on a bike.

'Yes,' she said.

And I waited in numbed silence until she'd finished her ice-cream and licked the spoon clean. Then I took her and myself to the bus. I walked all the way without once looking back.

I cried all the way home.

After a while I never stayed in bed again. I became the farmer's wife, the person everyone wanted me to be. And I was good at it. And Jimmy did bring me out to shows and he tried, he really did, to give my life some of the buzz he knew I craved.

But it was only at the end I knew how much he really loved me.

Jimmy died when —

★   ★   ★

Lily raised her hand and Carrie stopped.

Deirdre was glad Lily had made Carrie stop. The memory came back now, crystal clear, like a pot unearthed in a dig. Her mother had cried all the way home and all the way back to the house and all the next day and the next and Deirdre had pulled at her skirts and begged her to stop. Deirdre had grown frantic. Her dad had despaired, the first time she'd seen her daddy cry and it was her fault.

Eventually, Lily had to go to hospital to be put back together. 'I'm sorry you didn't have the life you craved, Mammy,' she whispered. 'I remember that day.' Then she added, 'Thanks for bringing me home.'

But the guilt had followed her through life, drifting in and out of everything, like a ghost that didn't know where to be. She didn't deserve to be happy, she had made her mother cry.

She knew in that moment, for definite, her mother had sacrificed herself for her, not for appearances or anything else, but for her. It made her feel good suddenly. As if something that had been twisted had suddenly been righted again.

CHAPTER 42

'Mam,' Zoe hissed when her mother arrived over the next day, 'will you stop flirting with the doctors. It's embarrassing.'

'He was flirting with me,' Mrs Killeen said smartly, as she waggled her fingers in a goodbye to the hunky doctor she'd come up in the lift with. 'He told me he was checking for a free bed.'

Zoe looked incredulously at her. 'Probably for a patient.'

Mrs Killeen flushed. 'Oh. Well, I thought it was joke. I told him he could come to my house if he liked.'

'Nooooo!'

'How's Abe today?'

Zoe let the subject change stand. 'Well, there's no change. They're attempting to wean him off some of his drugs today, so that's good apparently.'

'I see.' There was a pause as Mrs Killeen fiddled nervously with a button on her coat, twisting it this way and that, before finally blurting out, 'And you're sure you want to do this? You can't stay with Abe out of guilt, you know.'

Zoe flushed, 'I'm not feeling guilty.'

Mrs Killeen looked her daughter up and down. 'You've that much guilt coming off you, you'll do life. Now, I don't know why you feel that way, relationships break up all the time, but you can't stay with someone out of guilt, you know. Care for him by all means, but don't stay with him.'

'Abe was right, you do all hate him.'

'No we don't. But we love you and—'

'I was told Abel Kane is up here?'

A girl in her mid-twenties was standing in front of the nurses' station. She had dark brown shiny hair that hung in a veil to her shoulders before flipping out at the end. She was wearing flared pink jeans and pink converse trainers teamed with a frantic-looking T-shirt of blue and orange splodges against a red background.

'And you are?' the nurse asked.

'His sister.'

'Jesus,' Mrs Killeen whispered loudly.

Zoe was up and halfway across the gap before the nurse could reply. 'His sister?' she said, her heart booming, her skin pricking. 'You're Abe's sister?'

The girl swung around to face Zoe and Zoe's first thought was of course you are. They were so alike. This girl had Abe's upturned cheeky nose, his generous lips and his startling eyes. Her skin was the same creamy brown. 'Yes I am. Though I always called him Abel.'

'You sure you haven't mixed your Abel up with

our Abe?' Mrs Killeen spoke from behind Zoe. 'This Abe, he's twenty-eight and works for Aid for Africa and he—'

'This is my brother, Abel,' the girl produced a photograph. 'I haven't heard from him in about eight years, he lost touch with our family. I saw his picture on the news the other night.' She shoved the picture at Mrs Killeen, who took it.

It was a much younger Abe, sour and sullen, his arms crossed, a cap on his head that proclaimed him to be a member of God's Tipperary Church.

'It's the same boy,' Mrs Killeen pronounced. Then in another stage whisper, she added, 'There's a turn up for the books. A sister.'

Zoe ignored her. 'I'm Zoe,' she introduced herself.

'I'm Mary,' the girl said.

Mary did not suit her as a name at all, Zoe thought. She was too sparkly looking to be a Mary. 'Abe is in this room here. See.' She beckoned her over towards the room and pointed through the glass at Abe. 'You can go in if you like. I was just in there and came out for a breather. How long can she have, Ruth?'

The nurse glanced up, trying not to look astonished at the events unfolding before her. 'Half an hour,' she said.

Zoe helped Mary wash her hands and put on her mask. Then she pushed open the door and let her through.

Mrs Killeen opened her mouth to say something

and Zoe held up her hand. 'I do *not* want to hear it!'

'I was only going to say that she took her time coming,' Mrs Killeen said to Ruth.

'Let's go grab a cuppa,' Zoe pushed her mother in front of her, determined to be rid of her in the next half an hour.

Zoe waited until Mary had taken off her mask and deposited it in the bin before approaching her. 'You OK?'

Mary nodded, though her eyes were red. She avoided Zoe's gaze by pulling and tugging at her top.

'Fancy a coffee?'

Mary froze, then brought her eyes to Zoe's and studied her, trying no doubt to figure out where Zoe slotted into her brother's life. Finally she nodded.

'Well come this way so,' Zoe said as her phone vibrated in her pocket. She pulled it out and saw a message from her mother. *Tonight. Details on mystery sister. Your father is apoplectic. Love Mam.* Zoe deleted it, hoping that Mary hadn't been able to make it out. It had killed her mother to be ordered home, but she had gone after first pressing Zoe very close and telling her that she was to take care. 'They do nice coffee here,' Zoe babbled a little to Mary as they got into the lift.

'That's good,' Mary offered a smile. 'I'm gasping.'

The smile gave Zoe some hope and with a lighter heart she led Mary into the canteen and told her

458

to find a seat and that she'd shout her the coffee. Dominic was two in front of her in the queue and while Zoe pretended not to see him, he had no such qualms. 'Hi, you,' he said, having waited for her to pay.

Zoe made a big deal of putting her change into her pocket. 'Hi,' she mumbled without looking at him. 'How's your dad?'

'Worse.'

The simple answer made her look up and when she did her heart flip-flopped like a beached fish. He looked tired, heartbroken, and yet he looked so himself that her poor heart ached. 'I'm really sorry, Dom.'

'Yeah, well,' he gave a shrug that seemed to encompass hopelessness. 'It was always going to happen. How's Abe?'

'He's holding his own.'

'Good.'

There was a pause. It stretched on. Zoe made a move to go but he put a hand on her arm. 'Can we talk?' he asked.

'No,' Zoe made it sound final. She shrugged him off, hoping Mary wasn't watching. 'No, Dominic, it's not a good idea. I made a mistake, *we* made a mistake,' she corrected. 'And now, I have to think of Abe.'

'It wasn't a mistake for me,' he said.

Zoe said nothing, just pushed past him. When she sat down opposite Mary, she glanced up and saw with relief that Dominic had left. 'Just a guy

I work with,' she said to Mary, in a jolly voice that she most certainly did not feel. 'He was asking about Abe. His dad is in here too.'

'What guy?'

Mary hadn't even noticed the exchange. 'Oh, nothing . . .' She pushed Mary's coffee across to her along with some milk and sugar. 'Drink up.'

Mary smiled a thanks and took a sip.

Zoe was unsure how to begin, but was saved from trying by Mary asking, 'How do you fit into Abel's life, Zoe?'

So Zoe told her. As she narrated the tale of how she'd met Abe, Mary looked almost hurt, probably because it was all news to her. But then she got to the part about being pregnant with Lee and Mary gasped. 'Abel has a little boy?' she said, her voice almost singing with wonder. 'Really?'

'Uh-huh,' Zoe flipped open her mobile. Damn, a message from her mother again. She deleted it without reading it and instead searched for a picture of Lee. She chose one of him in his school uniform. 'That's him there.'

Mary took the phone and her small mouth puckered in an 'oh' of wonder as she looked at her new-found nephew. 'I am an auntie,' she whispered.

'Yes,' Zoe smiled, enjoying her delight.

'Can I meet him?'

Zoe hesitated. 'Abe never talked about you,' she said as delicately as she could. 'Lee doesn't even know you exist.'

Mary's hand trembled a little and she was forced to lay the phone back down on the table in case she might drop it. She sat very still for what seemed like ages, battling against the tears that stood out like diamonds in her eyes. Finally, when she'd got herself under control, she said, 'My brother is a selfish fucker.'

It was so unexpected that Zoe spluttered her coffee out all over the table. 'Jesus!'

Mary managed a smile.

Zoe smiled back.

'Sorry about that,' Mary said. Then asked, 'Has he told you about himself?'

'Only that he doesn't want to tell me anything,' Zoe said. 'Look, it's not my business.'

'But it is, he's living with you.'

Zoe shrugged.

'I'll tell you,' Mary said. 'I tell everyone. It's not a big secret. They all know down home anyway.'

Zoe wasn't even sure she wanted to know now. It would have meant more coming from Abe.

'Abel will never tell you,' Mary said, as if reading her thoughts. 'But it might help him if you knew, and he never needs to know I told you.'

Zoe was less sure about that. She wasn't good at pretending. 'I wanted Abe to tell me so he could see that he could trust me.'

'Abel trusts no one,' Mary said simply. 'How can he when our dad left us with a mentally ill mother for years?'

Zoe felt her stomach roll. It was scary hearing

461

this, discovering a new Abe underneath the one she'd always thought she knew.

'Abel and I had the worst childhood you could imagine,' Mary said without any trace of self-pity. It was almost as if she was used to trotting out her family story. 'Roald Dahl couldn't have bettered it. Abel likes to pretend it didn't happen, but you can't shut off part of yourself and not end up crippled.'

'He does that,' Zoe agreed.

'Our mother was a bit of a Bible thumper. She read the Bible morning to night, she prayed endlessly. She starved us. She accused me and Abel of all sorts of ridiculous sins. One time, she made us march in our bare feet in the snow to teach us how lucky we were to have socks. Abel got frostbite that time and had to be taken to hospital. He was about ten.'

Zoe didn't know what to say. Abe at ten must have been so cute. How could anyone . . .

'Abel got the worst of it. He was beaten and punished way more than I ever was. Then one of our neighbours reported her and she was committed. Abel and I were sent to a foster family. I loved it there.' She smiled as if remembering before she continued, 'Abel hated it though and he kept running away and having to be dragged back. I don't know why he did that. It was a lovely place, so normal. Being there changed Abel, though, he was never the same. I don't know what happened. Nine months later, Mammy came out of hospital and she was' – Mary swallowed hard – 'she was a *normal* person. She was calm and sensible and just lovely. On her first visit with us, she hugged us and told us how sorry she was, how she didn't know what she was doing, how she loved us. I cried but Abel just stood back, said nothing. He left home about a year later. He used to call in, but then he stopped.' She nodded at Zoe's phone. 'It must have been about the time your baby was born.'

Zoe took the phone up and thought of Lee and thought of Abe the same age and her heart ached for him and what he'd been through. 'And your mother?' she asked. 'How is she now?'

A tear trembled, then fell from Mary's eye. 'She died last year. I tried to find Abel for her, but I couldn't. She said she understood why he didn't want to be found.' Mary wiped some more tears that had dripped down her face and Zoe handed her a napkin.

'I'm really sorry, Mary.'

'Thank you.' She dabbed at her eyes again. 'I'm sorry for landing up here. I'll go home tomorrow.'

'No,' Zoe was horrified at the suggestion. 'He's your brother, you have a right to know how he is.' On impulse she added, 'You can stay with me.'

Mary shook her head. 'I couldn't. Abel doesn't want me here and your little boy—'

'He's your nephew and I'm sure he'll love to meet you.'

'But you said—'

'I know, but I didn't know that Abe is all you

have left. It wouldn't be right to leave now. Family matters.'

Mary's eyes watered again. 'It's all I ever wanted,' she sniffed.

And it's all her brother never wanted, Zoe thought despondently.

'So stay,' she urged.

'OK.'

Zoe caught her hand across the table. It felt good. She knew Lee would love her.

Zoe drove Mary back to her bed and breakfast to pick up her things and bring her back to the flat. It wasn't right, Abe's sister paying for accommodation when she had a perfectly good sofa she could use for free. 'Now, it's not a palace,' she warned her. 'In fact, it's a bit of a tip. We're hoping to get something better eventually.' It was only a little white lie.

Mary had protested but Zoe was adamant.

On the way, she picked up Lee from her parents' house. 'Just wait in the car, Mary, or my parents will smother you with questions. They've always been very curious about Abe.' Again another little white lie. Zoe hurried up the path and unlocking the front door she called, 'Only me.'

'Well?' Her mother appeared as if by magic from the kitchen. 'What's the story? Where has she been all this time?'

'Is Daddy better?' Lee asked. 'Can I go see him tomorrow?'

Zoe was glad of the change of subject. 'You can, honey,' she said, scooping him up. Then eyeing her parents warily, she added, 'And I have a big surprise for you in the car, Lee.'

'What?' her mother, father and Lee said together.

'Your auntie is in the car. Daddy's sister, Mary.' She tried to make it sound perfectly normal that a long-lost relative had shown up.

'Daddy has a sister?' Lee made a face.

'You have not got her in the car,' her mother tut-tutted. 'Honestly, Zoe, she could be anyone.'

'Your mother has a point there,' her father said.

'She is Abe's sister and I'm putting her up for a few nights,' Zoe said firmly, turning around and heading back out. 'And don't even think of calling over to check her out. You'll meet her at some stage.'

'Zoe, do you always have to take the waifs and strays of the world into your life?' her mother called.

'Yes, yes, I do,' she said with a grin, more to infuriate her mother than actually agree. 'I love waifs and strays.' She picked Lee's schoolbag from the hall and thanked her father for minding him.

'No problem. He's a little trouper.'

Their affection for Lee made her feel a little guilty for excluding them, they had a right to be worried about her. 'Mary seems perfectly nice, just give us some space. I'll fill you both in later.'

'Space,' her mother sniffed, a little annoyed. 'Well, it's not your flat you should be going to then, is it?'

'Space as in head space,' her father said.

'Head space? Is that a new-agey word you got from Lucy Lane?'

'Nana hates Lucy Lane,' Lee explained, as Zoe ushered him out the door. 'She wears tight shorts and T-shirts.'

Zoe barely heard him, instead she braced herself to introduce him to Mary and answer all the questions he'd have. Mary had pulled her window down. Lee paused mid-step and gawked at her.

'Hello, Lee,' Mary smiled. 'I believe I am your auntie. I'm so pleased to meet you.'

Lee stared at her shyly.

'Your T-shirt is cool.'

'It's not a T-shirt, it's a soccer jersey. Me and my granddad go to the matches. It's Bohemians. Do you know them?'

And Lee was off, seemingly happy to accept that a new auntie had shown up in his life out of nowhere.

CHAPTER 43

After her show the next day, Deirdre bought a bunch of flowers and made her way to St Catherine's hospital. She never normally went out on a limb, always afraid of going too far or doing too much and annoying people, but she figured that Zoe might like a bunch of flowers. It was just a token, to say she was thinking of her. Ann Morrisey had appreciated her mother's gesture all those years ago, and though this wasn't in the same league at all, Deirdre was sure that if Zoe asked for any more help she would give it. Hadn't Zoe been so nice to Lily?

Losing a man you lusted after was nothing to losing your partner, Deirdre had told herself sternly. Zoe had it a lot harder than she did.

She asked at reception and was told that she wouldn't be able to get in to see Abe because she wasn't family and it was strictly a one-visitor-only policy.

'Is there any way I could talk to Zoe?' she asked.

The receptionist rang up and told Deirdre to hang on. She stood nervously, unsure of her reception.

467

'Deirdre!'

Deirdre's first thought was that Zoe looked terrible. Her hair was flat and lifeless and she had huge circles under her eyes. Deirdre covered her shock and proffered the flowers. 'For you. Just to say I'm thinking of you.'

'Thank you,' Zoe buried her head in the blossoms and took a sniff. 'That's so nice. D'you fancy a coffee?'

'Only if you have time.'

'I've loads of time. There's a lot of waiting about in this place,' she smiled. 'Congratulations by the way.'

'On?'

'Your show. My dad was talking to Gary Sims the other night, he says they're all flabbergasted down at the station. It'll do Gary good to be knocked from his perch,' she giggled as she began to walk in the direction of the canteen.

'I resigned,' Deirdre said casually. 'I hate the bloody job.'

'No way!'

'Life's too short,' Deirdre said and then realised that she said the wrong thing because Zoe's eyes filled up. She clamped a hand over her mouth. 'Oh, I'm sorry, pet. Me and my big mouth. That's how the show is doing so well. I mess up big time, all the time.'

A splutter of a laugh. Then Zoe handed her the flowers, saying, 'You take these to a table and I'll grab us a coffee. It really is so nice of you.'

Deirdre found a table and watched as Zoe got them some drinks. She was joined by an elderly man whom she seemed a little impatient with. The man raised his hand and waved over and Deirdre waved back. The man crossed towards her. 'Deirdre Deegan,' he said. 'It's a pleasure.' He held out his hand and shook hers vigorously. 'I'm Liam, Zoe's dad. Your show makes me laugh my socks off. I never knew you could be so funny. That new producer brings out the best in you.'

Deirdre felt as if Zoe's dad had poked her hard in the heart.

'My dad wanted to join us,' Zoe said, rolling her eyes behind her dad's back as she handed out the coffees. 'Even though I said no.'

Before Deirdre could answer, Liam sat in saying, 'It's a bit of a hobby of mine, meeting celebs. When I was young I used to go chasing autographs. I've got a lot of good ones. If I'd known you were coming, I would have had a picture for you to sign, instead I only have this.' He took out a crumpled receipt and smoothed it on the table. Then he patted his pockets for a pen. 'Here we go.' He handed her the pen. 'I know it's a green one, so anyone who sees it will think you're a bit of a psycho, but I'll tell them it was my pen.'

'Wow, that'll be reassuring,' Zoe teased drily.

Liam watched with rapt attention as Deirdre signed her autograph. Then he folded it up carefully. 'What age would you be now? Probably not much younger than myself.'

'Dad!' Zoe winced.

'Fifty-five,' Deirdre said.

'You're looking well on it.'

'Thanks.'

'Though I suppose your single life isn't too stressful.'

'Bye, Dad,' Zoe said pointedly.

'Righto, I'll get out of your hair and go upstairs,' Mr Killeen patted Zoe's shoulder. 'You take your time.'

As he walked away, Zoe said, 'When I was a teenager, I used to be mortified by him, nothing has changed.'

Deirdre managed a laugh. 'My mother mortified me too. Your dad seems lovely.'

'Ah, he is. So was your dad, by all accounts.'

'Well, Jimmy was. The other guy was a dead loss.'

'Would you ever trace him?' Zoe knew she would if it was her. Hadn't she gone and tried to trace Abe's mother, for God's sake. What would she be like if it was a relation of her own?

'Nope,' Deirdre said grimly. 'Apparently, he wanted to meet me once but I told my mother I wanted nothing to do with him. I didn't even want to know his name. So she told him and that was that.'

'Wow, how did your mother feel when she saw him again?'

'I dunno,' Deirdre felt ashamed. 'I never asked her. She gave him his marching orders, though, I know that much.'

'Good enough for him.'

'Yeah, if a man isn't interested in staying with you, he isn't worth it.'

Deirdre had the weird sensation that she'd said the wrong thing. Again.

THE ELEVENTH WEDNESDAY

Carrie waited until there was perfect silence before she began to read.

Jimmy died when he got blood cancer. He was only fifty-five and all of a sudden he was complaining of being tired and falling asleep in the middle of the day. At first, I made him extra-special dinners or bought him fruit and made him eat it, but then he started losing weight and catching colds and finally he went to the doctor and despite all the medicine and all the hope they peddled, he just got sicker and sicker.

In the beginning, when he wasn't so sick, he was at home and I'd sit by his bed and hold his hand and I'd tell him news from the town. How there was a new shop selling fancy new clothes and of how everyone went to look but that the fashions were so risky, people were afraid to buy anything in it. I told him of the calves on the farm and of how his brother was doing a great job with them, I talked about the hens and how many eggs we'd had that day. I read to him sometimes, pieces from the paper or books. And all the time he got thinner and thinner and we'd blind ourselves to it.

He never complained, just stared up at me, his eyes almost caressing my face. I noticed that he smiled when I did, he laughed when I did and I felt closer to him at that time than I ever had before. I realised, like a slow bright-edged dawn, that love had crept up on me while I slept. This man that I had stayed with out of guilt had allowed love to wash across me day-by-day like a flannel; it had curled itself in my stomach, a shot of warm whiskey. This man had become my life. And as I realised it, the terror of losing him grew. I became determined that I would not lose him. I told him of all the people I'd read about who had been cured of this thing. I talked about all the things we'd do when he was better. We'd walk the farm, we'd tie up the fences, we'd birth the cows and drink their warm milk. We'd go into Cavan and I'd buy a shocking dress and wear it to mass. He laughed so much at that, I thought I had killed him. We'd buy seed for the fallow acres and watch the crops grow and get strong in the sunshine.

'You're a farmer's wife,' he said to me.

And I was. I had become someone I had never wanted to be and like a pair of jeans, it had eventually moulded itself to my form. 'I'm your wife,' I corrected. 'That's who I am.'

He smiled and drifted off to sleep.

There was a song I used to sing in those days. I was never much of a singer but I made it up for him. It was a song of the land, calling him back to it.

I can't grow my wheat/without your care/I can't feed your livestock/without you there/

473

I refuse to let the birds in/I refuse to hear their call/ I refuse to let you go/I refuse to let you fall.

Oh, stay with me my farmer boy/stay with me I cry/stay with me my farmer boy/without you I will die.

Jimmy liked that song.

About a week before he died, they moved him to the hospital. He was given a room to himself and all the painkillers he needed to be comfortable. Sometimes he hardly knew me; other times he was so there that I could almost feel his pain in my own body.

And then, one morning, really early, I woke to find him staring across at me. 'Jimmy?' I whispered. 'Are you OK?'

He beckoned me over to him. I clasped his hand and he smiled and I was reminded unexpectedly of that day in the street when he'd hidden on me and jumped out and frightened me. I'd never get that back, that time was gone and I hadn't valued it enough. Tears sparked the back of my eyes and he whispered, 'Don't. Don't cry, beautiful.'

'I'm sorry.'

He squeezed my hand in his. 'I just want to tell you that I always knew.'

'Knew what?' I gave a watery smile. 'That I loved you?'

'That she wasn't mine.'

At first I didn't think I'd heard right, then I didn't actually know what he was talking about. I suppose years of pretending had led me to believe, years of denial had led me to almost forget. 'Who?'

'Deirdre, I know she's not mine.'

'Oh, Jimmy. Oh, God.' Deep shame caught hold of me and I tried to pull away from him.

He caught my hand in a tighter grip. 'I didn't care. I loved you and because she was part of you, I knew I'd love her. I didn't want to see you hurt or thrown into one of those terrible places.'

'How did you know?'

He smiled, that teasing, annoying smile that drove me mad. 'Because I knew you, that's how.'

'And you never said?'

'No, because it didn't matter,' he said. 'Not then. But I just want you to know now, if you want to ever tell Deirdre, I won't mind. She's a young woman now, with her own life in Dublin and she'd be able for it.'

'You are her daddy,' I said fiercely. 'You and no one else.'

He ignored that. 'And I know at times you were unhappy but I think, in the end, we didn't do too bad, eh?'

I started to cry. 'We did great,' I said through my tears. 'We did absolutely great.' And I realised that for a long time in my marriage, I'd been looking into the sun, blinding myself and not able to see that the best thing I had was right in front of me. Jimmy was what I'd needed, what I'd wanted had never mattered. I held his face in my hands, 'You and me, we did good.'

He smiled and sighed and just like that, he was gone. I knew he was because the room seemed suddenly empty. My childhood friend, my tormentor, the best man in the world had died.

And I realised that song I sang for him was really all about me.

Carrie's voice trembled and she dissolved into tears, as did Deirdre. In fact the whole room was a sniffing, snuffling mess.

Her dad had always known and never cared. She wished she could have told him that when she'd known, she hadn't cared either.

But maybe he knew that too.

CHAPTER 45

Mary solemnly handed Lee five brightly wrapped presents. 'I missed five of your birthdays,' she said, 'so I got these for you.'

Greg, who had called over to the flat to babysit, uttered an impressed 'Wow.'

'So that's where you were yesterday,' Zoe smiled. 'You shouldn't have.'

'I'm a big boy,' Lee said, eyeing the gifts with suspicion, 'so I won't need stuff for a one-year-old. Thanks anyway.'

'Lee!' Zoe said, feigning embarrassment. 'That's rude.'

'I said, "Thanks anyway"!'

'Open them and then decide,' Mary giggled as Greg laughed.

Abe's sister had proved quite a big hit with her family, Zoe thought with a mixture of emotion. Her father had been charmed by her. His protective instinct had come to the fore when he'd heard about her rotten childhood. 'You're Lee's aunt,' he'd said, 'so now you are a part of our family.'

Mary had filled up and Zoe wanted to hug her dad hard for those words.

Mrs Killeen had started taking home-cooked meals to the hospital and insisting that Mary and Zoe take them home to eat. And just this morning, Greg had spent at least an hour telling her how he felt about being gay in Dublin. If only Abe had embraced their kindness so wholeheartedly, Zoe thought despondently as her phone pinged.

She answered as Lee, with Greg's help, started tearing the wrapping paper from present number one. 'Hello?'

'Hey, Zoe, it's Carrie.'

'Hi, what's up? Do you need me in there?' She half-hoped Carrie would say yes, she was beginning to feel a little hemmed in by the hospital routine.

'No, we're doing fine without you,' Carrie said. 'Oh, Zoe, you should have heard Lily's diary yesterday. Harry thought I was having a breakdown I cried so much. Jimmy died.'

Zoe was sure it would have been upsetting, but as there was a real possibility of Abe dying, she didn't want to hear the details. 'So what's up?' she asked instead.

'Oh, yeah,' Carrie's voice dipped. 'Dominic's dad died earlier this morning. The funeral is Friday at eleven.'

'Oh, that's awful,' Zoe said. 'Poor Dominic.'

'Yes, well, if you see him in the hospital today, give him a hug from us?' Carrie said. 'He sounded very down when he rang.'

'Will do,' Zoe said, knowing there was no hope of that. Since meeting him in the canteen that day, she checked and double-checked each time she went anywhere in the hospital so she could avoid bumping into him. Seeing him disturbed her and she couldn't say why. 'Thanks for letting me know. I'll see you at the funeral.'

'Mammy, look,' Lee waved five computer games in the air. 'Now all I need is for you to buy me a PS3.'

'Oh shit,' Mary looked stricken as Greg laughed.

Later that night, after Lee had gone to bed, Zoe poured Mary a glass of wine and began to regale her with tales of their horrible neighbours.

'When were you going to tell me, Zoe?' Mary interrupted suddenly.

'Tell you what?' Zoe laid her glass of wine on the crappy coffee table and pulled open a bag of crisps. They were only cheese and onion but Zoe liked cheese and onion with red wine.

'That you and Abel were breaking up?'

The crisp bag ripped and crisps fell all over the floor. 'Did my dad say that?' Zoe asked crossly. 'He had no business.' She began scooping up the crisps.

'It was Lee,' Mary answered. 'He told me that you and he were looking for a house and that his daddy was going to stay in this flat. He was quite excited about it actually.'

Zoe wasn't sure if Mary wanted to eat crisps that had fallen on the floor. She picked some from her clothes and thought about how to respond. 'It was discussed,' she muttered. 'Nothing was finalised. And now, well, things have changed.'

Mary stared at her for a very long time.

'What?' Zoe said, growing uncomfortable.

'Why were you breaking up in the first place?' Mary asked as she plucked a crisp from where it had fallen on the floor.

Zoe felt like telling her that it wasn't her business but instead she answered, 'Because he wasn't honest with me. I wanted him to talk about things and he wouldn't.'

'So if that changes you'll take him back?'

'I guess,' Zoe said. Then nodded, 'Of course.'

'Oh, right,' Mary said. 'And you think after this he'll start talking to you?'

'I dunno,' she hadn't thought about it really. She just assumed. 'I hope so,' she said, then added, 'Well, you're here now so maybe . . .' she let the sentence trail off. She hoped that when Abe woke up, which the doctors had said was possible in the next couple of days, that things would just slot into place.

'You can't stay with Abel just because he's Lee's dad or out of guilt, Zoe,' Mary said. 'I know he's my brother but you have to be happy too.'

Lily's words flashed into Zoe's mind. The man we think we want might not be the man we want. Trouble was, she didn't know what she wanted. 'No matter what happens,' Zoe attempted a grin, 'you'll always be Lee's auntie. And my mother will continue to feed you.'

Mary's snort of laughter was such a happy sound.

CHAPTER 46

The pond had been finished and now Deirdre had the job of christening the fish that were happily swimming about in their new home. Why couldn't her contract at the radio station have ended before now, Deirdre thought, as she plunged her hand into a hat of names chosen by listeners. Those whose fish names were pulled out would win a particularly crappy bird box.

'I'm picking the first name now,' Deirdre said as Paul cued up a drum roll. 'Now remember we'll inform all the winners after the show. Good luck, everyone.' She pulled out an entry. 'Cosmos,' she read.

'Fucking stupid name for a fish,' Paul said in her headphones. He'd seemed determined to be grumpy this past nine days. No one could understand why. Deirdre feigned ignorance too, even though he picked on her the most.

'Ping,' Deirdre read and ignored Paul's snort of derision. 'Shitface,' she read out before she realised what she'd done.

There was an explosion of laughter from Emma.

'And we can't use that name so, hard luck listener,'

Deirdre said flustered. 'Who vetted these?' she mouthed at Paul.

He shrugged, though there was a bit of a grin about his mouth.

'And the third one is Gay Byrne. Oh, I'll have a bit of competition in the talk-show stakes,' she joked feebly. 'And the next name up is Filo and finally, Dog.'

'Are our listeners stupid?' Paul grouched.

'So thanks, everyone, tune in tomorrow when we'll be reviewing some new gardening books.'

'OK, grand.' Paul pulled off his headphones and stalked off.

Deirdre watched him go.

This had gone far enough. Planting bogus names in the hat was not funny.

She found him in her office, smoking out the window. 'Caught,' she attempted some levity.

His sour expression killed it. 'I've quit my job so go ahead and report me.'

Deirdre sat opposite, determined to say her piece. 'I'm sorry I reacted badly last week,' she began. 'I'm mortified. I was out of my depth, I've never been . . .' – she tried to think of the word – 'propositioned before.' Oh shit, that made her sound like someone from the Victorian period.

Paul snorted as expected.

'But it's no excuse to plant "Shitface" in the hat. That's unprofessional.'

'I didn't. I wouldn't.' Standing up, he stubbed

out his cigarette in her fancy ashtray that she never used, because it was just way too good.

'Hey,' she grabbed it from under him.

He watched her. 'And that is you in a nutshell,' he declared.

'What? You've just ruined my ashtray. It's a decoration. Have you no bloody respect?'

'You have no bloody life,' he roared at her and she reared back. 'It's a frigging ashtray, so I used it.'

Deirdre pulled her cardigan around her defensively. He was really cross.

'Look at you,' he said, 'all buttoned up tight against the world. I thought it was just a thing you had going, it drove me wild.' He leaned his hands on the table and glared at her. 'But it isn't, is it? You really are . . .' – he paused, his eyes raked her up and down – 'I dunno what you are, Deirdre. I just don't know. I'm sorry I overstepped the mark. Let's just let it go.'

He walked out and closed the office door after him. It was as if he'd stripped her naked and she had to hold on to her tatters of dignity.

She started to declutter that night. Standing on a chair, she had to stretch to reach the top-most shelves. Sheaves and sheaves of old paper, contracts and bank statements and old newspapers that she'd kept for some long-ago startling news story tumbled out on top of her. Her house was clinging to the past. Every surface in it was adorned with memories of lives lived by people she barely knew. Pictures hung on walls showing places she'd never been. Knick-knacks people had bought her that she really should have known better than to keep. In the whole house, there was not one picture of her. Anywhere. Except for the one of her and John. And why would she want that hanging up? It brought her nothing but guilt whenever she looked at it. Because, hanging there, it was proof of a relationship, she thought suddenly. Proof of ancient happiness.

Stupid. Stupid.

Rick would be in for a surprise when he next visited – he'd gone home the night before.

She would make space in her house for the future, she thought as she piled all her rubbish higgledy-piggledy into great black rubbish sacks. Paul would never again think she had no life.

As she looked at her clutter, all piled up and ready to be discarded, Deirdre felt that on some warped level she had surrounded herself with objects to make up for the lack of people in her life and had grown a beautiful garden to make up for the lack of affection in her life. If only she'd known how much her mother loved her.

She wished her mother were still around to tell her what to do, because life had no signposts. Or rules.

It was a wilderness where anything could happen.

CHAPTER 47

Zoe slid into a seat beside Carrie just as the funeral mass got underway. Carrie was like a rainbow in a black sky, her bright clothes colourful against the sedate greys and blacks of everyone else. She beamed at Zoe. 'How's Abe? Did you get my card?'

'He's stable and we did, thanks. How are you?'

'Great,' Carrie whispered. 'Harry's mother bought us a car.'

'No way!'

'Excuse me,' the man in the seat behind tipped Carrie on the shoulder. 'I'm so happy that you've got a car' – he turned to Zoe – 'and that you got this lady's card and that Abe is OK, but there is a funeral going on here so can you shut up?'

Carrie reddened and glared at him.

'Sorry,' Zoe whispered as she sat back in the seat. Horrible as it was, it was nice to get time away from the hospital even if it was to go to a funeral. It was far more relaxing here than at the hospital and it smelled better too. She listened as the priest talked about the crash that had killed Dominic's mother and left his dad incapacitated.

He spoke of how Rosie had given up her job to look after her dad and the way Dominic had come home from a prestigious hotel in Paris to support the house. *A prestigious hotel? Dominic had never said that.* She watched hungrily as Dominic, clean shaven and white faced, got up to do a reading. His voice was low and he rushed his words, seeming embarrassed, but at the end he looked up and Zoe's breath caught in her throat. Her eyes wanted to latch on to him and never lose sight of him, but then he sat down and all she could see was the top of his dark head. His sister did the next reading. She was a plumper version of her brother and, unlike Dominic, her eyes were swollen and red from crying and in the final words of the reading, her voice broke.

'Aw,' Carrie whispered sympathetically, 'wouldn't you love to just hug her?'

And Dominic did when she stepped down. He stood up and embraced her and the two of them stayed like that for endless seconds in the silent church.

Finally the mass ended and Dominic, along with some members of his extended family, carried his father's coffin down the church. That was the part of the funeral service that always set Zoe crying, children bearing their parents on that final journey. To think that Dominic was now tall and big enough to carry his own dad. To think that once upon a time, Dominic's father had helped him grow into the man he was now, so that he was able to

486

provide this final homage. She wiped her face with the heel of her hand. Oh, God, she hated funerals.

'Here,' Carrie pushed a tissue at her.

'Thanks.' Zoe took it gratefully, but for some reason the tears wouldn't stop. 'We'll just go and hug Dom, then we'll leave.'

'Grand,' Carrie agreed. 'But I just want to talk to his sister too. Did you see her shoes, weren't they gorgeous?'

Zoe looked at her in disbelief.

'But they were,' Carrie said. 'I know it's a funeral and all, but great shoes are great shoes.'

'Well don't ask her where she got them, will you?' Zoe said, feeling like a granny lecturing a child, but it had to be said. Carrie was capable of doing it.

'It's a funeral.' Carrie made a face. 'Come on.' In annoyance, she stalked out in front.

Zoe tried her best to catch up but short of shoving people aside, she couldn't. Instead, she joined the queue to offer her condolences to Dominic. Her mouth was dry as she neared him and she would have given someone a million quid to do it for her. She was normally good at dealing with grief, having seen it so many times in the home, but Dominic's grief would be worse.

'Carrie, thanks for coming,' she heard him say as Carrie reached him.

'For the best chef in Lakelands, how could I not?' Carrie said, hugging him hard. 'I am so sorry, Dom. If there is anything I can do, let me know.'

He nodded. 'Yeah, I will, I'll be back next week.'

Zoe kept her gaze down, not wanting to catch his eye. Finally after three more people, it was Zoe's turn.

She looked at him, and he at her, for what seemed a long time. He looked lost, as if he didn't quite know what was happening. Zoe was unsure if she should hug him. She wanted to, just to let him know how sorry she was, but it was as if she was frozen. Finally, she said, 'I'm so sorry, Dominic. About everything.'

He flinched. 'Thanks for coming.'

And she moved on. She glanced around for Carrie but couldn't find her.

June caught up with her. She hadn't seen June in the church. They exchanged a few words before June gasped, 'Would you ever look at that!' She pointed across the churchyard.

Zoe looked and the angst she was feeling over Dominic and her inadequate words momentarily disappeared as Rosie took off her shoe and held it out for Carrie's inspection. Carrie was looking dead impressed and Rosie was smiling.

'I don't believe that she asked that girl to show her her shoes,' June gasped.

'I don't believe that she got that girl to smile,' Zoe said back, nudging June with her elbow. 'That's what you pay Carrie for, isn't it?'

'I know, but at a funeral!'

'Best place in the world for a smile.' Zoe linked

June's arm in hers. 'Come on, let's go get a coffee. I need one before I go back to the hospital.'

Zoe, along with her dad and Mary, waited anxiously outside Abe's room as the doctors attempted to wake Abe before taking him off the ventilator. All his blood tests had gone well and there was no reason for him not to wake up. Family were not allowed in, though, and so the three of them were confined to pacing the corridors.

After twenty minutes, a doctor came out. He was smiling. 'Abe woke briefly and is breathing on his own.'

Zoe had to sit down. Mary let out a sob and wrapped an arm about Zoe's shoulder and Mr Killeen, heaving a sigh of relief, asked, 'So what now, doctor?'

'Well, we'll let one person in at a time to see him. However, just be aware that if he wakens when you are there, he might get agitated or scared. On the other hand, he could be fine. Everyone is different. If Abe asks questions, answer them but don't overload him with information, OK?'

'Absolutely,' Mr Killeen nodded. 'No problem, doctor.'

'And don't give him anything to drink, just swab his mouth with water. Encourage him to keep the oxygen mask on as it will soothe his sore throat.'

'Absolutely,' Mr Killeen said again.

Zoe had to smile at his ingratiating tone. Her dad was in awe of the medical profession.

'So, who'd like to go in?'

'Well, I don't think he'd really want to see me,' Mr Killeen laughed a little.

'Or me,' Mary muttered.

The doctor looked a little startled.

Zoe wondered if Abe would even want to see her, but she so wanted to see him. 'I'll go in,' she said, standing up.

'Don't tell him about me,' Mary whispered, shooting a glance at the doctor. 'It might upset him.'

Zoe nodded. She hadn't been planning to and she was glad that Mary would be OK with that. Abe's possible negative reaction to his sister turning up had been worrying her a little.

'This way,' the doctor said as he ushered her into the room. The first thing Zoe noticed was that the sound of the ventilator was gone. Abe was breathing normally, his chest rising and falling in a perfect rhythm. There was no ugly tube in his mouth, only a mask over his face. Zoe let go a breath that she hadn't even been aware she was holding. Two ER nurses and another doctor were gathered at the bedside.

'I'm going to try and wake him again,' the doctor who had brought her in said. 'We'll see if he recognises you or understands us.'

Zoe nodded.

'Abe,' the doctor said loudly, 'Abe, can you hear me?'

Nothing. Abe continued to breathe but was otherwise motionless.

'Abe.' The doctor touched Abe's face and gently tapped his cheek. 'Can you wake up for us?'

'It's like waking someone after an anaesthetic,' one of the nurses whispered to Zoe. 'It takes a little time.'

Zoe's gaze was riveted to the bed.

Slowly Abe's eyelids flickered.

'That's it, Abe, well done,' the doctor said. 'Open up now.'

Abe blinked slowly and opened his eyes.

The doctor beckoned Zoe forward. When she was standing in Abe's line of sight, the doctor continued, 'Do you know who this is, Abe?'

Zoe inadvertently clenched her hands and held her breath.

Abe blinked again. 'Zoe,' he mouthed. 'Zoe.'

'Oh, God, yes,' she said, letting the air out with a whoosh and touching his hand. 'It is me. Oh, Abe, how are you?'

He blinked again and swallowed, then he closed his eyes and was gone.

'Fantastic,' the doctor said, though Zoe had thought for one horrible moment that he had died and she felt as if she was going to puke. She had to sit down. 'He'll improve every day.' The doctor patted Zoe on the shoulder. 'And you can finally relax.'

They left, and Zoe was alone in the room with Abe. She remained sitting, unsure of what to do. Was she just meant to wait until he woke again? It had been easier when she knew he was going to sleep all the time, she felt she could talk to him, but now she was half afraid to wake him. Her phone bleeped. Guiltily she pulled it from her pocket.

The docs all seem happy, her dad had texted.

She texted back: *Yes, he woke up and said my name. I'll hang on for a while. You go and get coffee.*

She knew her dad would like that. She sat back in the visitors' chair which was surprisingly comfortable and her mind ran through the events of the day, stubbornly focusing on Dominic. No matter how she tried to escape him, his face loomed before her. The guilt she felt at how she'd treated him was almost as bad as the guilt she felt over spending the night with him. Of course she hadn't felt guilty at the time, it was only since Abe had been hurt. For the first time since *that* night she replayed it in her head. Dominic had led her upstairs to his room. She teased him over his walls which had been adorned with pictures of food, she'd examined his scrapbooks and joked about his CD collection of heavy metal. He had taken it all with good grace, recognising it for the stalling tactic that it was. But the hungry way his eyes followed her about his room had turned her on and on and on . . . then, he had crossed towards her and undressed her and she him. Zoe recalled, in the dim light of the hospital room, every touch, every caress, every murmured endearment. Afterwards, she had gathered up her clothes, dressed hastily and told Dominic that he was a very bad boy. He'd told her, in that lazy drawling way of his, that was so damn sexy, that he'd always loved her. Then he paused and told her that if all she wanted was one night, that was fine. He didn't get too involved with girls, he said, because once they found out about his dad, they tended to leave him. 'I won't be leaving you,' she'd said, blowing him a kiss, which he'd caught. She'd gone home, full of new happiness, and ignored him ever since.

Zoe allowed her tears to fall unchecked. This would be the only time, she vowed, the first and last time that she would remember.

Abe needed her now.

THE TWELFTH WEDNESDAY

After Jimmy died, I was bereft. I never quite understood the full meaning of that word before but I knew only too well what it meant now. Jimmy had been my champion, my support, a man who believed in me, who accepted me without questions. He was the one true person in my life. It was an unconditional love he had offered and one I had gladly accepted. I had never felt worthy, having been thrown over by Patrick but, in Jimmy's eyes, I was a queen and when I looked into his eyes and saw my reflection there, I could believe it of myself too. He loved me. Really loved me. And sometimes all we need is one person to believe the best of us and the best we will be. That is who I became.

There was a huge Jimmy-shaped hole in my life.

I found that working on the farm would frequently make me cry, I'd imagine all the animals wondering where Jimmy had gone. Good kind Jimmy, who knew them all by name. I imagined the fields crying out for the sound of his feet on the earth, I had dreams of the house crumbling down about me.

I missed his voice, his smile, his habit of coming in in the evenings and clapping his hands together.

I missed the way he pushed doors open and broke the handles. I was reminded of him in every crack in the wall of the farmhouse, in the way the picture of the Sacred Heart hung proudly over the fireplace. He'd fixed that after it had been crooked for years. I missed the smell of him, the warmth of him, the humanity of him.

In the end, it was too much. And poor Deirdre was distracted worrying about me. I found that I was unable to get up in the mornings again for a while. I started to sleep all the time. But now there was no Jimmy to care for me, no Deirdre to curl up beside me in the bed and so, one day, at the start of spring about a year later, when a hint of the freshness outside stole in through my window, I decided to sell up and move to Dublin to be near my daughter. I'm not sure if Deirdre really wanted me there. I think she wanted to be free of me and my moods, but I swore to myself that Deirdre would never again have to care for me. No matter what happened, I would not burden her. It was the least I could do.

I'd watched her grow from a beautiful little girl into an anxious hyper-alert one. All the good Jimmy did for her I undid by my unhappiness. Jimmy told me that was nonsense, but a mother knows. I wanted my Deirdre to be happy, to have the life I never had. I encouraged her to go to Dublin, to spread her wings. I sometimes wonder if it was my dreams she followed.

★　　★　　★

Quite quickly, I sold the farm to Jimmy's younger brother, which I knew Jimmy would have liked. His brother told me that anytime I wanted, there would be a bed ready for me down there. In order to keep the farm in Jimmy's family, I sold it for less than it was worth but it was enough to get me a small terraced house on Dublin's southside. Six miles to the city centre on the bus.

Finally, I was living the life I'd craved and while I loved it, I also realised that without Jimmy, everything was a little washed out. Nothing had the bright spark that he gave it and I was so glad that Deirdre had the good sense to ask to go home to Daddy all those years ago. Deirdre darling, never feel guilty for that.

Then one day, after a year in Dublin, two years after Jimmy died, I got a telephone call. A voice that only took microseconds for me to recognise said, 'Well, you're a hard lady to track down.'

I froze.

'Lil, it's me. Patrick.'

I dropped the receiver, the phone toppled from the hall table and I backed away, pressing myself into the wall, as if by some miracle Patrick could actually see me down the phone. Only when I was sure that Patrick had hung up did I place phone and receiver back.

Of course he —

'Sorry, am I disturbing anything?' Zoe poked her head in the door. 'D'you mind?'

'Zoe,' Carrie smiled, 'you're back?'

'Just for the morning, I want to arrange the entertainment for the weekend. I'll be back properly next week.'

June, who was sitting in, flapped her hand. 'The entertainment is sorted. Ronnie offered and his daughter is accompanying him on the accordion.'

'Really? That's fantastic,' Zoe beamed. She glanced at the diary. 'Oh, you're nearly finished.'

'How's your boyfriend?' Deirdre asked. Her voice was a bit shaky after the diary. She hadn't realised that her mother had sold the farm for less than it was worth to keep it in Jimmy's family. That had been a lovely thing to do. Her dad would have appreciated it. She remembered giving her mother grief for letting it go, the one time she'd let fly at her mother and she'd never given her the chance to explain. And, really, how could she have expected her mother to stay in a place in which she'd been so unhappy? If only she'd listened more . . .

'He's awake and talking,' Zoe answered breaking into her thoughts. 'I'm bringing our little boy in to see him today. I wanted to be sure Abe would recognise him before I did. I thought it might upset both of them otherwise, but Abe has asked to see him.'

'Oh, that's wonderful,' Rick spoke from the corner of the room, where he'd been standing without Zoe noticing him. 'Nothing worse than not being recognised.'

As one, they all looked at Lily. She smiled absently.

'How you doing, gorgeous?' Zoe crouched down to her. 'Scandalising us all with your diary, eh?'

'Jimmy died and Patrick has rung her,' June said. 'Fecking nerve.'

'D'you mind, that's my biological father you're talking about,' Deirdre said with a smile. She was glad someone had good news.

'Here,' Carrie handed the diary to Zoe. 'You read it. She loves your voice.'

June filled Zoe in on what had been happening and Zoe found a place on the floor, beside Lily's chair and began to read. It was nice to come here and forget about her own life for a while.

Of course, being Patrick, he didn't give up. He kept ringing and writing, begging me to hear him out. At first I felt I owed him nothing. Had he considered me when he'd run away to London all those years ago? Had he thought about me when he'd got married? No, I thought, I will not let him explain. I don't need him to explain.

And then I was robbed.

A young boy snatched my bag on O'Connell Street. He was so young that he wasn't even a fast runner. Enraged, I ran after him, shouting at people to stop him. Eventually, a man caught him by the scruff of the neck and shook him like a dog. When I caught up with the boy, he was crying. He held out my bag and said he was sorry. And I was suddenly aware

498

that this man and I were frightening a small boy. Yes, he had stolen my bag, but the question of why he had done it suddenly seemed very important. He needed money, he said, so that the big boys would leave him alone. As he explained, his nose ran and his eyes ran and his voice broke and came back. And I realised that with understanding comes forgiveness. So I give him money and told him to tell the big boys that that was it. No more robbing. I don't know what happened, maybe it was foolish of me, but it felt right at the time.

After that I thought that, maybe, to get rid of my anger at Patrick, I should meet him and hear what he had to say.

And so we met on Grafton Street outside Bewley's. He arrived first and I noticed him when I was about ten feet away. It would be a lie to say that I didn't care how I looked. I bought new clothes and I'd had my hair done. I wanted him to see what he'd missed. He looked good and my traitorous heart leapt when he flicked his cigarette butt into a bin with his forefinger. How I'd loved that as a girl – it had seemed so sophisticated. He saw me and smiled, the same old Patrick smile but surprisingly, it didn't have any effect on me. In fact, it annoyed me that he could smile when he'd left my life in tatters all those years ago.

'After you,' he said, pushing open the door and in silence we bought a coffee and sat at a table in a fairly unoccupied part of the shop. I sipped my drink and he sipped his.

'You look well,' he said.

'I am well,' I replied.

There was more silence. His mouth worked about a bit as if he were trying out things he should say. I quite enjoyed it.

'Jimmy wrote to me,' he said eventually. It was so unexpected that I started choking on my coffee. Patrick had to jump up and thump me on the back. Yes, he thumped ME!

'Jimmy did not write to you,' I said when I'd recovered and my voice was furious and low. 'How dare you use him? He was a good man.'

'He was a great man,' Patrick agreed. 'You deserved him. I could never have given you what he did. And maybe you won't believe me, but I was always sorry about it.'

I said nothing.

'I was young and stupid,' Patrick went on. 'That is the only excuse I have. I've been ashamed my whole life for what happened.'

'You could have come back,' I said.

'You had Jimmy. I thought you were happy, I was not going to ruin that.'

I remained silent. I hadn't let myself be happy with Jimmy for years. What a waste of time it had been.

'My own marriage was to prove that I was good husband material, that I wasn't the weak, stupid man who'd let you down. But I couldn't let myself settle. The guilt was too much.'

'I'd say the money helped,' I muttered.

'The only good thing I did for you and your

500

daughter was to stay away,' he said, ignoring my barb. 'I am actually proud of that.'

I swallowed, moved despite myself. 'So why did Jimmy write to you?'

'Because he wanted me to explain to you. He said he thought you'd appreciate it. It took me a while to screw up the courage, another while to track you down.'

Even when he was dead, Jimmy had the ability to surprise and shock me. The man had known me so well. I stood up, afraid I might cry. 'Yes, well, he was right, I do appreciate it. Thanks.'

'Lily,' Patrick jumped up too.

We faced each other.

'Look,' he shook his head, 'I know I've done nothing for you or for my daughter—'

'Deirdre, that's her name, and she was Jimmy's, not yours.'

He dipped his head at my words. 'Well, I know I've done nothing,' he went on, talking now to his shoes, 'so, maybe it's too little too late, but here,' he pulled a card from his pocket and pressed it into my hand, 'if ever you want anything, and I mean anything, I will get it for you. I swear.'

'I won't want anything.'

'Still . . .' He let the word hang. Then he left.

I told Deirdre about him some weeks later. I felt I had no choice. She reacted badly, which is what I expected really. To find out that she wasn't part of Jimmy's blood must have come as a shock. She wanted nothing to do with Patrick, told me she never wanted to know him. Never wanted to hear his name.

Then she stormed out and though we spoke over the following years, it was never the same. I missed my girl.

I married Jimmy to save Deirdre. I ended up saving myself.

And for what I am about to do, dear daughter, forgive me.

'And that's it,' Zoe said, sounding puzzled. She flicked through it to see if she'd missed anything, but there was nothing, only the blank page at the end.

'I don't understand,' Deirdre said. 'Forgive her? For what?' She looked around at them.

They all looked blankly back.

'I did storm out,' Deirdre admitted. 'I told her I didn't want to know anything about this man. I was in my thirties, for God's sake.' She gulped a little tearfully. 'I should have let her tell me. I should have let her tell me that Dad had said it was OK. Anytime she broached the subject, I walked out. It ruined our relationship.' She looked at her mother. 'It's her that should be forgiving me. If she hadn't done what she did, I'd never have had such a lovely dad.' She took Lily's hand. 'What do I have to forgive you for, Mammy?' But Lily remained silent.

'It could have just been her disease,' June said

502

eventually. 'She might have imagined she did something wrong. Alzheimer's patients do that. And she did write the entries when she was getting ill.'

Deirdre looked doubtful. She took up the diary and scanned it to see what she'd missed. 'I just don't understand,' she muttered before eventually standing up and kissing her mother goodbye. 'I'll be back next week,' she said. Then smiling at the assembled staff members, she added, 'Now that Lily's diary is finished, I'll have to tell you my news, though I can guarantee there won't be a queue to hear it.'

Everyone laughed except Rick. He looked like a man trying to figure something out.

CHAPTER 49

Zoe pulled on her jacket. 'Well, that was a bit of an anticlimax,' she smiled. Fastening the zipper tight to her chin, she added, 'I'm heading off now; seeing as Ronnie has appointed himself entertainment manager you hardly need me.'

June laughed. 'OK, but I might ring you tonight for ideas for Dominic's leaving do.'

Zoe wondered if she'd heard right. 'Did you say Dominic's leaving do?'

'Yes, now Carrie did say that he mightn't be in the mood for a party, so it'll just be a meal and a few speeches and anything you might think of and we can take it from there.'

'Dominic is leaving?' Zoe asked, her mind still playing catch-up, 'He's going?'

'Well yeah,' June nodded, 'I rang you to tell you.'

'I never got it.'

'After his dad's funeral, he told me that he wanted to move. It's understandable, eh?'

'No it is not,' Zoe looked at June as if she was bonkers. 'He loves it here. He told me so.'

June looked a little taken aback by Zoe's

reaction. 'Well obviously not enough,' she said. 'Anyway, he's way too talented to be stuck here. It was only because of his dad—'

'We'll see,' Zoe snapped, 'we'll see. This is ridiculous.'

She whirled on her heel, leaving June standing open-mouthed in the middle of the corridor as she stomped all the way to the canteen. How dare he leave! Was it an attempt to make her feel guilty? She was going to leave, that was the plan. When she found a job, she was going to leave. But he couldn't go. He was so happy here. She was not going to have that on her conscience. She pushed open the door of the canteen.

Ronnie was playing cards with a new resident. Obviously a man on respite care. 'Watch him, he cheats,' she called out and Ronnie gave her an exasperated glare.

'That's OK, so do I,' the other man said mildly.

It should have made Zoe laugh, but she couldn't. How could she when she'd driven Dominic out of his job? Shoving open the door of the kitchen she said, more loudly than she intended, 'You're leaving?'

Dominic, who was carrying a pot of potatoes over to the cooker, jumped, splashing water all over the floor. He sighed in irritation and plonked the heavy saucepan down. 'Damn lucky that wasn't full of hot water,' he said.

'You're leaving?' Zoe said again, crossing towards him. She tried but was unable to help her cross tone.

'Yes.' Dominic nodded, as if he was discussing the weather. 'In a couple of weeks.' He flicked a switch under the potatoes and the gas flared. Turing to a mixture of root vegetables, he began to chop them with impressive speed.

'Why?'

He shrugged. 'I want to do other things.'

'My arse.'

'No, Zoe,' he said snottily, pausing briefly to glance at her. 'I don't want to do your arse, nice and all as it was.'

'Shut up!'

He slammed down his knife and glared at her. She recoiled slightly. There was genuine anger in his eyes. 'Do you have a problem with me leaving?'

'Yes, yes I do actually.' She was glad he'd put the knife down.

'Which is?' He poked his head towards her.

'You love it here. You told me that.' Zoe swallowed, then said softly, 'I don't want to be responsible for you leaving.'

He threw back his head and laughed so loudly that Zoe jumped. 'I don't believe you. I really don't.'

Zoe was unsure what that meant, so she said nothing.

'This is not about *you*, Zoe.' He emphasised the 'you', saying it so bitterly that she felt the spark of sudden tears. 'Who do you think you are, huh?'

He wasn't going to make her cry, Zoe thought indignantly. She had come here, out of concern for him, that he was making a mistake and she had to take this? 'I don't think I'm anything.'

'This is about me,' he jabbed his chest, 'Me!'

'Grand.' Zoe made a face.

'And the fact that you hurt me.'

'Yes, well, I'm sorry—'

'Sorry is no good,' he said and his voice dipped. 'You just dumped me, wouldn't even look at me, my dad died and you can't even bring yourself to touch me.' He shook his head and continued, still angry, 'And you think it's about you!'

Well, it kind of was, if he put it like that, Zoe thought but hadn't the nerve to say. 'Please don't leave,' she said softly. 'I know you love it here.'

'No, I don't.' Dominic picked up the knife and began slicing again.

'You do.'

'Right!' He gave the knife a bit of a flourish, and stomped towards her. 'Give me one good reason why I should stay. The best reason you can think of.'

Zoe swallowed. 'Can you put the knife down first?'

He ignored her request and came closer, 'Well?'

She could smell his aftershave mixed with the scent of spices and the hint of warm air. The combination made her feel a bit dizzy. 'One good reason?' her voice faltered.

'Yeah.' His body was about an inch from hers. He was looking down on her, his dark eyes narrowed.

She could feel the heat from him. The zing of electricity between them. 'Just one?' she croaked out, her voice quivering.

'That's all I need. But a good one.' His lashes were long, throwing faint shadows onto his cheeks. There was a scattering of freckles on his nose.

Zoe shifted uncomfortably. Did he mean what she thought? 'One reason?' she repeated weakly.

He nodded.

She opened her mouth, touched his shirt ever so gently with her finger. 'Because,' she answered, swallowing hard, 'because I' – her nerve faltered and she withdrew her finger – 'because you love it here,' she squeaked out.

The moment, so shiny only a second before, died like a leaf in autumn.

Dominic turned away. 'Not good enough,' he said.

She stood for a second, trying to think of something to add, but she couldn't. Dismissed, she left. She ignored Ronnie explaining to the newcomer about the lover's tiff they had just overheard.

Deirdre and Rick said very little to each other on the drive back. Deirdre was remembering that time her mother had told her about Jimmy. She was in her thirties, she'd started seeing John and suddenly a whole future of family and children seemed a possibility. John had crawled under her defences and set up camp. And then Lily had told Deirdre that she wasn't who she'd always thought she was.

508

She was not Jimmy's daughter. And suddenly, life crumbled. Things looked different. She was afraid to find out the full story and afraid if she didn't. Who was she? She was Deirdre Deegan and the only person she could depend upon was herself. And how could she put her trust in a man who said he loved her? How could she believe in him when all that she believed was gone? It was then, Deirdre realised, that her life had gone from mildly boring but deliriously happy to seriously stuck. Stuck because she hadn't known where she was going and in a desperate attempt to kick-start it, she'd become a radio show presenter and gone off in the wrong direction. If only she'd known that no matter who her dad was, Jimmy was still her guide and she was still Deirdre Deegan inside.

'Don't say anything to Daddy about Mary,' Zoe warned Lee, just before they went in to visit Abe that evening. 'It's a surprise for him, OK? If you mention anything you'll ruin it.'

'Swear on the leg of the Lamb of God,' Lee said solemnly.

Zoe decided not to ask him where he heard that one. 'OK, good boy. And, remember, Daddy gets tired really quickly, so no bouncing about.'

'No Mary, no bouncing about,' Lee agreed solemnly, and Zoe had to bite back a grin.

'OK, here you go.' She pushed open the door to Abe's room and Lee, suddenly high on the excitement of seeing his Daddy fully awake, ran headlong towards the bed. 'Lee,' Zoe called and at once he came to an abrupt stop, almost falling over himself before proceeding in a shuffling manner.

Abe saw them enter, he was lying sideways, his chin cupped in the palm of his hand. He grinned at his son. 'Hey, great to see you. You've grown.'

'Yep. I'm almost as big as Tom now.'

'Tom?'

'His friend in school,' Zoe explained. 'The obnoxious kid from the birthday party?'

Abe looked blank.

'Doesn't matter.' There was so much he didn't remember yet. Still, Tom's mother had turned out to be a lovely woman, asking Lee on sleepovers so that Zoe was free to spend nights at the hospital.

Abe lay back down, exhausted with the effort of propping himself up. He was weak but improving each day. He still talked a little like a kid blowing bubbles. 'Hop up here, Lee, and tell me all about what's been happening.'

Zoe hefted Lee up and he got comfortable snuggling in beside his dad. 'Where is the bullet hole?' he asked.

'Here,' Abe tapped the small bandage. 'It's getting better now.'

'Tom said you'd have a big massive hole that I could see through.' Lee sounded disappointed.

'Well, it was see-through but the doctors made it better,' Abe shot an amused look at Zoe. 'I should have got your mother to take a picture of it.'

'You'll be no good for show and tell now,' Lee said glumly.

'Sorry about that, mate,' Abe commiserated. 'Any other news for me?'

Lee scrunched up his face. 'I have cool new computer games,' he said. 'I even have one that no one else in my class has because they're all too young and it's too violent. Tom's mother wouldn't even let us play it.'

'Since when have you got computer games?' Abe grinned. 'Someone been buying you presents?'

Zoe stiffened as Lee clapped a hand over his mouth and looked at her in horror.

'I never said,' he blurted out.

'Never said what?' Abe asked, confused.

Zoe wondered if she should just tell him. She'd been looking for an opportunity and now it was here. And if she lied in front of Lee, he'd never let her forget it. And Abe had to find out sometime.

'When you got shot, it made the papers,' she said by way of gently introducing the topic.

'Yeah?' Abe looked a little pleased and then his features changed as he suddenly realised what that might mean. 'Oh?'

'Your sister saw the piece and she arrived at the hospital.'

'Mammy!' Lee sounded exasperated. 'It was a surprise. You ruined it.'

'I know, pet,' Zoe tousled his hair. She turned back to Abe, who was looking so pale he was almost transparent. 'Anyway, Mary has been a big hit with us all.'

Abe blinked and then closed his eyes, inhaling deeply. 'Is she still here?'

'Yes.'

He said nothing to that.

'I'll come in later and we'll talk,' Zoe said. 'I'll bring Mary—'

He shook his head. 'No, no not yet.'

She felt like shaking him. His only sister . . . But she made no comment, merely took Lee by the hand to help him down from the bed. 'Daddy's tired, Lee, you can come in tomorrow.'

'Aw,' Lee made a face, then threw his arms around Abe's neck and hugged him.

Abe held him tight, kissing him soundly on the cheek before letting him go.

Zoe stared for a second at this man who'd she'd only really begun to know in the past couple of weeks. She kissed her fingertips and pressed them to his cheek.

He held her hand briefly.

Abe had mountains of visitors that evening. If Zoe hadn't know better, she'd have sworn that Abe called them up and begged them to come in. Anything to get out of a personal conversation. First to arrive were her parents, who didn't stay long. They really were awkward around him, she realised. They had nothing to say to him nor he to them. Abe saw them as the enemy rather than the kind people they were. Her father ended up talking in a monotone about the weather while her mother wittered on about the washing machine breaking down again. Abe smiled politely but didn't contribute anything in the way of conversation to ease their discomfort. When they left, some workmates of Abe's arrived and he brightened considerably. Now it was Zoe's turn to sit in stony silence as she watched the transformation of Abe from the dour man of a few minutes previously. Finally, about twenty minutes before visiting ended, Audrey arrived with a massive jigsaw and some chocolates.

'I thought you could be doing with something to stretch your brain,' she said, winking at Zoe, 'seeing as how they found it and all.'

Abe laughed loudly and told Audrey that if her brain was twice as big as it was now, it'd still be small.

'That's gas,' she said, 'Zoe says the same thing about your dick.'

That made them all laugh. Zoe was thankful that Abe liked at least one of her friends. But then again, why wouldn't he like Audrey? Sassy, independent Audrey with her carefree, commitment-free life. As Zoe watched them bantering, a physical pain started somewhere in her gut and worked its way into her heart. Abe liked Audrey because she was so like him or the way he so longed to be. Abe was not a family man. The fact that he had a family wasn't the issue. Abe had been domesticated but he'd never be tamed. And maybe it was his early home life that had done it or maybe it was just who he was. Right now that was a devastating realisation but one, if she were honest, she'd always known. He'd stayed with her out of guilt and it had almost destroyed them both.

'Hey are you OK?' Audrey asked her.

'Don't mind me,' Zoe waved her concern away. 'I'm just going to grab a coffee. Back in a sec.'

She was glad to escape the room, everything was tumbling down around her. Yes, she'd been going to leave him because she didn't know him but, in reality, she'd known him all along. Maybe she hadn't known his background, his history, but if someone wanted to flee, they would flee and there was precious little knowing involved.

She'd wait until tomorrow. Abe, for the first time in his life, wasn't rushing off anywhere.

CHAPTER 50

Deirdre lay on her sofa in her decluttered living room and marvelled at the sheer size of it. And how bright it was and how the sun showed up all the worn spots on the frayed carpet. There was plenty of shelf space now for pictures and photos. She'd hung up the two taken from her mother's diary. It was all three of them, she realised – her mother, father and herself. She gazed up at them in their new silver frames and that weird sensation took her over again. The end of her mother's diary had caused it. Lily's story was over now and her voice was gone. Her mother had truly vanished into the haze of Alzheimer's. Her life flattened into the pages of time. But what a life it had been. In the end, she'd forged happiness for herself, which was all anyone really wanted anyway.

The ring of her mobile startled her. 'Hello?'

'Hello, Deirdre, it's Rick.'

'Hi. What's up?'

There was a pause. Then a voice, someone who sounded like Bert, urged, 'Go on.'

'I, eh, have something here for you Deirdre and I think it's best if you come over and collect it.'

515

He sounded strange. 'Are you OK?'

There was a deep sucking in of breath before he said, 'I'm grand. Grand. So, will you be over today then?'

'I can come now.'

More silence.

'Does now suit?'

Rick's voice, when it answered, caught her heart, 'Now is a good a time as any,' he said.

He met her at the door. Bert was just leaving. As she parked, she saw Bert clapping Rick on the back and giving him the thumbs up. Then, adjusting his hairpiece, he marched on down the drive. He caught sight of Deirdre and for some reason avoided her eye and pretended he hadn't seen her, so she called after him, 'Hello, Bert!'

He put his hand up in a wave but didn't detain her by asking if there was news on the gardening competition as he usually did. 'Have I offended him?' she asked Rick as she stepped into the house.

'Not at all, he's an odd man if ever there was one.' Rick led her into the kitchen.

And the glossiness of it hit her. The bounce of colour. The double-glazed windows. Modern. 'She liked to move with the times, didn't she?'

'Yes,' he answered and his voice was lost or sad.

Deirdre looked sharply at him. 'Is everything all right? Is it Mammy?'

'I've something for you,' Rick said. 'I think I

know what it is, so it's breaking my heart to give it to you. But your mother wanted you to have it and I respect that.'

'I don't understand.' Deirdre pulled off her coat and crossed towards Rick. 'Sit down, you look awful.'

He didn't sit, instead he pointed to an envelope on the table. 'It says "For Deirdre at the end"; I thought Lily meant at the end of her life, but I think now it means at the end of her diary.'

Deirdre turned and saw the envelope, large and brown and old, lying in the centre of the table. Picking it up she looked curiously at Rick. 'What's in it?'

'I can only speculate,' he shrugged and seemed a little tearful. 'Just remember that nothing has to change. And your mother only did what she thought was best.' Then he walked by her out of the kitchen.

Hesitantly, she pulled the envelope open and three things fell out. The first was some sort of a savings certificate. Deirdre unfolded it and glanced through it. The figure at the end made her gasp. More money than she had ever seen in her life. Where had her mother got that? Putting it aside, Deirdre turned to some sheets of pink paper, folded once and covered in her mother's handwriting. Her eyes filled up when she saw that the letter was addressed to her. She sat down, determined to savour every word.

* * *

Darling Deirdre,

By now you've heard most of my story, I hope the person I chose to read it was good. My mind is so terrible these days I am apt to pick a deaf mute. Anyway, this letter is between you and me. Just us. The two girls as we used to say when you weren't walking the fields with Jimmy.

Firstly I want to say how proud I am of you, you turned out so well despite my ham-fisted parenting. You were a joy – my joy and Jimmy's wonder. Your hugs kept me in the world, kept me sane. You saved my life, Deirdre.

As you read this letter, remember that. Keep it in your heart.

Did you look at the savings certificate? That's the money Patrick gave me before he left Cavan. He gave it to me for you and I have guarded it always. I invested it in things I would have liked to own like fashion houses and jewellery and gold. It's worth quite a lot now and you can choose to do with it what you will. I only ever took out three hundred pounds and unfortunately I never got to put it back in. It was given to a neighbour who needed it, so I know you won't mind that. Jimmy never knew about this money, or maybe he did, but as my mother said, a woman needs her secrets.

But some secrets are not good to keep. Some need to be let out into the open.

This is my secret, I hope you can forgive me.

*　　*　　*

Deirdre felt her stomach heave. It was as if something was crawling inside her. This letter had been so beautiful, did she need to read the rest? Would it taint everything? Upstairs she heard Rick making his bed, a radio playing. The normalcy of the sound reminded her that she was here, in this place and that nothing could harm her. Very slowly, she turned her eyes back to the page.

Some years ago, I went out and bought you a tutu for your birthday. It was your birthday all right, but you were fifty, not five. I came home utterly terrified. For a few hours I'd been convinced you were a child. I'd thought I was still young too. And then I stepped out on a busy Dublin street and I knew there was something wrong. I came home and I picked up the phone to call you, to beg you to come over. Then I realised you had your life. You were beginning your radio show. I had promised to listen in and I'd forgotten. You were not my carer. And neither was anyone else. And then I remembered a promise made in a street some years before. A promise that if ever I needed him, he'd be there. And I so wanted to talk to someone, Deirdre, and it seemed so much easier to confide in someone who owed me. To prove my mother wrong, to prove to her that Patrick wasn't just for the good times, I rang Patrick and we chatted. It was all a bit awkward, a bit stilted. Then one day he rang me again. Then I rang him. And then I went and got lost. I knew I was lost. I knew too that I shouldn't be lost. But I was lost in my head. All I could see was the time before I came to Dublin, and yet all my eyes could see was Dublin and they wouldn't match and I eventually sat down on a bench and at that moment Patrick rang. He went on the computer and looked up my street and he asked me where I was and he directed me home.

The next day he arrived at my door. He said he'd mind me. It was the least he could do. He agreed not to tell you, though he wanted to. We called him Rick after my favourite cousin who'd died. And because it's Patrick – shortened.

I am sorry.

There was more but Deirdre couldn't read it. She was stunned. Stuck to the chair in horror. Upstairs the radio played 'From the Candy Store On The Corner'.

That man upstairs calmly making the bed was her—

She flung down the letter and raced to the door and out of the house. Rick must have seen her because he called her from a bedroom window.

But she was gone.

She thought she might be sick.

Deirdre drove for hours, not sure where she was going, not really caring. She couldn't even cry as she wound her way up and up through the Dublin mountains. Eventually she pulled into a layby. It was getting dark and street lights and house lights flickered on, a magic carpet of yellow. Get enough distance and everything looked good, she thought.

Though she'd need miles and miles of it to recover from news like that. She sat for another few hours staring out as the night grew darker and the lights got brighter, listening to some radio show doing a sketch of her show. They had her voice unnervingly right, but they couldn't touch her for verbal clumsiness.

Finally, at about three the following morning, she drove home, wondering how her mother could have deceived her again.

Her phone was alight with missed calls.

She didn't care. She had no one now.

CHAPTER 51

'Talk to me,' Zoe sat beside Abe's bed the next evening and studied him. Whatever power he might have had over her had waned considerably. Maybe knowing Abe as she did now had turned her off him. Maybe if she'd always known him, they might not have got together. For years, Zoe had loved the fantasy she'd created around Abe, the funny, charming mystery man. Now she realised that the man she was with had created a fantasy of his own, an illusion, and kept himself well hidden from her. Like a bad magician, like Lily had to do so long ago. 'Talk to me.'

Abe's gaze flickered uncertainly. 'About?'

'You. What you really want. Where you see yourself going. I want to know.'

Abe turned his face away.

Zoe sighed. She hadn't slept the previous night wondering what she was going to say. And then she thought, to hell with it, let him talk. He'd never talked, it had always been her. He knew her feelings and desires like he knew the lines on his hands, whereas she didn't know him at all. Maybe he'd say something to kick-start her feelings again. 'I don't care what you say,' she said. 'I just need to hear it.'

'We were breaking up when I got hit,' he said instead.

'Yeah.' So he remembered that.

'So, there is nothing to say.'

The words were like a punch in her stomach. To think he cared that little after all this time. To think that he didn't even want to waste the effort of trying to make her understand. 'Don't you want me to understand?' she asked.

'Would it make a difference?'

'I don't know. I just feel, you know, after all we shared—'

'You shared,' he corrected her. 'I never wanted to.'

Just when she thought he couldn't hurt her any more.

Maybe Abe felt he'd been too harsh, but he blurted out, 'Mary told you what happened.'

She nodded, afraid to speak in case he stopped.

'It made me want to get away. I never wanted to be tied to anyone or anything ever again. I never wanted to trust anyone with, I dunno, my feelings, I guess, ever again.' He closed his eyes, heaved a huge sigh and stumbled on. 'You have no idea how hard it was when my mother came back from the hospital. It was as if I spent all my time waiting for her to go mad again. I couldn't stand it, it was easier to cut all ties.'

'But you still cared.'

'Nope.' A shutter came down.

'You did. You went to my mental-health night. You went to try and understand.'

Abe said nothing.

'Lee loves Mary.'

His face remained impassive.

'If you love your son, you'll try and incorporate her into your life.'

'I do love him, you know that.'

His solid declaration of love for Lee got her in the gut. 'Do you love me? I wasted five years on you.'

Abe looked like a cornered animal. 'Don't, Zoe.'

'Five years I wasted loving you and I got nothing back.' Her voice rose. 'All I wanted—'

'All *you* fucking wanted!' Abe hissed, startling her. 'It was all about what you wanted. I didn't want your family, Zoe. I didn't want huge networks of supportive aunts and fucking uncles. I wanted us to be on our own! I wanted to be on my own.'

'So I tied you down.'

'Yeah.'

'It wasn't all about me,' Zoe said. 'It was what I wanted for Lee. I wanted him to have what I had – a happy home.'

Abe turned away. 'Yeah, well, I couldn't give you what I never had.'

Zoe said nothing, the raw truth of the words made her wince.

'I tried, I did.' He returned his gaze to her face. 'I decided no more running away, no more ditching people, time to have roots. I wanted to do the honourable thing by you. But roots need food and water to survive and I didn't want to depend on anyone to give me that. And, yeah,' he nodded, 'I felt shit always running, but it's easier now to keep going than to stop.'

And with those words, she finally knew that what they had was over. Abe was never going to stay anywhere, he couldn't, it scared him too much. To admit it to herself was a relief.

'I'm sorry, babe,' he said.

He hadn't called her 'babe' in such a long time. The endearment made her eyes water but she knew what she had to do. She took his hand in hers. 'It's OK.'

He tipped her chin up with his finger. 'You deserve lots better, I know that. And if I could promise it to anyone, it'd be to you. I loved you as much as I could.'

The truth hurt, Zoe thought, but at least it had also set her free. At least now she understood. 'Thanks.'

'So? Friends?'

They hugged each other, a hello and a goodbye, both of them crying a little.

'Mary is outside,' Zoe said, eventually pulling away. 'Will you see her?'

Abe seemed frozen but then he dipped his head and he muttered, 'For Lee's sake, yeah.'

'Thank you.' She touched his cheek with her fingers and he leaned against it. 'I'll bring her in.'

★   ★   ★

A minute later, Zoe ushered Mary to Abe's bedside. The two stared at each other and Abe's eyes filled up with tears. 'I'm sorry, Mary,' he gulped out. 'I just—'

In answer, his sister wrapped her arms about him. 'It's OK, hon. I know you are.'

Zoe left them to it.

CHAPTER 52

The ring of the doorbell startled her. And it shouldn't have because she'd been expecting Rick, sorry, *Patrick* to come crawling over with some nonsensical explanation. She'd really been on the ball since the news in the letter, as she had come to call it. She hadn't fallen apart at all and she had gone into work every single day. Work was a distraction, especially now as Michael Allen was intent on finding out who had put 'Shitface' in the draw hat. Paul was denying it, as was she and her team and the media were having a field day with all the hoo-ha. You'd swear no one in the country ever said 'shitface' before.

'They're creating a hoo-ha,' Michael had proclaimed, throwing a paper across his desk.

'Hoo-ha,' Paul had repeated in a brilliant Al Pacino style.

Michael had glowered, she had smiled and Paul had winked at her. In fact, he'd been nice to her ever since the ashtray episode, but his wink only made her feel upset so she turned away.

There was another ring on the doorbell.

Deirdre had a peek from her kitchen. It wasn't Rick. It was someone small and squat.

Maybe it was a salesman. She hoped it was – she needed someone to talk to. But it was Bert. He was looking a little nervous.

'Hello there,' he said in a big, bright, patently forced tone, 'and how are you?'

Deirdre eyeballed him. 'I have no results for you,' she intoned.

He seemed confused. Then his face broke into a smile. 'That's not why I'm here,' he said before his smile faltered as he remembered why he was there. 'Rick knew you wouldn't want to see him—'

'How very astute of him.'

Bert's mouth opened and closed and opened again. Then he shook his head as if a fly had got trapped in it. 'Here.' From behind his back he produced a white envelope. 'Rick says it's yours now. And please look at the photograph. He says you couldn't have seen it properly.'

'I won't be doing what he says for a long time. And his name is Patrick.'

Bert was stumped. He obviously wasn't used to being embroiled in other people's domestics. 'OK.' He laid the envelope on the ground as she'd made no effort to take it. 'Bye now.'

And off he went, holding tight to his hair.

She had to get drunk to do it. She wasn't going to leave it another fifteen years. And so, one bottle of wine down and feeling a little queasy, she reached her hand into the envelope and pulled out the photograph. Four people. Two men. Two women. Lily and Jimmy, all dressed up. Jimmy looking at Lily. They were wearing the same clothes as they were in the picture Deirdre now had hanging up in her living room, so she concluded that it was taken the same night as that. The other girl in the picture was wearing a dress that should have been nice but just didn't quite cut it. Maybe it might have looked good if Lily hadn't been in the photo. The girl was holding the arm of the young man she was with quite possessively. The man, a stunningly beautiful youth, was staring at Lily as if she was the sun. *Oh, to have a man look at me like that*, Deirdre thought. And then, with slight shock, she saw who it was. Rick. *Patrick*. He appeared enchanted by Lily. The cameraman had captured a whole story in one fraction of time. Another second and there would have been nothing to tell. Had Patrick loved her then? Her eyes turned to her dad. Jimmy looked proud, happy to be with his future wife. Sure of his place in her life. Four people for whom life would be forever beginning.

Deirdre put the picture aside and picked up the letter.

Take a look at the picture, darling Deirdre. See how he loved me. Your dad and your other dad. Ann came into the shop two weeks after the dance and threw it at me. She told me to keep my hands off her man. I told her to tell her man to keep his eyes off me. The laugh I had. But I kept the picture for years after, hidden away. Foolishly, I'd take it out and tell myself that Patrick had loved me, that one day he would come back and prove it.

And that day came, only not like I'd ever planned.

I know you'll be angry with both of us, Deirdre. Patrick did want you to know, I didn't because I believed you should get to know the man before you stuck a title on him. Just like you did with Jimmy, your dad. I believe, just like that little boy who stole my bag that day in Dublin, that with understanding comes forgiveness.

Patrick was young, he was stupid. He left me. Not you. Life is short. Live it well. And don't be on your own. He's a good man to have in your life.

And even if I don't recognise you, I will always love you.

Mammy

She cried for an hour. Solid. When her doorbell rang again, she knew she couldn't answer it. She'd look a sight.

'Deirdre. Open up. It's Paul.'

'Fuck off.' Wow. So that's why people said it!

'Stop using that language.' Then he asked, 'Are you crying? Have I made you cry? I have, haven't I?'

The nerve. As if she had nothing going on in her life but him. 'Go away!'

'Will you just let me explain? Please.' A pause. 'I'll shout it out here, if you won't let me in.'

That would be uncivilised. And she was not uncivilised. She yanked open her door and there he was. As sexy as hell. Life is short. Live it well. What possessed her, she wasn't sure.

He made to come in.

She reached out and touched his T-shirt. *Oh my.* She grabbed a fistful of fabric. *Oh Holy Mother of God.* She pulled him stumbling into her hallway. 'Please, just kiss me.' She was Marilyn Monroe breathless.

There was a moment of shock before he detangled her hand ever so gently. 'You're a bit vulnerable-looking there. I don't want to take advantage.'

But she needed some comfort, some way to escape, and she was drunk and had an excuse. 'Please.' She pressed herself against him.

'I'm just a man,' Paul said a little raggedly. 'You can't keep throwing yourself at me. I'll give in in the end.'

She unbuttoned her top button. 'There's lots more where they came from.'

He groaned and moved beside her. Pinning her up against the wall, his knee between her legs, he pressed himself against her and began to kiss her. Then abruptly he pulled away and gawked around. 'What the fuck happened to this place. Where's your stuff? Were you burgled?'

'I got rid of it.' She pushed her hands up his T-shirt. 'You said I had no life so I got rid of it.' She pulled him to her.

He moved a little back and, breathing heavily, he began to undo her copious buttons. 'Oh,' he gulped. 'I was a bit angry about—'

'Explain later.' She kissed him harder.

'Oh, God, yes, I will.'

His hands on her body. She hadn't been touched in such a long time.

Afterwards, as they lay on the stairs, itchy carpet poking against their backs, Paul confessed that he'd called around to see if she was all right. 'I know I've been a bastard,' he muttered, 'and that I led you to believe it was you. Well it wasn't.'

'No?' She wanted it to be her. She ran a finger over his nipple and he caught her hand and kissed it.

'I did what you said, you know. Sent my son a birthday present. A letter. Everything came back, torn up, in an envelope. I was gutted, took it out on everyone. Blamed you for egging me on.'

Deirdre said nothing. Absentee parenting was not a subject she wished to discuss.

'I've come to the conclusion that whether he wants me or not, I'm going to keep trying.' Paul sat up.

'You are?' She moved away, a funny prickly feeling was making its way up her back.

'Yes. Because he's my son and I love him.'

'Even if you don't know him?'

'Yes.'

She wrapped her arms around him.

She told him everything. That's what happened when you had sex with someone, you tended to tell them things. Paul thought it would make great radio, a great documentary. The comment was designed to make her giggle and she did a little. The he said, all serious, as he looked at her with those sleepy eyes, 'I do feel a bit sorry for Rick. He seems a top guy and he's done so much for you. Like, why does anything have to change, he is who he is.'

'Yeah, a snake who left my mother.'

'You said he got scared so he ran. That's just normal.'

And she remembered a time when she'd got scared and run.

But it wasn't the same, was it?

CHAPTER 53

It was Friday, the end of the week, and Zoe was in the small garden at the back of the home. She was sitting in one of the white-painted benches that faced the sun, her head held upward to catch the rays. She turned as Carrie sat down.

'Spill,' Carrie ordered.

Her engagement ring caught the light and flashed, seeming to mock Zoe.

Zoe shrugged. 'Nothing to tell.'

'Did something happen between you and Dominic?' Carrie asked after a second. 'You've both been in terrible moods all weekend and, not wanting to make you feel bad, but his dad did die and no matter what, it seems the worst time to pick an argument with him. I heard you can't come to his going away do.'

'He doesn't want me there,' Zoe said, staring across at the distant mountains.

'So what happened?' Carrie shifted nearer and nudged her with her elbow. 'I need a happy person to be my . . .' – she paused for added dramatic effect – 'bridesmaid!'

At that, Zoe started to cry. The tears she'd somehow managed to hold back spilled out of her eyes like water from a kettle. So much had happened that she felt as if she'd never find her feet again. It was as if she'd been standing on the shore and a wave had swept her life out to sea and no matter how much swimming and threshing about she did, she could never reclaim it. She was washed up on a new shore now and while elements of it looked better, she'd lost a lot too. One of them was Dominic.

Carrie listened to her story, gobsmacked, interjecting a 'wow' and a 'I always knew he fancied you' every so often.

'I tried to apologise for how I treated him, but he won't listen,' Zoe gulped out. 'And I should have known he was the one. He was everything I'd been looking for. He loved his family, he was great with Lee. But I stuck with Abe. Why did I do that?'

'Because Abe was great with Lee too. Because Abe, even though he was scared, Zoe, he still tried to do the right thing.' Carrie shuffled a little closer and wrapped a plump arm about Zoe. 'Because you thought you were doing the right thing. It wasn't a total waste.' She paused, then went on, 'It's like Lily's story really, you know, only Abe stayed with you and messed up. Just keep trying with Dominic.'

'I have. He won't listen. He walks away. He talks over me. He's very stubborn.'

'You have to find a way to make him listen.'

Suddenly Carrie giggled a bit. All Zoe needed was a little help.

She scurried off to ring Deirdre.

CHAPTER 54

Five o'clock. Zoe sat in her office waiting for the phone to ring. Am I utterly mad, she wondered, to go along with this crazy scheme of Carrie's? Though Deirdre was in on it too and Deirdre seemed a sensible sort of person. Either way, in less than half an hour she would find out. Carrie sat opposite her and every time Zoe looked up, Carrie gave her the thumbs up. Carrie was glowing these days and it was as if she wanted to sprinkle her own happiness over everyone else. Zoe couldn't help but smile. But really was she bonkers to have listened to her?

In the kitchen, Carrie had asked Dominic to work late. 'I want to bring a nice romantic take-away meal home to Harry,' she'd said. 'I'll pay you.'

Dominic had agreed, delighted as Carrie knew he would be, to stretch his cooking muscles. He was still a dour specimen of manhood though, going about grumping at everyone. People let him away with it though because of his dad.

The phone rang and Zoe jumped. Carrie hopped up from the table, giving Zoe the thumbs up once more. 'Right, I'm off to make sure Dominic has the radio on in the kitchen,' she said.

Her heart pounding, Zoe picked up the receiver. 'Hello?'

'You OK, darling?' Gary Sims asked.

'Grand, Gar. Thanks for doing this for me.' Zoe gulped down some water.

'Not at all, this will send ratings sky high, audiences love this mush.'

'Thanks,' Zoe said drily.

'Aw, you know I love you, don't you? If he doesn't respond, I'll personally kick the crap out of him myself.'

'My hero,' Zoe managed a giggle.

'OK, we're on in two seconds,' Gary hissed.

Zoe drank some more water, which went down the wrong way and she started to cough. Shit! *Shit!*

'And now tonight,' Gary said, 'we have a girl who has treated the one she loves very badly and she's looking for his forgiveness. Is that right, Mystery Woman?'

'Yes.' It came out like a squeak.

'Off you go, Zoe! The airways are yours,' Gary boomed.

'Of course, Zoe is not my real name,' Zoe said rapidly.

There was a silence. 'Eh, no, of course not,' Gary back-pedalled, but his hesitation had cost him, he didn't sound convincing. 'Now, eh, Zoe, off you go. The airways are yours.'

Zoe haltingly began her tale, Gary interjecting every so often, saying inane stuff like, 'That must have been hard,' and 'I feel your confusion/pain/anxiety.'

'And I tried to apologise about three times,' Zoe said, 'but he wouldn't let me get a word in edgeways, he kept interrupting and—'

'For those of you who've only tuned in,' Gary interrupted, 'Zoe here is talking about her love life going a bit belly-up and she is going to make a heartfelt plea to a boy she's hurt. Stay tuned, we'll be back after the break.'

'Going great!' Gary said to her. 'Keep it up!'

Then she was put on hold.

Just then her mobile phone rang. It was her mother. Zoe debated whether to answer it and decided that she'd better, it might be something to do with Lee. 'Hello?'

'Zoe, was that you on Gary's show? What was going on? Did he pay you to make an idiot of yourself?' Her mother had recognised her, there was no telling who else might have. Zoe cringed.

'It *was* me,' Zoe decided to come clean, because in two minutes she was going back on. 'I asked to go on. I have to apologise to someone and I thought this might be the best way of getting him to listen to me. You know? Because he can't interrupt.'

There was a sharp intake of breath. 'Not Abe?' her mother said, as if the idea of it was akin to her husband fixing things around the house. 'Oh, surely not!' She didn't wait for Zoe to answer. 'When will you understand?' she said firmly. 'He doesn't love you and you don't love him. You only stayed with him because, I don't know, maybe you didn't want us to think you'd made a mistake, but we all knew it anyway. It was like Guinness Light.'

'Guinness Light?'

'Yes, you know that drink Guinness invented years ago. It seemed like a good idea at the time but it was doomed to failure.'

'Thanks,' Zoe said drily. 'Anyway, it's not—'

'I mean,' her mother interrupted as her voice dipped, 'your brother and his . . .' – she sought for the word – 'partner, they might be . . .' – another pause while she sought for a diplomatic phrase to describe Greg and Louis' relationship – 'weird but anyone, even a blind person, can see how right they are together. Even your father says it.'

'Says what?' her dad piped up.

'Says that Greg and Louis are a match made in heaven.'

'I certainly never said that,' her dad muttered. 'I only said that Zoe could take a leaf out of their book. I hope it's not that Abe fella you're chasing on the radio,' he shouted into the receiver. 'I'll have words with Gary if he's allowing it.'

'Zoe Killeen, are you ready?' the researcher on Gary's show twittered into the landline.

'Yes,' Zoe said.

'What?' her dad said.

'Good,' the researcher said.

'I have to go, Dad.' Without waiting for him to reply, she hung up.

'And now, we're back with the mystery girl who's going to make a plea to her one-night stand boyfriend.'

'One-night stand sounds all wrong,' Zoe said, knowing her mother would be on the floor with embarrassment. 'He was more than that. He was a great friend and I loved him only I didn't realise it until I let myself.'

'OK,' Gary said, 'and you have a letter to read to this guy.'

'I do.' Hands shaking, Zoe unfolded the letter. It had taken her hours to get it right. 'Here we go.

Dear D.

I'm copying L. because it worked for her. I feel that if you just listen to what I have to say, you will understand and you won't be angry. Last time I attempted to do this, I got too emotional and stumbled over my words. The bottom line is I love you. I've loved you forever. I've loved you ever since you arrived at my workplace only I'd never have done anything about it because I had a family. I didn't realise that in my heart, you are my family, the one I understand, the one who understands me. I'm sorry for shutting you out these past few weeks. It wasn't you, it was my guilt. Guilt for what happened to A. It was the fact that I might be tied to A for the rest of my life if he was badly injured. I couldn't ask you to be part of that in the same way you were scared of asking any girl to be part of caring for your own father. I needed to let you go for me and for you. Now, they say that if you let someone go, they always come back. I hope you will.'

There was a silence.

Zoe swallowed, glad it was over. Really glad she had done it. And a bit mortified too.

'Well done,' Gary said heartily. 'I'm almost in tears here.'

Zoe managed a shaky laugh.

'So, keep in touch. Let us know how it turns out.'

'I will.'

'We'll ring you next week and see if there are any developments.'

'OK.'

'Say hi to your father from me. He's a great—'

There was a loud pounding on the door. Zoe jumped, dropping the receiver.

'Zoe! Zoe, are you in there?'

It was Dominic. He sounded mad.

'Yes,' she tried to make her voice casual. 'What's wrong?' Hopping from her seat, she opened the office door.

Dominic, breathing heavily, stood before her in his chef's whites, a sheen of sweat on his brow.

His clothes reeked of oriental spices. 'Was that you on the radio?'

She thought of denying it, but what would be the point? 'Uh-huh.'

Dominic opened his mouth to say something, then shut it again. Then he blurted out, 'Did you have to go on the radio to say it? Jesus!'

'Actually, I did,' Zoe snapped back, 'you refused to listen to me. Three times. I even said that you should stay here for *me*. Isn't that the answer you wanted last week!'

'Eh, well, I wasn't expecting to have to wait a week for an answer. Like if it took you that long—'

'Oh, excuse me.' Zoe made a face. 'I never knew you possessed such a flipping big ego. No wonder your motorbike wouldn't start, the weight must kill it.'

'Oh shut up.'

'You shut up.'

There was a long, furious silence.

Zoe's mobile phone rang.

They glared some more at each other.

Zoe's mobile stopped ringing then started up again.

'Aren't you going to answer that?' Dominic asked.

'Yes,' she said, attempting to pull her last vestiges of dignity back. 'And whoever it is, I'm sure it'll be someone a lot more pleasant than you.'

She turned her back on him, wondering if he'd leave. It wasn't meant to be like this. He was meant to be flattered. He should kiss her and tell her how brilliant she was for doing that for him. Picking up her phone, she saw that it was her mother. On second thoughts, maybe she wouldn't be more pleasant than Dominic. 'Shit,' she said, unable to stop the quiver in her voice. Then she noticed the receiver of the landline lying on the floor. Oh double shit! Was it still connected to the radio station? 'Shit,' she said again, a tear slipping out. She swiped it away angrily.

'Zoe?' Dominic said uncertainly. 'Please don't cry.'

'What?' She was half afraid to pick up the phone. What if they were still live on the radio? Oh Jesus . . .

'I'm sorry.' He was behind her. 'I am. Don't cry. I'd hate to make you cry. I was hurt. I just . . . well, other girls treated me really badly when they found out about Dad, I guess I was just, well, anyway, that night with you was the best in a long time for me and—'

Zoe glanced at the phone. If she bent down to turn it off, it'd destroy the mood, maybe Dominic might chicken out. She decided to ignore it, hope that Gary Sims had cut her off. 'I'm not crying,' she managed, half-turning towards him. 'But I'm sorry if I hurt you, you know I am.'

'I know,' he turned her fully around to face him. 'I was going to talk to you eventually. I just wanted you to be sure. But I might as well just say it now. I'm mad about you too,' he touched her face with a fingertip, making her feel all shivery inside. 'I love you.'

'You do?'

A quirk of eyebrow, 'You want me to show you?'

'I think I'd like that.' That bloody phone better be off, she thought, a light sweat coating her palms.

'Come here so.' He bent his head and kissed her.

It was as delicious as his food. 'Yum,' she said.

Outside, from somewhere, there came the sound of cheering and clapping.

'What the fuck—'

'Don't stop.' Zoe pulled him towards her again. 'Baker Boy.'

Down the phoneline, in Gary Sims' studio, came the sound of more clapping and cheering.

CHAPTER 55

Deirdre found the note from Gary Sims on her desk.

Thanks for that peach of an interview. Listenership gold. I own up – I sneaked the name 'Shitface' into your hat. I suppose I was jealous. Report me if you like. Well, please don't. In fact I'm begging you not to.
Love Gary

Deirdre smiled and shoved the note into her bag. What a prat the man was, she thought. She didn't much care, she was leaving the show in a few months anyway and the media storm had moved on from the 'Shitface-gate' scandal as Paul had jokingly dubbed it to someone who'd dared to suggest that one of Ireland's literary greats wasn't actually that great at all.

Deirdre left her office, her handbag slung over her shoulder. She met Paul in the corridor.

'Hi, sexy,' he said. 'Heading home?'

'Yes,' Deirdre answered, blushing. He looked great, she thought, her knees growing week just looking into his face. Then she remembered, 'Oh, I have something to show you.'

'Not here,' he winked.

Oh Lord. She swallowed hard, composing herself. He was terrible. Then she drew Gary's note from her bag. 'It's only this,' she replied archly.

He read it and she smiled as he burst out laughing. 'I think we'll let him off. We couldn't have asked for better publicity for the show.'

'Nothing like that will happen when Emma takes over,' Deirdre said.

'Unfortunately,' Paul grinned. 'Are you there later?'

'I am.' Her voice shook. He was lust in human form. She couldn't get enough of him. Everything he did, from the way he drank his coffee to the look in his eyes when she screwed up another interview, turned her on.

'Wear loads of buttoned-up clothes,' he said.

'I will.' She tapped her shopping bag, a little shyly. 'I bought a big coat.'

'How big?'

'Forty buttons.' She cocked her eyebrows.

'Oh, Mammy!' Paul fisted his chest and groaned.

Deirdre laughed, blowing him a kiss, and pushed open the door to the car park. Her smile died when she saw that Rick was waiting for her. He was lounging beside her car and he straightened up as she approached. Her mouth went dry. She had pushed him out of her mind quite successfully. Or rather Paul had. 'I don't want to talk to you,' she said as she tried to get by.

'I love you,' he said. 'That's all.'

It halted her in her tracks. And then something weird happened. People she recognised started emerging from cars. It was like a scene from *Night of the Living Dead*. There was Mona, Pete, Adam, Bert, the woman with the big chest from the Alzheimer's group, Rick's four betting buddies, the shoppers from Lidl and the local GP.

'I didn't ask them to come,' Rick winced as they made a sort of semi-circle of support around him.

'Yes you did,' Deirdre stared at them in disbelief. 'I can't believe you told everybody.'

'Rick is a lovely man,' Mona said, putting her hand up in the air, like she was in school. 'He helps me look for Pete all the time.'

'He gave me half his winnings from the betting shop to buy my weekly shopping,' a Lidl person said.

'He told me how to avoid tax,' someone else piped up.

'Not a lot of tax,' Rick clarified.

'No, only a little bit,' the person hastily agreed.

'He babysits my kids when I visit Elle,' Adam contributed.

'He minded Lily better than any other carer I've come across,' the GP said.

Then there was silence.

'What am I doing here?' Pete shouted.

'Oh shut up,' Mona snapped.

He did.

'I know he's a good man,' Deirdre said to everyone. 'But—'

'That's all I want to be for you.' Rick sounded broken. 'You were never my daughter. Not really. You are nothing like me. You're Jimmy's girl, he gave you a love of the garden, of the countryside. He made you who you are.'

It was a beautiful thing for him to say, she thought. She looked hard at this man, a man who had abandoned her and yet somehow managed to attract so many loyal friends. So many people to speak up for him. 'I need time, Rick.'

He stood aside. 'That's fine. Totally fine.'

Then she sat into her car and drove away.

CHAPTER 56

'And now to the last story of the morning, "Mystery Girl Gets Her Man"!' the newscaster said, giving a recap of the Gary Sims show the day before. 'And this is what happened afterwards,' she announced as she played a tape of Dominic and Zoe's conversation after he'd burst into her office. 'Jesus wept, how did that happen?' Dominic looked at Zoe in horror.

They were in his house having breakfast, his sister having tactfully stayed in her friend's the night before. Zoe stared into her bowl of cornflakes.

'Was the phone still on?' he asked.

'My folks will kill me,' Zoe said weakly. 'They already think I'm a basket case.'

'Did you forget to hang up the phone?' Dominic asked.

Zoe finally raised her eyes to his. 'It fell on the floor,' she offered him a contrite smile. 'You know when you hammered on the door? I got a fright and dropped it.'

'So, like it's my fault?'

'I guess it is.' Zoe grinned.

'It's not funny,' Dominic said, though there was a trace of a grin on his face. 'It so isn't funny.'

'You'll never live it down,' Zoe said, poking him in the chest. 'Ronnie will be on your case forever now.' She flicked him a look. 'That's assuming you're staying in Lakelands.'

'I dunno,' Dominic screwed up his face. 'Can you show me why I should stay?'

'Come over here,' she took a fistful of his T-shirt and pulled him towards her, planting a kiss on his lips.

'I love you,' he said, pulling away slightly.

Her heart flipped over like one of his delicious pancakes. It had taken a while, but, like Lily, she had finally found what real love meant.

Her, Lee and Dominic. A perfect combination.

Paul was leaving. For the moment anyhow. He was heading to England to see if he could talk to his son. When he got back, they'd talk. See where it all might lead. So far, it had just been to bed and Deirdre knew that buying stuff he could unbutton was costing her a fortune and there had to be more to a relationship than tearing buttons off clothes. But for now, she revelled in him, in his humour and his sarcasm and his body. She had blossomed, everyone said it. Like a flower facing the sun after a long winter. She wondered if they knew it was just touch that had done it. And lust, lots of lust. And a future full of possibility and loss and love.

★   ★   ★

Some weeks later, or it could have been a day later, or a month – she wasn't sure, because time meant nothing now – Lily lay in bed and looked at the two people in front of her. She knew she should know them, and by the way they were talking to her she felt that they definitely knew her. They looked like two nice people, both tall and dark with wide sunny smiles and a lot of affection for each other. She tried to ask who they were, but her words got all muddled.

The woman sat beside her. 'Thanks for the diary,' she said. 'I'm glad you made me listen after all these years. I should have listened before. And if my dad had to be anyone, I'm glad it was Rick.'

The man placed a hand on the girl's shoulder, his eyes suspiciously shiny.

Lily gasped, the dark rooms of her mind suddenly illuminated. She tried to tell them how glad she was that they were happy now, how important it was that they had found each other. How she and Jimmy and Deirdre were once a family, but how it was now Rick and Deirdre. How it didn't matter a jot what a family consisted of, mother, father, children, or just a man and woman, or even a group of people who cared for each other. It didn't matter. Love mattered. Love made a family of perfect strangers. She longed so much to say all this; she tried but all that came out was, 'Love you both.'

Their answer was to enfold her in the warmth of their embrace.

EPILOGUE

This is the last page of my mother's diary. She has left it blank and so I'm filling it in for her.

My mother was Lily Flynn and Lily Deegan. One sometimes did not sit easy with the other. She made mistakes, but she forged on. And when the end came, I finally had the chance to tell her what a great mother she'd been, because though she never blasted into the Dublin social scene, though the bright lights eluded her, though she remained a humble unknown housewife all her life, she became the thing that at five years old, I'd wanted to be.

And now, in my dreams, it's my mother and father I see walking towards me, telling me how jackdaws are the most social and loved of all the birds.

And when I say that's what I want to be, I don't wake up crying anymore.

Deirdre Deegan